FORBIDDEN HARMONY

HARMONY FALLS BOOK THREE

ELIZABETH KELLY

EK PUBLISHING INC.

Edited by:
L. Nunn Editing

Cover art by
The Final Wrap

FORBIDDEN HARMONY

She's done being the good girl.

Addison's life was perfectly planned...

Until she caught her fiancé in bed with another woman.

Her ex-fiancé's claim that she's terrible in bed left her reeling. Now, the self-proclaimed good girl is looking for someone to help her be very bad.

And the sexy as hell, Preacher, is the perfect choice.

Asking Preacher to show her how to be a sexy vixen isn't her worst idea. But falling in love with the secretive tattoo artist most definitely is.

Preacher's attraction to the prim and proper schoolteacher isn't something he ever planned to act on. The town's good girl has starred in all of his dirtiest fantasies, but he's certain his obsession is one-sided.

Until she approaches him with an offer promising to bring even his most deviant fantasies to life.

It's only supposed to be sex. But as Addison chips away at Preacher's tough outer shell, she begins to see the real him.

But will Preacher's past secrets destroy their chance at happiness? Or can Addison convince him that he can outrun his past?

Author's Note: "Forbidden Harmony" is Book Three in The Harmony Falls Series. It is a stand-alone story in the series.

CHAPTER 1

"Addie, this is terrible timing."

"It's fine, Mom. Honestly."

Her mother brushed a strand of hair away from her face. "It was bad timing when the wedding was happening, and it's even worse now. I should stay. You know what? I'm going to stay."

Addison smiled at her mother. "You're not staying. We are literally at the airport, and your flight leaves in three hours."

"It's not the time to be leaving you. Your father will understand."

Addison glanced at her father. He was standing at a kiosk a few feet away, purchasing two neck pillows. He waved at her before shuffling forward in the line.

"Dad's work trip is six weeks long. You'll miss him like crazy. Besides, you retired early for a reason, remember? You wanted to go with Dad on his work trips."

"I know, but..." her mother touched Addie's hair again, the auburn colour the exact same shade as her own, "you're my baby, and you're hurting."

"I'm fine," Addie said.

"Honey." Her mother's look of exasperation was kind of sweet. "Your fiancé cheated on you. You're not fine. And it's okay that you're not. Gosh, I hate Harrison for what he did to you. I'm so glad that Daniel broke his nose."

"Daniel almost went to jail for breaking his nose," Addison said. "You would have been forking out bail money for your son."

"Totally worth it," her mother said. "Harrison is the jerk here, honey. You know that, right?"

"I do."

"Spend lots of time with Gracie and Kira, okay? Don't lock yourself away for the entire summer vacation in your apartment watching bad reality television and knitting Harrison voodoo dolls."

"I won't," Addison said with a small smile.

"Maybe you should go and visit Harper in New York. She's your best friend, and she -"

"I was just there, Mom. You know that. Besides, she has her own stuff going on and doesn't need me moping around her apartment."

"So, instead, you'll mope around your apartment? What if you've gone feral by the time your father and I return from Tokyo?"

Addison laughed so hard that a short woman with 'Hawaii or Bust' written across her t-shirt stared at them as she walked past.

"I'm not going to go feral, Mom. I promise."

Her mother smoothed her fingers across the neckline of Addie's t-shirt, studying the space where pearls usually graced Addie's neck. "Sweetie, you wore jeans and a t-shirt to drive us to the airport. You're not even wearing makeup. Honestly, you're halfway to being feral already."

"I got up late, that's all," Addie said. "I promise I'm okay."

"I know I'm your mom, and I'm old, but will you humour me and take some advice?"

"Yes," Addie said.

Her mother glanced over at her father, who was still in line at the kiosk. "The best way to get over someone is to get under someone else. Find yourself a nice boy and sex him up, sweetheart. Nothing serious, just some casual banging. You'll forget all about that nasty dickface Harrison."

Addison's jaw dropped. She'd never once heard her mother say a swear word, and hearing dickface come out of her mother's mouth was more shocking than her suggestion that Addison should do some 'casual banging'.

"Did you just say dickface?" Addison said.

Her mother laughed. "Just promise me you'll think about it. Casual sex is a good thing."

"You married Daddy right out of high school. How do you know that casual sex is a good thing?" Addison said.

"I read a lot. It'll be good for you, honey. And it'll give the town gossips something else to gossip about."

Addison winced. Directly after she'd caught Harrison cheating and they'd broken up, there'd been a period where it seemed like she wouldn't be the talk of the town. It had lulled her into a false sense of security.

She rubbed at her suddenly throbbing temples. What an idiot she'd been to think she could avoid being the town's hottest gossip topic.

She chewed at the inside of her cheek. Once she'd returned from New York and realized that the gossip had started, she'd been very tempted to take Kira's advice and *accidentally* spill the beans about Harrison's penchant for wearing a dog collar and being spanked, but in the end, she couldn't do it.

Not because she felt any lingering love for Harrison – that ship had sailed after the shock of seeing him cheating with his legal assistant had worn off. No, she'd kept her mouth shut purely for one reason – she was ashamed. Harrison had straight up told her she sucked in bed and that he'd cheated on her because she didn't do it for him.

It was bad enough that the whole town was talking about poor little Addison, whose fiancé had dumped her. If she spread the rumour about Harrison's tastes, he'd retaliate immediately. She didn't need them knowing he'd cheated on her because she was terrible in bed.

"Honey?" Her mother touched her cheek. "Don't worry about the gossip. They'll move on to the next juicy story soon enough. Maybe about how you're banging a new guy and having the time of your life doing it."

Addison shook her head, a small grin playing on her lips. "Yeah, maybe."

"Ready to go?" Her father joined them, the neck pillows swinging from one meaty hand.

"I think so," her mother said. "Addie, are you sure you'll be okay?"

"I'm positive." Addison took her mother's arm and steered her toward the security line. "I'll see you guys in six weeks. I love you both."

"YOUR MOM IS THE BEST, ADDIE." GRACIE COLLAPSED IN THE armchair in Kira's living room and swung her legs over the arm. She took a swig of beer from the bottle in her hand.

"And she's right. You need to find someone to, as Harper says, hit it and quit it with, sweetie."

Addie grimaced, folding her legs up under her on the couch and staring at the liquid in her wine glass. "Why would I want another guy telling me that I suck in bed?"

Kira snorted and dropped onto the couch beside her. Beer burbled up out of her bottle, and she licked it off the side before pointing the bottle at Addison. "Just because Harrison says you suck in bed doesn't mean you do, Addie."

Addison toyed with the multiple friendship bracelets tied around her wrist. "It doesn't mean that I don't, though."

"Oh please," Grace said, "Harrison is not the end all and be all decision maker of what makes a woman good in the sack. Trust me, most guys are not as picky as your asshole ex-fiancé."

"Great," Addie said.

Grace leaned forward. "Okay, that came out wrong. I was trying to say that you're super hot and sweet and funny, and the guys will be falling over themselves to be in your bed. Trust me, sweetie. You hold all the power here when it comes to sex. Half the guys in this town think you're a total hottie. I'm surprised they haven't been banging down your door now that they know you and Harrison are finished."

Addie traced her finger around the rim of her glass. "Maybe Harrison told them how much I sucked in bed."

"Maybe Harrison can suck a big fat hairy monkey dick," Grace said.

Kira laughed. "He'd probably be into that, the kinky son of a bitch."

Grace took another drink of beer. "Look, you don't have to do anything you don't want to do, but -"

"I want to do it," Addison said.

Kira blinked at her. "Seriously?"

"Yes." Her stomach was churning, and she felt a little sick, but she did want to do this. She *needed* to do this. Harrison's words about her being stiff in bed and not sexy kept echoing in her head, and if it took banging some random dude to get his voice out of her head, she'd do it.

Maybe you should ask Preacher if he wants a casual bang.

Her face flushed fire engine red immediately. Thinking about the tattoo artist was a terrible idea. She might have had the occasional fantasy about him while engaged to Harrison, but that was because it'd been safe to fantasize about him. She'd been an engaged woman, and there was no chance of that fantasy ever coming true.

And you think now that you're single, it might? Grow up, Addison. Preacher wouldn't have sex with you if you were the last woman on Earth. If strait-laced Harrison thought you were bland and boring in bed, you can sure as hell believe that Preacher would feel the same. He probably sleeps with a different woman every weekend.

Kira poked her in the arm. "Why are you blushing?"

"I'm not," Addison said.

"You are."

"Just thinking about, uh, my night of casual sex," Addison said.

"Anyone in particular you want to sleep with?" Kira said.

"No." Addison glanced at Grace. The curvy hygienist's face wore a neutral expression, but she knew damn well what Grace was thinking. Grace was too perceptive and already suspected that Addie had a crush on Preacher.

Her face flushed again. God, she would be crushing on the exact wrong man for her. She and Preacher had zero in common.

6

You don't need to have anything in common to fuck him, Addie.

She cringed at her inner crudeness, but it did make a valid point. Casual sex wasn't about a connection with someone. It was about fulfilling a need. But regardless, Preacher was not the man for her.

"You're still blushing," Kira said. "If you don't want to do this, you don't -"

"I want to," Addison said. "In fact, Daniel mentioned the other day that a few of the firefighters will be at the Thirsty Beaver tomorrow night watching the baseball game."

Kira clapped her hands. "Banging a hunky firefighter is totally the right call. Oh shit! I'm going to Willington tomorrow night with Connor to have dinner with his parents. Damn."

"Willington, ugh." Grace pretended to spit on the floor.

Kira laughed. "Hey, it's not my fault my boyfriend is from Willington. You're the one who set me up with your boss, Grace."

"You're welcome," Grace said before raising her beer bottle toward Kira.

Addie smiled a little. Her two best friends were happier than she'd ever seen them. After over a decade of crushing on Addie's older brother, Daniel, Kira finally tried to make him jealous by faking a relationship with Grace's boss, Connor, a handsome dentist who'd moved here from their rival town of Willington. It didn't take long before Kira and Connor fell in love for real.

"Shit, what time is it?" Grace glanced at her watch. "I told Gideon I'd be home by seven."

"You really gonna let my big brother tell you what to do?" Kira said with a grin. "I know he's the sheriff, but it's not like he'll arrest you for being a few minutes late."

Grace laughed. "Nope, but he might give my burger to Tank."

Addison smiled at her. "Have I told you how happy it makes me to see you so happy, Gracie?"

"Thanks, Addie," Grace said. "Gideon's the best thing that ever happened to me, and I still can't believe we're finally together. The other night in bed, he -"

"Ew!" Kira said. "No sex talk, Grace. I'm super glad you and my brother are together, but I don't want to hear anything about your sex life."

Gracie laughed. "I *know*. It wasn't about sex, you dork. Anyway, Gideon's working tomorrow night, so I'll go with you to the Beav, Addison."

"You don't have to," Addie said.

"I want to." Grace stood and finished off the last of her beer before leaning over and kissing Addison's forehead. "I'll meet you there around seven, okay?"

"Okay, thanks, Gracie."

"Don't mention it." Grace held up her arm and pointed to the friendship bracelets wrapped around it. "We're besties, remember?"

Addison laughed. "I love you guys for wearing the silly bracelets I made."

"They're not silly," Kira said. "I love them, and you're mad talented. Connor and Gideon are still wearing theirs, too. Hell, even Preacher still has his on his wrist."

"He does?" Addie said.

Shit, did she sound weird? She sounded weird.

"Yep," Kira said. "He was over the other night with Gideon, and I saw it on his wrist. I'm sorry I can't go with you tomorrow night, but I fully expect you to text me in the morning with all the details of who you banged."

CHAPTER 2

"Yo, Preacher, that guy is here."

Preacher finished spraying the metal side table in the room he used for piercing. He wiped up the disinfectant spray with a clean cloth. "Can you be a little more specific, Nolan?"

"The interview guy. Shit, he told me his name, uh…"

"Nix," Preacher said. He liked his apprentice, and Nolan wasn't stupid, but sometimes he acted like a complete idiot. "Tell him I'll be a few minutes."

"Right." Nolan lingered in the doorway. "Hey, uh, you're happy with the shit I do around here, right?

"I'm hiring another tattoo artist because the shop is busy," Preacher said. "It has nothing to do with you or your work."

"Okay, good, 'cause I know I kind of messed up that tattoo the other day, but I learned from it, and it won't happen again."

Preacher shrugged. "It was your buddy you were tattoo-ing. I don't give a fuck if you messed it up."

He could almost see Nolan's body deflate in front of him. "Right."

He turned to leave, and Preacher said, "You're doing fine. Stop fucking worrying so much. You've got talent. It was a hard tattoo, and you did better with it than ninety percent of the artists I've worked with would have done."

Nolan's face brightened. "Yeah? Thanks, man, I appreciate that. I really like it here, and I want to say thanks again for letting me apprentice. It means a lot to me and -"

"Jesus Christ, knock it off with that sappy shit, or I'll end your apprenticeship, and you'll start paying me a chair rental fee," Preacher said.

Nolan laughed and left the room. Preacher finished cleaning the table before tossing the rag in the hamper to be washed. He'd interview in this room. He had no clients booked for the rest of the day, but the shop would still be busy. People were constantly dropping in to book appointments, browse the art on the walls, and look over his tattoo books.

Even more so now that it was tourist season. After his first summer here, he'd learned to leave a few spots open daily for walk-ins. It was the only time of the year that he did walk-ins, but it helped make his shop more popular with tourists if they thought they had a chance to get a tattoo while on vacation.

He hoped this Nix guy was good. He'd interviewed two other people this week, and neither had strong enough tattooing skills. He wanted only the very best for his shop.

His shop.

A brief smile crossed his face. He'd never thought he'd be saying those words. Even now, some days, he still couldn't believe it. After living his entire life in New Cassel, Gideon had to work hard to convince him to move to Harmony Falls. And, if Preacher was honest, despite how much he missed

Gideon, he'd moved here because it was his only chance to get his own tattoo shop.

Maybe, but you love this stupid little town now, and you know it.

Yeah, maybe he did. He'd convinced himself he was a city boy, but fuck, if there wasn't something appealing about living in a small town.

Something or someone?

He stared down at the friendship bracelet on his wrist. The blue and green threads were woven into a simple diamond design. He touched the bracelet, a flash of heat hitting his groin. He rolled his eyes, annoyed with himself for lusting after the little schoolteacher who'd made the bracelet.

She wants to fuck you.

He snorted before walking toward the door of the piercing room. Maybe she was just as hot for him as he was for her, but it didn't mean he had a chance with her. Even if Addison didn't have an idiot fiancé, she'd never actually let him touch her. Not outside of her fantasies, anyway.

He'd met plenty of women like her, and as soon as he made it clear he'd be happy to fuck them, their flirting stopped, and their interest dropped off as sharply as tourist shop sales in September. He never spoke about his past to anyone, but he was confident that more than one of those proper ladies who flirted with him suspected he was an ex-con.

Addison's different.

He yanked open the door and stepped into the main part of the shop. She wasn't different, and he was a fucking fool if he tried to convince himself otherwise.

Besides, it didn't matter. Addison was engaged, and in a couple of months, she'd be forever tied to that wanker of a lawyer.

A dark-haired man, his body nearly as large and imposing as Preacher's own 6'5", stood at the front desk. He held out his hand as Preacher approached, and Preacher shook it firmly.

"Hello, I'm Nix Cordell. You must be Preacher."

"I am," Preacher said. "You want a coffee or some water?"

"No thanks," Nix said.

He wore a dark green dress shirt with a grey tie and jeans. Like Preacher, his face was clear of tattoos, but a few were peeking out from his shirt collar, and Preacher had no doubt that the rest of his body was fully inked.

"Follow me," Preacher said.

He returned to the piercing room, shutting the door behind Nix and pointing to the chair he'd brought in from the lobby. "Go ahead and have a seat."

Despite himself, he was already impressed with Nix. Hell, just the fact that he was wearing clean clothes and didn't reek of weed and alcohol was a minor miracle. He grabbed a stool and set it a few feet in front of Nix. The tattoo artist looked close to his age and projected an aura of confidence.

Nix handed over the black binder he carried. "Some of my work."

"Thanks." Preacher flipped through the binder, concealing the pleased look on his face. The guy could tattoo, and as long as he didn't completely fuck up the question portion of the interview, Preacher was fucking hiring him.

He closed the binder and returned it to Nix. "How long have you been tattooing?"

"Since I was twenty-three, so eight years now. I apprenticed with Akio Morimoto."

Preacher made a low whistle. "You serious?"

Nix nodded. "I got lucky. My old man was a delivery driver. Used to deliver Morimoto's supplies to his shop. They became friends."

"You originally from New Cassel?" Preacher said.

"Yes. Moved to Maine for a few years and worked in a shop there. Returned to New Cassel about six months ago and tattooed at a shop on the west side. Then I saw your posting online."

"Harmony Falls is a lot different from New Cassel. You lived in a small town before?"

"In Maine," Nix said.

I know the town seems busy, but it's tourist season," Preacher said. "I'm looking for someone who isn't gonna quit on me once it's winter and shit dies down."

"I won't quit." Nix stared steadily at him. "I hate the city, and I'm deliberately looking for something smaller."

"All right. The shop's usually open from eleven to seven, Tuesday to Saturday. You can set your own hours, but for the first three months, you won't be allowed to tattoo outside the regular shop hours. Once the three-month probation period ends, you'll get a key to the shop and can work outside of regular hours, if necessary."

"Sounds good," Nix said.

"I charge a chair rental fee. It's high but fair. Shop rules are pretty simple – no tattooing drunks, people high on drugs, or underage kids."

"What about tattooing faces and hands?" Nix said.

"I try to discourage it, but it isn't outright banned from the shop," Preacher said. "I expect high-quality tattoos. If you're consistently fucking up a tattoo, or if you show up drunk or high, I'll kick you out of the shop. It's a small town, and a tattoo shop that has unreliable artists, bad tattoos, or tattoo drunks and underage kids will sink fast. You get what I'm saying?"

"I do," Nix said. "I'll follow the rules."

"We get a lot of walk-ins during the summer. Enough that I can't keep up. You good with tattooing walk-ins? Even when they want stupid shit?"

"Yes," Nix said. "I saw on the website that the shop does body piercings. You have someone come in to do that?"

"Nah, I do it," Preacher said. "I apprenticed in piercing at the same time I apprenticed in tattooing. You certified to pierce?"

Nix shook his head. "No."

"That's fine. Mostly, I get requests for nose and belly button piercings and not enough that I can't handle them on my own. You got any other questions for me?"

"Not at the moment," Nix said.

"Okay, well, I have a couple more interviews, but I'll call you once I've decided." He didn't have any other interviews, and he was ninety percent certain he would offer Nix the job, but if he'd learned anything, it was that making rash decisions had a way of backfiring on a guy.

"Perfect." Nix stood and shook his hand. "Nice to meet you."

"You as well." Preacher walked him into the main tattooing area. "Email the shop if you think of any questions."

Nix's big body had gone still, and Preacher followed his gaze to where Gideon, wearing his sheriff's uniform, leaned against the front counter. The tension in Nix's body and the expression on his face suggested he might also be an ex-con. Preacher filed that information away and brushed past Nix to join Gideon.

"Hey," he nodded to Gideon, "what's up?"

"Not much. I was downtown, figured I'd stop in and say hi." Gideon clapped him on the back as Nix joined them.

"Nix Cordell, this is Gideon Walker. He's the sheriff of Harmony Falls," Preacher said. "Nix is interviewing for a job at the shop."

"Nice to meet you." Gideon held out his hand, and Nix shook it, the tension in his body easing slightly.

"You as well, Sheriff. Preacher, thanks again." Nix shook his hand a second time before heading toward the door. "I look forward to hearing from you."

He left the shop, and Gideon leaned against the counter. "He looked… normal."

"Fuck off," Preacher said.

Gideon laughed. "He wore a tie and didn't smell like he just finished a three-day bender in a swamp like the last guy you interviewed. If he can tattoo, you'll hire him, right?"

"Dude can fucking tattoo," Nolan said from his spot behind the counter. "You see that tiger in his book? Fucking sick, man."

"That's good," Gideon said. "You offer him the job?"

"Not yet." Preacher glanced at his watch. "I'm done for the day. You want to grab a beer?"

"I can't. I'm working the late shift this weekend," Gideon said.

"You're the fucking sheriff," Preacher said. "Get one of your peon deputies to work the late shift. Isn't that the benefit of being the sheriff? You get the day shift?"

Gideon laughed. "It's called being part of a team. Besides, the night shift isn't that bad. I have to go. Later, buddy." He clapped Preacher on the back before leaving the shop.

Nolan grinned at Preacher. "Hey, I'm free. I'll hit the bars with you if you want."

"Not going to a fuckin' bar," Preacher said. "That shit's too loud for me. I'm going to the Beaver if you wanna go."

Nolan laughed. "Jesus Christ, Preacher, you're such an old man now."

"Yeah, yeah, you comin' to the Beaver or not?"

"Hell, yes." Nolan grabbed his phone and followed him to the door.

CHAPTER 3

"Honey, we can just go home."

Addison studied herself in the dirty, spotted mirror before applying more gloss to her lips. "No, I'm doing this, Gracie."

"Look," Grace leaned against the counter, "I know me and Kira and Harper all said the best way to get over Harrison was to get under someone else, but if you don't *want* a night of rebound sex, you shouldn't do it. Like, don't do this because we say you should."

"I'm not." Addison smiled at Grace, trying to ignore how her head pounded and throbbed. "I promise, Gracie."

"Are you sure?"

Man, she hated that her friends knew her so well.

"I'm sure. Brad's into me, right?"

Grace's face wrinkled like she'd eaten something bad. "Yeah, he's into you."

"Good. So, I'll sleep with him tonight."

"He's kind of a douchebag, Addie."

"He's totally a douchebag." Addison smoothed down her dress and tugged at the pearls around her neck. "Which

17

makes him perfect for rebound sex. I absolutely, positively will not want to date him, even if he's amazing in bed."

"He does have a great body," Grace said.

"He's a firefighter. Of course he has a great body. Probably good stamina, too. That's important, right?"

She hated how dumb she sounded. She'd been with her lying, cheating dick of a fiancé for years, and she was remarkably naïve about sex. She'd known that she and Harrison hadn't had the most... provocative sex life, but she'd had no idea just how bad she was in bed.

Her cheeks flamed bright red, and the bathroom suddenly seemed too loud and bright. A woman came out of a stall, washed her hands, and checked her makeup before leaving, all while Addison stood frozen at the counter.

"Addie?" Grace said. "Honey, you okay?"

"Fine."

Pain danced along the front of her skull, making her feel a little sick to her stomach.

"You don't have to -"

"Enough, Grace!" The headache was making her short-tempered and irritable. "I'm doing this. I need to know if I'm... if I'm as bad in bed as Harrison said I was. Okay? You don't know what it's like to hear your fiancé, the man who's supposed to love you, tell you that he cheated because you suck in bed. You have no idea what I'm going through right now, so just stop!"

"All right," Grace said.

Grace was the one with the temper, but her voice stayed calm, and she didn't look angry. Addison reached out and took her hand, squeezing it tight. "I'm sorry. I was being a bitch."

"No, you weren't," Grace said.

"I was, and I'm sorry." Addison toyed with the pearls

around her neck again. "C'mon, let's get back to the table so I can use my rusty flirting skills on Brad."

"All right." Grace kissed her forehead. "But if you change your mind any time, let me know, and we'll leave."

"I won't change my mind," Addison said.

SHE WAS ON THE VERGE OF CHANGING HER MIND. IT WASN'T because of Brad's bad breath or the way he acted like he was God's gift to women. It wasn't even because her headache had worsened exponentially in the last hour.

She wanted to change her mind because Grace was right – this wasn't her. She wasn't the type of girl who had random sex with a guy and then never talked to him again. She was a nice girl. She was a...

Proper lady?

She cringed at the term and could almost hear Harrison saying it in her head. Her head throbbed with fresh pain, and she rubbed at her temples. Screw that. She was tired of being a proper lady. She was having sex with Brad tonight, and that was that.

But first... she needed to do something about her headache. She'd never relax and enjoy herself if her head was aching like a rotting tooth.

She squinted around the pub. Grace had gone to the bar, and it looked like she was talking to the woman who ran the animal rescue. Rain or Raylene, maybe...

She touched Brad's arm. He might be into her, but even his lust took a backseat when it was the bottom of the eighth, and the score was tied. For the last half hour, he and every other guy at the table were glued to the big screen television on the wall.

"Brad, I have a bad headache. There's some Advil in the glovebox of my car. Will you walk me out to get it?"

"Uh, the game is almost over. Can you give me half an hour?" Brad said without taking his eyes off the screen. "Oh, come the fuck on! You call that a fucking strike? What kind of ump is this guy?"

"A shit one," Jesse said.

"It won't take long," Addison said. "It's late, and it's dark out. It'll take a few minutes to walk to my car and back. I'm not comfortable walking in the parking lot by myself."

"Nothing's going to happen," Brad said. "This is Harmony Falls. Nothing bad ever happens here."

She waited another few seconds before standing. Brad was right. She didn't need an escort. She was being a silly little girl.

Addison made her way to the front door of the pub as there was a round of cheers from the people watching the game. She opened the door, stepped into the warm night air, and breathed deeply.

She rubbed at her temples as she leaned against the brick exterior. God, what was wrong with her? Why did she have such a need to be protected? Being a helpless female was so outdated, and she should be ashamed that she even wanted Brad to act like her hero. She needed to be her own hero. Needed to take care of herself for a change.

She'd been so used to having Harrison at her side that some days, it seemed overwhelming to be alone.

Still rubbing at her temples, she walked across the dark parking lot to her car. She opened the car and rummaged through the glovebox, breathing a sigh of relief when she found the Advil. Clutching it in one hand, she slid out of the car and locked it before walking toward the bar. She would feel better and more like herself when this horrible headache was –

"Well, hi there, pretty lady."

She turned around and stared at the four men trailing behind her. She had no idea where they'd come from or who they were, and her headache surged into almost unbearable pain as a rush of adrenaline went through her.

"Whatcha' doin' out here all by yourself?" The biggest of the men drawled.

Fear spiking in her veins, she backed away, the bottle of Advil slipping from her fingers to land on the pavement as the men wandered a little closer. "Just grabbing something from my car."

Her mouth was cotton-dry, and her legs shook as her body went into flight or fight mode. Predictably, it chose flight.

"You thinking about running, little lady? Guarantee you, we're faster than you," the leader said.

More adrenaline surged through her as she slipped out of her heels. No one else was around, and the noise in the pub was too loud for anyone to hear her scream. Grace didn't know where she'd gone, and Brad was completely absorbed in the baseball game and wouldn't notice if she was gone too long. Her only chance was to run.

The men watched her in amusement as she took a few deep breaths and calculated the distance to the pub in her head. She ran track in high school. She could beat them. She just had to keep a level head and not look back.

"Looks like we got ourselves a runner, boys," the leader said with a cold grin. "Truth be told – we like it when you run. We like the -"

She turned and fled. She could hear the men chasing after her, and she had taken maybe a dozen steps when a large body stepped out from behind a truck. She ran face-first into a wall of hard and unforgiving muscle, and she screamed piercingly as an arm wrapped around her waist and held her immobile.

PREACHER HAD NO IDEA WHY THE SCHOOLTEACHER WAS leaving the pub on her own, but he didn't like it. She was little, and it was late and dark outside. Where the hell was her dickhead fiancé, anyway? Sure as shit, if Preacher had a woman like her, he wouldn't let her sit at a table full of firefighters who kept looking her over like she was a piece of meat. He stared at the blue and green bracelet tied around his wrist before swallowing the last of his whiskey, pushing his chair back, and standing.

Nolan looked away from the television screen. "You leaving?"

"Just hittin' the head," he grunted.

He bypassed the bathroom and headed straight for the exit. He stepped out of the pub. The schoolteacher was walking across the parking lot, and he eyed her firm ass as he leaned against the wall.

He watched the schoolteacher slide into the passenger seat of her crappy little car. He was too far away, and it was too dark to see what she was doing, but he kept watching her anyway.

He wondered idly what she looked like under those prim and proper dresses she always wore. She was a real lady. The kind who would never have anything to do with him, but it didn't stop him from imagining her naked in his bed. She smelled so fucking good that day at the school. Jesus, he'd forgotten just how good a woman like her smelled. The women he took to his bed couldn't afford fancy perfume.

Fuck, half the time, he wasn't even sure they showered on a daily basis.

The little schoolteacher, though, he bet she had a big tub in her place, one of those fancy ones with jets. He bet she took a bath every night, maybe even let her small-dicked fiancé fuck her in it. The thought sent jealousy shooting through him, and he shook it off.

So the pretty lady with more class in her baby finger than any of the women he'd been with had been nice to him. Didn't mean she wanted to fuck him. She was nice to everyone. That was apparent. Nice and sweet and polite.

What he wouldn't fucking do to see her with her neat and tidy hair messed up from his hands, her perfectly applied lipstick smeared from his kisses, and her pale, slender thighs spread wide around his hips. He'd fuck her until her politeness was gone, until she was pounding on his back and begging him to fuck her harder.

The schoolteacher slammed her car door and started walking across the parking lot. His gaze had dropped to her tits, so when she suddenly stopped and swung around, he blinked in surprise. He stared at the four men standing behind her before cursing. His anger rising, he walked toward the schoolteacher, his long strides eating up the distance.

ADDISON'S SCREAM WAS MUFFLED AGAINST THE MAN'S CHEST. She tried to squirm away, punching frantically at her captor's hard chest.

"It's okay," he said.

She froze at the familiar voice. She raised her head and stared at the man holding her.

"Hello, Sunshine," Preacher said in a low voice.

Relief flooded through her. It made her knees weak, and she sagged against him as he stroked her hair back from her face with a surprisingly gentle touch.

"Please help me," she whispered.

He smiled reassuringly at her and turned her in his arms until her spine was against his chest. He kept his arm around her waist, his big hand gripping her hip possessively. She clung to his forearm, staring up at his face as he said, "Good evening, assholes."

"Get lost," the leader advised. "This don't concern you."

Preacher laughed. "You're bugging my woman, and it doesn't concern me?"

"We didn't know she was yours." One of the other men tugged on the leader's arm. "C'mon, Gary. It's time to leave."

"Yeah, Gary," Preacher said. "It's time to leave."

Gary pulled his arm free. "No way she's with you. Not a woman like her."

Addison didn't object when Preacher nuzzled his face into her hair. She leaned against him and tried to look like she belonged to him as he said, "The woman's mine. Leave. I won't ask you again."

"There's four of us and only one of you," Gary said.

"Fucking Christ, Gary. Do you have a goddamn death wish? Look at that guy," his friend said. "Let's go."

"You fucking pussy," Gary said. "He can't take all of us."

"Yeah, he fucking can," the third man said. "You're just too drunk to fucking realize it."

Gary glared at his friends. They were already starting to back away, and he gave them a look of disgust before muttering "pussies" under his breath. He turned and followed them to a large black truck.

As the four of them climbed in and started the engine, Addison continued to cling to Preacher's forearm. His hand was smoothing up and down her hip, and when Gary and the others roared out of the parking lot in a cloud of exhaust and dust, she jerked wildly.

"It's fine, Sunshine. Let's get you back inside," Preacher said.

He released her and took a step back. He grabbed her hand when she swayed a little, and she held it in a death grip. "My shoes. I – I need my shoes."

He led her to where her shoes were, and she watched numbly as he bent and helped her slip into her heels. He grinned up at her. "There you go, Cinderella."

She tried to laugh, but all that came out was a weird coughing, hiccupping noise. Stupidly, tears were threatening, and she blinked them back grimly as Preacher stood and reached for her hand again. It was lost in his big one, and she stared at their linked hands as he walked her slowly back to the pub.

She shook her head when he reached for the door and dropped his hand. She backed up until she felt the cold brick wall against her back as the tattoo artist stared silently at her.

"I – I just need a minute," she gasped.

Her head was spinning, and she felt sick to her stomach. If Preacher hadn't been outside, if he hadn't come to her rescue...

Her stomach roiled, and she bent over, clutching at her stomach and willing herself not to vomit. She'd die of shame if she threw up on Preacher's boots. His warm hand gripped the back of her neck as he bent down and said, "Take deep breaths, Sunshine."

She was feeling faint, and there was a tightness in her chest that made her feel like she couldn't breathe.

"Deep breaths." Oddly enough, the command in Preacher's voice got her lungs working again, and she gulped in air as his hand kneaded her neck.

"Nice and slow," he demanded.

She slowed her breathing, concentrating on pushing air in and out of her lungs and on the feel of his fingers massaging her neck. When she no longer felt like she was going to throw up or faint, she straightened slowly. He was still cupping the back of her neck, and she stared up at him as he studied her.

She was suddenly aware of how close he was standing to her. Her breasts were nearly brushing against him, and the heat of his body felt like it was warming her to her core. Her nipples tightened, and her pussy tingled in an unfamiliar but decidedly enjoyable way.

Addison! Say thank you and leave!

"I – thank you for rescuing me," she whispered.

He cocked his head and studied her for a moment longer before leaning down, his deep voice a low rasp. "If you were mine, you'd always be safe."

His words made the muscles of her pussy clench in agonizing pleasure. For a moment, she could almost imagine what it would be like to belong to this man. To know that he would always take care of her, to know that every night, he would take her to his bed and show her more pleasure than she could ever imagine. Her lips parted at the thought of being naked underneath him, and Preacher's gaze dropped to her mouth.

"Do you know what you do to me, Sunshine?" he said.

Before she could reply, his hard mouth was on hers, and his tongue was pushing past her lips to take what belonged to him.

WHAT HE WAS DOING WAS ALL SORTS OF WRONG. THE schoolteacher had a goddamn fiancé, and here he was, shoving his tongue down her throat. Preacher pulled away with regret. He wasn't going to steal another man's woman – not even a douche like Harrison Frank – no matter how much he wanted her.

Of course, he hadn't counted on the little schoolteacher standing on her tiptoes, fisting her hands in his shirt, and mashing her mouth back onto his. At the first tentative swipe of her tongue against his lips, he groaned and reached down to grip her ass with both hands. He lifted her, and she wrapped her legs around his waist as he pushed her against the wall and angled his mouth over hers. He kissed her hard, exploring every inch of her warm mouth with his tongue as his hands squeezed and kneaded her perfect ass.

Fuck she tasted good. He kissed down her throat, nipping at the soft skin before sucking on the spot where her neck met her shoulder. If he applied even a little more pressure, it would leave a mark, and without thinking about it, he sucked hard. He ground his erection against her crotch, and the little gasp she made sent his lust into overdrive.

He dry-humped her against the wall, pressing rhythmically against her pussy as he shoved his hands under her dress and caressed her ass through her soft panties. He curled his fingers around the waistband. All it would take was one tug to rip them off. Once she was bare for him, he could unzip his jeans, pull out his dick, and he'd be balls-deep in her hot pussy with one twist of his hips. He'd bet his left nut she was wet for him. The way she was rocking her pussy against his dick made it more than obvious she wanted to be fucked.

His hand tightened around her panties, but before he could go any further, the pub door opened. He froze against the wall, his brain screaming at him as Grace stared wide-eyed at them.

"Preacher? What are you doing to Addie?"

With a wince, he dropped Addison to her feet and backed away. She was panting, her cheeks red and her eyes bright with a combination of lust and embarrassment. His dick throbbing in his pants, he pushed past Grace without saying a word and went into the pub.

CHAPTER 4

Addison knocked on Gideon and Grace's front door. The booming bark of Gideon's Great Dane, Tank, rang out from the backyard. Her hands were trembling, and she wanted to turn and sprint back to her car, but she stayed where she was. Grace drove her home last night from the Thirsty Beaver. After Addison refused to talk about what Grace saw her doing with Preacher, she made Addison promise to come over today after Grace finished her shift at the dental clinic.

The door opened, and Grace smiled at her. "Hey, honey. Come in."

She followed Grace down the hallway and toward the backyard. She could see Tank bouncing around in front of the door, and she braced herself for his enthusiastic greeting as she stepped out into the yard.

Tail wagging and bum wiggling, Tank crowded up against her, his one hundred-and-seventy-five-pound body nearly knocking her on her ass. Grace grabbed her arm to steady her when Addie staggered back.

"Tank, go on."

"It's okay." Addison petted Tank's head. He was so tall that all he had to do was lift his head to sniff her chin. "Hi, buddy. Who's a good boy?"

His tail wagged harder, and Grace patted him on the hip. "Okay, you said hi. Go lay down, big guy."

Tank wandered away to the patch of evening sun that beamed down on the yard's far corner. Grace handed Addison a glass of wine and sat in one of the deck chairs. "Sit down, babe."

"Where's Gideon?" Addison sat in the chair next to Grace.

"He's working the late shift this weekend."

"Oh, right, you told me that." She toyed with the bracelets around her waist and took a big gulp of wine. Crickets chirped, and Grace swatted at a mosquito.

"How was work?" Addison said.

"Good. What did you do today?"

"Cleaned my apartment, washed my car, and Facetimed with Harper."

"Did you tell her what happened between you and Preacher last night?" Grace said.

"Yeah."

"And?"

"She was excited, kind of giddy, demanded to know every last detail," Addison said.

Grace laughed. "That sounds like Harper. Will you tell *me* why I found you outside with Preacher's hands on your ass and his tongue down your throat?"

"It all started because I had a stupid headache…"

ADDISON RESISTED HER TEMPTATION TO DRAIN THE HALF A glass of wine she had left, sipping at it instead. "Well, is this where you call me a slut?"

Grace blinked at her. "What? Why would I call you a slut?"

"Because I – I made out with Preacher in a parking lot! He gave me a hickey!"

"Oh yeah? Let me see it."

Addison pulled aside the collar of her shirt, and Grace studied the dark purple mark at the base of her neck. "Preacher, you dirty boy."

"I can't believe I made out with Preacher," Addison said.

"He kissed you first," Grace said.

"Yeah, but he pulled back right away and then I practically threw myself at him."

"Didn't look like he minded," Grace said. "Why do you look like you're going to barf?"

"Because I made out with Preacher! Oh my God, Gracie. Harrison is the only guy I've ever kissed, and I... I had my tongue shoved into the mouth of a guy whose name I don't even know! I mean, his real name can't be Preacher, can it? It can't be. What kind of mother names her kid Preacher? And what kind of woman kisses a guy whose name she doesn't even know!"

She could hear the hysteria in her voice, and she knew she was overreacting, but the numbness she'd felt when she told Harper about what happened this morning had completely disappeared. It'd been replaced by confusion and embarrassment and, God help her, just the tiniest bit of lust.

She drank the rest of her wine in three large swallows before grabbing the bottle on the small table between their chairs and pouring herself another full glass. Screw it, she'd Uber home tonight.

"Simon," Grace said.

"What?" Addison stopped with the wine glass to her mouth, her hand visibly shaking.

"Preacher's real name is Simon." Grace glanced at the fence that separated their yard from the neighbours as if she thought Preacher might be peeking over it. "I don't know his last name, though."

"How do you know his first name?"

"Gideon told me. But," Grace took a drink of beer, "you can't tell Gideon or Preacher that I told you. Gideon told me with the understanding that I wouldn't tell anyone, but I feel like knowing his actual name might help you stop freaking out."

Addison took a deep breath and then a sip of wine. Weirdly, knowing his name did help a little.

"Better?" Grace said.

"Yes."

"Good. Listen to me, you're not a slut, okay? Last night, you had a very traumatic and scary experience that Preacher rescued you from. It's natural in that moment to have strong feelings for the person who saved you, and if the overwhelming feeling was lust... so what? You have a crush on Preacher. It's not surprising that you made out with him."

"I don't have a crush on him," Addison said.

Grace rolled her eyes. "Addie, c'mon. You're not with Harrison anymore. It's perfectly fine to admit you have a crush on Preacher. Hell, what did Harper say? Half the women in this town – single and married – masturbate to fantasies of him in their bed."

Her face red, Addison watched as Tank stood, circled a few times, and then stretched out in the soft grass again. "Yeah, okay. I have a small crush on Preacher."

"Plus, you were determined to have rebound sex last night, so sex was on your mind anyway, right?"

Her blush deepening, Addison said, "Maybe, uh, Preacher should be my rebound person."

"I don't think that's a good idea, honey."

"Yeah, I know. Preacher can have any woman he wants. I doubt sex with me has ever crossed his mind. He was probably just drunk last night."

"Well, that's some horseshit." Grace took another swig of beer. "The sexual tension between you two is off the charts, and I don't think Preacher is the kind of guy to kiss a woman the way he was kissing you if he didn't want to bang their brains out."

"Unless he was drunk."

"You had your tongue shoved down his throat. Was there an overwhelming taste of liquor?" Grace said.

"Don't be crude, Gracie."

"Answer the question, Addie."

"He tasted like whiskey, but not crazy strong or anything."

"He wasn't drunk. And the reason I said it wasn't a good idea is because we all hang out together, and the two of you having casual sex could get awkward. I don't want the band broken up."

Addison smiled a little. "You make a good point."

"Addie?" Grace leaned forward and stared solemnly at her. "Your little crush on Preacher is just that, right? A crush?"

"Of course it is," Addison said. "One, I just ended a long-term relationship, and two, it would never work between Preacher and me."

"It wouldn't," Grace said. "Preacher is a good man, probably better than any of us even realize, but you two have incredibly different lifestyles. Not to mention, he doesn't show any indication that he wants to settle down. He's lived here almost three years, and we've never seen him with an actual girlfriend. Just a random woman here and there who is never from Harmony Falls."

"I know," Addison said. "It's just a crush, Gracie, nothing more."

Is it? Then explain why you masturbated in the shower this morning after reliving what happened between you and Preacher.

Addison drank some wine, hoping Grace would think her deepening flush was because of the wine. So, she had masturbated this morning – a*nd last night when you got home from the pub* - so what? It was like Harper said, plenty of women in their small town masturbated to thoughts of Preacher. She was no different than them.

Except you know what it's like to kiss Preacher.

Did she ever. And it'd been the hottest and best kiss of her life. She'd kissed Harrison thousands of times, and it had never once been like that. She'd never felt so alive or turned on or even –

"Addie?"

She cleared her throat. "Sorry. Just, uh, thinking. Hey, what are you doing tomorrow afternoon? I was thinking of texting Kira and seeing if she wanted to hike at the Falls. I know it'll be busy with tourists, but I could use some exercise and fresh air."

"Sorry, honey. Kira and Connor are coming over for a barbeque tomorrow afternoon and to play cards."

"Oh, okay," Addison said.

"Why don't you come over too? There will be plenty of food and -"

"Nope, this is obviously a couples thing," Addison said.

"I'm sorry," Grace said.

"Don't be. It's all good. I'll do my own thing tomorrow," Addie said.

She plastered a smile on her face, determined not to let Grace see how upset or left out she was feeling. It wasn't Grace's fault Addison wasn't part of a couple anymore. Besides, she needed to get used to being alone and enjoying her own company. She didn't need a guy to have a good time. She could have a great time alone.

―――

"I AM HAVING A GREAT TIME ALONE," ADDISON MUTTERED. She opened the door to Twisted Stitches and stepped inside. The air conditioning hummed in the store, and the cold air was a welcome relief from the hot mugginess of main street.

During the winter months, Harmony Falls' only yarn shop was closed on Sundays, but Emma, Twisted Stitches' owner, kept the shop open seven days a week during tourist season. Not surprisingly, the yarn shop was busy with a mixture of both tourists and locals. Some were just there to escape the heat for a few blissful minutes, while others carried small baskets loaded down with colourful hanks of yarn.

"Addie, hey, how are you?" Wearing a 'Twisted Stitches' t-shirt, Emma squeezed her curvy body past a couple of tourists. She carried a few hanks of yarn, a couple of sets of knitting needles, and a pattern book in her hands. Her usual calm vibe was a little frazzled. "Good to see you."

"You too, Emma. Busy in here today," Addison said.

"It is. I'm a bit swamped because Cora called in sick."

"Ma'am? Excuse me, ma'am?" A woman wearing an 'I love Harmony Falls' t-shirt and a large sunhat jammed onto her head waved at Emma with one sunburned arm. "Do you have this yarn in chartreuse?" She turned to face the bored looking teenager standing next to her. "The yarn place in New York just has so many more colours. I knew I should have brought extra yarn to the cabin, but your father insisted there wasn't enough room in the car. Probably because he filled it with his fishing gear. I swear, next year, we're renting a trailer when we come up for our summer holidays. If your father gets to bring fifty different fishing rods, I should get to bring more than a bagful of yarn."

The teenager mumbled a reply that Addison couldn't hear as the woman waved at Emma again. "Ma'am, I'm really looking for chartreuse yarn."

Emma turned to face them, and Addison winced when the woman twitched in surprise, and the teenager said, "Dude, what's up with your face?"

"Rodney! Car, now!" the woman snapped.

He was still staring at Emma, and his mother elbowed him hard. "Go to the car and wait for me there."

"Fine." The teenager rubbed his ribs. "God, it was just a question."

"I'm so sorry," the woman said as the teenager slouched out of the store. She smiled apologetically, her gaze skittering away from Emma's face.

"It's fine," Emma said in the 'it's no big deal, it happens all the time' voice that Addison suspected she had perfected by the age of ten.

She wanted to glare at the woman when she continued to stare at Emma. The curvy yarn shop owner had a large port stain birthmark that started at her left temple, covered almost the entirety of her left cheek, and followed a meandering path down the left side of her throat to disappear under the collar of her shirt.

Addison had always admired Emma's ability to deal with

the constant questions and looks from tourists and even locals who'd known her all her life. Secretly, she was surprised that Emma hadn't moved away from Harmony Falls. Living in a large city or even a mid-size one like New Cassel would probably have been easier for her to blend in. There, she would have just been another slightly different looking face in the crowd. Here, her birthmark meant she was often considered or talked about like she was the town freak.

As Emma, a smile tacked on her face, and her head turned to minimize the amount of birthmark the tourist would have to see, helped the woman, Addison moved deeper into the shop. It wasn't that big of a space, but Emma had maxed out the space she did have by hanging yarn on the walls almost to the ceiling. Addison rummaged through a bin of discount yarn, studying each hank of yarn and reminding herself that she didn't need any more.

Her job as a schoolteacher paid her rent and her bills, but it didn't leave much extra. She tried to be frugal and didn't eat out much or take a lot of vacations, but she admittedly had a yarn addiction. She stroked the soft cotton yarn she was holding before putting it back.

Her car had been making that weird clicking noise again, and she needed to consider returning it to the mechanic. She would try Nuts and Bolts Auto Repair this time instead of the shop owned by Gordon Rampton. She took her car to Gordon because that's where Harrison took his Mercedes, but her crappy Honda Civic had looked ridiculously out of place among the gleaming Mercedes and BMWs that Gordon primarily serviced.

Gordon was always perfectly polite and never made her feel embarrassed about her piece of crap car, but now that she wasn't with Harrison anymore, she could try a cheaper alternative. Harrison was always so concerned about appearance, always wanted people to look at them and see wealth and luxury, that he'd balked at her doing anything others might consider cheap.

She sighed and moved down the far aisle to study the selection of sock yarn. Harrison had expensive taste, and while he made good money, she knew he carried a lot of credit card debt. They'd always kept their finances separate at Harrison's insistence – some days, he acted like *she* was the one with money issues – and she supposed not having to take on his debt was another reason to be thankful they'd separated.

There were a lot of reasons she should be thankful they'd separated, and she needed to concentrate on those instead of obsessing over the fact that Harrison said she was stiff and unsexy and terrible in the sack. So she wasn't a great lover. It wasn't the end of the world. There were probably plenty of women who weren't amazing at sex.

She studied the wall of yarn, not registering anything she was seeing. Maybe she needed to order a couple of books online to give her some tips and ideas on how to be better at sex. Her idea of rebound sex had seemed like a good one on Friday night, but now, she wasn't quite so sure. If the only person she'd slept with was Harrison, she could hold on to the hope that maybe it wasn't all her fault. Maybe Harrison wasn't so great at it either, or –

Crystal seemed to be enjoying herself. It's you, girl. Face it. You suck in bed. You were worried about that long before Harrison finally told you the truth. You need to get better at this sex thing, and you know reading a few books isn't going to cut it. You need some hands-on experience with a real penis. A penis that's attached to say... I dunno... Preacher?

She grabbed a random ball of yarn from the wall and stared at it. She needed to get over her stupid crush on

Preacher. It was starting to border on obsessive. Last night, she'd had this shameful little fantasy where Preacher had shown up at her place and, without a word, picked her up like she was some damn princess in a fairy tale, carried her to her bedroom, and...

Say it, Addison.

Her face flushed hot. No, she wouldn't say it. A proper lady did not have dirty thoughts about a man's head between her thighs, about his tongue –

"Girl, are you serious? How can you not know that Harrison dumped her? Have you been living under a rock?"

The voice drifting over from the aisle next to her killed her dirty thoughts as quickly as if she'd been doused with a bucket of cold water. She stood frozen in the aisle, staring wide-eyed at the yarn in front of her, her fingers squeezing compulsively around the ball of yarn in her hands.

"I've been busy. God, don't be a bitch. Why did he dump little Miss Goody Two Shoes anyway?"

Addison didn't recognize the two women's voices, but it didn't matter. She dropped the yarn she held into the basket on the shelf before her. Her hands were too shaky and clammy to attempt to hang it in the right spot.

Her ears burning and her heart thumping, she told herself to walk away. Instead, she remained frozen to the spot like her feet were dipped in concrete.

"Well, I heard from Doris Sindle that Harrison dumped her because Addison has, like, a serious shopping addiction and debt problem, and he didn't want to be saddled with it. But, Shelly, over at the Walgreens, said that Harrison dumped her because he caught her in bed with some guy from Willington."

"No fucking way." The voice was high-pitched with excitement. "Addison Moore is such a prim little good girl.

She would never cheat on Harrison. Hell, I'd be surprised if she even fucked Harrison."

The other woman laughed. "You're telling me. She does have that 'only missionary position, under the covers, with the lights off and showering immediately after' look to her. Maybe old Harrison dumped her 'cause she refused to use that good girl mouth of hers to blow him."

"That seems more likely than her banging some gross dude from Willington. Although, just between you and me, I always thought Harrison could do better than her. He's, like, good looking and rich and apparently about to make partner at his firm. Honestly, she would have just weighed him down if they'd gotten married."

Feeling sick to her stomach, unable to stand there a second longer, Addison stumbled down the aisle toward the front of the store. She weaved around a group of tourists and staggered toward the front door, tears pricking her eyes.

"Addie?" Emma was standing by a rack of buttons near the front door. "Are you okay?"

"Yes. I have to go." She pushed her way out of the shop, the hot, muggy air slapping her in the face like a wet rag. Sweat prickled along her hairline, and she hurried down the street to her car. She climbed in and turned it on, blasting the air conditioning and pressing the heels of her hands against her eyes.

She wouldn't cry. She would not fucking cry.

She took a few hitching breaths and threw the car into reverse before backing out of the parking spot and driving down the street. She needed to leave. She needed to leave this stupid town, even if it was only for a few hours.

CHAPTER 5

"Sorry, hon. It's gonna be at least a couple of hours. Wade's got two other cars he needs to tow before he can get to you."

Addison banged her hand on the steering wheel before blowing her breath out. "Okay. I'll wait here until -"

"Don't do that, sweetheart." Roberta, Wade's wife and co-owner of Wade and Roberta's Tow Truck Services, popped her gum so loud Addison could hear it through the phone. "You said you were out on Watkins Road, right? That road ain't very busy, even with tourist season, so your car will be fine until Wade gets there. No point in you sitting and sweltering by the side of the road. Get a friend to pick you up, and leave your car unlocked with the keys in the glove box. I'll get Wade to tow it straight to the Nuts and Bolts shop. Give me your credit card number, and I'll ring it through once he picks up your car."

"Um, sure, okay." She dug her card out of her purse and recited the number to Roberta before ending the call. She climbed out of her car. Even a few minutes without air conditioning had made her dress stick to her back.

She kicked the front tire of her car and then slammed her hand on the hood. She'd driven to Willington before turning the car around and heading back to Harmony Falls. Her decision to take the back roads instead of the main highway seemed like a good one until the ticking noise grew increasingly louder, and her car made a horrible grinding noise and then completely died. She'd steered it to the side of the road and tried to start it a few times before giving up and calling for a tow.

She kicked the tire again, pulled at the front of her dress, and fanned herself. God, it was so damn muggy and hot. She wore a lightweight button-up skater dress that she rarely wore because it fell to mid-thigh rather than her knee. Harrison always said the short hem made her look like a prostitute for a second-rate escort agency, but it was the only dress she owned with a collar. She pulled the collar aside and touched the hickey on her neck before tucking the collar back into place to hide the dark blotch.

She grabbed her phone and stared at her contacts. Her parents were in Tokyo, Daniel was working a shift at the fire station, and Kira and Gracie were busy with their boyfriends. She pressed her lips together, embarrassed at how weepy she was.

She didn't have anyone to call.

Call Grace and Kira. They won't care, Addie. They'll come to pick you up, and you can join them at their barbeque and stop feeling so goddamn sorry for yourself.

No, she wouldn't call them. She would get a ride home from Wade. She needed to realize that she was alone now and start taking care of her problems herself.

You'll stand at the side of a road in ninety-degree heat because why? To prove you're an independent woman? Don't be an idiot. Call your friends and –

The distant roar of a motorcycle made her stiffen. She studied the Harley flying down the road toward her, her stomach dropping. It was him. Of course, it was him.

For a moment, she had the stupidest urge to run to the ditch and fling her body into it. To hide and hope he didn't see her. Thankfully, it passed quickly. She smoothed her dress with suddenly trembling hands and patted her cheeks, hoping her makeup hadn't completely sweated off.

Why did it have to be him? Why couldn't it have been anyone else? Her stomach clenched with nerves as the Harley grew closer. Maybe it wasn't him. Maybe it was some other large, tattoo-covered motorcycle driving badass.

He slowed down as he approached and stopped the bike behind her car. She leaned against her car, and he shut off the motorcycle. Her ears rang in the sudden silence. He put the kickstand down and swung his leg over the bike with practiced ease. He wore a navy blue t-shirt, a worn leather vest, and faded jeans that clung to his thick thighs.

Did his jeans have to be so tight?

He took off his helmet and scrubbed his hands through his hair. He left the helmet on the seat and ambled toward her.

"Uh, hi, Mr. Preacher." Her voice was nervous and high-pitched, and she winced inwardly. Calling him mister seemed ridiculous after she'd had his tongue in her mouth, but it just popped out.

"Afternoon, Miss Moore," he said.

Her breath caught in her throat when he moved closer, but he simply walked by her, popped the hood latch and lifted the hood. He bent over her car, staring at the engine.

"It was making a ticking sound and then a grinding sound, and then it died," she said.

"Your car is a piece of shit," he said.

"Um, yes, I know."

She watched silently as he poked and prodded at the engine before straightening. "Your engine is shot."

"How do you know that?"

"I'm good with cars," he said. "You'll probably need a whole new engine."

"Shoot. Okay, well, thanks."

He stared at the phone in her hands. "You call your fiancé?"

She jerked in surprise, nearly dropping her phone on the hot pavement at her feet. He didn't know she and Harrison had broken up. Holy crap. He didn't know. How could he not know? Relief mixed with shame twisted through her.

She realized she didn't want to tell him. She didn't want him to know that Harrison had dumped her, even if she skipped over the reason why. Telling Preacher that a man like Harrison had left her made her feel like the biggest loser in the world.

So, instead, you'll let him think you're the type of woman who makes out with another guy while she's engaged to someone else?

She swallowed hard. Wrong or right, letting Preacher think she was a cheating whore somehow felt less pathetic than telling him Harrison dumped her.

"Miss Moore?" Preacher stared at her, and she realized she'd been standing there silently for nearly a minute.

Her hands sweating and her voice a bit shaky, she said, "I want to apologize for the other night, Mr. Preacher. What I did was completely inappropriate, and I am very embarrassed."

He didn't reply, and she babbled on. "I think – I think I was just so grateful to you for saving me that I, um, took it a little too far. I hope you don't think poorly of me."

"Why would I?" he asked with genuine puzzlement.

"Well, because I threw myself at you when you were just trying to be nice, and I…"

He stared silently at her. Any idea that he might have been attracted to her had flown out the window with how he was acting now, and why did that make her feel like crying? It wasn't surprising he would regret what happened or consider it the worst mistake of his life.

"I'm sorry," she blurted again. "It was a huge mistake, and I -"

"Of course, it was," he said. "Good girls like you don't fuck men like me, do they?"

The weird bitterness in his voice made her feel even worse, and her stomach churned with nausea. She backed away a couple of steps in case she just casually vomited on his damn boots.

His voice tight and guilt etched into his face, he said, "Are you afraid of me? I wouldn't hurt you."

"I'm not afraid of you." She knew without a doubt that Preacher would never hurt her. "But I feel bad about leading you on the other night, and I wouldn't blame you for being angry with me."

"I'm not angry. You were afraid, and sometimes people do crazy shit when they're afraid." He leaned against her car and folded his arms across his broad chest. "I'll wait with you until your fiancé gets here."

"He's not coming," she said.

He scowled, and his gaze dropped to her neck. Her breath caught in her throat when he stalked toward her and pulled her dress collar away from her throat.

"He mad because of this?" His callused fingers brushed against the pearls around her throat before he touched the hickey he had branded her with. Goosebumps skittered to life on her skin despite the cloying heat.

"He hasn't noticed it," she whispered.

An odd look crossed his face. "His woman's got another man's mark on her, and he hasn't noticed?"

She didn't know what to say to that, so she just clutched her phone and said, "I called Wade for a tow, but he's got a few other calls, so he'll be a couple of hours. He said I could leave the keys in the glovebox, but I think I'll wait until he arrives. Just to keep an eye on the car."

"No one's going to do anything to your junk car. C'mon, I'll give you a ride home. You can text Wade and tell him to take this piece of shit straight to the junkyard."

"Oh no, that's okay," she said immediately. "I don't mind waiting."

"You're in the middle of nowhere," he said. "It's unsafe for a little thing like you to be out here alone."

"It's fine," she said. "This is Harmony Falls. Nothing bad ever happens here."

"We both know that isn't true."

She flushed and stared at her phone for a moment. "Okay. If you're sure you don't mind?"

"I don't," he said.

"Okay, well, uh, thank you, Mr. Preacher."

DECIDING TO TAKE A RIDE THIS AFTERNOON WAS TURNING OUT to be the best fucking decision of his life. Finding the little schoolteacher stranded on the side of the road wearing a pretty green dress that showed off her delectable thighs and clung to her perfect tits shouldn't have made him as fucking happy as it did, but here they were.

He studied her smooth thighs, immediately transported back to Friday night and the way they'd felt clamped around his waist. What he wouldn't fucking give to be between those pretty thighs again.

Cool it, asshole. She's engaged.

"Mr. Preacher?" Addison was tugging at the pearls around her neck, and that image in his head, the one that always seemed to be lurking in his brain, popped up to say hello.

He'd never actually seen Addison naked, but goddamn, it was easy to imagine it. Easy to imagine what she'd look like on her knees on his bed, wearing nothing but those pearls around her neck. Her firm tits bouncing, her voice moaning his name, those pearls tangled around his fingers as he fucked her tight pussy from behind. He'd jacked off so many times to that fantasy it was a surprise his dick wasn't raw. He was going through goddamn lube like a thirteen-year-old boy who'd just discovered internet porn.

"Mr. Preacher?" Addison repeated. She sounded nervous, and despite her earlier reassurance, he hated even the idea that she might be afraid of him.

"It's just Preacher," he said, standing beside his bike. "You ready?"

The little schoolteacher drifted closer – Christ, she smelled so fucking good. How did a woman smell that good in this heat? He wasn't surprised when she said, "I've never ridden on a motorcycle before."

She slipped her purse over her head, newsboy style. He unstrapped his extra helmet from the bike and said, "C'mere."

"You know what," she said with another look at his bike. "I think I'll just wait for Wade."

"It's perfectly safe," he said.

"Did you know that a motorcyclist's risk of a fatal crash is thirty-five times higher than a passenger car?" Her usual low voice had gone up an octave.

He couldn't help but laugh. "Nah, I didn't know that."

"It's true," she said.

"I'm a very safe driver," he said.

"Are you?" She bit at her bottom lip.

"Yes, Sunshine," he said.

Her face flushed at the nickname, and she didn't object when he slipped the helmet over her head and buckled it under her chin. He kept his movements brisk and detached, but even grazing his knuckles against her throat gave him half a goddamn stiffy. He put on his helmet and turned on the intercom system in his helmet and hers. He sat down and patted the spot behind him.

"Swing your leg over and put your feet on the pegs."

She did what he asked, pulling at the hem of her dress when it rode up even higher on her thighs. He reached behind him, grabbed her legs just above her knees, and pulled her up snugly against him. Her crotch was pressed against his lower back, and her thighs rested against his hips. He had an over-whelming urge to rest his hand on her thigh, to show the world that she was his woman, which was stupid because a woman like her would never be with a man like him.

Not to mention she has a man, you dickhead.

Right. It was strange how easy it was for him to forget that fucking detail about her.

She was trying to wiggle back, and he used that as an excuse to reach back and slide his hand around her thigh, holding her in place. "Nope, sit nice and close, Sunshine. You don't want to fall off, do you?"

Her legs tightened around his hips at his words, and he tried not to groan. What he wouldn't give to have her legs tighten like that while he was fucking her. "What's your address?"

She recited her address, and he said, "Hands around my waist. Hold on tight."

"Will you drive slowly?" She put her arms around him and linked her fingers together across his flat abdomen.

God, she felt way too good pressed up against his back with her arms around him. He started the motorcycle, and she jumped. Her thighs squeezed his hips even tighter, and her voice through the intercom turned high pitched. "Preacher, will you drive slowly?"

"I'll drive carefully," he said before lifting the kickstand. With a quick throttle twist, he had the bike flying down the road. The little schoolteacher squealed and clung to him like the world's sexiest piggyback ride. He could feel her helmet pressing against his back, and he reached down and patted her hand.

"Both hands on the wheel!" she said hysterically, and he laughed before gunning the engine.

She squealed again, but this time, he thought he might have detected a little bit of excitement mixed in with the fear. She lifted her head from his back. Thanks to the intercom, he could hear her soft and weirdly sexy gasps in his ear.

"You okay?" he said after about five minutes.

"Yes." The excitement was palpable in her voice. "Yes, this is… lovely! Can you go faster?"

He grinned. "Yes, Sunshine, I can."

———

THE RIDE TO HER HOUSE WAS OVER FAR TOO QUICKLY. Addison's terror had turned first to excitement and then pure delight in the time it took Preacher to get her home. As he slowed to a stop and put the kickstand down before shutting off the bike, she tried to ignore her disappointment at the end of the ride.

She was ashamed to admit that it wasn't only the ride she

enjoyed. Pushed up against Preacher's back, feeling the hard muscles of his abdomen under her hands, and the vibration of the bike between her thighs had made her horny as hell. She was half-fantasizing that Preacher was driving her to some secluded part of town so he could make love to her when he turned onto her street.

She realized she was still sitting on the bike, still clinging to Preacher's back like a monkey, and with a flush of embarrassment, she climbed off the bike. Preacher stood and unbuckled her helmet, removing it and letting it dangle from two fingers as she self-consciously fluffed her hair.

She knew she had a huge grin as she stared up at him. "That was so much fun! Thank you, Preacher."

"You're welcome, Sunshine."

She cleared her throat and patted her hair again. "Do I look funny with helmet hair?"

He shook his head. "You look good. Real good."

She flushed. "I look wind-blown, I'm sure."

"I like it," he said. "The only time a woman looks better than after her first motorcycle ride is after her first orga -"

He abruptly cut the sentence short as his tanned skin turned red. She hid her smile as he turned and strapped the helmet to the back of his bike.

She studied the friendship bracelet she'd given him as he looked at her apartment building.

"This is a nice area," he said.

"It is," she said. "I like that it's kind of close to downtown. Sometimes, I'll walk from my place to downtown just for, um, exercise. You know."

Lord, she sounded like such an idiot.

Her nerves were getting the best of her. She couldn't stop talking. "I like the building. It's quiet, and my neighbours are friendly. I live in apartment 427."

He stared at her, and oh my God, why did she say that?

"Anyway, thank you again," she said. "I appreciate your help."

He nodded, and she hesitated a moment longer before saying, "Well, I'll see you around, okay?"

"Bye."

"Okay, bye," she said.

"Bye."

Cursing herself for being an idiot, she turned and walked up the pathway to her apartment building, pulling her keys out of her purse. Before opening the door, she looked behind her. Preacher was back on his bike but hadn't started it yet.

She waved, he nodded, and she shoved the key in the lock and opened the door. She peeked again at Preacher. He was still sitting on his bike and staring at her. Ignoring her urge to return to him, she shut the door and headed for the stairs.

CHAPTER 6

"You look terrible, pinky-pie, what's wrong?" Harper's face stared out at Addison from the screen of her iPad.

Addison grimaced. "I talked to the mechanic today about my car, and it's toast. Totally toast. Preacher was right. I need a new engine, which will cost more than the car is worth. So, now I have to buy a new car, and I seriously do not have the money right now."

"Wait, wait, back up... what do you mean Preacher was right?" Harper raised one perfectly manicured brow.

"Oh, um, Preacher happened to drive by on his motorcycle yesterday while I was stranded on the side of the road, and he gave me a ride to my place because Wade was going to be a few hours."

"Are you fucking kidding me right now?" Harper gave her the hairy eyeball. "Bitch, you did not text that part of the 'my car broke down' story to me last night. What the hell?"

Addison couldn't help but laugh. "I didn't... I mean...it wasn't that big of a deal."

"Fucking hell, it wasn't that big of a deal," Harper said.

"You rode Preacher's Harley. What else aren't you telling me? Was it just his bike you rode, or did you take a spin on his dick too?"

"Harper!" Addison propped the iPad on the table before grabbing juice from the fridge. "Don't be crude."

"Well?" Harper leaned forward until all Addison could see was her nose and mouth. "Did you or did you not bang Preacher like a screen door yesterday?"

"No, of course I didn't. He just gave me a ride back to my place. It was no big deal, all right?"

"What were you wearing? What was he wearing? Did he do that sexy thing where the guy rests his hand on the woman's thigh while he steers his big ole' hog with one hand?"

"Oh my God, what is up with you tonight?" Addison said.

Harper laughed. "Sorry, honey. I went out with Angie and Pooja, and I might still be a teensy bit high."

Addison stared at her watch. "It's, like, five-thirty. I don't think you're supposed to smoke weed until after seven."

Harper laughed so hard that she dropped her phone, and Addison was treated to a view of the ceiling until Harper scooped it back up and pointed it at her face again. "There's no appointed time for weed, you dork. It can be weed time anytime."

"Until you get arrested for it," Addison said.

"Okay, Mom," Harper said. "Anyway, why didn't you mention that Preacher rescued you."

"I don't know. I think it's because I suddenly feel obsessed with him, and it's ridiculous. He's not attracted to me, and half the time, I end up looking and sounding like a fool when I'm around him."

"One, he's attracted to you – all guys are attracted to you. You're a hot and sexy little number, and you're sweet, and you're smart. You're the perfect package. I get why Gracie-Lou is discouraging you from picking Preacher as your casual sex partner, but I disagree. You're both adults, and it doesn't have to be weird unless you make it weird, right? You find him sexy as hell. Why not fuck his brains out?"

"It's not a good idea," Addison said.

"Why not?" Harper persisted. "Give me one valid reason."

"Because I'm terrible in bed, and I will die of shame if Preacher finds out?"

Harper shook her head. "Babe, that butterface fuck goblin, Harrison, is not the be all and end all of what makes someone a good sex partner. You can't just take his word that you're bad in bed. Maybe he's the one who's bad in bed."

"Maybe," Addison hesitated, "but he was right about one thing – I was often kind of stiff and awkward and most of the time I didn't climax and -"

"What.The.Fuck." Harper's face was a mixture of disbelief and anger. "What do you mean most of the time you didn't climax?"

Her face so hot, she half-expected it to catch on fire, Addison said, "Forget I said anything."

"Oh no," Harper said. "Look, I respected your wishes not to talk about boning when you were with Harrison because I knew he didn't like you talking about it, but, girl, that ship has sailed. Spill it."

"There isn't much to say about it. It takes me a long time to orgasm, and sometimes Harrison got tired of how long I was taking, so I told him to finish up and not worry about it."

"That tone deaf turd pirate is lucky I'm not there right now." Harper's face had disgust written across it.

"Oh my God, Harper, it isn't that big of a deal. I told him

to do it. It doesn't matter all that much. Some women don't climax every time they have sex."

"They fucking should be, and if they're not, their man is doing something wrong. How long does it take you to come when you masturbate?"

Now she was positive her cheeks were actually on fire. "Harper!"

"How long, pinky-pie?"

"Well, it depends…"

A wicked grin crossed Harper's face. "When it's Preacher with his amazingly hard tattooed body and that sexy deep voice in your fantasy, how long does it take?"

"Not that long," Addison admitted.

Harper grinned triumphantly. "Ladies and gentlemen of the jury, the council rests."

"Your case can be torn apart easily," Addison said. "All women come faster when they're masturbating. We know exactly what we like, right?"

"You might have me on that," Harper said. "Still, it's an outrage that Harrison didn't make you come every time you had sex, and I think you should hop on some Preacher dick and feel the magic."

Addison laughed. "Preacher's dick isn't magical."

"It might be," Harper said. "Only one way to find out." She suddenly slid off the bed. "Oh shit, girl, I gotta go. I said I'd meet Francisco at six at Donatello's."

"Wait, who's Francisco?"

Harper grinned at her. "He's a fun guy and attached to the totally casual, totally magical dick I'm riding. Later, sexy."

Harper made a kissy sound and ended the call. Addison sat back in her chair, staring at her unopened juice. She was feeling sorry for herself and more than a little lonely. After a moment, she jumped up and grabbed her purse from the side table in the hallway.

The weather was a little cooler today. She would walk to the Walgreens downtown and pick up more facial wash. Maybe stop at the bakery and pick a little treat to have while she watched Netflix later.

Okay, great plan, but maybe you should change first and do something with your hair.

She glanced at her reflection in the hallway mirror. Her hair was up in a messy bun, and she wore a t-shirt, jeans, and no makeup.

She did kind of look like shit, but she realized with a weary sort of resignation that she didn't care tonight. She shoved her phone into her purse, slipped into her sneakers, and walked out the door.

BLINKING BACK TEARS, HER STOMACH ROLLING WITH NAUSEA, Addison practically ran out of the Walgreens. She pushed past a group of tourists standing near the bus stop and dodged a teenager flying down the street on a skateboard, his elbow pads flapping uselessly from one hand.

She glanced up and down the street before crossing to the other side, which was quieter and in the shade. She planned to go to Grind My Beans, find a quiet corner at the back of the café and cry into an iced coffee, but her footsteps slowed as she stared at the bright red door in front of her.

Crimson Door Tattoo.

She'd never been inside Preacher's shop. Why would she? She was a good girl, and good girls didn't get tattoos. She hitched in a breath as a hot tear slid down her cheek.

So, stop being a good girl. For once in your life, show the small-minded assholes in this town that you're more than Harrison's ex-fiancé, more than a schoolteacher, more than just a good girl.

She reached for the handle, yanked the door open and stepped inside before she could change her mind. The shop was larger than she thought. To her right was a seating area with an oversized leather couch and a matching armchair. Binders, a few of them open to show the tattoo drawings they contained, were scattered across a glass coffee table in front of the couch.

Tattoo drawings covered the walls. The ones featuring women in the nude, their legs spread in invitation and their large breasts bordering on obscene, sent a flush of colour to her cheeks, and she looked hastily away.

A glass counter was to her left. A laptop and a small printer/scanner sat at one end of the counter, and a display of white mugs with 'Crimson Door Tattoo' was sitting on the other end next to a spinning rack of 'Crimson Door Tattoo' keychains. Inside the counter were two glass shelves displaying gleaming jewelry.

A long table with sketchpads and pencils was tucked against one wall, and the far wall had three doors, one marked discreetly with a washroom sign.

The air smelled strongly of antiseptic, and she found that oddly comforting. The tile floor was cleaner than her floor at home, and the glass counter was free of fingerprints and gleamed in the light. The whole place was much cleaner than she pictured, and some of her nerves eased slightly. She didn't know why she expected Preacher's tattoo shop to be small and grungy. He was a man who took pride in his work. She knew that just by how he spoke to her class on career day.

There were three curtained stations, although all three

curtains were pulled back at the moment. Each station had a tattoo chair, a small rolling stool, a large rolling cart with a tattoo machine, an autoclave, and a small bookshelf filled with boxes of disposable gloves, stacks of towels, different coloured ink and scraps of paper, some with tattoo drawings. Biohazard and sharp containers were screwed into the wall behind each station.

Music from a New Cassel rock station drifted from small speakers affixed to the ceiling. She waited a few minutes, and when no one appeared from the other rooms, she stepped over to the counter, her hand hovering over the small 'ring for service' bell sitting next to the rack of keychains. She bent and stared into the top of the glass counter at the jewelry. There were rows of silver barbells and hoops, belly button rings, and some she didn't even know where they would go. She had her ears pierced, but she'd never gone beyond that.

"Can I help you?"

She jumped, her hand smacking the bell in her surprise, making it yell out a strangled 'ding'.

"Sorry," she said before smiling at the man. He had neon green hair pulled into a man bun on the top of his head, revealing a dark brown undercut. His septum was pierced with a big metal hoop, and stretchers had turned the holes in his lobes large enough that she could have shoved one of the markers from her classroom through it with room to spare.

She stared in fascination at the full sleeve of tattoos on his left arm until he made a sound of annoyance and moved behind the counter. "Can I help you, lady?"

"Oh, uh, yes, I'm here for…"

He arched an eyebrow at her before pointing at the jewelry. "Let me guess… belly button piercing. Or maybe you're gonna get real wild and get a nipple pierced?"

Hot colour flooded her cheeks. "No, no, I'm here for a tattoo."

"Shop's closing in ten minutes," the young man said.

"Oh, right. Of course. Could I book an appointment for tomorrow?" Her resolve to do something crazy, like permanently altering her body, would probably fade by tomorrow, but maybe if she had an appointment, she wouldn't chicken out.

The guy laughed. "Lady, this ain't like TV. We do walk-ins during tourist season, but we're already fully booked for those for the rest of the week. And Preacher's regular appointment schedule is booked three months in advance."

"Three months?" She blinked at him in surprise. Were there that many people in Harmony Falls who wanted tattoos?

"Yep," he said. "I can book you for then if you'd like."

"I'd like to try to get it done sooner," she said. "I don't want a very big tattoo. Is there any way that Preacher could squeeze me in tomorrow?"

"Nope."

"Are you sure?" she wheedled. "We're friends, he knows me."

The man laughed out loud. "Yeah, sure you are."

"No, really, we are." She supposed that making out with Preacher once didn't exactly qualify them as friends, but a little white lie never hurt anyone. "If you just mention my name to him, I'm sure he'll make an exception and -"

"Nope, he won't," the man said. "You know how many women come in here daily telling me they know Preacher personally? You ain't the first to try, and you won't be the last. Now, you can book for three months, or you can leave. Makes no difference to me what you do as long as you leave so I can close the goddamn shop and get the hell -"

"Nolan, enough."

Preacher's low voice washed over her, and she turned and stared at him as he stepped out of one of the unmarked rooms and closed the door.

"Hi there." Her voice was too loud, and she winced as Nolan stared at her and then at Preacher.

"You know her, Preacher?"

Preacher nodded. "Good evening, Miss Moore."

"Hi," she said.

"She wants a tattoo," Nolan said.

If Preacher was surprised, it didn't show on his face.

"Not a very big one," she said. "Um, just a small one."

"I told her we're booking three months in advance," Nolan said.

"I can tattoo you tonight," Preacher said.

Nolan's mouth dropped open. "Tonight? I told Monica I'd meet her at the Falls in ten minutes and -"

"Go on, Nolan," Preacher said. "I'll close up when I'm done."

Nolan frowned. "You sure?"

"I am. See you tomorrow."

"Yeah, sure, okay. I haven't cashed out yet," Nolan said as he grabbed his jacket.

Addison smiled a little smugly at Nolan as he walked past her and out the door. Her pulse sped up when Preacher walked toward her, but he passed by her and turned the open sign to close before locking the door and pulling the shade down over the big picture window.

"What kind of tattoo are you looking for?" he asked.

She licked her lips. "I was thinking of a flower."

"You want colour?"

"Yes, I think so."

He walked to the seating area and brought back one of the

black binders. He set it on the counter before her and flipped it open. "These are all flowers."

She looked through the book as he walked to the closest station and laid out some equipment. He returned just as she was flipping the last page.

"Find anything you like?"

She hesitated and shook her head. "No, I'm sorry. Do you have anything else?"

He stared silently at her for a moment before saying, "Follow me."

She followed him to the table with the sketchbooks and watched as he opened one to a blank page and picked up a pencil. "What's your favourite flower?"

"Orchids." She watched in amazement as he quickly sketched an orchid. In less than ten minutes, he had sketched out a small, perfectly shaped orchid, and her mouth dropped open. "That's beautiful."

"You like it?" he said.

"I love it."

"Then it's yours," he said. "Do you want it bigger or smaller than this?"

"I don't know. What do you think?"

"Where are you getting it?"

"I thought maybe the back of my right shoulder."

"Maybe a little bigger than this. Have a seat on the couch while I detail it out." He pointed to a bar fridge that was close to the table. "There's bottled water if you're thirsty."

She took a bottle of water before wandering to the couch and sitting. Her throat was bone dry from nerves, and she gulped half the water before capping the bottle and setting it on the floor. She stuck her hands between her knees to try and quell the shaking. He was printing something off the laptop, and she took the clipboard and pen from him when he handed it to her. It was a consent form, and she read it carefully before answering the health questions and signing at the bottom of the page.

He was back at the table working silently, and she placed the clipboard on the table before studying the other books. One of them was full of pictures of body piercings, and she looked over a few of them, staring in fascination at the nipple piercings, before clearing her throat.

"Do you do body piercings as well?"

He nodded, and she cleared her throat again. "When did you learn to do all of this?"

"I was always good at art," he said. "I apprenticed at a New Cassel tattoo and body modification shop."

"Right, that's where you met Gideon," she said. "Why did you decide to move here?"

He shrugged. "I was tired of big city living, and Gideon is my best friend."

"Kind of strange that you two are best friends," she said.

"Is it?" He glanced at her, and she flushed at the look on his face.

"No, I guess not."

He didn't reply, and feeling stupid, she changed the subject. "You must be pretty good if you're booked three months in advance."

He just shrugged again, and she lapsed into silence. After a few minutes, without looking at her, he said, "Your fiancé know you're doing this?"

Shit. She considered lying to him again, but lying wasn't exactly her strong suit. Besides, it was a friggin' miracle he still didn't know, but that wouldn't last forever.

"We're not together anymore."

The tip of his pencil snapped. He cursed and tossed it

aside before grabbing another one. Still not looking at her, he said, "Why'd you break up?"

Now's your chance, Addie. Tell him you're not very good at sex and ask if he'd like to help you change that.

"I'd rather not talk about it," she said.

He didn't say anything else, and she sat back against the couch and studied the art on the walls as she listened to the faint pencil scratching. It took him nearly forty minutes, and she was vibrating from nerves by the time he took the clipboard and glanced through her consent form.

He had transferred the drawing to a stencil, and she studied it nervously. It was bigger than she had pictured, but she didn't say anything as he led her to a full-length mirror bolted to the wall.

"Turn around," he said.

She turned, and he waited a beat before saying, "You'll have to remove your shirt."

"Oh right, of course," she said.

She cursed herself in her head. Why hadn't she worn a tank or camisole under her shirt? And why the hell was she wearing her oldest, ugliest bra? Feeling incredibly self-conscious, she stripped off her shirt before crossing her arms over her chest. It was a pointless gesture. Preacher had already moved behind her to study her back.

"Can I touch you?" he said.

"Yes."

He was all business, and she wondered why she was feeling disappointed.

His warm fingers slid across the back of her shoulder and hooked under the shoulder strap of her bra. He slid it down her arm, and she tried not to shiver at his touch. He pressed the stencil against her skin before carefully peeling it away. He picked up a large hand mirror and stepped in front of her, holding it up so she could see her back in the full-length mirror.

"What do you think of placement?"

"It looks good."

"Too big?"

"No, I don't think so," she said.

"You sure?"

She nodded. It looked exactly the right size, and she was a little amazed by Preacher's ability to gauge the correct size. "I like it."

"Let's get started then."

"How much?" she said.

He paused. "What?"

"How much for the tattoo?"

"Hundred," he said.

She had been prepared to pay a lot more and was already planning how long she'd have to eat ramen to pay for this little moment of madness. "That seems too low."

"It isn't."

She crossed to the couch, incredibly aware that she was in just her jeans and a spectacularly ugly beige bra and grabbed her wallet from her purse. "Should I pay you now?"

"It doesn't matter. You can pay me after if you prefer."

"I'll do it now."

His crooked little grin was weirdly sexy. "No refunds if you hate it."

She smiled at him. "I'm sure I won't hate it."

He ran her card through and printed a receipt that she stuffed into her purse. He walked away to his station, and after a moment, she followed him. She studied the tattoo bed as he pulled a rolling chair out from under the drawing table and brought it to the station.

"Can you straddle this?" he said.

"Yes." Holding the back of the chair to keep it steady, she straddled it and tried not to flinch when Preacher sat on the stool behind her, and she felt his warm breath on her back.

"What colour would you like?"

"Pink," she said. "I like pink. Is that too, um, girlie, do you think?"

"It's your body and your ink," he said.

"Right. Pink it is, then."

It took him another twenty minutes to set up his equipment. Before pulling on gloves, he showed her the needles he would be using, all still encased in their new wrapping.

"This is my first tattoo," she said.

"Yeah, I figured. Are you afraid of needles?"

"No, why?"

"You're shaking," he said.

"Just nervous. I'm not worried about the pain or anything, though."

He was silent behind her, and she nearly jumped out of her skin when his gloved hand traced over her lower back. "You need to relax, Sunshine. I can't tattoo you if you're shaking like this."

"I'm sorry," she said.

"It's fine," he said. "If you don't want this, it isn't too late to change your mind."

"I want this."

Preacher continued to rub her lower back. His touch was soothing, and she felt much calmer and more in control after a few minutes.

"Better?" he said.

"Yes, thank you."

"Good. I have some tequila I could give you if you want a shot to calm your nerves further."

She laughed. "Probably not a good idea. I'm a cheap drunk."

His low chuckle sent a zing of heat to her core. "No tequila then. I have a rule about not tattooing my clients when they're drunk."

"Good rule," she said.

He stroked her back a final time before rolling closer. "Here we go. Ready?"

She nodded and breathed deeply as the tattoo gun buzzed to life.

CHAPTER 7

P reacher was impressed with his little schoolteacher. It was an hour later, and he was almost finished with the tattoo. Her soft skin was bright red, and it was evident that it was becoming more painful, but she hadn't complained once or asked for a break. He wiped at her skin, and she made a soft hiss of pain.

"Sorry," he said.

"It's fine," she said. "I'm just being a wimp."

He traced his finger down her spine, liking how it made goosebumps rise on her skin. "I'm almost done."

"O-okay," she said.

He resisted the temptation to trace her skin again and resumed the shading. The orchid was perfect and looked beautiful on her. He'd almost fallen over when he heard her soft voice in his tattoo shop. He wondered if she had seen his surprise when she said she wanted a tattoo.

He probably should have told her no. He had a feeling that later she would regret being inked, but he couldn't refuse her pleading gaze. Never mind the fact that he was itching to tattoo her. When she allowed him to draw an original for her, an even deeper sense of possessiveness and pride washed over him.

She would be marked forever by him. His ink would always be etched in her soft skin. Every time she looked at it, she would be reminded of him.

He wanted desperately to know why she wasn't engaged anymore. Was it because of him? Had the dirtbag lawyer finally seen his mark on her neck and broken it off with her? Guilt rolled over him, and he stopped tattooing. Fuck, what if it was his fault? He could try to ignore it all he wanted, but his little Sunshine didn't look as sunshiny as usual.

Was her heart broken? Was she regretting that fleeting moment with him outside of the pub? Even the way she dressed was different. She wasn't wearing her customary string of pearls, and instead of her usual dress, she wore a plain t-shirt and skinny jeans. He'd never seen her in jeans before. Her auburn hair was in a messy bun, pinned haphazardly against her scalp, and her skin was free of makeup.

"Is it my fault?" He had to know.

She didn't ask him what he meant. "No."

"Are you telling me the truth?" He could still see his fading mark on her throat, and more guilt flooded through him.

"I am," she said. "It had nothing to do with you."

He resumed tattooing, and after a moment, she spoke over the sound of the gun.

"That night outside of the Beaver, when you, um, when you helped me?"

"I remember." Like he'd ever fucking forget it.

"I wasn't with Harrison then either. I would never have kissed you like that if I'd been with him. I'm not a cheater. I'm a good girl." She made a weird hiccupping laugh. "I didn't tell you when you helped me with my car yesterday because I was embarrassed and thought everyone in this stupid town already knew."

"Why did you break up with him?" It wasn't any of his fucking business, but he couldn't help asking.

"I didn't. He ended it with me."

Jesus, the guy was an even bigger idiot than he thought.

She sighed, and then her shoulders straightened as if she was steeling herself. "Back in the spring, I discovered Harrison was having an affair with his legal assistant."

"You're fucking kidding me," he said.

"No." She seemed emboldened by his outrage and continued. "I went to his house when he wasn't expecting it and found him naked on his hands and knees wearing a dog collar and leash while Crystal beat his butt with a leather crop."

"Fucking hell," he said.

"Yeah, I guess he had certain kinks that he didn't share with me," she said.

He shut off the gun and gently wiped the tattoo as she stared at the wall for a few seconds before the words tumbled out of her. "I was so upset. Not that he had certain tastes in bed, but he thought I couldn't handle them. He said that the only reason he slept with Crystal was because he knew I was too much of a good girl even to try those things in bed. He said I was too uptight and stiff in the bedroom. He made it sound like all I did was lie there while he rutted away at me. But I," her entire body stiffened, "I was a good girl because I thought that's what he wanted. I was proper and *demure* in the bedroom because he expected me to be that way. He disapproved if I wore too revealing lingerie, for God's sake. Said it wasn't me and that I shouldn't try to be sexy because I just ended up looking ridiculous, and it was a turn-off for him."

She was breathing heavily, and he rubbed her lower back again as her tiny hands clenched into fists.

"You're sexy," he murmured.

She didn't seem to hear him as she slumped against the chair. "Anyway, it's been kind of a bad day. You were right about my car. The engine is shot, so I have to buy a new one, which will be such a stupid hassle. I was sitting at home alone and feeling sorry for myself, so I decided to walk downtown to Walgreens. While there, I overheard a couple of people talking about me and Harrison, just like on Sunday at the yarn shop, and they were saying the same thing. That I was a goodie-two-shoes and boring, and Harrison probably broke up with me because I wouldn't give him oral sex, but I did do stuff like that in the bedroom. I swear! I would have been willing to try whatever he asked. But he never asked."

She sucked in a gulp of oxygen. "I ran out of the Walgreens and saw your tattoo shop and thought to myself – Self, get a tattoo. That'll prove to stupid Harrison and everyone else that you're not such a good girl. I was trying to be a rebel, but I suppose getting a tattoo's not rebellious anymore, is it?"

Before he could reply, she sighed again. "I've been with him since high school. All that time wasted, and for what? To be tossed aside for a big-breasted blonde woman who whips his ass and calls him Harry."

He snorted laughter, and she glanced over her shoulder before giving him a slight grin. "He looked ridiculous in that dog collar."

He laughed again, and she giggled before trying to look at the back of her shoulder. "Are you done?"

"Yes. Just let me clean it, and then you can take a look."

She waited patiently as he cleaned it and then followed

him to the mirror. He handed her the hand mirror and watched as she held it up.

"Oh my goodness," she whispered. "It's so beautiful."

"You like it," he said.

"I love it," she said.

The tension he didn't realize he carried vanished, and he grinned at her. "It's red and a little swollen right now. That's normal. Give it a few days, and it'll look even better."

She set the mirror down, and he grunted in surprise when she threw her arms around him and hugged him. "Preacher, thank you. I don't know what I expected, but I didn't expect to love it this much."

He really should have stepped back, but instead, he put his arms around her slender waist and pulled her in tight. "You're welcome," he said as he breathed in the scent of her hair. "It was my pleasure."

"I can't wait to show Kira and Grace. They'll flip out. Maybe I'll get you to take a picture, and I'll text them tonight." She tried to step back and gave him a confused look when he kept his arms around her. "Preacher? What's wrong?"

"Nothing," he said. "Nothing's wrong, Sunshine."

She studied him silently, and he told himself to let her go. To release her and walk away, but then she was pressing her body against his, and her tiny hands were tugging at his neck. He bent his head, and she kissed him hard on the mouth. He groaned and opened it, letting her push her small tongue deep into his mouth.

ADDISON WAS MAKING A MISTAKE. KISSING PREACHER WAS the wrong decision, but the thought was lost when he groaned and opened his mouth. She pushed her tongue into his mouth, eager to taste him again. This time he tasted like mint with no trace of whiskey, and she moaned happily when he sucked hard on her tongue.

His big hand cupped her left breast and squeezed. She arched her back, ignoring the dim pain it caused her freshly inked skin. When his fingers moved to the front clasp and unhooked it, she helped him peel back the cups of her bra. He stared at her breasts before cupping her left one again and rubbing his thumb over the tip of her nipple. It beaded into a hard point immediately, and she made a low cry of pleasure.

"So beautiful," he muttered.

He bent his head and sucked on her nipple, teasing the tip of it with his tongue as his rough fingers pulled on her right nipple.

"Oh my gosh," she whispered. "Preacher, please…"

He suddenly tensed and lifted his head to stare cautiously at her. "Sunshine, this probably isn't a good idea."

No! She wouldn't be rejected by this man. The thought that he didn't want her hurt more than discovering that her fiancé didn't want her.

"You don't want me?" she said.

His big hands cupped her ass, and he lifted her to her tiptoes before pressing her crotch against his erection. "I want you so fucking bad I can't think straight, Sunshine."

"Then take me," she said in a low voice. "Please."

He hesitated a moment longer. She was getting ready to beg when he grabbed her arm and steered her back to the tattoo bed. He bent her face-first over the bed, and she rested her heated cheek against the smooth leather as he unzipped her jeans and yanked them and her panties down to her ankles.

"Preacher, what if your assistant comes back?" she gasped as a little of her sanity reappeared.

"He won't," he said.

"Are you sure?"

"Yes."

She could hear him unzipping his jeans, and she peered over her shoulder at him. "We need a condom."

He was already reaching into his pocket, and she turned her face away as he tore open the packaging and stepped back. She didn't want to see his penis. He was a big man, and she was sure he was just as big in the downstairs department.

She'd never seen any penis but Harrison's. She didn't think he was small, but Harrison was average size physically which meant his penis was probably an average size too. It always hurt at the beginning to make love with Harrison, so if she saw Preacher's and it was bigger, she might be tempted to call the whole thing off.

Is now really the time to be thinking of this? You're about to be fucked by Preacher!

She winced at the foul language of her inner voice, but it was right. Preacher wasn't making love to her. He was fucking her. And being fucked was what she needed right now. Right?

She clutched at the tattoo bed as Preacher shoved her feet apart. She was starting to lose some of her lust, her thoughts crowding in and overriding her need for him.

"Maybe we," she started to say, and then his hand was between her legs, and his rough fingers were caressing her clit.

"Oh my goodness!" She arched up off the bed when he slid one thick finger into her. Shamefully, she was already wet. Hell, she'd been wet since he ran his gloved fingers down her back.

"You're so tight and wet, Sunshine," he moaned. "I need to fuck you right now."

The need in his voice made her desire flare back to life, and she widened her legs even more as he pressed the head of his cock against her. She probably wouldn't have an orgasm from sex. It took a miracle for her to have an internal orgasm, and experience had proven that once the fucking started, her clit was forgotten about entirely.

For a moment, she wished she was brave enough to ask Preacher to make her come first, but she ignored her feelings. Being fucked by Preacher was something she wanted, regardless of whether she came or not. Still, she couldn't help but tense a bit from nerves as he traced her naked ass with his fingers.

He paused and then echoed his words from earlier, "If you don't want this, it isn't too late to change your mind."

"I want this," she said.

THE MOMENT ADDISON TOLD HIM SHE WANTED IT, PREACHER shoved his cock into her sweet pussy. Her entire body stiffened, and she cried out. It was a sound of pain, not pleasure, and he immediately froze.

"Fuck!" He'd hurt her. He was so desperate to fuck her that he hadn't given a thought to how little she was. She was soaking wet when he touched her, but he should have at least made her come first. He'd hurt his sweet Sunshine, and he'd never forgive himself.

He started to pull out and grunted in surprise when she wrapped her hand around his wrist.

"No, don't stop," she said.

"I've hurt you."

"It's fine. It always hurts at first." She spoke in a matter-of-fact tone that made him feel even worse. "It's already fading. Go ahead."

He didn't know what was worse – hurting her or finding out that she expected it to hurt. He muttered a curse under his breath and made himself stay perfectly still.

"Go on," she said again.

"Just give me a minute," he said through gritted teeth. It wasn't only his worry that he would hurt her again. She was so goddamn tight around him that he wasn't confident he wouldn't just blow his load if he took even one stroke.

He made himself take a few deep breaths and think about motherfucking baseball until the need to come had eased. He stroked Addison's warm back, staring at his ink on her pale skin.

"Okay?" he asked hoarsely.

"Just fine," she said. "Do it, Preacher."

While she didn't sound like she was in pain any longer, she also didn't sound like a woman who was dying to be fucked. Jesus, he was messing this up in the worst way. He was starting to lose his erection, and he reached around her and cupped her pussy.

He pressed against her clit before caressing it lightly. She jerked and twitched, her pussy squeezing him tight, and just like that, his dick was back in the game.

"Wh-what are you doing?" she squeaked.

He rubbed her clit again as she lifted her upper body and braced herself on her hands. "Preacher, what…"

Her voice died out, her slender body shaking wildly when he cupped her breast in one big hand and toyed with her nipple. His other hand was still between her legs, and he groaned when she wiggled and squirmed on his aching dick.

"Oh! Oh my goodness!" She kept repeating herself in a

soft little voice as she rocked her pussy against his fingers. "Oh, that feels so good. You're so big, Preacher."

He grinned as she continued to talk. He usually preferred his women not to be so goddamn chatty in bed, but it was fucking adorable the way she couldn't seem to stop voicing her opinions.

"Oh my goodness! I've never had something so big in me before. It feels good, it feels really…"

She moaned when he pinched her clit, and then she shoved her ass against his pelvis. "Oh my gosh! Do that again! Right now!"

His grin widening, he pinched her clit again, and she made a loud squeal of pleasure. "I like that very much."

He rubbed her clit roughly, listening to her soft squeals and moans of delight. She was growing steadily wetter, and he made a few slow, experimental thrusts to gauge her reaction. She squealed again and thrust back and forth on his dick when he stopped.

"Oh, don't stop!" she begged. "Please, Preacher, don't stop."

Fuck, what her soft, polite schoolteacher voice did to him. He slid in and out of her in a firm rhythm as she moaned happily. She was tiny and tight, but her pussy swallowed every inch of him like it was made for his dick. He bottomed out in her, gave her clit a rough little pinch, and then pulled out until just the head was encased in her warmth.

She was wiggling and moaning and babbling at him, and he thrust back in to the hilt. Watching her pussy lips stretch around his width nearly made him come, and he tore his gaze away and stared at her back again. Jesus, if he didn't make her come soon, he would embarrass himself by coming before she did. He *never* let that happen, but then he'd never been in a pussy as smooth and tight as his little Sunshine's.

Gritting his teeth, he rubbed firmly at her clit, willing her to fucking come already as she moaned and writhed on his dick and dug her hands into the tattoo bed. Thank fucking Christ, she stiffened only a few minutes later, her back arching and a loud cry escaping her mouth as she climaxed. She shook wildly around him, and muttering a low curse, he thrust in and out of her pulsing pussy and followed her to his climax less than fifteen seconds later.

He dug his hands into her narrow hips and threw his head back as his orgasm flowed through him. It might not have been one of his better performances but holy fuck, if it wasn't one of the best orgasms of his damn life. By the time he came down from the high, his little sunshine was collapsed against the tattoo bed and panting harshly.

He rubbed her lower back as his racing heart slowed. Fuck, she was so goddamn beautiful. She wiggled against him, and he pulled out reluctantly as she straightened. She turned around, and the look on her face had the apology falling immediately from his lips.

"Sunshine, I'm sorry." He pulled off the condom and dropped it into the waste basket.

"It's fine." Her voice was too loud and high-pitched as she yanked up her jeans and panties. She fumbled with her bra and winced when the shoulder strap dragged across her tattoo.

"Wait, hold on," he said, pulling up his jeans and buttoning them.

"I really should be going now," she said. He could hear the tears in her voice, and he cursed inwardly.

"Addison, I'm sorry."

"Please don't," she said in a strangled voice as she finished putting on her bra. "Please stop saying you're sorry."

"Can we just talk about this?"

"No, I don't think that's a good idea. It's late, and I need to go."

She pushed past him and grabbed her shirt from the counter.

"You need a bandage on the tattoo."

"I don't, it's fine, really."

"Addison!" His sharp tone made her freeze as she reached for her purse. "Just wait for a minute."

She stayed where she was, her hands clamped together across her flat abdomen as she stared blindly at the door. He quickly grabbed a bandage, a damp cloth, and the paper with cleaning instructions. He wiped her tattoo and placed the bandage over it, taping it in place.

"Take this off in the morning." He shoved the piece of paper at her. "Here are the cleaning instructions. Follow them carefully."

"Okay," she said as she pulled her t-shirt on.

He walked around her and unlocked the front door. She refused to look him in the eye, but he could see that her cheeks were bright red, and there were tears in her eyes as she hurried out the door.

"Goodbye, Preacher," she said. Without waiting for a response, she nearly ran down the street and disappeared into the darkness.

"Goodbye, Sunshine."

CHAPTER 8

"You did what?" Kira sank into a kitchen chair and stared at her.

"I also got a tattoo," Addison said.

"Addie, who cares about the damn tattoo!" Kira shouted. "You slept with Preacher last night. Preacher!"

"You guys were the ones who told me I needed to have rebound sex," Addison said.

"Yeah, but not with Preacher!" Kira stared at Grace. "Gracie, why don't you look surprised?"

Grace shrugged. "There's always been tons of sexual tension between them, and I caught Addie and Preacher making out at the Beaver on Friday night."

"Grace!" Addison said as Kira's mouth dropped open. "You promised you wouldn't say anything!"

"Does it matter at this point? You just told us you boned him. Who cares if he was kissing you and feeling you up outside the pub?"

"He was feeling you up outside the pub? I, like, go to Willington for one Friday night and miss Addison losing her mind," Kira said.

"He saved me from a bunch of drunk guys in the parking lot, okay? I was grateful to him."

"So, you let him kiss you and grope you as a thank you?" Kira said.

"Yes," Addie said.

There was a long silence, and then Kira said, "Okay."

Grace burst out laughing. "Okay?"

"What?" Kira said.

"That's a rapid change in thinking," Grace said.

It was Kira's turn to shrug. "I replayed my freak out back in my head, and I sounded like a ninety-year-old grandma. Addie is a grown woman, and besides, it's about time she got laid by someone other than boring old Harrison."

"He was only boring because I was boring," Addison said. "Crystal doesn't find him boring."

"Fuck Crystal," Grace said. "And you're not boring in bed."

"You don't know that," Addie said.

"What happened when you finished banging each other?" Kira asked.

"I left right away."

"What? Why?"

"Because it suddenly felt awkward and weird, and I had just let him bend me over a tattoo bed and screw me," Addison said. "Nice girls don't do that."

"Who says?" Grace said. "Nice girls do all sorts of bad things in bed."

"Not to mention, he apologized after. When he pulled out, he was all, 'Sunshine, I'm sorry'."

"Sunshine?" Kira said.

"He calls me sunshine," Addie said.

"That's adorable," Kira said. "Who would have thought big, bad Preacher would be into nicknames."

"Did you hear me?" Addie said. "He apologized. I mean, how bad does a girl have to be at sex for a guy to apologize to her?"

"That doesn't make any sense," Grace said. "Men don't apologize because a girl is bad in bed, Addie."

"Whatever," Addie said. "The point is, it was just a one-time thing, and I only did it because you guys told me I needed to have rebound sex."

"Bullshit," Grace said with a cheerful grin. "Don't blame your desire to see Preacher's dick on us, girlie. How was it, by the way? It was big, right? Really big?"

Addison blushed furiously as Kira leaned in. "From the look on her face – yep, it was big."

"I don't know for sure," Addie said. "I was bent over the tattoo bed, remember? I didn't see it."

"Yeah, but you felt it," Grace said with a cheeky wiggle of her eyebrows. "Did it feel big?"

Addison's cheeks burned. "Yes. It hurt."

"Uh oh," Grace said. "That's not good. He hurt you?"

"He didn't mean to," Addie said. "When he realized he hurt me, he tried to, um, pull out right away, but I told him not to."

Grace frowned at Kira, and Addison said, "What? It always hurts the first few strokes."

"No, it doesn't," Grace said. "Gideon has never hurt me when he's -"

"Nope!" Kira said. "Nope, don't you dare say it, Gracie."

Grace laughed. "Sorry, honey. Anyway, it isn't supposed to hurt, Addie. Did it hurt with Harrison every time?"

"Yes," Addie said. "Not for very long, but it was always a little painful at first."

"Okay, so I don't have much experience," Kira said, "but the only time it hurt for me was the first time Connor and I had sex. After that, it didn't hurt at all. Connor's a damn good size, so, like, how big are Harrison and Preacher's dicks?"

"Well, Harrison was average size, I think," Addison said, "and I told you, I didn't see Preacher's. He did feel bad about it. Harrison never seemed to notice that it hurt. But Preacher stopped moving immediately and touched me until I had an orgasm."

"Okay, Preacher has moved off my hit list," Grace said.

Addison rolled her eyes. "He didn't mean to hurt me. Honestly, even if he had done more to prepare me, it would have hurt."

"Will you give him another opportunity to test your theory?" Kira asked.

"No, of course not," Addison said. "I keep telling you – it's a one-time thing. Besides, he won't want to sleep with me again. I couldn't stop talking the whole damn time."

Kira blinked at her. "Talking about what?"

"The weather?" Grace said.

Addison swatted her on the arm. "I wasn't talking about the weather. Look, when I was with Harrison, once he was, um, inside of me, he didn't touch me or try and make me climax. He just did his thing, and we were done."

"Selfish bastard," Grace said.

"Well, I usually had an orgasm before we started having sex," Addie said.

"Usually?" Grace scowled at her. "What percentage?"

"What?"

"How often did you have an orgasm with Harrison?"

"God, I don't know," Addie said. "What does it matter?"

"Throw out a number," Grace said.

"Fine!" Addison scowled at the table for a moment. "I'd say at least forty percent of the time."

Both Grace and Kira made identical groans of dismay.

"What?" Addie said.

"Honey, if you're not having an orgasm *every* time, he's not doing it right," Grace said.

"You watch too many romance movies," Addison said.

Grace rolled her eyes. "Get back to the 'you couldn't stop talking' part."

Addison traced the worn wood of Kira's kitchen table. The years long habit of not sharing intimate details was still difficult to break.

"Honey," Kira reached out and squeezed her arm, "if you don't want to tell us, you don't have to. We know you don't like to share this kind of stuff."

"No, Harrison didn't like me to share it," Addison said.

"I'm beginning to understand why," Grace said. "That guy is such an asshole."

"Anyway, I want to share, I'm just… it feels weird and a bit embarrassing, I guess. Especially after what I said to Preacher."

"Oh, now you *have* to tell us," Grace said.

"Gracie!" Kira squeezed Addie's arm again. "You don't have to tell us, honey."

"I want to." She took a deep breath. "So, um, Preacher was already inside of me, and I hadn't come yet, but I wasn't that upset about it or anything. Except, then he started touching me, and the combination of that and his, um, penis felt so good that I kind of lost my mind and started babbling. I mean, I couldn't shut up. It was so embarrassing. I kept telling him it felt really good and begging him to keep going. I mean, I was begging!"

Her embarrassment was at an all-time high, but she dropped her gaze to the table and kept talking. "I felt like I might die if Preacher stopped and I didn't have an orgasm. How stupid is that? I didn't shut up once the whole time he was, um, screwing me. Half the time, I was pleading for him not to stop, and the other half, I was telling him he was big. I even told him that I... oh God, this is humiliating... I'd never had anything so big in me before."

She was still staring at the table and lifted her head when there was only silence. Kira had herself under better control, but Grace's face was so red, and her body was shaking so violently that Addie thought she might have a stroke.

"It's not funny!" she said.

The laughter spilled out of Grace. "Oh honey, it's awesome. It's like you were auditioning for a bad porn movie."

She bent over and pressed her hands against the table before fluttering her eyelashes at Kira and Addie. "Oh, Preacher," she said, her voice a remarkably accurate impression of Addie's, "I've never had something so big in me before. You're such a stud!"

Kira laughed so hard that tears came to her eyes. Addie tried to glare at Grace but giggled instead. "Oh God, it's funny because it's true. That's exactly how I sounded!"

Grace sat beside her and howled with laughter as Kira wiped at the tears on her cheeks. When their laughter finally eased, Addie said, "I'm so embarrassed."

"Don't be," Kira said. "I'm sure guys love hearing a woman tell them they're big."

"True," Grace said. "But maybe you should try to avoid sounding like a cheesy porn script the next time, honey."

Addison groaned and buried her face in her hands. "There won't be a next time. I keep telling you that."

"Well, the good news is – you got your first try at rebound

sex over and done with, and you can concentrate on finding other pretty boys to have meaningless sex with and gain some confidence," Kira said. "This is your time to shine, Addie."

Addison laughed. "Yeah, I don't think casual sex is for me. As good as it felt with Preacher, the awkwardness and the way he kept apologizing after was terrible."

She turned her head from side to side, easing the tense muscles. "You were right, Gracie. Sleeping with Preacher was a bad idea, and now I have no idea how I'll even look him in the eye at the next barbeque."

"It'll be okay," Grace said. "I mean, yeah, it'll be awkward at first, but sleeping with women once is kind of what Preacher does, right? He'll probably be much cooler about it than you think."

"Maybe you're right," Addison said. "Besides, we barely spoke at the barbeques or when we were all hanging out together before we slept together. So that's not going to change. I was just a warm place to put his penis."

Grace snorted laughter. "Sweetie, call it a dick at least, would you?"

"I... I can't be crude."

"You should try it. It's lots of fun," Grace said. "Remember when I texted you last night?"

"Yeah. I'd just gotten home from the tattoo shop."

"Gideon asked me to text you."

"What? Why?" Addison said.

"That's the weird thing. He wouldn't say. He just asked me to text you and make sure you were at home and safe."

"Oh my God," Kira said. "Preacher asked Gideon to ask you to text Addison."

"I think so," Grace said. "He knew you were walking home in the dark, and he was worried. Which means you were more than just a warm place for him to put his," she smiled teasingly at Addison, "penis."

Addison didn't reply, but she couldn't ignore the tiny spark of warmth in her belly. It was stupid, but the idea that Preacher might have been worried about her walking home in the dark made some of her regret and embarrassment about what happened last night ease.

"All right, now that the sex talk is over show us this tattoo, you wild woman," Grace said.

Smiling, Addison turned and lifted the back of her shirt so that Grace and Kira could see her tattoo.

"Oh my gosh, it's gorgeous," Kira said. "I love it."

"It looks great," Grace said. "It's so... you."

"Thank you. I love it, too. Preacher drew it last night after I couldn't find a flower that I liked from the choices he showed me. He's a crazy good artist."

"Holy shit," Grace said. "You have a Preacher original? Girl, you're going to be eating Kraft Dinner for months. You must have maxed out your credit card to pay for it."

Addison fixed her shirt. "What do you mean? It only cost a hundred dollars."

Kira turned to Grace. "Did she just say a hundred bucks?"

"What?" Addison said.

"Addie, the minimum charge for a tattoo from Preacher is one-seventy-five. That's the *minimum* charge." Kira pointed to the butterfly tattoo just above her ankle. "Remember when Preacher did this last year? This tattoo, which is smaller than your orchid, cost me two hundred bucks, and Preacher gave me a discount."

"What?" Addison touched the tattoo on her back. "No, that can't be right."

"Oh, it's right," Kira said. "And I just picked this out of

the book. He didn't draw it or anything. Also, I'm pretty sure his price has increased since then."

"Gideon told me an original drawing by Preacher is ridiculously expensive because Preacher's one of the top tattoo artists in the state. Last year, he was number three on a list of top ten tattoo artists on a popular tattoo website. Since then, his business has doubled, and people are coming all the way from New York to get a tattoo from him. He's hiring another artist to work in the shop," Grace said.

"Honestly, I'm surprised he even tattooed you last night," Kira said. "Connor tried to book him for August, and Preacher is booked solid until late October."

"His assistant guy did say he was booked, but then Preacher said he would tattoo me last night," Addison touched the tattoo again. "Shoot, now I feel bad about paying so little for the tattoo. I told him it seemed too low, but he said it wasn't."

"Don't feel bad," Grace said. "You asked him the price, and he's the one who said it was a hundred bucks. Besides, you more than made up for the low price by banging him. Hell, he should have been paying *you* for the great sex … wait, that didn't come out right."

Both Kira and Addison laughed as Grace slapped herself on the forehead.

"Thanks, you guys. It helped to talk about this," Addison said.

"Girl, any time you want to talk about sex, just call. I'm always up for talking about dick," Grace said.

Kira laughed again. "Oh God, Grace. I love you."

"Love you too, Kira-baby. Love you too."

"So, are you going to tell me why you texted me last night asking me to ask Grace to make sure Addie was safe at home without telling either of them you were asking? Because," Gideon drank a swallow of beer, "it feels like some next-level teenage girl drama bullshit."

"Busy in here tonight." Preacher studied the people crowded into the pub. Like it always was in the summer, the Thirsty Beaver was overrun with tourists and locals. Hell, he was lucky he'd found a table for him and Gideon near the back that was relatively quiet.

"Always is this time of year. What was up with the Addison thing?" Gideon said.

Jesus, his best friend was like a dog with a bone. He supposed Gideon couldn't help it – he was a goddamn cop after all.

You invited him out tonight, knowing he would ask. You want to tell him what happened with Addie last night, you dickhead. So fucking tell him.

"Preacher?" Gideon leaned in. "What the hell is going on, buddy?"

"I fucked Addison last night."

Gideon's mouth dropped open, and the look of shock on his face almost made Preacher laugh. Would have made him laugh if he could get the look of regret on Addie's face after they were done fucking out of his head for one goddamn second. His apologies had only made it worse, and after she'd taken off, his worry about her walking home in the dark had kicked in. He'd almost grabbed his bike and gone after her, but what the hell would he have done if she refused to get on the bike? Just followed her home at a snail's pace like some fucking weirdo stalker?

He'd done the next best thing he could. He texted Gideon and asked for his help. He hadn't stopped pacing his small apartment until Gideon texted him with an update that Addison was safe at home.

"Close your mouth, asshole," Preacher said when Gideon continued to gape at him.

"What the fuck, Preacher?" Gideon said. "You seriously had sex with Addison Moore last night?"

"Yeah. She came into the shop just as it was closing and wanted a tattoo."

"Okay, even that's fucking weird, but how the hell did you go from her wanting a tattoo to having sex?"

Preacher glanced around. None of the tables nearby had locals sitting at them, but he lowered his voice anyway. "It just happened. I finished the tattoo, she hugged me, and then she kissed me, and then we had sex."

"There's so much more to this story than you're telling me," Gideon said.

Preacher cracked his knuckles and drank two big swallows of beer. "Fine. Here's the entire fucking story, you nosy bastard."

Ten minutes later, he was finished telling Gideon about Friday night at the pub and Sunday afternoon.

He drank another swallow of beer to ease his dry throat. "Why the hell didn't you tell me she and that lawyer had broken up?"

"One, I thought you knew, and two, I didn't think you'd care. I had no idea you were into Addison," Gideon said.

"I'm not into her," Preacher said. "We fucked, it doesn't mean anything, and it'll never happen again."

"She's not your usual type," Gideon said.

Preacher just shrugged. The little schoolteacher wasn't his usual type, and maybe that's why he found her so damn hot. Maybe that's why he couldn't stop thinking about her and had masturbated three goddamn times this morning to the memory of fucking her.

Being in her pussy had been better than all of his fantasies about her. She was tighter and wetter than any woman he'd fucked before. All day he could barely concentrate on tattooing, and he'd stared at that goddamn tattoo bed so many fucking times that Nolan had finally asked him what the fuck was up.

"You really shouldn't sleep with her again," Gideon said. "You're a good guy, but she just got out of a long-term relationship, and you two are," he paused, "very different."

"I know," Preacher said. "Jesus, Gideon, I don't want a fucking relationship with her. I told you it was just sex, and it's not going to happen again."

Of course, it'd be nice if he could stop thinking about fucking her again. Just the memory of her sweet little pussy had him half-hard right here in the goddamn pub. He knew where she lived, knew her apartment number. Maybe he could stop in and pretend he was checking on her tattoo or some shit like that, and –

And what? You hurt her when you fucked her, remember? You were such an impatient asshole that you hurt her. If you think she's ever going to let you near her pussy again, you're crazy. You've fantasized for months about fucking the little schoolteacher, and when you finally get the chance, you screw it up. You're such an asshole.

Guilt replaced the lust, and his dick went limp immediately. Shit, he *was* an asshole.

"Jesus, the next few barbeques are gonna be awkward as shit," Gideon said.

"No, they won't," Preacher said. "We didn't talk much before this, and now I guarantee she'll avoid me. She regretted fucking me the minute it was done. Women like her don't let men like me between their legs."

"Shut the fuck up," Gideon said. "This, 'I'm not worthy of someone like Addison Moore,' is complete bullshit. If you'd let someone get close to you other than me, you'd realize that plenty of people would care about you if you let them. Your past doesn't define you. How many fucking times do I have to tell you that?"

Preacher just grunted, but, like always, there was a sense of relief at hearing what Gideon had said to him a hundred times before. Maybe it would only take another hundred times before he started to believe it.

"The only reason I'm saying to stay away from Addison is because she's been with Harrison since they were teenagers, and they've only been broken up since the spring. There's no way she's ready to be in another relationship yet," Gideon said. "I don't want you getting hurt."

Preacher laughed. "Only you would worry about me being the one to get hurt by her."

Gideon didn't laugh. "It's because I love you, man."

Preacher could admit that it'd taken him a bit to get used to how freely and without any reservation or self-conscious-ness Gideon told him he loved him. After a lifetime of neglect from his parents and betrayal from men he thought were friends, his relationship with Gideon had evolved into the most important one of his life. If it weren't for Gideon, he'd be in a fucking prison cell again right now. He knew that as well as he knew his own name.

And, as fucking cheesy as this sounded, he would die for Gideon Walker. The sheriff had saved his life in more ways than he could count, and Preacher could spend a lifetime trying to repay the favour.

"Yeah, I know. I love you too," he said, a little amazed all over again that he genuinely meant it and by how easy it was to say. "But you have to stop worrying about me like you're my goddamn mother. I'm not going to get hurt by Addison Moore. She doesn't mean anything to me, and I sure as shit don't mean anything to her."

"All right. Did you hire that Nix guy?"

Relieved at the change in subject, Preacher said, "Yeah, called him Monday and offered him the job. He accepted and starts Thursday."

A guy in a cowboy hat and a belt buckle nearly the size of Preacher's head stopped at their table. He stuck out his hand. "Hey, Sheriff."

"Hey, Tom. Good to see you again. How's Ronnie and the kids?" Gideon shook his hand.

Preacher sat back and waited patiently. He didn't think he'd ever had a public conversation with Gideon that didn't get interrupted. Gideon was a popular sheriff, and people in the town were always eager to talk to him.

"Oh good, good. You should come by the farm sometime, have a visit. We got some new puppies looking for a home."

Gideon laughed. "Tank's enough for me. Say hi to Ronnie for me and tell him I'm still waiting for that drink he owes me."

"Will do." Tom glanced at Preacher. His face was permanently red from years in the sun, and his big hand was rough as sandpaper when he held it out for Preacher to shake. "Our oldest boy turns eighteen in January and says he wants a tattoo for a birthday gift."

"Call the shop, and we'll get him booked in," Preacher said.

"Ayuh, I'll do that," Tom said.

"Do it sooner than later," Gideon said. "Preacher's booking for…what… November?"

94

"Yeah," Preacher said.

"Jaysus." Tom made a low whistle. "You must be some good."

"He's the best," Gideon said.

"Well, I'll get Ronnie to book it in before the end of the week. Good seeing you." With a tip of his hat, Tom strolled away.

Gideon took a drink of beer and picked up where they'd left off. "I thought you said Nix lived in New Cassel. How the hell is he starting on Thursday?"

Preacher shrugged. "Don't know and didn't ask. I asked when he could start. He said right away, so he's starting on Thursday. Maybe he'll drive in from New Cassel until he finds a place to live here."

"Maybe," Gideon said. "You see the way he looked at me?"

"Yeah. He's probably an ex-con."

"Probably. Will it piss you off if I do a background check on him?"

"Nah."

"Cool." Gideon looked around before fishing something out of his pocket. It was a ring box, and he opened it and showed Preacher the ring inside.

"Holy fuck. Is that what I think it is?"

"Yeah. I'm asking Gracie to marry me this weekend." Gideon tucked the ring box away.

Preacher couldn't help but grin at Gideon's boyish look of excitement. "Congratulations, man."

"You don't think it's too soon?" Gideon said.

"Fuck no. You've been in love with Grace Larken for years. I'm fucking surprised it's taken you this long to ask her to marry you."

Gideon relaxed in his chair. "If she doesn't say yes -"

"She's gonna say yes, you idiot," Preacher said. "She looks at you, and you can practically see those goddamn cartoon hearts in her eyes. It's gross."

Gideon laughed, and Preacher clinked his beer bottle against Gideon's. "All kidding aside, I'm happy for you, buddy."

"Thanks, Preacher."

CHAPTER 9

Addison, her tablet propped up beside her on a couch pillow and her laptop balanced on her knees, clicked through the pages on the Crimson Door Tattoo's website, landing on the piercing information page again.

"You should probably go with a belly button piercing." Harper was painting her toes, and she wiggled them at Addison through the iPad screen. "What do you think of this colour?"

"I love it," Addison said. "Paint your fingernails the same colour."

Harper stroked the brush over her nail. "Seriously though, babe, a nipple piercing probably isn't the way to go for your first piercing."

"It's not my first. I have my ears pierced."

Harper rolled her eyes. "You know what I meant."

"Navel piercing seems so pedestrian, though. Like every girl has one, you know? It's the safe choice."

"Hey!" Harper lifted her shirt to stare at the small silver hoop in her belly button. "I like my belly button ring."

"I don't mean it in a bad way. I just mean – if I'm going

to get pierced, go big or go home, right? Do something different."

"Honestly, the fact that you want to get a piercing is blowing my mind," Harper said. The screen on the tablet froze for a few seconds before returning to normal. "You still there?"

"Yes," Addison said. "Hey, why aren't you at work? It's one in the afternoon."

"Why aren't *you* at work," Harper said before laughing. "God, if being a teacher wasn't so damn difficult, I'd become one. Summers off would be fucking awesome."

"Why aren't you at work?" Addison repeated.

"Switched my days off with Antonio so he and Mark could go fishing," Harper said. "Back to the piercing thing. You sure you want to do this?"

"I always liked the idea of getting my navel pierced, but Harrison freaked out the one time I mentioned it."

"Okay, but you keep talking about a nipple piercing, not a navel piercing," Harper said. She switched to her other foot and resumed painting. "Are you doing this just because you want to give Preacher a look at your tits again?"

"Harper! Of course not!"

"You sure? Because maybe you're thinking if he gets a look at your perfect girls, he'll ask if you want to play another round of hide the bishop."

"That isn't it," Addison said.

Harper paused with the nail brush in her hand, a drop of bright red polish clinging to the end of it. "Isn't it?"

"It's mostly not that," Addie said.

Harper grinned. "It's fine if it is. Hell, I think you *should* fuck Preacher again. It sounds like it was the best orgasm of your life, and, girl, you need more of those."

"He's not going to have sex with me again," Addison said.

"But you're still gonna show him your tits and get him to pierce a nipple."

"Well, maybe his assistant guy, Nolan, does piercings too," Addison said. "Maybe I'll be booked in with him. If that's the case, I'm still going to get my nipple pierced, so that proves I'm not doing this in the hopes of having sex with Preacher again. Right?"

"Right," Harper said. "But if it is Preacher who does the piercing, there's nothing wrong with asking him if he wants to have sex again."

Addison swallowed. "You know I could never ask him something like that."

"You gotta be bold, pinky-pie. If you can pierce your nipple, you can ask Preacher for casual sex." Harper blew on her toenails.

"Oh my God."

"What?"

"He does, um, clit piercings." Addison's face had gone hot. Lord, had she ever blushed this much in her life as she had in the last few days?

"Oh yeah? Lemme see." Harper leaned closer to her phone, squinting at the image. "Look at that, a pierced clit."

"I didn't even know you could pierce something like that." Addison stared at her crotch. "My God, it must hurt so much."

"Honey, whatever body part you can think of, I guarantee someone has pierced it. Whatever you do, do not Google a Prince Albert piercing."

"Thanks for the tip," Addison said. "Okay, I'm gonna call and book an appointment."

"Pinky-pie," Harper's voice had turned serious, "are you certain you want to do this? I love that you're getting tattoos and trying new things, but body modification is a big step outside your comfort box, especially if you're only doing it as an excuse to see Preacher again. Because, holy shit, wait a couple of days, and you'll see him at the barbeque this weekend."

"It's not that," Addison said. "I'm tired of living as if I'm still engaged to Harrison. I've spent years doing what he wanted me to do, and now... now I want to do something that I want because no one's allowed to tell me I can't. You know?"

"I do," Harper said. "Go get that nipple pierced. Live your authentic self, you sexy beast."

"Thanks, Harper. I love you."

"Love you too, pinky-pie. Send me pics of your pierced nip."

She ended the video call before Addison could tell her she absolutely would not send her a picture of her nipple.

Her fingers trembling a little, she called Preacher's shop. It rang twice before a voice said, "Crimson Door Tattoo."

"Um, yes, hi. I'd like to book a piercing, please."

"Sure, what are you looking for?"

She swallowed hard. "Nipple piercing, please."

"Sure." She could hear the clicking of a mouse. "Preacher's got some spots open for piercings next month. I can book you in... oh, hold on. We had a cancellation for today at the end of the day. I can book you in at six forty-five."

"Today?" She didn't want to admit this, but part of her ease in phoning for an appointment was because she was confident it would take a few weeks, and by then, her weird obsession with seeing Preacher would probably be over, and she would cancel the appointment.

"Yeah. Today work for you?"

"Yes." Her voice sounded shaky, but she cleared her throat and repeated, "Yes, I can do it today."

"Great. Nipple piercing is fifty bucks, but you have to pay the cost of the jewelry, too. You going barbell or hoop?"

"Barbell, please. It's better, right?"

"Yeah, it's what we recommend. We carry titanium, gold and platinum barbells. Titanium's the cheapest and the one we recommend for new piercings. If your body rejects the piercing, you're not out a lot of cash. They only run about fifty bucks."

"Right. Okay."

"Be here ten minutes before your appointment as there's paperwork to fill out, and you need to pick your jewelry."

"Oh, I was there the other day," Addison pulled nervously at a thread on her couch, "and I saw the jewelry. Just a plain titanium barbell will be fine."

"Okay. But come early to fill out the paperwork. I need your name and a phone number."

She recited her name and number, waiting patiently as he typed it in. "All good. See you around six-thirty."

"Bye," she said, but he'd already ended the call.

Her heart was thumping, and she was sweating despite the air conditioning in her apartment. She was getting her nipple pierced. Tonight.

Holy crap.

She was getting her nipple pierced.

PREACHER STOPPED AT THE COUNTER. NOLAN HAD THE PHONE stuck between his shoulder and his ear as he typed into the computer. "All good. See you around six thirty."

He ended the call and turned to Preacher. "Yo, what's up?"

"I'm running over to Nan's to grab lunch. You want anything?"

"Nah, I ate my lunch earlier. I gotta set up for Rory. He'll be here at one thirty. I got maybe a couple hours left of work on the tattoo, and then that motherfucker is done." He flipped his neon green hair out of his eyes. "Your nose piercing for the end of the day cancelled, but I booked a nipple piercing in its place."

"Sure, okay." Preacher was checking his email on his phone and barely listening.

"I think it might be that chick who came in the other night at closing wanting a tattoo. Her last name was Moore."

"What?" Preacher's head snapped up. "What did you just say?"

"Your nipple piercing. I think it might be the same -"

"What's the name?" Preacher practically laid across the counter to try and see the laptop screen.

"Jesus, dude, chill out," Nolan said. "Addison Moore. Is that the chick?"

"Yeah. You sure she said nipple piercing?"

"Yes." Nolan pointed to the side of his head. "I got ears, don't I?"

Preacher ignored him, staring down at the body jewelry on display. "She say what kind of jewelry she wanted?"

"Yeah, titanium barbell." Nolan headed to his station and spritzed the leather tattoo chair with disinfectant.

Preacher stepped behind the counter, unlocking the case and opening one glass door. He picked up one of the titanium barbells and slipped it into his pocket before sliding the door back into place and locking it.

He left the shop. The switch from the cold air-conditioned

shop into the muggy heat of the summer day sent sweat immediately sliding down his back. Jesus, it was the hottest day yet. He was supposed to watch Gideon play ball tonight, but if the heat didn't let up, he was skipping it.

Addison might be there.

Would she? She wasn't with her fiancé anymore, so why would she bother going to the games?

Maybe because she loves baseball just like everyone else in this town? You're the only one who can't stand baseball in Harmony Falls. It's just another reason why you and the little schoolteacher are so different.

It didn't fucking matter. He would see Addison at the shop in roughly five hours anyway. A little thread of excitement wormed into his stomach. Even better, he'd be seeing those perfect tits of hers. He immediately berated himself. He would be seeing her tits because of his fucking job, and he'd make damn sure to be professional.

Oh yeah? Because what you're about to do sure as fuck isn't strictly professional.

He ignored his inner voice, and instead of crossing the street to Nan's, he turned right and walked four blocks down Main Street. The street was crowded, but he barely noticed. When you were as big as he was and covered in tattoos, people tended to get out of your way. By the time he opened the door to the fine jewelry and engraving store, his shirt was sticking to his back with sweat.

The store was almost empty except for a couple sitting on small stools in front of the engagement ring section. A pretty young Indian woman with long dark hair and wearing a sleeveless dress that showed off the full tattoo sleeve on her left arm and the half sleeve on her right was showing the couple various rings. She glanced up and waved at Preacher. "Hey, Preacher."

"Hi, Diya."

She pointed to her half-sleeve. "I'm booked in September to finish this off."

"I saw that," Preacher said. "Looking forward to working on it."

"Me too. Dad's just in the back. Give him a minute, and he'll be out to help you." She waved again before returning her attention to the couple. A small and compact Indian man came out from the curtained off area behind the counter. "Mr. Preacher, it's good to see you again."

"It's good to see you too, Samar."

He shook the older man's hand. He towered over the jeweler and outweighed him by at least a hundred pounds, but he wasn't fooled by the man's slight stature or age. Samar was a jiu-jitsu expert, and Preacher had seen him take down men twice his size at the local sparring gym.

"How can I help you today?" Samar asked.

He fished the barbell out of his pocket and held it out to the jeweller. "I was wondering if I could get this engraved."

"Of course, of course." Samar took the barbell from him, and Preacher followed him to the front counter. "What do you want engraved on it?"

"Initials on either end of the barbell. SW on each, please."

"Do you want a script font or something thicker and bolder?" Samar asked. "With the small area, I would suggest you skip the script. It'll be more difficult to read."

"Plain lettering is good," he said. He wanted the next guy Addison Moore slept with to know what the initials said.

One – no one in this town but Gideon knows your real name, so it doesn't matter if they know it's an S and a W or not, and two, you want someone who isn't you, looking at her tits?

No, he fucking didn't, and the intensity of his feelings on the subject was a little alarming.

So, you think putting a barbell in her nipple with your initials engraved on it, like you're branding her as yours or some happy horseshit like that, is going to stop her from fucking another guy? Is that it?

Of course not. She wouldn't have a clue what the SW stood for. Hell, she might not even notice the initials.

Then why the fuck are you doing this?

The hell of it was, he didn't know why. But the second he found out she was getting a piercing, the urge to have his initials engraved on her barbell was too fucking great to ignore.

"I need it by six at the latest," he said to Samar. "Is that doable?"

"For you? Of course," Samar said. "I'll ask Diya to drop it off at your shop when it's finished."

"Great, thank you." He pulled out his wallet and paid for the engraving before leaving the store and heading to Nan's Diner. He didn't have to put that barbell in Addison, he reasoned. Maybe by the time she arrived for her appointment, some of his sanity would have returned, and he'd keep the marked barbell the fuck out of her nipple.

Maybe.

CHAPTER 10

Addison glanced at the clock on the wall of the tattoo shop. It was ten after seven, and she'd been sitting on the couch in the seating area since six-thirty, her nerves fraying like cheap yarn and her resolve to pierce her nipple weakening by the minute.

She'd borrowed her brother Daniel's truck to drive here. The weather was too friggin' hot to walk. She'd snagged a spot right outside the shop and glanced at the truck through the big front window behind her, tempted to jump up and run out of the shop.

The two young women sitting on the couch beside her were on their phones, taking selfies, texting, and talking in high-pitched giggles about some guy named Doug, who may or may not have a large penis.

She tuned them out, staring at the curtain drawn around the station farthest from her before her gaze drifted to the tattoo bed in the first tattoo station. That was the tattoo bed Preacher had bent her over and –

"Shouldn't be too much longer," Nolan said from behind

the counter. "Preacher's just finishing up his last tattoo. Don't know why it's taking so long."

"We know," the girls beside her said in unison before breaking into high-pitched giggles that made Addison want to throw a tattoo binder at them.

The girl closest to her on the couch grinned at her. "Our friend is getting tattooed by him, and she's, like, got a total crush on him. They're probably making out behind the curtain right now."

"I can hear the tattoo gun," Addison said.

The girl blinked at her. "Oh, right. Well, whatever. Bethany wants him, and what Bethany wants, Bethany gets."

The other girl laughed. "Get it, girlfriend."

The two girls bumped fists, and Addison stared at the curtain again. She could hear the buzz of the gun and the high murmur of Bethany's voice as she talked non-stop. She was annoyed to realize that the feeling in her stomach was jealousy.

"Are you guys from Harmony Falls?" she asked abruptly.

"No, we're here camping for a couple of weeks. We come down here, like, almost every summer," one of the girls said. "It's so good to get away from, like, technology."

She twirled her hair as she stared at her phone. "Oh my God. Brittany and Jeff broke up."

"You're kidding me?" Her friend stared at her phone. "How do you know that?"

"It's all over Facebook."

Nolan made a low snort, and when she glanced at him, he rolled his eyes and made a wanking off motion with his hand. She grinned, and he winked at her.

She looked up when she heard the curtain being drawn back, her breath catching in her throat at the sight of Preacher's big body. Good gravy, it wasn't right that a man looked that good in a t-shirt and a pair of jeans.

"Preacher, I love it so much. Thank you!" Bethany was blonde-haired and slender with sun-kissed skin and a perfect complexion. Addison hated her on sight.

Her jealousy went from pale green to an alarming shade of emerald when Bethany leaned toward Preacher with her arms open. It was obvious she was going to hug him, and Addie had no idea how to process her immediate and confusing 'get away from my man' feelings.

Luckily, she didn't have to. Preacher stepped back, shaking his head and pointing toward the counter. "You're welcome. Nolan will take your payment."

"Are you sure you don't want to stop by our campsite later? We're close to the front of the park and have marshmallows and chocolate." Bethany cocked her hip and thrust her admittedly lovely breasts in Preacher's general direction. "It'll be, like, so much fun. We're gonna go skinny dipping, too."

"You can't get the tattoo wet today. It'll ruin it," Preacher said.

"Oh, right. Of course. Well, if you change your mind, you, like, totally have my number, so text me," Bethany said.

Preacher walked away without replying, disappearing into one of the rooms at the back of the shop as Bethany paid Nolan before joining her friends.

"How's it look?" The woman sitting next to Addison leaned forward.

Bethany pulled down the front of her jean shorts until it was so low Addison could almost see the top of her damn vagina. A bandage covered her smooth skin, and Addison suddenly wondered if she should wax her entire muff like Bethany.

Did Preacher like that look?

"It's covered by the bandage. What did you even get?" her other friend said.

"Oh, just a little four-leaf clover." Bethany glanced at Addison and then Nolan before saying in a slightly softer voice. "Mostly, I just wanted to give him a look at the goods, let him know what he was gonna get if he popped by the campsite later tonight."

The two girls screamed laughter, and Addison forced a smile when Bethany grinned at her. "He's hot, right?"

"Um, sure," Addison said.

"You think he's gonna show up?" The other girls stood and followed Bethany to the door.

Bethany smiled at them over her shoulder. "He was playing hard to get while he was tattooing, but have you ever met a guy who could resist the Bethany charm? He'll show up."

Addison didn't catch their reply as the door swung shut behind them. A blast of warm air settled over her skin. The thought of Preacher joining Bethany and her friends, of him touching and kissing her like he'd kissed Addison not two days ago, made her sick to her stomach.

Doubt crashed into her like she'd taken a direct hit from a roller derby queen. She couldn't do this. She couldn't pierce her nipple. What was she thinking? She was judging Bethany, and she was exactly like her, modifying her body just to try to get Preacher's attention.

You're not. Yeah, maybe you're a little excited at the thought of Preacher seeing you half-naked, but if you really examine your feelings on it, that's not the reason. You're doing this because you're tired of living under someone else's expectations. It's time to do what you want. So, pierce that nipple, girl. Hell, pierce your clit too.

She had to clamp her mouth shut around the giggle. Pierce her clit? No damn way.

"Hey, sorry for the delay." Preacher had returned, and Addison stood up, clutching her purse tightly in one hand.

"Uh, that's fine."

Preacher turned to Nolan. "You can cash out and head home."

"You sure?" Nolan said.

Preacher nodded. "Just lock up and turn the sign to close." He glanced at Addison. "Follow me."

She followed him across the shop to the room he'd disappeared into earlier. It was a small room with a tattoo chair already in the bed position, a counter with a sink, a rolling stool, an autoclave, bio-hazard and sharps containers bolted to the wall, and a metal rolling cart next to the bed.

She swallowed hard as she stared at the cart. The top of it had a box of disposable gloves, bandages, gauze, some packages of alcohol wipes, a pen and – her pulse sped up – a pair of clamps. A small barbell and an unopened needle were on a paper towel.

"If you want to rebook because the shop is closed now, I understand," she said.

He shook his head. "It's fine. It won't take long." He paused and gave her an assessing look. "Unless you've changed your mind about having your nipple pierced?"

The look on his face suggested he was positive she had. She lifted her chin and straightened her back. "I haven't."

He studied her a moment longer before saying, "All right. Take off your shirt and your bra."

Her nerves returned in full force, like a punch to the gut by a championship boxer. She smoothed her sweaty hands over her skirt before quickly unbuttoning her shirt.

She'd worn her practical cotton panties -why break out

the silk thong when no one would see it - but she'd made sure to wear her prettiest bra, a lacy pink thing. It didn't matter because Preacher had turned away and was washing his hands at the sink. She unhooked her bra and placed it neatly on the second shelf of the utility cart with her shirt.

Feeling incredibly self-conscious, she crossed her arms over her breasts as Preacher turned around. Without looking at her, he pulled on a pair of gloves and tore open an alcohol wipe.

"Um, should I lie on the bed?" she said.

"Not yet." He sat down on the stool and indicated for her to stand in front of him. "This is an alcohol wipe. First, I'll clean your nipple, and then I'll mark it with a pen. You want a horizontal piercing, right?"

"Yes," she said.

"Okay." He paused and said, "You need to drop your arms."

"Right." Oh, excellent, she was blushing again. She dropped her arms, staring at a spot over Preacher's left shoulder. She'd spent some time this afternoon wondering what would happen if her nipple wasn't hard when he tried to pierce it. Would he touch it to make it hard, maybe suck on it or lick it? The perverted version of Addison had certainly hoped so.

Unfortunately for pervert Addison, it wasn't a concern. Whether it was nerves, the coldness of the room, or just because Preacher's mouth was agonizingly close, her nipples were diamond hard.

"Right or left?"

"S-sorry?" She stared at the top of Preacher's head, wondering what he would do if she threaded her fingers through that thick dark hair.

"Which nipple do you want pierced?"

"Oh, um, the right one, please."

She jerked, a soft gasp escaping her mouth when he wiped her nipple with the alcohol wipe. "You okay?"

"Yes. Nervous," she said.

"That's normal. It'll hurt, but the pain fades fast," he said.

His head moved closer, she could feel his warm breath on her nipple, and it took everything in her not to arch her back. He used the pen to draw a mark on either side of her nipple before rolling the stool back.

"Good, lie on the bed."

She laid on the bed, the paper covering crinkling beneath her.

"I cleaned and sanitized the barbell before you got here. All right?"

She nodded. "Okay."

"I'll clamp your nipple first, then pierce it with the needle, and then put the barbell in," he said as he opened the needle package. "Last chance to change your mind."

"I'm not changing my mind," she said.

He clamped her nipple, and she stared at the ceiling, her hands in tight fists at her side, her spine a rigid line of tense nerves.

"Take a few deep breaths," he said.

She forced air in and out of her lungs, and on the third exhale, he slid the needle neatly into her nipple. It hurt much more than she expected, and she bit back her soft cry, making a strangled *mmpf* instead.

"Good girl," he said. "Almost finished, Sunshine."

He placed the barbell in, working quickly and efficiently, before using the gauze to clean up the blood and applying pressure for a few minutes.

"You okay?"

Addison blew her breath out. Her nipple felt hot, but the pain had faded. "Yes. It doesn't hurt anymore."

"Good."

He checked her nipple. The bleeding had stopped, and he placed the bandage over her nipple before peeling off his gloves. "You'll remove the bandage and clean the piercing in four to five hours. I'm sending you home with a care sheet and a small bottle of Castile tea tree soap. Clean your nipple with it and warm water very gently. Do that once a day in the shower. It's normal for your nipple to swell a bit and crust over. It will be very sore the first few days. If your nipple swells to the point where it's touching either end of the barbell, come back, and I'll put in a longer post."

"Okay."

He tossed the needle into the sharps container and threw the paper towel and alcohol wipe packages into the garbage.

"Can I wear my bra?"

He glanced at the lacy piece of fabric. "Not for twenty-four hours, and not that one. The barbell might get caught in it and rip out the piercing."

She winced as he rolled his chair back to toss away his gloves. "Sports bra or cotton bra only until it heals. It can take up to a year to heal, but most clients find by six months it's healed."

"Okay," she said.

"Don't touch it unless you're cleaning it. Don't play with the barbell."

"I won't," she said.

"Don't let anyone else touch it either," he suddenly said. "No one licking or sucking on your nipple for at least a month. At least."

She turned a brilliant shade of red. The last person who had sucked on her nipple was the very man who had just pierced it, and as his gaze suddenly drifted over her naked chest, her left nipple turned as hard as her right nipple.

"Did you hear me, Sunshine?"

She nodded and closed her eyes. She really should get up and put her shirt on. The piercing was over. Why was she still lying here half-naked, letting Preacher ogle her?

Instead of getting dressed, she said, "Do you do other body piercings?"

Addie! What are you doing?

"What else do you want to pierce?"

She opened her eyes and made a vague motion toward her crotch. "I was thinking maybe, you know…"

He grinned at her, and her blush, beginning to fade, flared back to life. "You'll have to be more specific, Sunshine."

She bit at her bottom lip. "You know, down there."

"Down there?" His grin widened, and she sat up abruptly. "Forget it."

"Hold on." His hand wrapped around her arm, and she almost moaned at the contact. "I didn't say I wouldn't do it. I just need to hear you say you want your clit hood pierced. Clear communication is important with my piercing clients, Addison."

She shivered all over, and his gaze dropped to her naked breasts for a moment before he raised his eyebrow at her.

Addison Mabel Moore! Don't you dare say it! Don't you -

She took a deep breath. "I – I want to get my clit hood pierced…please."

CHAPTER 11

Preacher stared at Addison. He'd kept it professional while he was piercing her nipple, but her clit piercing request had thrown him over the edge. Fuck, did he want her. The first time he fucked her, it ended badly, and despite her acting like he'd never been inside her pretty little pussy, he really should be talking to her about it.

Or better yet, telling her to go the hell home. Unfortunately, his willpower seemed to have flown out the window.

He'd spent the last two days thinking obsessively about how he messed it up with her. He'd hurt her, for God's sake. Now she was here again, and he had the chance to fix what he'd done the last time. He could make it good for her. He could show her that it wouldn't – *shouldn't* – hurt her to be with him. He had no intention of piercing her perfect pink clit, but he'd be an idiot not to take advantage of the opportunity to fix his mistake.

"Will – will you do it?" Addison asked a bit breathlessly.

The only thing he wanted to do was her... repeatedly. "Well, Sunshine, here's the thing. Not every woman's clit hood is pierceable, so I'll need to look at your clit before I say yes."

God, he loved the way she blushed.

"I – you've already seen it," she said.

"No, I've touched it," he corrected.

Her hands clenched into tight fists, and her entire body shivered as if she were remembering that moment two days ago. His dick was as hard as a rock and straining against the front of his jeans. If she looked at his crotch, she'd see how much he wanted her. He wondered if she was wet, and he tried not to look too desperate as she returned to lying on her back and studying the ceiling.

"Okay," she said.

"Okay, what?"

"You can look at me down there."

He pressed his lips together to keep from smiling at her shyness. "I can look at your clit. Say it, Sunshine. Clear communication, remember?"

"You can look at my clit," she said in a low voice.

His dick practically screamed hallelujah, and he rolled his stool to the end of the table before she could change her mind. Now was the time to hand her a sheet to cover herself, instruct her to remove her skirt and panties and leave until she called for him.

Instead, he said, "Lift your skirt."

He wondered if she could hear the harsh need in his voice.

Breathing hard, she pulled her skirt up around her waist. He stared at her panties as fresh lust roared through him. He had expected to see something lacy like her bra. Women like her always wore matching underwear sets. Instead of lace, her panties were cotton and light pink in colour. A tiny green bow adorned the waistband just below her belly button. They were sweet and practical, just like her. A silky scrap of a thong on a woman was usually what got his motor running, but damn if the sight of those practical, soft pink panties didn't make him want to come in his jeans.

He was more than thankful she was still staring up at the ceiling and couldn't see how his hands were shaking. Willing himself not to rip those soft panties right off of her, he cleared his throat and said, "Hips up."

She lifted her hips immediately, her slender body jerking when his fingers curled in the waistband of her panties. He pulled them down her thighs, his knuckles gliding across her satiny, soft skin, and tugged them down her calves and off her feet.

She was panting harshly, and her legs were locked together. He resisted the urge to sniff her panties and instead folded them neatly and set them on top of the cart. He studied the small patch of reddish curls at the top of her pussy before grabbing her ankles. He pushed her legs up until her feet were resting on the bed. Her body was trembling like mad, and he ran his fingertips down her shins.

"Open your legs, Addison."

She made a low moan and parted her legs. He stared at her pussy, and his cock twitched. She was wet. Soaking wet, in fact. He squeezed his hands together in a tight fist before saying, "Wider, Sunshine."

"I – I'm sorry?" she said.

"I need you to spread your legs nice and wide for me." He stroked her inner thigh with the tips of his fingers.

She moaned again – he didn't think she even realized the sounds she was making – and let her legs drop open.

"That's my good girl," he said in a low voice.

He stood and leaned over her, rubbing her inner thigh with one big hand as she stared up at him. Her nipples were hard, and he wanted to bend over and suck on her left one until she was making those same sweet cries she made two days ago.

Instead, he stared down at her pussy again as she cleared her throat. "Does it, uh, look okay?"

"Your pussy looks perfect." He was deliberately crude, a part of him loving how it made her blush. She didn't disappoint. He watched the red rise from her newly pierced nipple up her throat to her cheeks.

"I meant, can it be pierced," she whispered.

He smiled at her as his fingers traced circles on both her inner thighs. "Let me take a closer look."

"A closer look?" she squeaked. "What do you – oh my goodness!"

His hands holding her thighs open, he bent until his face hovered inches from his idea of heaven. He inhaled deeply – fuck, he loved the smell of pussy – as she made another nervous squeak.

"Mr. Preacher, wh-what are you doing?"

He didn't reply. Instead, he thumbed back the hood of her clit. She cried out, her hips rising a little, and he smiled at how swollen and wet her perfect pink clit was. He could feel her thighs trembling and told himself to walk away. Nothing good could come of this.

Instead, he leaned in and licked her clit with a wide, flat stroke of his tongue.

Her reaction was off the charts. She made a hoarse cry of pleasure, and her entire body jerked like a live wire. She would have fallen off the bed if he hadn't grabbed her hips.

"Liked that, did you?" He grinned up at her, the smile faltering a little when she stared at him with shock all over her beautiful face.

"Wh-what did you do?" she whispered.

"Jesus, Sunshine, you act like you've never had a tongue in your pussy before," he teased.

Her red cheeks flamed even brighter, and she licked her bottom lip before looking away. He muttered a curse under his breath and squeezed her thigh. "Look at me."

She returned her gaze to his, and he hated the embarrassment he could see in her eyes.

"Are you fucking kidding me?" he said.

"Harrison said a proper lady doesn't like that type of -"

"Fuck proper," he growled and buried his face in her pussy.

THE SECOND STROKE OF PREACHER'S TONGUE ON HER CLIT was even better than the first one. Addison gripped the sides of the tattoo bed and tried not to scream with pleasure as he spread her pussy wide with his rough fingers and licked her clit with stiff, short strokes.

When he thrust his tongue into her narrow entrance, she cried out and tried to scramble away. He hooked his arms around her thighs and held her immobile before lifting his head to stare at her. More embarrassment swept through her. His face was soaking wet, and she stared at him in shame. "I don't think -"

"Stop thinking," he rasped before burying his face in her pussy again. He pressed his chest against the bed and tossed her legs over his shoulders. His large hands gripped her ass, preventing her from wiggling away as he feasted on her pussy.

His tongue was so soft, so wet, and, oh my goodness, every touch against her clit made her want to jump out of her skin. Pleasure and tension coiled together in her belly as her orgasm hovered just beyond her reach. She needed more, and she had the feeling he was deliberately holding back. Teasing her until she couldn't think straight.

She could hear someone begging shamelessly and was shocked to realize the pleading and begging was coming from her. She tried to take back her self-control, but when Preacher pushed one thick finger into her opening, she screamed and resumed her babbling, incoherent begging.

"Shh, Sunshine." His voice was muffled. "I know you need to come."

"Please, oh please, Simon," she moaned.

He stiffened and stared up at her. "What did you say?"

"Please make me come, Simon. Please!"

He lowered his head. She felt his warm breath against the lips of her pussy, and then his lips were wrapped around her clit. He pulled firmly, rubbing her clit with his tongue at the same time, and she screamed as her orgasm washed over her in a tidal wave of indescribable pleasure. She bucked and writhed against his mouth as he pinned her down with one big hand and continued to lick and suck at her clit while he pushed two fingers into her core and stretched her lightly.

She pulled his hair, pounded on his back with her feet, and squeezed her thighs around his head until he pulled them apart with a low grunt. He rubbed her thighs as she collapsed against the bed. She barely heard the crinkle of the condom wrapper over the rapid pounding of her heartbeat. She stared at him when he sat her up and eased her down to the end of the bed so that her legs were hanging off it. His shirt was gone, and he had pushed his jeans down to his ankles.

"Are you going to fuck me again?" she said.

"Yes, Sunshine. I am."

A tingle of delight went down her spine at his reply. He had given her pleasure, and now she would give him pleasure. The thought brought on another weird surge of desire in her belly, this one so strong it almost hurt. Before she could stop to consider why, he had spread her legs and pushed the wide head of his cock against her entrance.

"It won't hurt this time, I promise," he said in a low voice.

She dug her nails into his biceps as he put his arm around her waist and pushed again. To her complete shock, the head slipped in easily without any pain at all. She stared up at him as he made a low groan.

"Okay?" he muttered before threading his fingers through her hair and gripping it tightly.

"Yes, it – it doesn't hurt."

"Good," he said hoarsely. He nuzzled her throat before whispering in her ear, "I guess this means every time I fuck you, I'll need to eat your sweet pussy first."

She clenched around him at the thought, and he groaned again before cupping her left breast and toying with her nipple. "Relax and let me in, Sunshine."

She tried to relax around him, but it was difficult with the way his fingers were tugging on her nipple. It sent waves of need through her, and her pussy kept clenching rhythmically around him. He pulled her head back and kissed her. She could taste herself on his mouth, and when he pushed his tongue between her lips, she sucked eagerly at it. He was pushing steadily into her, and she made a small squeak of pain when he sheathed himself entirely, and her right nipple brushed against his chest.

"I'm sorry," he said immediately. Addison wrapped her legs around his waist when he tried to withdraw.

"No, it's my, um, my nipple," she said.

He glanced at the bandage that covered it. "Right, sorry."

"It's okay." She touched his chest tentatively, tracing her

fingers over the cross tattooed just below the hollow of his throat. If she hadn't been stuffed full of his cock, she supposed she would have wanted to study each of the tattoos that covered his upper body.

Instead, she was starting to feel a slow pulse of pleasure in her lower belly as Preacher cupped her left breast again and kneaded it. He kissed her slowly, sucking on her tongue and her lips until she was thrusting her hips against him.

He released her mouth and pushed lightly on her upper chest. "Lean back and brace yourself on your hands."

She did what he asked, digging her fingers into the paper sheet that covered the tattoo bed as he curled his big hand around the back of her neck and gripped firmly. His thumb rubbed against her fluttering pulse as he stared at her pussy. Her skirt had slipped down a little, and he pushed it back up around her waist to see all of her.

He was breathing harshly as he thrust back and forth. She glanced down and was mesmerized by the way his cock slid in and out of her. Just watching the way her pussy stretched around his thick cock, the way she took every inch of him, was making her hot.

"You feel so good on my dick," Preacher suddenly groaned before thrusting harder. "Can you come again for me, baby?"

She stared wide-eyed at him. She never came more than once, and certainly not after she'd had that intense of an orgasm. Besides, she'd always been hit and miss when it came to an orgasm from sex. More often miss.

"I – I don't think so." Her desire was rapidly disappearing under her anxiety that she would disappoint Preacher. It shouldn't have mattered since she was nothing but an easy lay for him, but she couldn't help it. The anxiety was there and impossible to ignore.

He cupped her cheek and stroked her cheekbone with his thumb before pushing her flat onto her back. The bed was at the perfect height for him to fuck her, and she wondered vaguely if he had raised it that high on purpose. Had he planned this from the moment she'd booked the appointment?

The thought that he might have been planning to fuck her all along sent fresh wetness surging out of her, and she squeezed tightly around his dick. Preacher groaned and took her right hand, pushing it to her pussy and pressing her fingers against her clit.

"Try to come again for me, baby."

"Simon, I can't," she said. The thought of touching herself in front of him made her cringe with embarrassment. What if she looked stupid? What if she didn't do it right or –

"Sunshine." His low voice urged her to look at him. He leaned over her, his hand still holding hers to her core and his dick still embedded deep within her. "Touch yourself, baby."

Unable to resist him, she rubbed tentatively at her clit. He straightened and held her hips, gliding in and out of her slowly as he watched her fingers caress her throbbing clit.

"Good," he said, "just like that. Fuck, baby, do you have any idea how goddamn hot you look right now? Keep touching that sweet little clit."

His hoarse voice and the look of lust in his eyes emboldened her, and she rubbed her clit more firmly. It sent sparks of pleasure darting up her spine, and he groaned again when she thrust her hips at him. "Feel good?"

"Yes," she gasped.

"Keep going." He was starting to lose his control. She could see it in the way his eyes were glazing over and feel it in the harder thrusts of his dick. She closed her eyes and concentrated on touching herself the way she liked best, gentle caresses followed by firmer ones with a slight tug every few seconds. Preacher had pushed her legs up again, resting her feet on the bed as he held her thighs open wide. She could feel his big, hard hands kneading and pressing against her inner thighs.

She opened her eyes and made a soft cry of pleasure at the look on Preacher's face. He was staring at her pussy, alternating between watching her fingers rub her clit and his cock slide in and out of her narrow opening. She was close to coming, her fingers rubbing steadily against that little pink nub, and she studied Preacher intently. His mouth dropped open, and he sucked in breath in harsh gasps as he almost absentmindedly cupped her left breast and pulled on her nipple.

She cried out, her body arching as that one little tug pushed her over the edge. Her second orgasm rolled through her, making her body shake, and her brain short-circuit. Vaguely, she was aware of Preacher's harsh shout, of his fingers digging into her hips and his cock slamming into her so deeply that there was a brief flash of pain before more pleasure shuddered its way through her.

She quivered and moaned beneath him as he thrust back and forth a few more times, his body shaking from the pleasure of his release, before leaning over her and resting his head just below her breasts. She stroked his thick hair tentatively as his breath blew across her ribs, lighting up goose bumps across her flesh.

"You okay?" he rasped.

She nodded. "Yes. I – I've never had two orgasms in a row before."

Addie, shut up! You sound like an idiot!

Preacher raised his head and stared at her. "Maybe we should try for three."

Her mouth dropped open as she tried to decide if he was

serious. He looked serious, and she licked her lips. "Um, I don't think – I mean, I'm pretty sure I can't do that."

"You thought you couldn't do two," he said with a wicked grin.

"I know, but I'm quite positive that three is -"

"Preacher! Yo, you still here?"

Addison's eyes widened at the sound of Nolan's voice. She stared blankly at Preacher as he muttered a curse. He straightened and pulled out of her, yanking off the condom before tossing it in the garbage and throwing paper towels over top of it. He hauled up his jeans and buttoned them as he muttered, "Get dressed."

She nearly fell off the table as she tried to get down. The protective paper was stuck to her ass, and she yanked at it futilely as Preacher uttered another curse. He pulled the paper away from her bare butt and off the table, wadding it up and throwing it on the floor as she shoved her skirt down, and he yanked his shirt over his head. She grabbed her shirt and stuffed her arms into the sleeves.

"Preacher? You back here, man? I forgot my fucking phone. Jesus, I'd forget my goddamn head if it wasn't attached."

"My panties." Addison pulled her shirt over her head. They were still sitting on the cart in plain view. Preacher snatched them up and stuffed them into his pocket just as the door opened, and Nolan walked in.

"Hey, didn't you hear me calling or…"

He trailed off as he stared at Addison and then at Preacher. "What's going on?"

"What do you think is going on?" Preacher snarled at him. "I'm finishing up the piercing."

Nolan blinked at him. "Finishing up the piercing."

"Are you a fucking parrot now? Yes. Next time fucking knock before you come in when I'm with a client."

"Sorry." Nolan stared at Addison. "Sorry, Miss Moore."

She smiled weakly at him and tucked her bra into her purse as Preacher handed her a plastic bag with some paper and a small bottle inside. "Cleaning instructions," he said. "Follow the instructions exactly. If your nipple starts to look infected, come see me immediately."

"Right, okay," she said.

Nolan was eyeing her hair, and, oh shit, did she have the *I just had sex* hair happening? Forcing herself not to pat it down, she made herself smile at Preacher.

"Thank you, Preacher."

"You're welcome."

She hesitated a moment longer. She hadn't paid him, and she needed her damn underwear back, but Preacher took her by the elbow and steered her past Nolan and out into the main part of the tattoo shop.

"I need my underwear," she said under her breath. Nolan had followed them out, and Preacher just gave her a cocky grin before opening the door and ushering her into the warm night air.

"Good night, Miss Moore." His gaze dropped to her crotch. "Remember to keep it clean for me."

Damn him. Why did he have to make everything sound so dirty, and why did it have to turn her on?

"I will," she whispered.

"That's my good girl." He grinned again at her. Suddenly feeling awkward and cheap, she turned and stumbled toward Daniel's truck. She was on the verge of tears, and as she fumbled open the car door, she glanced up at Preacher.

The grin dropped from his face, and he cocked his head at her. "What's wrong?"

"Nothing," she said. "Good-bye."

She slid behind the wheel and started the truck as he walked toward her. She threw it in reverse and stomped on the gas as he stopped on the sidewalk outside the shop. Blinking back the hot tears, she drove away without a backward glance.

CHAPTER 12

*Y*ou're acting both pathetic and stalkerish, Addie. You'll see him on Sunday at Kira's place, for God's sake. Go home.

She hesitated just outside the Crimson Door Tattoo shop. Preacher's shop was open until seven, and she hadn't deliberately shown up just before he closed… that was just how the bus schedule worked out.

Uh-huh, keep telling yourself that, little Miss Denial.

She continued to hesitate, studying the people milling about on Main Street. It might have been almost seven in the evening, but the street was still packed. Most carried melting ice cream cones from Licks Ice Cream Shop two blocks down.

All of them looked hot, sweaty, and exhausted.

The last two times you had sex with Preacher, you felt weird and cheap afterwards. Do you want to be with a guy who makes you feel like that?

No, but if she was honest with herself, it wasn't Preacher who made her feel cheap. It was herself. She was judging herself in the same way Harrison would judge her, and, dammit, she didn't want to do that anymore. There was nothing wrong with a woman having casual sex with a man. Maybe if she kept having casual sex, it would help her get over her stupid inner judgment about it.

There's also nothing wrong with being a woman who doesn't want to have casual sex. Go home, Addie.

No, she wouldn't. Her nipple piercing was maybe – *possibly* – looking infected, and the responsible thing to do was to have Preacher take a quick look at it once he'd finished with his other clients and closed up the shop. Once he gave her the okay, she'd hop on the bus and return home.

Oh yeah? So, you're not hoping that Preacher will take one look at your tits and immediately fuck you again?

Of course, she wasn't. She would pay Preacher for the piercing, have him check it for infection and then leave.

You going to ask for your panties back?

Nope, she was not. Looking Preacher in the eye and asking him to return her underwear was an impossible task. Besides, nothing sexual was going to happen between them. This was just her being cautious.

Bullsh-

She muzzled her inner voice and stepped aside as a larger man, his bald head gleaming in the sun, stepped out of the shop. A bandage covered his right arm from his wrist to his elbow. He held the door for her, and she nodded in thanks before stepping into the sweet coolness of the tattoo shop. A dark-haired man almost as large as Preacher stood behind the counter, tucking a receipt into a cash box.

"Hi, can I help you?" he asked.

She blinked at him before her gaze was drawn to the inked art on his arms. He wore a short-sleeved t-shirt, and tattoos covered every inch of his skin, from his wrists to the edge of his sleeves.

"Miss?"

She dragged her gaze back to his face to catch a brief look of annoyance crossing it. He was handsome, maybe even better looking than Preacher, but she didn't feel any sexual attraction to him. Apparently, her vagina was only hot for a particular grumpy tattoo artist.

"Sorry, I thought... does Nolan not work here anymore?"

"He's off today. How can I help you?"

"Oh, um, I'm here to see Preacher."

"He's with a client. Do you have an appointment?"

She stared at the curtained off tattoo station. "No, but -"

"He's fully booked for walk-in appointments until after next week," the man said. "You can book with him for mid-August, or you can book with me."

"You work here?" She winced at her stupidity. Obviously, he worked there.

"I'm Nix." He held out his hand, and she shook it.

"Addison."

"Nice to meet you. What kind of tattoo were you thinking of getting?"

"Oh, I wasn't here for -"

"Are you fucking kidding me? You have to give me a refund!"

Their heads swiveled toward the tattoo station as the curtain drew back with a rattle. Bethany - she of the four-leaf clover tattoo and naked vagina – glared at Preacher, her hands fisted on her hips and her lips thin.

"I told you not to get it wet. You did. You didn't follow my advice, and you ruined your tattoo. You don't get a refund." Preacher's voice was calm, but Addison could see a muscle ticking in his jaw.

"You asshole!" Bethany shouted. "You didn't say anything about not getting the tattoo wet."

"Yes, I did. It's in the written care instructions you were given, and I specifically told you not to get it wet as well."

"It doesn't even look like a four-leaf clover anymore. It looks like a… like a smeared piece of snot on my fucking pussy!"

"Not my problem," Preacher said. "Next time, pay attention to the care instructions."

"You're seriously not going to give me a fucking refund?" Bethany's face was bright red, and her slender body was as stiff as a rabid dog's.

"Fucking right, I'm not," Preacher said.

"You asshole!" Bethany screeched. "I'm gonna tell everyone that you're a shit tattoo artist who doesn't know shit about tattooing."

"Have a nice day." Preacher folded his arms across his massive chest. A bored look had settled on his face, but the muscle in his jaw tick-tick-ticked in rapid succession.

For a moment, Addison was sure Bethany would try to claw Preacher's eyes out. Instead, she turned and stomped toward the door, pushing past Addison with an irritated huff before pausing at the door and glaring again at Preacher. "I'm glad you didn't show up at my tent. I wouldn't fuck you if you were the last man on earth. You're a pathetic loser who probably doesn't know shit about making a woman come."

When Preacher didn't reply, her face went a darker shade of crimson, and, with a final muttered 'asshole', Bethany flounced out of the shop.

Silence descended over the shop. The muscle in his jaw still ticking, Preacher frowned at Addison. "What are you doing here?"

Shit. Could she have had worse timing?

"I'll come back on Monday," she said, groping for the door handle behind her.

His scowl deepened, and she swallowed hard when he stalked forward and stopped in front of her. "What's going on?"

She licked her lips. Now that he was closer, she could see how angry Preacher was. It should have frightened her. Instead, she wondered how much hotter sex would be with a pissed-off Preacher.

"I think it's infected," she said.

"Tattoo or piercing?"

"Piercing."

A muscle in his temple joined the jaw muscle in ticking solidarity. He took a deep breath, his nostrils flaring before he reached behind her and flipped the open sign to close. His hard chest nearly touched her breasts, and … God help her, why did he always have to smell so good?

He turned away to stare at Nix. "You can head out. I'll close up the shop."

"All right. See you tomorrow." Nix headed toward the door. "Nice to meet you, Addison."

"You too."

When he was gone, Preacher locked the door behind him. "C'mon." Without looking at her, he walked toward the piercing room.

She followed him to the piercing room. Shamefully, her pussy was already tingling, and her nipples were hardening as he pointed to the piercing bed. "Sit down and take off your shirt."

She hopped up on the bed and unbuttoned her shirt with trembling hands. He had his back to her and was rummaging through a cupboard, pulling out some gauze and a small spray bottle of yellow-tinged liquid. She removed her soft cotton bra and sat straight, arching her back a little as he snapped on gloves.

"I still need to pay you for the piercing," she said.

"Have you been touching it?" He turned around.

"No," she said. "Only to clean it."

She searched his face, but if he found the sight of her tits to be an enjoyable one, it didn't show. He was all business as he approached her and bent down to study her right nipple.

"Have you let anyone else touch it?" His warm breath sent goosebumps scuttling to life on her skin, and she promptly forgot what he'd just asked.

"Have you?" he asked as something dark flared in his eyes.

"Have I what?" she whispered.

"Let someone else touch it? Lick it? Suck on it?" he almost growled.

Her panties were suddenly so wet she was afraid she would drip on the bed.

"No," she said. "No one has done those things."

"Good," he said briskly. "A human mouth is full of germs."

She blinked at him as he straightened. "It isn't infected."

"Are you sure?" she said a little breathlessly. "It looks kind of red to me."

"It isn't," he said. "It looks really good. The swelling is already down significantly."

She couldn't hold back her moan when his gloved fingers grasped one end of the silver barbell and turned it gently back and forth.

"Did that hurt?" he said.

"N-no," she said. Her nipple was incredibly sore Wednesday night and all of Thursday, but she'd woken up this morning with no pain at all and no goo crusted over her nipple either. She cleaned it in the shower this morning but hadn't turned the barbell like Preacher.

She was utterly unprepared for the lightning bolt of pleasure it sent straight from her right nipple to her crotch. Holy mother of Mary's ghost, who knew piercing a nipple would do that. What would having Preacher's lips tugging on the barbell feel like?

"You okay?"

She nodded, not trusting herself to speak. She wasn't entirely certain she wouldn't beg him to suck on her nipple.

"You sure?" he asked as his fingers turned the barbell again. More pleasure speared straight to her core.

"Yes," she almost moaned. "It feels a little, uh, strange. In a good way."

"A piercing can make your nipple more sensitive," he said.

She wondered if he could see her disappointment when he stopped twisting the barbell.

"Maybe I should pierce the other one," she said.

"It's your body." He held up the bottle he'd taken from the cupboard. "This is an antibacterial spray. It's not infected, but it won't hurt to give it a couple of sprays."

"Okay," she said.

He sprayed her right nipple, using some gauze to wipe away the drips. She clamped her mouth shut against the stupid little moans that wanted to escape. This wasn't foreplay. He was working for God's sake.

Desperate to take her mind off the fact that she was nearly climaxing from his touch to her nipple alone, she said, "What does SW mean?"

"I don't know what you're talking about," he said, but something flickered in his eyes.

"SW is engraved into both ends of the barbell. I noticed it in the shower this morning." She pointed to it, and he glanced at it before shrugging.

"Must be a manufacturer thing."

She frowned. "I don't remember seeing any initials engraved on the display jewelry."

"I can put a new barbell in if you want."

"It doesn't matter," she said. "I just wondered."

He threw the gauze and the gloves in the garbage and tucked the spray into the cupboard. "You can get dressed now."

"Actually, I'd like to get my clit hood pierced." She was proud of how steady her voice was.

He didn't turn around. "No."

"What do you mean?"

"I mean, no," he said. "Get dressed. The shop's closed, and I'm tired."

"I didn't mean tonight," she said. "I'll book another appointment. When's your next availability?"

"No," he repeated.

"Stop saying that," she said. "I want my clit hood pierced, and you have to do it."

He barked harsh laughter before turning around and stalking toward her. He placed his hands on the bed on either side of her as she stared wide-eyed at him. "No, I don't. Listen carefully, Sunshine. You might be used to using sex to get your ex-fiancé to do whatever you want, but I'm not him. I don't care how many times you offer up your tight pussy, I'm not piercing your pretty little clit, and that's final. Got it?"

"You're so rude," she whispered.

"That's right, I am," he said. "I'm not a good guy, and I never will be. This isn't a goddamn Hallmark movie where the bad boy with a secret heart of gold is tamed by the town's good girl. This is real life. I'm an asshole who only wants one thing from you."

His gaze drifted to her crotch, and she flushed with a combination of embarrassment and, shamefully, excitement.

"I won't be your boyfriend," he said. "I won't bring you soup when you're sick or go to family dinner. I won't run to the drugstore to buy you fucking tampons, and I won't watch those stupid chick flicks with you."

He leaned in even closer, his eyes burning with anger and lust. "The only thing I want to do to you is spread those soft little thighs and fuck you. Do you understand?"

"Yes," she whispered.

"Good." He straightened and stepped away before turning his back to her. "Then we're done. Have a good life, Sunshine."

She took a deep breath and said, "What if I want that too?"

IT TOOK EVERY OUNCE OF PREACHER'S WILLPOWER NOT TO pick up Addison and carry her to his apartment upstairs. He had purposely been crude and tried to scare her off with his little speech.

He wasn't lying to her. He didn't want to be her man. He wanted to fuck her, pure and simple.

Sure, the little schoolteacher might set off some protective vibes in him, but it didn't mean anything. She was small and sweet and a little naïve. She needed someone to look out for her. That's all it was.

Besides, the look of regret and shame on her face every time they finished fucking, made him feel fucking terrible, and feeling fucking terrible was not an emotion he was used to.

Of course, it didn't stop his cock from nearly busting out of his jeans when she said, "What if I want that too?"

He couldn't turn around and look at her again. Not when she was sitting there half-naked with her nipples hard and begging to be sucked. Not when he was sure her little pussy would be soaking wet for him. The way she had moaned when he twisted the barbell...

Fuck! Stop thinking about it, you asshole!

Smart fucking idea.

"You don't want that," he said.

"Yes, I do," she huffed at him.

Thank fucking Christ, he could hear her getting dressed. He turned and stared down at her when she tapped him on the back.

"That's exactly what I want," she said. "I've had a fiancé, remember? I'm not looking for that. I don't need you to take care of me when I'm sick or buy me stupid flowers or tampons! I want someone who will teach me how to not be boring in bed."

His mouth dropped open, and she blushed furiously. "Look, I know I'm not great in the sack, okay? Harrison cheated on me because I couldn't," she paused and then forced the words out, "satisfy him in bed. I don't want another boyfriend until I'm good at sex. Teach me how to be good in bed, and then I promise I won't bother you again."

He stared blankly at her, and she licked her lips. "I'm a fast learner. All I would need is a few lessons. I'm not asking for anything super kinky. I just want a few pointers on giving a blow job and how to be sexy in the bedroom and more, uh, responsive when I'm having sex. We could get together even just once a week for a month, and you can show me some stuff. I'll be discreet, I promise. I won't ask you to stay the night or anything, or text or contact you outside of our weekly meetup. I know I'm not your usual type, but heck, it's, uh, free pussy for a month, right?"

"Are you fucking kidding me?" he rasped.

She flushed bright red but shook her head. "No, I'm not. I want to get better in bed. You seem pretty, um, knowledgeable, and you like having sex. Say yes, Preacher. I promise I won't tell anyone – not even Gracie and Kira."

He continued to stare at her, and she blurted out, "I won't talk during sex."

"What?"

"I know I babbled and said some stupid stuff when we were having sex," she said. "It was dumb and distracting, and I won't do it again. I'll keep my mouth shut the whole time. Unless, you know, you want it open for something else."

She dropped her gaze to his dick, and he almost groaned out loud. God, she was trying to kill him. He was unbelievably tempted to give her what she asked. Although, as far as he was concerned, she didn't need to be taught how to be sexy. Nor did she need to be coached on being more responsive in bed. That bastard of a fiancé had done a real number on his little sunshine.

Not your problem, Preacher. The girl is nothing but trouble, and you know it. The two of you are oil and water.

His inner voice was right. As much as he wanted to fuck Addison, as much as he wanted her on her knees in front of him with her mouth wrapped around his dick, he couldn't. She talked a good game about not wanting more, but after a few weeks of fucking, she'd want more.

He reined in his libido and shook his head. "No."

"Why not?"

"Because you'll want more."

"You don't know that."

"Women like you always want more."

He waited for her to pout and whine and do her little speech again. Instead, her shoulders slumped, and she stared at the floor for a moment before straightening her spine and staring up at him. "Okay. Thanks for hearing me out. Good-bye, Preacher."

She slipped by him and walked out of the room without looking back.

CHAPTER 13

"Hey, man. Why aren't you at work?" Gideon stared at him in surprise.

Preacher petted Tank when the big dog squeezed past Gideon in the doorway and leaned against him. His tail whacked him in the thigh, and Preacher winced before rubbing the Great Dane's ears. "Took the afternoon off."

"Seriously? You have a Saturday afternoon off in the middle of tourist season?" Gideon said.

Preacher just shrugged, and after a second, Gideon said. "C'mon in. Gracie and I were having beers in the backyard."

"She's not at work?"

"She has the weekend off," Gideon said.

Preacher took a step back and said in a low voice. "Shit. Are you proposing to her today? Did I ruin the fucking moment?"

Gideon glanced behind him before shaking his head. "No, tomorrow. I was going to do it today, but the tap in the upstairs bathroom started leaking, and I had to fix that first, and then I have this whole cardboard note thing with Tank I want to do when I ask Gracie, and… anyway, tomorrow. I'm doing it tomorrow morning. Come in."

He followed Gideon and Tank down the hall toward the door that led to the backyard. Grace stepped inside, and she smiled at him. "Hey, Preacher."

"Hi, Grace."

"Preacher has the afternoon off," Gideon said.

"Cool. Head into the yard with Gideon. I'll bring us all fresh beers." Grace said.

She grinned at Gideon when he patted her ass as she walked by. Preacher followed Gideon into the yard and settled into a lawn chair, grunting when Tank immediately sat in this lap.

"Tank, go on," Gideon said.

"It's fine." He petted the heavy dog and tried to shift in his chair. "As long as he stops trying to crush my fucking balls."

Gideon laughed and pointed to a patch of sunlight. "Go lay in the sun, Tank."

The big dog woofed before standing up and ambling to the sun. He stretched out on his side and closed his eyes. The snoring started almost immediately, and Preacher envied the dog's ability to sleep. He hadn't slept a fucking wink last night. Instead, he'd tossed and turned, Addison's request for lessons on fucking rattling around in his brain until he thought he'd go insane.

His shop didn't open until eleven, and he'd finally gotten up at six and gone for a workout at the gym. It hadn't helped clear his mind the way working out usually did. He couldn't concentrate on tattooing worth shit, and he'd finally done something he rarely did. He'd cancelled on his client for the afternoon, told Nolan to close the shop when Nix had finished his last tattoo, and then left.

Knowing Gideon had the weekend off, he'd come here to talk to him about Addison's request, but, he grimaced and glanced at the wide open kitchen window, he couldn't talk to Gideon about it with Grace here.

He could hear the soft ring of a phone, and then Grace's voice drifted out of the open kitchen window. "Hey, Kira. Yup, I know. Yes, I've already made the potato salad. Wait… what? She went where? To Willington? Seriously?"

He tuned Grace out as Gideon said, "I'll get your beer."

"I can wait," Preacher said. He'd had no appetite today, and the idea of mixing beer with his churning stomach acid made him want to barf.

They sat silently for a few minutes, Gideon sipping at his beer, Preacher picking at some threads on the lawn chair.

"You gonna tell me what's wrong or just sit there?" Gideon said.

"Nothing's wrong."

"Bullshit," Gideon said. "You don't just take the afternoon off. What's going on?"

Preacher glanced at the open window and lowered his voice. "Addison asked me to -"

"Gideon?" Grace stuck her head out the window. "Can you come in here and help me carry some stuff out? I've got the beers, but I want to do some munchies for us, too, and I need you to grab the chips from the top shelf."

"Sure." Gideon stood. "Be right back." He squeezed Preacher's shoulder before disappearing into the house.

Preacher stared moodily at Tank. Fuck, what was he thinking? He couldn't talk to Gideon about this. Addison would be embarrassed if people knew she'd asked him for sex lessons, and just the idea of causing her embarrassment made that churning stomach acid rise and burn his throat.

"You're kidding me." Gideon's voice drifted out of the kitchen window.

"I'm not," Grace said. "She took the bus to Willington. Kira just told me when she called. Said she offered to drive her because she still doesn't have a car, but Addison said she was fine to go alone."

Preacher sat up straight when he heard Addison's name.

"Why didn't she just book an appointment with Preacher?" Gideon said.

"I don't know," Grace said after a slight hesitation. "Maybe he was all booked up."

"Yeah, but to go to Willington just for a piercing? What's she getting pierced anyway?"

Preacher jumped out of the lawn chair and headed for the door. He stalked down the hallway and stood in the kitchen doorway.

"She didn't say. I'm assuming her belly button." Grace poured chips into a bowl.

"That doesn't seem like Addison," Gideon said. "Is it just me, or has she been acting weird the last little while?"

"It's been tough for her since she and Harrison broke up," Grace said. "She had her life all planned out, and now -"

"What piercing shop did she go to?"

Grace and Gideon turned at the sound of his voice.

"What's wrong?" Gideon said.

"What shop did she go to?" Preacher stared hard at Grace, who gave him a thoughtful look.

"I don't know the shop's name, but Addison told Kira it was on Peach Street."

"I have to go." He turned and strode out of the kitchen, slamming the front door behind him.

THE USUAL FORTY-MINUTE DRIVE TO WILLINGTON TOOK HIM twenty minutes. His bike roared down Peach Street, and he parked in front of Paul's Piercing Palace. He yanked off his helmet, threw it on his bike seat, and stalked toward the door. If anyone in that goddamn place had their hands anywhere near Addison's pussy, he'd cut them off and shove them up their own goddamn ass.

He whipped open the door. There was no sign of Addison, and he stomped up to reception. "Where is she?"

"I'm sorry?" The woman, who was short with bright blue hair and multiple piercings on her face, stared nervously at him.

"Addison Moore. Where is she?"

The woman just shook her head, but her gaze darted to a door to their left. He glared at her and marched toward the door.

"Mister, you can't go in there!"

He ignored the receptionist and pulled open the door. Addison was sitting on the piercing bed talking to a bearded man. She was fully clothed, thank God, and she gave him a startled look when he walked into the room.

"Preacher? What are you doing here?"

"Taking you home."

He lifted her off the bed and set her on her feet, holding her arm in a tight grip as she glared up at him. "Let me go."

"No. We're leaving, Addison."

"I'm a grown woman. You can't tell me what to do!"

"Like fucking hell, I can't," he growled.

In desperation, she stared at the piercer who stood up. Preacher stared him down and said, "She's my woman, and you're not piercing her. Is that a problem?"

"I am not your woman!" Addison said.

"Hey, man," the piercer held up his hands, "it's not a

problem for me. I got me an independent woman myself. I get it."

"I am not his woman," Addison repeated. "I'm getting pierced, and you can't stop me, Preacher!"

"If she comes back here and I find out you pierced any part of her, do I have to tell you what I'll do to you?" Preacher said.

The piercer shook his head. "Nope. Consider her banned from the shop, brother."

Preacher gave him a curt nod of thanks.

"You jerk!" Addison shouted. She whacked Preacher on the chest and then muttered a curse and rubbed her hand.

"Watch your piercing," he said.

"What? What do you -"

She gasped and pressed her hand over her right breast to protect her nipple when he bent and tossed her over his shoulder. She pounded him on the back as he walked back into reception. He grunted when Addie bit him on the back and gave her a slap to the ass.

She squealed in outrage, and he smiled politely at the receptionist as he walked to the door. "Later, sweetheart."

The moment they stepped outside into the hot sunshine and Addison saw the people staring at them, she stopped struggling. She cleared her throat and said, "Please put me down, Preacher."

He set her on her feet next to his bike, and she straightened her dress. "Why are you here?"

"Stopping you from getting your goddamn clit pierced," he snapped.

"Keep your voice down," she muttered before smiling at the older woman walking past them.

He glared at her and stepped closer before saying in a low

voice, "You are not getting your clit pierced, Addison. I won't allow it."

"You don't get a say in it."

He wanted to spank her ass in frustration, but instead, he made himself take a deep breath. "Please, Sunshine. Don't get your clit pierced."

"Why not?"

"Because it's perfect just the way it is."

She blinked at him before sighing and looking away. "I wasn't here to get my clit pierced anyway."

Relief rushed through Preacher. Not just because she wasn't piercing her clit but because fucking goddamn Paul from Paul's Piercing Palace wouldn't see her clit. He didn't want anyone to see her perfect pussy but him.

"What were you piercing?" he said.

"My other nipple."

Stupidly, another wave of jealousy went through him. Thinking that some other guy might see her tits was just as bad.

He tried not to scowl at her and failed. "I'll pierce it for you. Let's go."

"No, I don't -"

"Let's go, Addison," he said. He pulled her gently to his bike and put the helmet on her before buckling it. He put his helmet on, sat on the bike, and patted the seat behind him. "Get on."

"Preacher, I don't want you to -"

He switched off the comm and then pointed to the helmet before shrugging and making a 'I can't hear you' gesture.

She glared at him, and he again pointed at the seat behind him. She flipped him the bird, and he had to hide his grin from her as she straddled the seat behind him. She put her feet on the pegs and her arms around his waist. He grunted when she smacked him on the abdomen before clasping her hands together. He checked for traffic, pulled out on the street, and headed home.

HE DROVE STRAIGHT TO HIS SHOP. IT WAS ONLY FOUR, BUT the blind in the front window was down, and the closed sign was on the door. Nolan had closed the shop like he'd asked.

Addison followed him inside and flounced to the couch, collapsing dramatically on it as he closed the door and locked it. She scrolled through her phone, and he said, "What are you looking at?"

"I'm looking for another piercing place," she said.

"You're not allowed to let anyone else pierce your nipple but me," he snarled.

"I don't want you piercing my nipple or my clit," she said.

He ignored the trickle of hurt that went through him. "You said you weren't getting your clit pierced."

"No, I said I wasn't getting my clit pierced today."

"You're not getting your clit pierced, Addison, and that's final."

She laughed. "Do you seriously think I'm just going to do what you tell me?"

He stared at her in frustration before being hit with sudden inspiration. "If you pierce your clit, you can't have sex for at least six weeks."

She blinked at him. "What? That isn't true."

"Yes, it is," he said. "It has to heal completely, and sometimes that can take months."

"Bullcrap," she said. "You're just saying that."

He shrugged. "Look it up. You'll see I'm telling you the

truth. No sex for possibly months, Sunshine. Is that what you want?"

"Shoot. No. I guess I won't be getting my clit pierced any time soon."

He was instantly jealous. It had barely been twenty-four hours since she'd asked him for lessons. Had she found someone else already? Was his little schoolteacher fucking some moron who didn't know how to make her come? How to eat her little pussy until she was screaming with pleasure?

He folded his arms across his broad chest and glared at her. "Who are you fucking?"

"Excuse me?"

He stalked over to her and leaned down as she pressed back into the couch cushions. He placed his hands on either side of her head and said, "Who did you find to teach you how to suck dick? To teach you how to fuck properly?"

She flushed bright red and returned his scowl. "That's none of your darn business, Preacher."

Her scent and the heat of her body were driving him insane. He had to touch her. He traced her exposed collarbone with the tip of his finger, immediately satisfied when desire flared in her eyes.

"Tell me his name, Sunshine." As soon as she did, he'd track the guy down and warn him to stay away from Addison unless he wanted a goddamn broken kneecap.

"Obviously, there isn't anyone yet. It's been barely a day since I asked you. But I have a few different men I'm considering."

"No," he said.

"Yes."

"You're not fucking them."

"Why do you care?" she said. "I offered you the opportunity first, and you turned me down flat. So, why do you even care who I have sex with?"

"I've changed my mind."

"I… what? Why?"

"Does it matter? I've thought it over and changed my mind about giving you lessons on fucking."

"Maybe I've changed my mind too. Maybe I don't want your help anymore," she said.

He leaned closer and licked her bottom lip. She moaned, her mouth parting immediately, and he grinned before nipping at her lip. "Liar."

She licked the spot he nipped and glared at him. "You're not playing fair."

"I never do." He straightened and pulled her to her feet before taking her phone and dropping it into her purse. "Let's go, Sunshine."

"Go where?" she said as he led her toward the back of the shop.

"It's time for lesson one."

"I don't want to keep having sex at your shop," she said. "It seems like it might be unsanitary for your business."

That made him laugh, and she smiled timidly at him. He led her down the hallway and unlocked the door at the end of it before leading her up the narrow staircase. He opened the door, and she stared in surprise at his small apartment.

"You live above the shop?"

"Yeah." He kicked off his boots as she removed her heels and placed them neatly on the mat.

His place was a bachelor pad with a tiny living room and an even tinier kitchen. There was a TV, a coffee table, a small bookshelf stuffed with books and a loveseat in the living space. His double bed was against the far wall with a nightstand on one side and a dresser on the other, and that was it for furniture.

He kept his place clean and tidy but was suddenly a little embarrassed by its size. Not to mention the seventies décor. The orange shag carpeting that covered the floor was gaudy and ugly, the beige linoleum in the tiny kitchen was chipped and faded, and the avocado green fridge was hideous. But it was furnished and decorated when he bought the shop, and he'd never gotten around to updating it. Didn't seem necessary. No one but Gideon ever saw this place anyway.

This was his sanctuary from the outside world, and he never brought the women he fucked here. He either fucked them at whatever grungy place they lived at or took them to a motel. He should be doing the same with Addison, but he was too goddamn horny to wait. He could make an exception just this once.

"I like your place," Addison said.

"Yeah, right," he said.

"No, I do," she said. "It's small, but I like its seventies feel."

She smiled at him before walking to the large window that overlooked main street. He followed her and yanked down the blinds. She glanced at him, and he shrugged.

"No one needs to know you're up here."

"Right," she said. "I'm sorry. I promised to be discreet, and I'm already breaking that promise."

She walked a couple of steps to the kitchen. "Could I get a drink?"

He opened the fridge. It had beer, a few takeout boxes from a Chinese food restaurant, and a bottle of hot sauce.

"I've got beer or water," he said.

"Water is fine."

"It's just from the tap," he said as he grabbed one of his two glasses from the cupboard.

"That's fine with me." She studied the kitchen before saying, "You don't have a stove or a microwave."

He filled the glass with water and handed it to her. She took a few sips. "How do you cook your meals?"

"I eat out," he said.

"Oh. I'm a good cook if you ever want a home-cooked meal. My mom taught me, and -"

"I don't need or want you to be my girlfriend," he said. "This is just fucking, remember?"

"I remember," she said before drinking the water in three large gulps. "I was just trying to be nice."

"Don't bother."

"Fine by me," she said, but he could hear the hurt in her voice.

"C'mon." He walked to the bed and stripped off his shirt before yanking off his socks. He turned to see her standing behind him, fully dressed, and he raised his eyebrow at her. "Are you going to get naked?"

She flushed. "I thought you would, I mean…"

He unbuttoned his jeans. "You have two hands. You don't need me to undress you."

"Right," she said.

He turned away from her and dropped his jeans and his briefs. He picked them both up and tossed his underwear in the hamper before folding his jeans and placing them on the dresser. When he turned around, she was still in her dress and struggling to pull the zipper down.

He rolled his eyes, and she said, "The zipper is stuck."

"Turn around."

She turned around, and he pushed her hair over her shoulder, resisting the urge to bury his face in the soft strands. The zipper was caught in the lining of her dress, and he tried to pull the lining free. It refused to budge, and he yanked on the zipper with a grunt of effort. It broke off in his hand, and he cursed. "I broke the zipper."

"Oh, uh, that's okay." She sounded like she was on the verge of tears.

Of course she is! You're being a complete asshole. For fuck's sake, she's a lady – treat her like one!

Guilt coursed through him. He didn't want Addison to think he was her goddamn boyfriend, but that didn't mean he should treat her like she was nothing. He took a deep breath and pulled on the edges of her dress. The broken zipper pulled apart easily, and he eased her dress down her arms to her waist. She didn't protest, but she immediately crossed her arms over her breasts. Her entire body trembled, and he didn't think it was because she wanted him.

He leaned forward to brush a light kiss against her upper back. "You okay, Sunshine?"

CHAPTER 14

She was making a mistake. She wanted Preacher a lot, but she couldn't do this. He didn't want to be her boyfriend, and she was fine with that, but how he treated her now was humiliating. She blinked back the tears as Preacher pulled on the stuck zipper. Maybe he hadn't been romantic the first two times they'd had sex, but he'd been sweet, at least. There was no sweetness in him at all now.

You said this was what you wanted. He laid out the rules, and you agreed to them. Don't go changing your mind now just because he isn't sweet. Harrison was sweet, and look what he was doing behind your back. You have a month to learn everything you can from Preacher. Pay attention, figure out how to be good in bed, and then you can forget all about him and move on with your life with a nice man who you can wow in bed so he won't cheat on you.

Preacher spit out an expletive. "I broke the zipper."

"Oh, uh, that's okay." She could hear the tears in her voice, and she tried to swallow past the boulder sized lump in her throat.

Get it together, you idiot!

Preacher pulled on her dress, and she allowed him to ease it down her arms until it bunched at her waist. She folded her arms across her small breasts. She was wearing a bra, but she was suddenly self-conscious.

God, what was she doing? She had to put a stop to this. She opened her mouth to tell him she had changed her mind when Preacher brushed his mouth across her bare back and said, "You okay, Sunshine?"

Hearing his nickname for her made her release her breath in a shaky sigh. Before she could reply, he put his arm around her waist and brought her back against his chest. He pressed a soft kiss against her neck.

"Okay?"

"Yes," she said.

"Your tattoo looks good."

"It's crusted over."

"That's normal. Just keep moisturizing it." He hesitated and then said, "I was being an asshole."

"Yeah, you were," she said.

He pressed another kiss against her bare skin. "I'll make it up to you when you sit on my face."

"Wh-what?" She squeaked out as his big hands tugged her dress down her hips. It pooled on the floor at her feet, and while she had to wear her plain cotton bra because of the nipple piercing, she wished she had worn prettier underwear. She had her usual cotton ones on, and she had a feeling that Preacher would find them unappealing.

You sure about that? He stole your last cotton panties.

He was unhooking her bra, and still not certain she'd heard him correctly, she said, "What did you say?"

"Lesson number one, Sunshine, is you sitting on my face." He pulled her bra off and dropped it to the floor before peering over her shoulder. He cupped her left breast and pulled on the nipple. Her back arched, and she moaned.

"I don't see how that will teach me how to be good at sex," she said.

He didn't reply. Instead, he turned her to face him and bent to study her right nipple. "It's still looking good."

"Thank you." She hoped that he would twist the barbell again, it was ridiculous how good that felt, but instead, he licked the tip of her left nipple.

"OH!" Her hips jerked, and his erection pressed against her stomach for a moment before she pulled back.

His hand tightened around her waist, and he held her steady before he tugged on her nipple with his teeth.

"Oh my gosh!" Her hips bucked again as white-hot pleasure went straight from her nipple to her pussy. "Will you do that to my other nipple? Please?"

"No," he said. "No touching or licking it for a few more weeks."

He glanced up at her and grinned. "No pouting, Sunshine."

"It doesn't hurt anymore."

"Don't care. It's not healed yet, and I'm not touching or sucking on it. But I guess that means your left nipple gets all the attention." His hot mouth closed around said nipple and sucked hard.

"Oh, oh my gosh, oh please, Simon!" She was already starting to babble, and she clamped her mouth shut and gripped his hair as he sucked and licked at her nipple.

"You like that, baby?"

She nodded and arched her back when he lightly bit her nipple. He straightened and kissed her hard on the mouth. She opened to his tongue, and he gave her a slow, deep kiss that made her toes curl. His hand squeezed her ass, and when his chest brushed against her right nipple, she moaned. "It's so sensitive. Please, will you touch it?"

"When this one heals, we are definitely piercing your other nipple, Sunshine," he growled.

He sucked on her bottom lip before pulling on her thigh. "Spread your legs."

She spread them, clinging to his upper arms as he pushed his hand into her panties and cupped her. "Nice and wet. That's my good girl."

She buried her face in his chest and used his hard flesh to muffle her moans – God, why had she told him she'd keep her mouth shut – as he rubbed at her clit with light strokes of his fingertips.

"You ready to sit on my face, Sunshine?"

She nodded, even though a part of her cringed at letting him see her that up close and personal.

He slid his hand out of her panties and grinned at her. "Let's get you out of your good girl panties."

She flushed at his teasing but let him pull her panties down her legs. She kicked them off her feet and followed him to the bed. He laid on his back in the middle and crooked his finger at her. "Come here."

She hesitated before kneeling on the bed beside him. He tugged on her thigh. "Climb on. I want your pussy in my mouth."

"Are you – are you sure?"

"Yes. Get over here now." His voice was impatient.

She took a deep breath and straddled his head a bit awkwardly. He peered up at her from between her thighs and grinned wickedly as he wrapped his big hands around her slender thighs. "Hang on tight, baby."

"Hang on to what?" she said as he tugged her to his mouth.

He didn't tease or tantalize. He sucked her clit into his mouth and sucked hard. She screamed at the sudden burst of pleasure in her belly and clutched frantically at the wall in front of her. His mouth was hot and wet, and the rough scrape of his stubble against the wet lips of her pussy only inflamed her more. She rocked frantically against his mouth as she begged and pleaded and cried his name repeatedly.

He changed the pressure of his tongue against her clit, licking her lightly instead of the heavy, firm strokes she needed. She wailed her displeasure and pulled on his hair. He growled against her pussy and cupped her bare ass, digging his fingers into her soft flesh as he pulled her even closer before lightly licking her clit again.

"More!" she shouted. "Please, I need more!" She pulled on his hair again, and he gave her what she wanted when he sucked firmly on her clit. He tugged on it with his teeth, and she screamed again before arching her body and coming all over his face. Shameless in her need, she ground her pussy against his mouth as she rode out her release.

He patted her on the thigh and lifted her a little. "Move down, baby."

Her body trembling madly, she scooted down his body until she was straddling his abdomen. He wiped his face with the sheet before sitting up. She nearly fell off of him, and he grabbed her around the waist, making a low groan when her pussy rubbed against his dick.

"Steady, Sunshine."

"That - that was so good," she whispered.

"Of course it was," he said with an arrogant grin. He patted her naked ass before leaning over and grabbing a condom from the nightstand drawer.

"Put this on me, Sunshine."

PREACHER WATCHED AS ADDISON REACHED FOR THE CONDOM. Her fingers shook like crazy, and he pulled the package out of her reach. "On second thought, I'll do it this time. You're shaking too badly."

"Sorry," she said.

He pushed on her hips. "Straddle my thighs."

She did what he asked and watched as he rolled the condom onto his dick. When it was in place, he rubbed her smooth thighs. "You been on top before?"

She nodded, and he said, "You like it?"

"It was fine." She was staring at his dick, and he hated that the look of bliss on her face was being replaced with apprehension.

"It won't hurt, baby," he said.

"I know," she said, but there was doubt in her voice.

"We'll go slow," he said. "I won't move, and you can take my cock as slow as you want, okay?"

"Okay," she said. He relaxed on his back as she moved up until she was straddling his hips. He helped her position his cock at her entrance. Biting her bottom lip, she pushed experimentally. It took every ounce of his willpower not to thrust upward when the head of his cock slid into her warmth.

She gasped, and he squeezed her narrow hips. "Okay?"

She nodded and pushed again. He slipped into her wet tightness easily, and she moaned as she sheathed him entirely in one final push. She stared at his cock seated snugly inside of her, before glancing up at him.

"Didn't hurt," she said.

"Good." He tried not to think about how goddamn tight her pussy was. For how small she was compared to him, her pussy took his dick like a fucking champ. He wanted to thrust hard and fast into her and find the release his body had been craving the last two days.

"Like not at all," she said.

"Good," he spit out. "I'm fucking glad it didn't hurt. Think you could start moving before I lose my fucking mind?"

She flushed, and her knees squeezed his hips. "Um, yes. I'm sorry."

"Don't apologize. Just move," he groaned.

She braced her hands on his abdomen and moved her slender body up and down. His hands tightened on her hips, and she watched him closely as she moved a little faster. "Does this feel okay?"

He nodded and cupped her ass. "Faster."

She twitched all over when he moved his right hand to her pussy and rubbed at her clit. She stopped moving and tried to tug his hand away.

"I already had one," she said.

"You're going to have two for me," he said through gritted teeth.

"But I want to concentrate on you," she said. "I want to make sure I'm doing this right."

"Fucking hell, you are," he groaned. "Just keep doing what you're doing."

She hesitated for a moment longer and then started fucking him again. He watched his cock slide in and out of her before rubbing her swollen clit. Her breath quickened, and two little spots of red appeared high on her cheeks.

She made little moans of pleasure, and he grinned when she said, "You're so big, Preacher. You're so thick and big, and it feels really good. I love how big you -"

She threw one hand over her mouth and stared anxiously at him before mumbling, "I'm sorry, I was babbling."

He didn't reply. Secretly, he was starting to love the way she didn't shut up when he was fucking her. He loved that she said whatever the hell she felt when he got her all amped up.

"I'm sorry," she repeated.

"Fuck me harder," he said.

She obeyed, thrusting her slender body up and down as he reached for her clit again. He tugged on it and watched as she cried out and then clamped her mouth shut again. She was trying desperately not to say anything, and, with a small grin on his face, he reached up with his other hand and pulled on her left nipple.

She cried out, her hips rocking faster and harder against him as she lost all of her inhibition. "Oh my gosh! Oh my goodness! Simon, please!"

"Please, what, Addie?" Jesus, he really shouldn't like the sound of his name on her lips as much as he did. He sat up and wrapped his arm around her waist. She bounced on his cock like a woman possessed as he bent his head and sucked on her left nipple. She screamed again as his other hand rubbed her clit hard and fast.

"Oh my gosh! Oh, Simon! I'm going to come again, I'm going to…"

Her voice trailed off as her entire body stiffened, and then she climaxed again, her pussy squeezing him so tightly that it pulled a groan from his throat. He released her nipple and used both hands to hold her hips as he pumped in and out of her. She clutched at his shoulders, her nails digging into his flesh as she moaned repeatedly and her body shook.

He made one last hard thrust, roaring hoarsely as his climax washed over him. He gripped her tight against him, keeping her sheathed completely around his cock as he came. When the last of his climax had finished pulsing through him, he fell onto his back, dragging her with him. He stroked her damp back as she rested her head on his chest and panted harshly.

He was softening inside of her, and after a few minutes, he lifted her off of him. She sprawled on the bed beside him, and he disposed of the condom and relaxed on his back. She immediately snuggled up to him, wrapping her arm around his waist and resting her head on his shoulder. He stroked her back as she yawned.

His night of insomnia had caught up to him, and that, combined with his orgasm, made him sleepy, too. He closed his eyes, listening to how Addison's breathing slowed and deepened, and he made a low noise of contentment.

What the fuck are you doing? You can't let her stay with you.

His eyes popped open, and he stared at the ceiling as his drowsiness disappeared instantly. Fuck, what *was* he doing? He had specifically told her he wouldn't be her boyfriend. Besides, he didn't fucking cuddle with a woman. Ever.

Letting Addison sleep in his bed or snuggle up to him was a terrible goddamn idea. Especially if he wanted to keep things simple and uncomplicated.

He shook her arm. "Hey, don't fall asleep."

"Hmm?" Her sleepy smile was stupidly adorable, and she tried to snuggle closer.

"Addison, wake up," he said.

The tone of his voice made her sit up. "What? What's wrong?"

"You can't stay," he said.

"What?" She stared at him in confusion before understanding dawned. "Oh, right. I'm sorry."

She slid out of bed and grabbed her clothes. "Do you mind if I use the bathroom?"

He shook his head, and she disappeared into the bathroom. While she was gone, he threw on his jeans and grabbed a beer from the fridge. He wanted to tell her he would give her a ride home, but that was just stupid. Still, the thought of making her walk or take the bus made him feel like an asshole.

She came out of the bathroom. She was dressed, and her auburn hair was pulled into a ponytail. Her face was still a little flushed, but other than that, you couldn't tell at all that she'd just been fucked.

That thought bothered him, and he grimaced inwardly. What the hell? They didn't want the town to know they were fucking – that was the last thing they wanted.

"I'm sorry, but do you have a shirt I can borrow? The zipper is still, uh…."

He set his beer on the counter before crossing to the dresser. "Right. I'll pay for a new dress."

"Oh no," she said, "you don't have to do that. I think the zipper can probably be fixed on it. I just need something to throw on over the top of it because I can't, you know, zip it up."

He rummaged through the dresser and found a long-sleeved dress shirt he'd forgotten he had. He handed it to Addison, and she slipped it on. He watched as she rolled the sleeves to her elbows. She bunched the bottom of the shirt around her waist and tied it before smiling hesitantly at him.

"How's it look?"

"Fine," he said.

Truthfully, she looked damn hot in his shirt, and he had the sudden urge to strip her down and take her right back to his bed. Instead, he grabbed his beer and took another long swallow as she walked to the door, grabbed her purse, and put her heels on.

"Okay, well, uh, bye, Preacher," she said.

"I'll walk you downstairs," he said.

He followed her down the staircase. She paused at the bottom of it. "I still owe you for the piercing."

"Don't worry about it," he said.

"Oh, I can't do that. I know you charged me less than you normally do for a tattoo and -"

"I said don't worry about it."

He could hear the annoyance in his voice, and obviously, she could too because she winced and hurried out into the hallway. She peered down the connecting hallway at the service door. "Is that the back entrance into the alley?"

He nodded, and she said, "I'll slip out that door."

"You don't have to do that," he said. Jesus, now he really felt like a dick.

"I don't mind," she said. "It'll be busy out front, and there's no point in a bunch of people seeing me leave your shop wearing your shirt."

She walked down the hallway. "Bye, Preacher."

"Addison, wait."

She paused with her hands on the door's exit bar.

"I'll give you a ride home."

"That's okay," she said. "I bought a bus pass."

"You don't need to take the bus," he snapped.

"I don't mind. Besides, it's not keeping a low profile if I'm riding around on the back of your bike." She glanced over her shoulder at him. "Was I, um, okay in bed?"

He stared at her in surprise. How the hell could she think she wasn't? He'd come like a fucking fire hydrant, hadn't he? "You were fine."

She winced again, and he cursed inwardly. What the fuck was wrong with him?

"Sounds like I need more lessons," she said, her eyes bright with unshed tears.

"I didn't mean -"

"I really should get going," she said. "Let me know if you're interested in, uh, doing another lesson next week. But I'll understand if you're not."

"Addison -"

"Bye, Preacher." She gave him a little wave, pushed open the door, and disappeared into the alley.

CHAPTER 15

"Thanks for picking me up, loser." Addison buckled her seat belt as Daniel pulled away from her apartment building.

"No problem." He laughed when she reached over and tied a friendship bracelet around his wrist. "Another one? I already have three on my wrist. You're not just sitting at home making friendship bracelets and pining for that asshole Harrison, are you?"

"No. Honestly, I'm over making the bracelets now, and I'm back to knitting. But I have a pile of friendship bracelets to hand out."

She sat back in her seat, staring out the window as her brother drove toward Kira's place.

"You doing okay, butthead?" Daniel said. "I know I haven't been around much, but I've been busy at work and…"

She reached over and patted his arm. "And since Kira stopped inviting you to the barbeques, we don't hang out as much. I'm sorry. I should be making more effort to do stuff with you, too."

"It's cool," Daniel said. "It's my fault I got kicked out of the Scooby gang."

"You weren't kicked out," she said. "Kira just needed some time to…"

"To get over thinking I'm the biggest asshole in the world for taking advantage of her crush on me for years?"

"Yeah," Addison said.

She studied her brother. His blond hair was too long, dark circles were under his eyes, and he hadn't shaved. "Are *you* okay? You look rough."

He laughed. "I'm fine. Just got off a three-day shift, and baseball kicked my ass last night."

"Are you feeling nervous?"

He shrugged. "Maybe a little."

"Don't be. Kira invited you because she's a good person and wants to try being friends. But you know she's with Connor and loves him so…"

"I know," he said. "I'm happy for her. She deserves someone great who treats her well. Didn't think it would be a dentist, but, hey, whoever floats her boat."

"Will you behave yourself?" she said. "Don't say anything to Connor to piss him off. He's open to you coming to the barbeque, but you need to behave yourself, okay?"

"I always do." It was said with his usual teasing grin, but she could see something lurking underneath that grin. Something dark and dank and worrisome.

"Daniel, honey, is something going on?" she said.

"No, I'm fine. And don't worry. I'll behave at the barbeque. Besides, you're worrying for nothing. I already had a beer with Connor and apologized."

"Seriously? When?"

"Last week after ball one night. Look, I'll never be

friends with the guy or anything, but we're not mortal enemies. It'll be fine."

"Okay," she said.

He glanced over at her. "Why are you so dressed up? You out trolling for a man now that you and Harrison are kaput?"

She wrinkled her nose at him. "No, and I'm not dressed up."

"You look like you've made more of an effort than usual. Your face isn't quite as hideous as normal."

"Shut up, gator breath."

"Hey, I can't help it if I got all the looks in the family," Daniel said.

Addison rolled her eyes and stared out the window as Daniel hit a button on the steering wheel and rock music blasted out of the speakers.

She had made more of an effort than usual for the barbeque, and she knew exactly why she had.

Preacher.

Which was stupid because, after yesterday afternoon, it was more than apparent that he was not going to be offering any more sex lessons. God, why had she let him do so much stuff to her? She was supposed to be learning how to be sexy and how to make sure the guy was having a great time.

Instead, she'd sat on Preacher's face, had a stupidly intense orgasm, and then had another damn orgasm not fifteen minutes later while she rode him like a horse. She honestly couldn't remember if Preacher had even climaxed.

Maybe he hadn't. Maybe that's why he'd seemed so meh afterward about her performance. She sighed and tugged at the friendship bracelets around her wrist as Daniel pulled onto Kira's street. If Preacher gave her another chance, she would make darn sure she made it all about him and didn't get distracted by his mouth and hands and his ability to make her come until her brain nearly exploded.

PREACHER HATED THAT FUCKING GAMER DUDE. HATED HIM. How the fuck Connor, who seemed like a decent guy, could be best friends with the prick, he'd never know.

His hand clenched around the beer bottle, and for the first time in his life, he wished he did play baseball. Then maybe he could launch the bottle across the yard and knock some sense into the fucking douchebag of a gamer.

"You're going to shatter that beer bottle." Gideon settled into the lawn chair beside his and stretched his long legs out. Tank had followed him over, and he crowded up against Preacher, sniffing at his face and pressing his big head against Preacher's chest until Preacher gave in and scratched the top of Tank's head. "What's got you so pissed?"

"I'm not pissed. Congratulations on the engagement." He held up the beer bottle, and they clinked them together.

"Thanks." Gideon stared across the yard at Grace, who was talking to Kira and some other chick Preacher didn't know. The rock on her hand gleamed in the sun, and Gideon laughed when Kira grabbed Grace's hand and admired the ring again.

"Who's the chick with Grace and Kira?" Preacher said.

"Rayna. She runs the animal rescue and works for Sneaky Leaks Plumbing. She and Grace became friends while we were volunteering for the cancer fundraiser that Wanda organized."

Wanda was a dispatcher at the sheriff's department, and while Preacher barely knew her, he knew she meant a great deal to Gideon. "How's she doing?"

"Okay. She's back to work now. It's been rough on her since Murray died, but the fundraiser auction and dinner went well, and they raised a lot of money. That seemed to help. They had a PowerPoint tribute thing for Murray at the dinner. There wasn't a dry eye in the house after. Has the person who won the bid on your tattoo at the auction contacted you yet?"

"Nah." Preacher's gaze drifted back to Lucas. He and Addison were by the folding table that the food was set out on. He was standing too close to Addison, and hot jealousy flowed like lava into Preacher's gut when Lucas tugged on Addison's hair.

"Asshole," he muttered.

Gideon laughed. "He's a nice guy. I had a beer with him and Connor last week."

"You didn't think he was so great when he was hitting on your woman," Preacher said.

"And now you have a problem with him because he's hitting on your woman," Gideon said.

"She's not my woman."

"No, she isn't. So, why are you sitting here looking like you're about to crack Lucas in half?"

"Fuck off, Gideon."

Gideon took a drink of beer. "Don't worry about it. Addison isn't going to go out with him. One, he's not her type, and two, Grace told me she isn't looking to jump into another relationship immediately. What did she say when you showed up at the piercing place in Willington?"

"Who says I showed up at the piercing place?"

Gideon snorted. "I've known you seven years, asshole. You're like an open book to me. What did she say?"

"She was surprised and then pissed with me," Preacher said.

"You must have done something stupid then. Addison is the sweetest woman in Harmony Falls."

"I refused to let her get pierced and carried her out of the shop over my shoulder."

Gideon choked on his swallow of beer, spitting it out in a fine spray. Tank lifted his head from Preacher's chest and sniffed the air before squeezing between their lawn chairs and licking at the spilled beer on Gideon's t-shirt.

Gideon wiped at his mouth. "Are you serious?"

He shrugged. "If she wants another piercing, I'll do it. The fucker in Willington has a rating below three on goddamn Yelp."

"Another piercing?" Gideon raised one eyebrow at him.

"Addison didn't tell Grace she got pierced?"

"If she did, Grace didn't mention it to me. What did she get pierced?"

"That falls under the piercer/client confidentiality agreement," Preacher said.

Gideon laughed. "Asshole. Fine, keep your little secrets. Just remember that Addison and you won't work."

"I know," Preacher said. "I love you, but I'm getting real tired of you being on my ass about this."

"Pookie bear, I haven't even climbed onto your ass yet. Trust me, you'll know when I do."

Despite his sudden bad mood, Preacher couldn't help but grin. "You're such a shithead."

"Yeah, but I'm your shithead." Gideon drank beer before pushing Tank and his tongue away from the front of his shirt. "Go on, Tank. Lie down."

As Tank settled in the grass at their feet, Gideon said, "Daniel is drunk."

Preacher glanced across the yard. Daniel and another firefighter, Jesse, sat in lawn chairs near the firepit. Daniel gestured wildly to Jesse with one hand while holding a beer in the other.

"How many has he had?" Preacher said.

"At least six," Gideon said. "Enough that he's not driving home. On Tuesday night, Ian got called out to The Hitching Post to break up a fight between a couple of drunks. Daniel was one of them. Ian said the same thing happened the week before."

"Shit." Preacher glanced at Addison. "His sister know he's drinking that much?"

"I don't think so. But if he keeps this up, we'll have to -"

Preacher stopped listening. The asshole gamer was holding Addison's hand and studying the friendship bracelets on her wrist. He stood and stalked toward them. Without speaking, he grabbed a paper plate and dumped some raw veggies onto it before standing beside Addison.

He stared at Lucas's hand holding Addison's hand before giving Lucas his best *what the fuck do you think you're doing?* look.

Addison pulled her hand away from Lucas and smiled at Preacher. "Hi there."

"Hey, Preacher." Lucas held out his hand, and Preacher shook it. "How's it going?"

"Fine. You just here for the weekend?"

"I'm living here now. Moved in last weekend into a fantastic condo that Kira helped me find," Lucas said.

"She's so good at her job," Addison said.

"That she is. There isn't much for rentals right now, but she found me the perfect place." Lucas grinned at Addison. "There's only one condo full of rowdy college students in the building. They had one hell of a party Friday night."

Addison laughed. "Did you join them?"

His grin widened. "Nah. My days of hard partying are over. I'm looking to settle down in my small-town life."

"Well, you've picked the perfect small town," Addison said. "We're so much better than Willington."

Lucas clapped his hand over his heart. "All this trash talk about my hometown is crushing to my soul."

"I can't help it if Harmony Falls is superior to Willington in every way," Addison said with a grin, "but I do feel a little bad about the soul crushing."

"Tell you what, give me one of those friendship bracelets you've made for all your friends but poor old me, and we'll call it even." Lucas reached toward Addison's hand again.

Preacher clamped his hand around Lucas's wrist without thinking about it. He glared at the gamer as Lucas raised his eyebrows, and Addison said, "Preacher, what are you doing?"

"Since when did you and Addison become friends?" Preacher said to Lucas.

Lucas glanced at Preacher's hand still wrapped around his wrist. "You wanna let go of my hand, big guy? I think it's a little soon in our relationship for hand holding. Don't you?"

Addison tugged on his wrist. "Preacher, let him go."

"Don't touch her," he said before releasing his grip.

"You're being rude," Addison said to him.

"It's all good," Lucas said.

Addison rolled her eyes before digging into the small handbag looped around her forearm. She was wearing a bright green dress with a distractingly low neckline. The pearls were around her neck like usual, and when Lucas glanced at them, Preacher scowled at him and could barely control the urge to bare his teeth. He knew what the prick was thinking about – fuck, it was the same thing he thought every time he looked at those goddamn pearls – and if Lucas didn't stop picturing a naked, pearl-wearing Addison in his bed, Preacher would rearrange his fucking teeth.

"Here, Lucas." Addison pulled two friendship bracelets from her purse and quickly tied them around his wrist.

Lucas grinned at her. "You're too sweet, Addison. Thank you."

"You're welcome," Addison said. "Oh, and here, I'll give you my number now, and you can text me about Tuesday afternoon."

"What's happening Tuesday afternoon?" Preacher said.

"You sure you don't mind?" Lucas said.

"I really don't," Addison said.

"What's happening Tuesday?" Preacher said again.

"Well, I appreciate your help," Lucas said.

"Addison," Preacher cupped her arm just above her elbow – fuck, her skin was soft – and squeezed gently, "what are you doing with him on Tuesday?"

"I'm taking him to the yarn shop to help him pick out yarn for his mom's birthday," she said. "Why?"

"Addie! Hey, Addie!" Kira was waving at her from across the yard. "Come over here for a second."

"One minute," she called. "Lucas, do you want my number?"

"Yep." Lucas added her number to his phone, and with a final look at Preacher, Addison walked away.

Ignoring his urge to stare at her ass, Preacher instead glared at Lucas. He had Addison's phone number – Preacher didn't even have her fucking number. His gaze dropped to the two braided bracelets around Lucas's wrist. She'd given him two. She'd given him two of her bracelets, and Preacher only had one.

For fuck's sake. Are you twelve? You're seriously jealous over a goddamn friendship bracelet?

"Addison is great, don't you think?" Lucas said with an infuriating grin. "It's a shame about her and her fiancé."

"Stay away from her," Preacher said. "She's not looking for a relationship with a man-child who plays video games all fucking day."

"Develops them, actually," Lucas said, that annoying grin still planted on his face, "but it's still a remarkably fair description of me, so I'll give you that."

"She's not interested in you," Preacher said.

"She's more into tortured tattoo artists? Is that what you're saying?" Lucas said.

Preacher could feel his face reddening. His urge to punch Lucas was growing by the minute, and what the hell was wrong with him? He never got jealous.

"Look, man," Lucas clapped him on the arm, "in the interest of not having you punch my face into mincemeat, I'm going to stop being a dickhead and tell you the truth. I'm not interested in Addison. I like to flirt, and Addison is a pretty girl, but I like curvy girls. Okay? It's not going to go beyond flirting with her. So, you can stop picturing how it'll look when you shove my head up my own ass and relax about the whole situation."

He fucking hated it, but just hearing Lucas say he wasn't interested in Addison made the steam cooker in his brain cool off a couple of degrees.

"Friends again?" Lucas held out his hand, the two bracelets around his wrist taunting Preacher.

"If I find out you touched her on Tuesday, even one goddamn time, you'll regret moving to Harmony Falls," Preacher said. "You understand?"

Lucas's laid-back grin didn't waver. In an exaggerated French accent, he said, "Aye, aye, mon capitaine."

Preacher rolled his eyes and stalked away.

CHAPTER 16

"Thanks for inviting Daniel," Addison said. "I appreciate it, and I know he does too. He's been lonely without us, even if he won't admit it."

Kira smiled at her. "It's going well, I think. I talked with Connor beforehand, and he was good with it. He's not jealous, which I'm grateful for because he has nothing to be jealous about, you know?"

"I do. Daniel said he and Connor had a beer, and he apologized."

"He did. I still don't know what exactly Daniel said to make Connor punch him – Connor won't say – but I know that Connor appreciated the apology."

"Speaking of, how's his hand doing?"

"Well, considering how hard your brother's face is, Connor's hand is improving. Obviously, it's still not fully healed, and the cast isn't even close to coming off yet, but the fingers are no longer swollen, there's no numbness in them, and he can wiggle them. Which the specialist said is fantastic news. He thinks with even just a few weeks of physical therapy, Connor will have enough range of motion to start working on patients again. Although he did manage a dental checkup one-handed on a very patient client the other day," Kira said.

"That's good," Addison said.

"It is." She swept the lemon rinds into the compost bin under the kitchen sink. "Daniel's had too much to drink."

"I know," Addison said. "He's already given me his keys. I'll drive him home."

"Okay, good. I could see Gideon giving him the old cop eye."

"Daniel wouldn't drive drunk," Addison said. "He's not perfect, but he would never do something that stupid."

"I know," Kira said quickly. "I just want to make sure he stays safe. Now, let's talk about Lucas."

"What about him?"

"I saw how you two were flirting up a storm by the food table." Kira stirred the fresh pitcher of lemonade she'd just made.

"We weren't flirting," Addison said.

"Oh yeah? Because you gave him a couple of friendship bracelets," Kira said.

"Oh my God, I've given all my friends the bracelets."

"Girl, seriously, just consider him," Kira said.

Addison leaned against the kitchen counter. It was only her and Kira in the kitchen, everyone else was in the back-yard, but she lowered her voice anyway. "Lucas isn't inter-ested in me."

"Are you kidding? He asked you to go yarn shopping with him," Kira said.

Addison laughed. "It's for his mom's birthday present. She's been knitting since Lucas was a kid."

"He's good looking and sweet," Kira said. "You really should at least consider him as your new casual lover. He's not in a relationship right now, and I don't think he's looking for one. Plus, he's the exact opposite of Harrison. He's easygoing, funny, and probably a lot of fun in bed."

"He's not my type," Addison said.

"You don't know that. Maybe you secretly love the fun and flirty guy. Besides, you're not looking for a relationship, just a casual banging partner. Right?"

"Right," Addison said. "But he's just not..."

"Not flicking your bean for you?" Kira said.

Addison laughed again. "Now you sound like Gracie."

"Don't I?" Kira said with a grin. "You know what we need to do? We need to take you out to the bars. We need to introduce you to a bunch of different guys and figure out what kind of guy you want to get dirty with just for fun. What do you think?"

"Um, yeah, sure, why not," Addison said.

"Look at you!" Kira put her arm around Addison's shoulders and squeezed. "Stepping out of your comfort box and trying new things. I'm so proud of you, honey."

"Thanks."

"You okay?" Kira studied her. "You've been on the quiet side this afternoon. Did the news about Grace and Gideon's engagement upset you?"

"What? No, of course not."

"It's okay if it did," Kira said. "That's natural and -"

"It didn't upset me. I'm happy for both of them," Addison said. "I swear, Kira."

"Okay." Kira hugged her again and picked up the pitcher of lemonade. "C'mon, let's get back out there."

"You go ahead. I'm going to use the washroom first."

"All right."

She waited until Kira left the kitchen before walking toward the guest bathroom. She wasn't upset about Grace's engagement - she was thrilled for her. It was being around Preacher that had her all tied up in knots. He'd ignored her for the entire barbeque, which wasn't unusual. They rarely talked at the social gatherings. Why would they? They had nothing in common.

But that was before she knew what it was like to have him inside of her, and now that she had, his ability to pretend that there was nothing different between them was… well, it was kind of hurtful.

Stop it, Addie. See, this is why a casual thing isn't good for you. You're not in a relationship with Preacher. Hell, he won't even continue lessons with you, so stop acting like such a baby. You got to have sex with him a couple of times, enjoy it for what it was and move on.

She stopped in front of the bathroom door, worrying at her bottom lip with her teeth. Inner Addie was right. The weird little interaction with Lucas aside, Preacher was sending her a message, and that message was –

"Hello, Sunshine."

Preacher's low voice brought immediate lust to her belly in a slow wave. She froze with her hand on the handle of the bathroom door as his hand smoothed around her hip and rested against her lower abdomen. He brushed her hair away from her throat and pressed a kiss against her skin.

"You smell good," he said.

"Th-thank you," she said. "Are you enjoying the barbeque?"

"Hmm," he said as he traced her throat with the tip of his tongue. "What are you doing in here all by yourself?"

"Just going to wash my hands," she said.

"I'll come with you," he said.

"What? No, that's not a good idea," she said.

He opened the bathroom door and pushed her inside

before following her and closing it behind them. He crowded her up against the wall, and she moaned softly when he pressed his erection against her stomach.

"Everyone is just outside," she murmured, glancing at the open window. It didn't face directly into the backyard, but they could hear the voices of the others. "Gideon and Grace and – and my brother."

"I know," he said. "It's the perfect time for lesson two."

"Lesson two?" She stared at him in shock. "I – we just had lesson one yesterday."

"I remember. I was the guy whose face you were sitting on," he said.

She flushed bright red as he grinned wickedly at her. "Seems like you remember too."

"I didn't think you wanted…"

"Wanted what?"

"To keep going with the lessons."

He tugged on the pearls around her neck before rubbing his thumb along her collarbone, and just like that, she was soaking wet.

"That's odd," he said. "Why would you think that?"

"Well, because…" laughter drifted through the open window of the bathroom, and she tensed against him. "Everyone is just out there," she whispered.

"Like I said, perfect time for lesson two."

"Wh-what's lesson two?"

"How to have public sex without getting caught," he said.

"Not a chance!" She pushed at his chest. "We'll be caught and -"

He kissed her softly on the mouth, licking at the seam of her lips until she moaned and parted them.

"Good girl," he whispered before kissing her again.

She kissed him feverishly and didn't object when he reached under her dress and stroked her panties.

"Are you wet for me, Sunshine?"

"Yes."

"Good. Let's get these off."

He tugged on her panties, and she let him pull them down her legs. She stepped out of them and glanced at the window when more laughter drifted in.

"I want to take you bare," he said in a low voice.

"I – you don't have a condom?"

"I do," he said, "but I want you bare. I get tested regularly. I can show you my results later. Are you on the pill?"

She nodded. "Yes. I, um, I was tested too… after I found out Harrison was cheating on me. I didn't, uh, get anything from him."

"You good with not using a condom?"

She hesitated, and he pressed a kiss against her neck. "It's fine if you're not. I'll use a condom, Addison."

"No, I don't want to use one." It was true. She didn't. The idea of nothing being between her and Preacher was intoxicating.

He kissed her throat again, then pushed her dress up around her waist. He pressed his hand between her legs and cupped her pussy. "I don't have time to eat your sweet pussy."

She arched into his hand. "That's, um, that's all right."

He rubbed at her clit. "I'm going to make you come first. I want you very wet when I fuck you, baby."

Her moan was too loud, and he nipped her neck. "Quiet, Sunshine."

He rubbed her clit with firm pressure as he pressed his cock against her hip. "Do you need me to suck on your nipples, baby? Or can you come without it?"

She buried her face in his throat. "I'm already close."

She could hear the embarrassment in her voice, and he threaded his free hand through her hair and pulled her head back. "Don't be embarrassed."

He slid two fingers deep into her warmth, and she ground her pussy against his hand. "Oh gosh, that feels so good."

He grinned and slanted his mouth over hers. He continued to kiss her as he stretched her narrow entrance with his fingers and rubbed her clit with the ball of his thumb. Her body tensed against him, her hands dug into his arms, and he swallowed her cry of pleasure when she came against his hand. He gently eased his fingers out of her as he licked her lips and then pulled his head back.

"Feel good, Sunshine?" he said.

She nodded and leaned against the wall, her legs quivering as he unbuttoned his jeans. He tugged his t-shirt off before pushing down his jeans and underwear. He put his hands on her hips.

"Legs around my waist," he said in a low voice as he lifted her. She obeyed him, and he braced her against the wall before reaching between them and guiding his dick into her pussy. He pushed the head in and paused. "Does it hurt?"

She shook her head, and he kissed her again as he slowly eased his dick into her warmth. When she was pinned against the wall with his hard cock deep inside her, he released her mouth and brushed her hair back from her face.

"It feels good," she whispered before he could ask. "Please don't stop."

FUCK, BEING IN ADDISON WITHOUT A CONDOM WAS HIS OWN personal heaven. The hot warmth and the silky feel of her inner walls were enough to make him almost blow his load. He'd never had sex without a condom before, and while asking Addison to let him take her bare was a total impulse decision, he knew he couldn't go back to fucking her with a condom after this.

Not when she felt this fucking good around his dick.

Addison rubbed his back and stared pleadingly at him as she rocked her pelvis against his. "Please."

"Say my name," he said.

"Please, Preacher."

He cupped her left breast through her dress. "Try again."

She paused and then said, "Please, Simon."

He thrust back and forth. Her moan was way too loud, and he glanced at the open window before he clapped his hand over her mouth and put his mouth to her ear. "I'm going to fuck you hard and fast, Sunshine. We've been gone too long, haven't we? The others will start wondering where we are. Don't you think?"

She nodded, and he thrust again as he lowered his hand from her mouth. "Can you be a good girl and be quiet?"

She hesitated before shaking her head. "No, I don't think so."

He grinned at her. "Bury your face in my neck and hang on."

She did what he said, clinging to him with all of her limbs as he fucked her hard. Her back hit the wall with rhythmic thuds, and she squealed into his throat when he shoved his hand between their bodies and rubbed her clit.

"Come for me, baby," he muttered into her ear. "I want your hot pussy to squeeze my dick while I'm coming."

She moaned into his throat, and only a few minutes later, she was climaxing again, her cry of pleasure muffled against his skin. He groaned and buried his face into her neck as he thrust roughly before pinning her to the wall and coming with another low groan. He pumped hard, a part deep down inside of him loving the idea that she'd be filled with his come.

She was panting, her trembling arms still wrapped around his shoulders and her face still buried in his neck. He moved his hand to her ass and gave it a quick squeeze before easing out of her and setting her on her feet.

His cock was glistening with her sweet cream, and he could see the blush rising in her cheeks when she glanced at it. He grinned at her and yanked up his briefs and jeans, tucking his cock away and buttoning them. "You good, Sunshine?"

"Yes," she said. "Are you?"

Now that he'd fucked her, he was fucking incredible. Now that she smelled like him and was marked by him, his weird and overwhelming jealousy had faded. He might get through the rest of the barbeque without feeling like he was on the verge of insanity.

"I am." He pressed a kiss against her mouth. "Thank you."

"Oh, um," her blush deepened, "you're welcome."

Remembering her doubt from yesterday, he said, "It was fantastic."

The pleased look on her face made him feel like a fucking superhero. "Good. I, um, really enjoyed it, too."

They stood in awkward silence for a few seconds before he eased open the door and checked the hallway. "It's empty."

She was holding her panties in her hand, and she said, "I'll be out in a minute. I need to, uh... I need a minute."

He grinned at her and slid one arm around her waist, drawing her close. "Do you have any idea how much I like knowing that you'll spend the rest of the afternoon with my come dripping out of your sweet pussy?"

She blushed furiously, just like he knew she would, and he laughed before pressing a kiss against her mouth. "See you out there, Sunshine."

CHAPTER 17

"I think I'm allergic to this face mask. It's itchy." Her face covered by a moisturizing mask, Harper peered at her from Addison's iPad screen. "Also, you kind of look like Jason Voorhees."

"Quiet, you," Addison rearranged the mask on her face so she could see better from the eyeholes. The mask was slimy and starting to get cold. "Just a few more minutes, and we can take them off."

"It feels like I've got cold semen all over my face," Harper complained.

"Don't be gross." Addison wanted to take a sip of her tea, but she didn't fancy the idea of getting whatever was on the mask potentially in her mouth. "How was work today?"

Harper shrugged. "Typical Monday. It was slow in the gallery. I might get laid off."

"Shit." Addison shifted on the bed and smoothed the mask again when it slipped down her forehead. "Are you serious?"

"Yeah." Harper didn't sound worried, but Addie knew her best friend better than anyone.

"Have you sold any more art online?" she said.

Harper shrugged. "A couple of smaller pieces. Nothing that I can live on."

"It's going to happen for you, honey," Addison said. "You just need to be patient. By this time next year, you'll be one of the most famous artists in New York City."

Harper laughed, and the underlying bitterness beneath it hurt Addison's heart. "Doubtful. My shit looks like a fucking toddler drew it compared to the artists here."

"You can't compare yourself to others," Addie said.

"Yeah, I know." Harper sat back on her bed. "I'm worried about Dad."

"Is he still acting kind of weird?"

"So weird. He's still talking about retiring and selling the clinic," Harper said.

Addison could see the hurt and the confusion on Harper's face, even with the mask covering it.

"I don't understand why he keeps talking about selling the clinic. He loves being a vet, always has, and he's not even sixty yet. Ever since Mom died," Harper paused, "he hasn't been the same. It's been six years, and he still hasn't cleaned out her side of the closet. That's not normal, right?"

"He loved your mom a lot."

"He did," Harper said. "Even when she didn't deserve it."

The pain in Harper's voice made Addie wish she was there to hug her. "I'm sorry, honey."

"Thanks. I think that the new vet he hired is pressuring him into selling. Dad didn't start talking about it until this guy started working there. Only a month after he started working with Dad, he told him he would be interested in buying the clinic if Dad ever wanted to sell it. Next thing you know, Dad's talking about selling the clinic."

"Okay, but your dad wouldn't do anything he didn't want to," Addie said.

Harper pushed at the mask on her face. "Wouldn't he? Mom walked all over him for years."

"Your mom had a very," Addie paused, "strong personality."

"Yeah, just like me," Harper said.

Addison scowled at her, making the mask wrinkle and sag, "Stop it. You're nothing like your mom. She was selfish, and I know it's not nice to speak ill of the dead, but she was a real asshole for what she did to you and your dad."

"Whoa," Harper said with a small smile. "Look at the mouth on you now. Looks like teaching you the joys of a good pussy eating isn't the only thing Preacher's taught you."

Addison was thankful the cold and gooey mask hid the bright blush on her cheeks. "Harper!"

Harper's usual cheerful attitude was coming back in full force. "What? I'm just saying that I think this casual fucking thing you've got going on with Preacher is good for you. When is your next," she made quotation marks with her fingers, "lesson?"

"Well, um, I guess this weekend," Addison said. "We just had lesson two yesterday, and I proposed a once a week thing for a month, so…"

"But you've had two lessons in two days," Harper said. "So, maybe Preacher will just do what he wants when rocking your world. Hell, maybe -"

She glanced down at her phone before yanking the mask off her face. "Sorry, pinky-pie, I gotta go."

"Is there something wrong?" Addie said.

Harper grinned, her face shiny from the moisturizing mask. "Nope. Francisco just texted me. I texted him earlier to see if he wanted a booty call tonight, and he's on his way over. I'm about to get me some D."

"Oh." Addie blinked at her. "Oh, well, um, okay. Have fun."

"I plan on it," Harper said with a laugh. "Text me when Preacher calls you for another lesson. Let me know if you're planning on doing something outrageous like having sex in a hot tub or something."

"Ha, ha," Addison said. "One, Preacher doesn't even have my number, and two, I would never have sex in a hot tub. Water is a terrible lubricant, and do you know how many germs are floating around in the average hot tub?"

Harper laughed. "Oh, how I love you, Addison Mabel Moore. I'll talk to you later!"

She blew Addie a kiss and ended the call. Addison went to the bathroom and peeled off the mask. She tossed it in the garbage and rinsed her face before patting it dry. She supposed her face looked less dry… it was kind of hard to tell with how shiny it was now. She scooped her hair into an unflattering bun on top of her head and brushed and flossed her teeth before returning to the bedroom.

It was only eight-thirty, but she was already in her pink cotton pajama bottoms with a matching tank top and had been since four. She studied the orange splotch at the bottom of her tank top before sniffing it. Yup, that was a Cheetos stain. Sadly, it was from Friday night.

She briefly considered changing her tank top before climbing into bed. What did it matter? It wasn't like she had anyone to impress. She picked up the scarf she was knitting and knit a couple of rows. Usually, knitting soothed her, but it wasn't doing anything for her tonight.

She was feeling restless and lonely and… horny. She stared blankly at her knitting. She'd just gotten laid two days in a row, and she was still horny. What was wrong with her? She and Harrison used to have sex once every couple of weeks, and nine times out of ten, it was because she initiated it. That had always seemed like enough for her, especially if it was one of the times she actually had an orgasm, so what was going on with her?

You know what good sex is like now?

She scowled and set her knitting on the bed beside her. Okay, so maybe sex with Preacher was a little – *a thousand times* – better than it'd been with Harrison, but that still didn't completely explain her sudden voracious sex drive. Did it? Did good sex make a girl's sex drive change that drastically?

Maybe you always had a high sex drive and didn't know it because sex with Harrison was so blah.

She leaned against the headboard. She wasn't being fair. Sex with Harrison was so blah because of her.

Don't be that naïve, girl. It takes two people to make good sex happen. Stop blaming yourself entirely for the terrible sex with Harrison. Preacher can make you come in, like, four minutes. Harrison could never do that. Hell, he wouldn't even consider the idea of eating your pussy. Ten years together, and he didn't put his tongue on your pussy once. That's selfish and rude.

She swallowed hard. The memory of being in Preacher's shop, of how he looked with his head between her thighs, of how it *felt* when his tongue and lips were on her clit, was flooding through her.

She shifted restlessly. God, if she'd thought she was horny before...

She wished she was brave like Harper and could text Preacher about a booty call. She stared at her phone, knowing she was being ridiculous. She would never have the guts to call any guy, let alone someone as hot as Preacher, to ask about a booty call. Besides, she didn't have Preacher's number anyway, so even if she was brave enough to text, she couldn't.

You could call Gideon and get Preacher's number from him.

Oh yeah, that would go over well. What if Gideon asked why she wanted Preacher's number? What would she tell him? Even if she thought of a plausible excuse, if Gideon told Preacher that she got his number from him, it might piss Preacher off enough to stop having sex with her.

The thought of not having sex with Preacher ever again was disturbingly upsetting.

She shifted on the bed again. Her thoughts might be confused and in turmoil, but her body wasn't. It was looking for relief.

She leaned over and opened the bedside drawer, staring at what was inside it with trepidation. The silk scarves, the massage oil, and the wand vibrator from her planned night of seducing Harrison that had ended so horribly.

She pushed aside the wand vibrator and stared at the object tucked below it. She had purchased this one when she'd discovered Harrison cheating on her, and she fled to New York to stay with Harper for a while.

She'd been a little drunk on wine, and Harper had been a little high on weed, and before Addison knew it, they were walking into one of the many – *many* – sex shops in Harper's neighbourhood to pick out a vibrator.

"Those wand vibrators are fantastic for clitoral stimulation," Harper said as they perused the wall of dildos and vibrators, "but when you're craving the D, you need a dildo – the bigger the better."

Mortified by how loud her best friend was, Addison shushed her and hurriedly picked out something. She couldn't quite bring herself to purchase one of the flesh-coloured, horrifically giant and weirdly realistic dildos that Harper was urging her to buy, but Harper wouldn't let her buy the comfortingly smaller vibrator she was eyeing either.

"It's too small," Harper said.

"It isn't," Addison said. "It's a good size."

"Girl, how teeny was Harrison's wiener if you think that's a good size?" Harper said with a mock look of horror. "Seriously. How many inches was he?"

"I never measured," Addison said.

"Was it smaller than this?" Harper held up the vibrator Addie had been eyeing.

"No, he was bigger." She'd picked the smaller one, hoping it wouldn't hurt like it did with Harrison.

"This big?" Harper held up the next size vibrator.

"Um, a little smaller than that." Her face was bright red, and she wished Harper would talk a little more quietly.

"Oh my God. So, it was only slightly larger than this?" Harper pointed to the smaller vibrator.

"Yes. But that seems like a pretty good size to me."

"Oh, my sweet summer child," Harper said. "You poor thing."

Addison rolled her eyes. "Size isn't everything, Harper."

"Says the girl whose cheating cunt of an ex-fiancé had a dick the size of a pencil," Harper said.

"It was bigger than a pencil," Addison said.

"Honey," a large woman wearing a skin-tight dress and stilettos paused as she walked by them, one hand clutching a bottle of lube and two dick lollipops, "if his dick isn't at least the size of a flashlight, you can do better."

"Yaass, queen." Harper held out her fist. The woman bumped it and walked on.

Now, Addison took the vibrator from the nightstand and

set it on her lap. She'd let Harper convince her to buy the slightly larger vibrator, but just like the wand vibrator, she hadn't used it yet.

Once she'd returned from New York, she hadn't exactly had much of a sexual appetite. The humiliation of being the gossip of the town, the constant worry that she'd run into Harrison or – God forbid – Crystal, had killed her libido. The one night she thought she might try it, her interest had waned by the time she got it out of the packaging and put batteries in.

She turned the vibrator on, resting it in the palm of her hand as she played with the settings to get an idea of the different vibration levels. Before Preacher, this vibrator had seemed almost impossibly large to her, but now...

Preacher's dick is twice the size of this thing.

That was true. A grin crossed her face. The idea that not only would she be able to take a dick the size of Preacher's but crave it was actually funny to her. She'd only had sex with him four times, but her usual anxiety she felt right when she was about to have a penis inside of her was already lessening. The realization that it didn't have to hurt to have sex and that she could have multiple orgasms was friggin' magical. She wasn't sure she'd ever get used to how amazing that was.

Right. You think this little thing is going to satisfy you? You should have listened to Harper and got the giant dildo.

It probably wouldn't be enough, not after Preacher. But beggars couldn't be choosers, right? It would do until Preacher contacted her for another hook-up. She had to do something. The ache in her crotch – *pussy, it's called a pussy, and you loved having it eaten out by Preacher, you dirty girl* – was maddening.

She took a deep breath and laid on her back on the bed.

She cupped her left breast, pulling on the nipple as she closed her eyes and thought about Preacher. She had the urge to tug on the barbell in her right nipple. God, it had felt so good when Preacher twisted it, but she kept her fingers away. She didn't want to have to explain to a pissed-off Preacher why her nipple piercing was infected.

Maybe he'll spank you for being a bad girl.

Her face flushed bright red, but her nipples were stiff peaks, and her pussy was suddenly soaking wet. She had no desire to be spanked, not even by Preacher, but that's what fantasies were for... to imagine doing something you would never do in real life.

She rubbed at her nipple through the thin material of her tank top and thought about what it would be like to be draped over Preacher's lap with her bare ass in the air and ready for his spanking. To have his outrageously large dick digging into her stomach as he spanked her with sexy little slaps that just drove her need higher.

She pulled at her nipple again, her pussy aching and wet, and her other hand gripping the vibrator. She could hear Preacher's low voice telling her she was his good girl, could see his big hand sliding between her legs to feel how wet she was, how much she needed him.

She turned the vibrator on, the low buzz against her palm making her jump a little. She slid it under her pajama bottoms and rubbed it along her panty-covered clit. The vibration made her moan, and she hurriedly pulled the vibrator free and reached for the waistband of her pajamas. She needed to be naked for this. Yes, definitely naked.

There was a knock on her front door, and she made a soft shriek of surprise and dropped the vibrator. It buzzed against the quilt, and she quickly turned it off before shoving it under the quilt and staring wide-eyed at the open bedroom door.

Her heart hammering in her chest and feeling weirdly guilty, she climbed out of bed, grabbed her robe, and walked down the short hallway toward the front door.

It was probably Mrs. Garnet from next door. She was always making fresh bread and bringing a loaf or two over. Or maybe it was Kira or Grace. She'd finally gotten around to giving them keys to her building and apartment. Of course, they usually just knocked and let themselves in, so… she peered through the peephole, and another startled sound escaped her mouth.

What was he doing here?

He knocked again, and she opened the door, staring wide-eyed at him.

"Hello, Sunshine."

"Um, hi," she said.

There were a few seconds of silence before Preacher raised an eyebrow at her. "Can I come in?"

"Right, yes, of course. Come in."

He stepped inside, and she shut and locked the door behind him. He wore his usual jeans and t-shirt with a leather vest over the shirt. He smelled like hot sun and warm leather and his unique smell, and holy crap, if she hadn't been wet before, she was wet now.

"How did you get into my building?" she said.

"Someone was leaving. You busy?"

"Um, no, I was just, uh, knitting."

"Right," he said.

His gaze dipped to the front of her robe, and she clutched at it. "Would you like a drink? I have wine or juice or water. I don't have any beer, I'm sorry."

He stepped closer, and she was suddenly aware of how awful she looked. Her face was shiny, she wore her bulky terrycloth robe, and her hair looked stupid and –

He pressed his hands against the wall on either side of her head, penning her in. She stared up at him. Her heart had gone from hammering against her ribs to possibly busting through them, and the heat of his body and the good, clean smell of him made her head swim.

He moved one hand to her waist and traced the knot of her robe ties. "What are you wearing under this very practical looking robe, Sunshine?"

"Oh, um…"

He tugged on the knot, pulling it loose with a hard jerk. Her robe opened, and he stared at her tank top and pink cotton pajama bottoms with the tiny parrots stamped onto them. A grin crossed his face, and she covered the orange stain on her tank top with one hand as her face flushed bright red.

"Are those birds on your pants?" he said.

"Yes," she said.

His gaze lingered on her breasts, on the way her nipples pressed against the thin fabric. "You always answer your door without wearing a bra?"

"I thought you were Mrs. Garnet from next door, and besides, I was wearing a robe, so… oh!"

His finger traced a slow circle around her left nipple through the fabric, and she arched into his touch.

His satisfied grin made her squirm with need. "I love how sensitive your nipples are."

"I didn't – I mean, why are you here?"

"It's time for lesson number three," he said.

"What's lesson three?"

"You'll see."

He picked her up and carried her past her tiny living room, galley kitchen, and down the hallway. Her bedroom door was open, and he carried her into the room and set her next to the bed before tugging her robe off.

He pulled her in close until she could feel the heat of the sun on his vest and kissed her. She returned his kiss, moaning into his mouth when he licked at her tongue and then sucked on it.

He stepped back and shrugged out of his vest and then his t-shirt, letting them join her robe on the floor. "Move your knitting, Sunshine."

"What?" She was distracted by all the rippling, glorious tattooed muscle in front of her.

"Your knitting. Move it off the bed. I don't want a knitting needle in the ass while we're fucking."

She giggled nervously before grabbing the knitting and bending over to stuff it into the knitting bag beside the bed. Preacher stepped behind her, his hands cupping her hips and pulling her into an upright position as he pressed his cock against her ass.

He kissed the back of her neck and along the back of her shoulder with warm, open-mouthed kisses that made her quiver and moan.

"You always smell so fucking good," he said before nipping her neck. "Lift your arms."

She lifted them, and he pulled her tank top over her head before cupping her left breast and teasing the nipple. She clutched at his arm, letting her head fall back against his chest and grinding her ass against his erection.

He groaned into her ear and then reached for the waistband of her pajamas. He shoved them down her legs, and dammit, why couldn't she just once be wearing a sexy silk thong when Preacher saw her underwear?

He traced the waistband of her cotton panties as she kicked her pajamas off her feet. His fingers toyed with the little ribbon bow at the front of it before he slid his hand beneath her panties and cupped her pussy.

His grunt of surprise made her want to die of embarrassment.

He kissed the side of her neck and tugged on her earlobe with his teeth. "You're very wet, Sunshine. I know that isn't just from me undressing you. You wanna tell me what you were doing before I came by?"

"I'd rather not," she said and then cried out with pleasure when he rubbed her clit.

He laughed as his fingers brushed over her wet clit again before withdrawing. "You want me to leave so you can keep touching yourself?"

"No!" She was embarrassed by the whine in her voice, but it didn't stop her from grabbing his hand and sticking it back inside her panties. "No, I want you to touch me."

He peeled off her panties, sliding them down her thighs until they slipped past her knees and pooled at her ankles. She stepped out of them, arching into Preacher's hand when he cupped her pussy again and rubbed her clit with the heel of his hand.

"Oh God, oh God, please," she said.

He chuckled into her ear, the sound spiking new pleasure in her belly. "You like it when I rub your clit, baby?"

"Yes," she said. "Very much."

He laughed again and teased her clit with the pad of his finger. It felt amazing, and she desperately wanted more.

Addie, no! Pay attention. You need to make this about him, remember?

Right. About him. She pretty much had the more responsive thing down. Now, she needed to learn how to be sexier and give a better blow job. Her Cheetos stained tank top and ridiculous pajama bottoms had ruined the be sexier part, but she could get some oral sex tips from him.

She turned in his arms, ignoring his scowl of disapproval when it knocked his hand out from between her thighs and kissed his chest. "How about we make lesson three giving a blow job?"

His breath hissed out between his teeth when she reached between them and rubbed his dick through his jeans. "Fuck, Sunshine. That feels good."

"My mouth will feel better." She tried to sound bold, but she came off sounding nervous, maybe even bordering on scared, which was ridiculous. She wasn't scared. She was just really worried that she would make a fool of herself trying to blow him. According to Harrison, she was terrible at them, and the thought that she might disappoint Preacher in any way in the bedroom made her feel a little nauseous.

Preacher eyed her thoughtfully, and when she rubbed his dick again, he reached down and took her hand, pulling it away. "Lesson three is pussy eating."

"But I – that was lesson one," she said.

He grinned and picked her up, dumping her on the bed unceremoniously and pushing her thighs apart before stretching out between her legs. "I know you're the teacher, but I'm in charge of this lesson plan."

"But," she reached down and pressed on his forehead to stop him from sticking his face between her thighs, "this isn't a lesson for me. I think you've proven that you can make me come with, um, oral sex, so maybe we should concentrate on you this time."

"Sunshine," he shook off her hand impatiently, "I've been dreaming all fucking day about eating your sweet tasting pussy. So, be my good girl and spread those smooth thighs of yours and give me what I want."

Hot fire dancing at her nerve endings, she let her legs drop open without another word. He grinned up at her. "There's my good girl." He kissed the patch of auburn curls at the top of her mound. "Fuck, I love these pretty little curls."

"I thought maybe I would wax them," she said. "Guys like a cleaner look, right?"

"Don't you fucking dare," he said. "You leave your pussy just like this. Do you hear me, Addison?"

He stared up at her, and she nodded. "It was just an idea. It doesn't matter to me if... oh God! Oh, Simon!"

Her hand reached down and clamped around his head, pressing his mouth harder against her clit as his hot tongue slicked across the throbbing bundle of nerves again. He grabbed her hand and then her other one, his hard fingers wrapping around her wrists and pinning them against the outside of her thighs before he licked her swollen pussy lips clean.

She writhed and wriggled, already amped up to unbearable levels. "Simon! Please!"

"Please, what, Addie?" He licked her entrance before stiffening his tongue and sliding it inside of her.

"My clit! Please, my clit, Simon!"

His voice was muffled as he licked and nipped her inner thighs. "What about it?"

"Don't be a jerk!" She kicked him in the butt with her foot, and he lifted his head and grinned at her.

"Considering this is only the third time you've had your pussy eaten, you're being pretty demanding about it."

"Simon!" She glared at him, her pussy throbbing and aching so much that she couldn't stand it. "Don't tease!"

"Ask me nicely," he said.

She kicked him in the butt again and made a snort of

anger. He laughed and nipped her inner thigh. "Ask me nicely to eat your pussy, and I'll suck on your sweet clit until you come all over my face. I promise."

She sucked in a lungful of air. "Please, will you eat my pussy, Simon?"

"Yes, baby, I will." He pushed his face between her thighs, and she bit back her scream of pleasure when he sucked on her clit just like he promised.

He released her hands, and she grabbed the back of his head, grinding her pussy against his mouth as he sucked and licked. Her earlier fantasy about Preacher had her panting and aching and close to climaxing in only a few minutes.

When Preacher reached up and cupped her left breast before tweaking her nipple, it threw her over the edge. She screamed again, not caring if her neighbours heard her, and climaxed in a roaring, blinding rush of pleasure that blotted out everything else.

She was only vaguely aware of Preacher stripping off the rest of his clothes, of him pushing her thighs apart and kneeling between her legs. He bent over her, his hands braced on either side of her head as he pressed light kisses against her left nipple.

When he sucked gently on it, her hips bucked, and he hissed out another breath when his erection rubbed against her abdomen. "Fuck, baby. I could watch you come all fucking day."

She moaned when he kissed the tip of her nipple before nudging at her thighs with one of his. "Spread your legs wider, baby."

She spread her legs again, still trying to catch her breath, as he lined up his cock at her entrance. He pushed the head in and immediately paused, studying her face. "Okay?"

"Yes." The way he checked in with her to make sure he didn't hurt her was the sweetest damn thing. "Keep going."

He slid in and out, rocking his hips back and forth as he eased further into her pussy with every stroke. He didn't have to go that slow, she was so wet he could have entered her with one push despite his size, but she loved that he took his time. Loved that every few strokes, he would give her that assessing look to ensure she was okay. Loved that he treated her like she was as fragile and precious as spun glass.

He made one final push, sheathing himself right to the balls. They moaned in unison, and she gripped his narrow waist as he shifted his hands on the bed. "Baby, you feel so good around my -"

"What's wrong?" She stared up at him as a weird look crossed his face.

Without speaking, he braced himself on one hand above her and stuck the other under the quilt. He brought out her vibrator, staring at the slender pink piece of plastic in his hand as horror filled her body.

"Oh God," she said. "That's um…"

"I know what it is," he said with a grin.

She wanted to die. She wanted to flee from the sight of the vibrator in Preacher's big hand but pinned under him and stuffed full of his cock, she could only stare at him in horrified silence.

"Were you using this on your pretty pussy before I knocked?" He dropped the vibrator on the bed and braced his hand beside her.

"No, I -"

He made a hard thrust, and she gasped and clung to his waist as fresh pleasure washed over her.

"Be honest with me, Sunshine."

"I wasn't. I was going to, but you knocked before I could."

He leaned down and kissed the tip of her nipple. "How often do you use that vibrator?"

"I don't, I mean, I…"

Oh God, she could not talk about using a vibrator while she had Preacher's dick inside of her. "Can we please talk about this later?"

"How often?" He punctuated each word with a slow pump of his hips.

"I haven't used it." She clutched at his waist when he continued to fuck her with slow and measured strokes. "I bought it when I was in New York, but I hadn't used it yet because it was bigger than what Harrison was, and I was afraid it would hurt. But then I had sex with you, and it didn't hurt, and you were way bigger than Harrison or the vibrator, so… oh God, that feels so good, Simon."

She braced her feet on the bed, her hips rising and falling with the rhythm of Preacher's hips. He felt so good inside of her, so perfect and right.

"Why were you using it tonight?" His voice was strained now, a vein in his temple pulsing and sweat covering his chest in a fine sheen.

"I don't want to talk about this."

"Tell me," he said. "Tell me or I'll stop fucking you."

He wouldn't.

He couldn't.

When his thrusts slowed, she folded faster than a cardboard house. "Because I was horny. I was horny, and I needed something to help."

She closed her eyes, shame eclipsing her lust.

"Look at me, Addie."

"I don't want to," she whispered.

"Look at me."

She opened her eyes, staring up into his dark ones as he thrust harder. "You call me the next time you're horny. You don't need to use a piece of plastic if you need your pretty little pussy filled. Got it?"

"I don't have your number," she moaned. "Oh, I think… I think I might come this way."

She sounded surprised, but honestly, she was. An internal orgasm was incredibly rare for her. Like, only happened once before, kind of occurrence.

"That's the idea," he groaned. "You coming on my cock needs to happen every time. The way you fucking squeeze…"

He trailed off and made four hard thrusts that had her crying out with pleasure.

"What will you do, Sunshine, when you need your tight pussy filled?" he groaned out.

"Call you," she moaned. "I'll call you."

"That's right. It doesn't matter what time it is. You call me, and I'll come over and give you my cock."

She cried out, clinging to him with her legs and her arms when his thrusts turned hard and rough. The pleasure peaked inside of her, peaked and then spilled over, and she cried his name as her orgasm made her quiver and tighten around him.

He groaned in pleasure, his hips pumping and straining as he emptied himself into her. He collapsed against her with a soft grunt, and she rubbed his back, enjoying his heavy weight on top of her. Too quickly, he rolled off of her and onto his back.

She wanted to snuggle up to him but made herself stay on her side. She stared at the ceiling, waiting for her heartbeat to return to normal and her breathing to slow. Preacher didn't cuddle. That was obvious from his reaction to her attempts to snuggle at his apartment.

It didn't bother her. This was just sex and nothing else. There was no reason to cuddle, and besides, Harrison had never enjoyed cuddling either. Her clinginess after sex was annoying to him, and she'd learned quickly to give him his space in the bed if she didn't want him leaving immediately after they made love.

Preacher was no different, and that was fine with her. But if Harper, Gracie, and Kira kept telling her anything, it was that she deserved to get what she wanted, too. So, when she went looking for a boyfriend, she would make sure they liked to cuddle after sex. Some guys had to enjoy cuddling, right? She made a mental note to ask Harper if Francisco liked cuddling after sex.

She sat up when Preacher did, pulling the sheet up to hide her nakedness and hugging her knees to her chest as she watched Preacher pull his boxer briefs and jeans on.

"I gotta go," he said.

"Okay, bye." She thought she sounded normal and cool about it. No big deal. Just a round of casual sex. Lesson number three completed.

What exactly did you learn, Addison?

Preacher glanced at her with what looked like irritation before he pulled his shirt over his head and grabbed his vest from the floor. He pulled his phone out of his pocket. "What's your number?"

She recited her number, a little surprised that he wanted it. Wasn't she supposed to get his number and call him?

"Um, what's yours?" she said as she grabbed her phone from the nightstand.

"Just sent you a text." He shoved his phone into his back pocket. "See you later."

"Bye, Preacher."

CHAPTER 18

"**P**reacher, yo, dude, are you even listening to me?" Nolan leaned against the counter.

"You talk so fucking much, I'd go insane if I listened to everything that fell out of your goddamn mouth," Preacher growled.

Nolan laughed. "Hey, I got shit to say, okay? Anyway, I said the new guy is doing good."

Preacher glanced at the tattoo station where Nix was setting up for his next client. The client, a dweeby tourist who, Preacher had no doubt, was probably an accountant or an engineer, sat on the couch, his knee jiggling and his fingers tapping out a nervous beat on his thigh as he stared at the screen of his phone.

"Don't you think?"

"He hasn't been here that long," Preacher said.

"Yeah, I know, but he's already booked solid with walk-ins this week," Nolan said. "And some locals are meeting with him next week to discuss tattoos. You did good hiring him, man. I approve."

"Since when did I start caring what you thought or approved of?" Preacher said.

Nolan laughed again before clapping him on the back. "Christ, you're being a little bitch today. What crawled into your Wheaties and died?"

"Fuck off, Nolan." Preacher made a show of looking at the appointment schedule on the laptop, hoping Nolan would take the hint and leave.

"I'm just saying, you start being even more of a grumpy little bear than you usually are, and your clients are gonna abandon ship to new guy."

Preacher cut him a look, and Nolan grinned and held his hands up before backing away. "I went too far. I realize that now. I'm gonna mop the floor before you rip out my tongue and tack it to my forehead."

The dweeby tourist was staring at them, his fingers paused in their beat against his thigh, his entire body as stiff and alert as a deer smelling a predator.

"Just kidding," Nolan said to him. "Preacher wouldn't do that."

The man relaxed a fraction, and Nolan grinned at him. "He'd tack it to the wall.'

As Nolan walked away and Nix waved the client over to his station, Preacher stared moodily out the tattoo shop window. It was just after two, and the sidewalk was packed with tourists. He watched them scurry past, his mood worsening every minute.

Nolan was right, he was being a little bitch today. He shouldn't have been. The tattoo he'd just finished had been one of his best, and his client had been almost delirious with happiness. The extra hundred he'd tipped Preacher should have been enough to drive away Preacher's bad mood.

It wasn't.

He rubbed at the back of his neck. He had the beginning of a tension headache, and he was starving. He needed to grab a bite before his next client came in. Instead, he leaned against the counter and stared at the tourists.

He knew why he was in a bad mood, even if he refused to admit it.

Addison was hanging out with the asshole gamer this afternoon, and despite what Lucas had said, Preacher couldn't get the idea out of his head that maybe Addison and him would hook up. Lucas had the clean-cut look that women liked, he probably didn't have a single fucking tattoo, and he probably made an ass load of money with that video game shit he did.

Don't forget he hasn't spent four years in prison.

The muscle under Preacher's left eye twitched, and he gritted his teeth. No, he probably fucking hadn't. Which is why he was much more suitable for Addison than Preacher was. If the little schoolteacher ever found out he was an ex-con, she'd drop him so fast his fucking head would spin.

Drop you? You're not dating, idiot. You're fucking, that's it. And it's only for a month, remember?

Of course he fucking remembered. He was there when she proposed the deal, wasn't he?

Yeah, well, she also said once a week, but that didn't stop you from driving over there last night. Three days in a row, you've fucked her now.

He rubbed the back of his neck again. He'd thought about eating Addison's sweet pussy all day yesterday, and not a workout at the gym or a hike at the Falls had helped his restless energy. He'd paced his apartment last night until just after eight, thinking of nothing but burying his face in Addie's pussy, before finally giving in and driving to her place.

It was a good job he had, too. She'd been about to use a vibrator, for God's sake. A goddamn vibrator. When he had a perfectly good cock she could use.

Maybe she's not as into you as you think. She didn't even try to do that post-sex cuddling shit that women want, did she?

No, she hadn't, and why the fuck it bothered him, he didn't know. He should have been happy she hadn't tried. He didn't cuddle with women after sex. It made them think what was happening between them was more than it was. He should have been happy that Addison picked up so quickly on his preference for not having a woman glom onto him after sex.

Instead, he'd laid in her bed, getting all worked up that she was lying on her side of the bed and not even trying to touch him. It had completely ruined his fucking high from having her come on his face and his dick. He'd abandoned his plan to have her come on his fingers and seal the hat trick deal and left her place like a huffy toddler.

She didn't seem to mind. Didn't even ask if you would stay, did she? You're just a vibrator to her, buddy, and guess what? It's better this way. The two of you would never work, so stop acting like such a fucking baby and stop showing up at her place uninvited. Stick to the fucking deal. A lesson a week for a month. That's it.

Yeah, that's what he needed to do. His obsession with the sweet little schoolteacher needed to be reined in. There was no future for them, and -

His body stiffened, and he watched with a weird mixture of anxiety and anger as the very object of his obsession walked by the shop. She was with Lucas, and Preacher's hands turned into fists when he said something to her, and she laughed. She wore a pretty blue dress with her usual pearls around her neck, and her soft hair was in a high ponytail. She looked fucking amazing, and hot jealousy flooded through him as they continued down the sidewalk and disappeared from his view.

She didn't even glance into your shop, did she? She was too busy laughing at whatever Lucas was saying, wasn't she?

Had she dressed up for Lucas? Did she plan on taking him back to her place later and showing him those practical and weirdly sexy cotton panties she was always wearing? The jealousy was a fire-breathing dragon inside of him. It would be a cold fucking day in hell before Lucas saw Addie's goddamn panties. He headed for the front door as Nolan swirled the mop on the floor in front of the counter.

"Where you off to?" Nolan said.

"Getting some lunch." Preacher pushed open the shop door.

The heat settled over him like a warm, wet glove. He headed after Addison and Lucas, cursing inwardly at the crowds of tourists lingering on the sidewalks and walking about as fast as fucking turtles.

He gritted his teeth and tried not to break the guy in half who had stopped in the middle of the sidewalk to take a picture of the barrel of flowers in front of Grind My Beans. Jesus Christ, had he never seen fucking flowers before?

He pushed his way past the tourist. He could see the back of Lucas's head about a block ahead and, occasionally, a glimpse of Addison's dress through the crowd of people. He quickened his pace, sweat starting to collect at his temples.

By the time he reached the yarn shop, Lucas and Addison were already inside. Preacher reached for the door handle.

What the fuck are you doing? Have you lost your fucking mind? What kind of excuse will you give Addison for showing up in a yarn shop? And what if he is touching her? What if she's having a good time with him? You have no fucking right to be jealous, and if she wants to start dating Lucas, it isn't any of your business. Walk away before you make a complete fool of yourself.

He backed away from the yarn shop like it was on fire. What the fuck? He'd been about to storm into a goddamn yarn shop just because a woman he was casually fucking was in there with another guy.

His headache surged forward, a blinding and pulsing pain that threatened to become a full-blown migraine. Sick to his stomach at even the thought of getting a migraine, he turned and walked back toward Nan's. He'd grab a bite to eat and try not to think about Addison and what she may or may not do with that asshole gamer.

"Can I just say I'm happy I brought you with me?" Lucas touched a hank of yarn hanging on the wall. "My mom's been knitting since I was a kid, and I'm still a complete idiot about yarn."

Addison laughed. "Well, there is a lot to choose from. What does your mom -"

"Hi there!"

Addison hid her smile when Cora, one of the yarn shop employees, stopped beside Lucas. Honestly, she was surprised it had taken this long. Lucas was a good looking guy, and Cora was single. If Addison were single, she'd hit on Lucas, too.

You are single. Harrison and you are over, remember?

Right. She glanced at her bare ring finger. She wasn't engaged anymore. She was free to date anyone she wanted, and that included Lucas.

You know what's weird, Addie-baby? It wasn't Harrison you were thinking of, was it?

She needed to shut that thought down and quick, but it refused to be quieted. It was right, anyway. It hadn't been Harrison. It was Preacher's face that popped into her head. Which was ridiculous because they weren't dating, and she was free to go out with any guy she wanted. Just like Preacher could go out with any woman he wanted.

Jealousy licked at her stomach like a hungry tiger, and she swallowed hard. The thought of Preacher having sex with another woman shouldn't upset her so much. Hell, for all she knew, he could be banging some other chick at this very minute. They had never spoken about him not sleeping with other women while he was giving her lessons.

Yeah, well, if you'd looked in the damn tattoo shop when you were walking by earlier like I told you to do, you'd know if he was working or potentially out banging another chick at this very minute.

It'd taken every last ounce of willpower not to peer into Preacher's shop as she walked by with Lucas. She'd been proud of herself in the moment, but now she just wished she'd done it, if even to catch a glimpse of Preacher.

Yikes. You're moving into obsession territory. You know that, right?

Moving? Hell, she'd moved into obsession two days ago after he fucked her in the bathroom. Moved in, unpacked all her belongings, and was thinking of getting a cat.

"You're buying a gift for your mom? That's so sweet," Cora said. Her hand lingered on Lucas's arm, and he grinned at her.

"Us Willington boys know how to be sweet to our mamas."

Cora's hand dropped off his arm, the smile on her face faltering. "You're from Willington?"

Lucas glanced at Addison, his grin widening before he turned back to Cora. "I am. You're not going to judge me for that, are you? Because I live here now, and it's been my impression so far that the Falls girls are all about being sweet."

Cora laughed. "Sounds like you haven't met the right Falls girls yet."

"Maybe not," Lucas said.

Cora stared up at him for a few seconds. She was starting to look a little flustered. Addison didn't blame her. She was surprised that Lucas was even single. He was a good looking guy. He had a model's cheekbones, a swimmer's tight, lean body, and the little flecks of green in his hazel eyes were very pretty.

You prefer dark eyes.

She did. Dark eyes and dark hair and a muscled tattoo-covered body with rough, talented hands that knew exactly how to touch her, and a mouth and tongue that knew where to kiss and where to lick and…

The yarn shop had suddenly heated up about a thousand degrees. Maybe the air conditioner was broken. Addison fanned herself with her hand as a now familiar ache started in her lower belly. Maybe she'd text Preacher tonight. He did say anytime she needed him for, uh, stuff, she could call.

No, what he said was anytime you needed your tight pussy filled, he'd come over and give you his cock.

Her face flushed. Harrison never talked during sex, and he'd certainly never said anything dirty to her. Ever. She'd always thought she preferred that, always thought that having a man talking about her body so crudely would be a huge turn-off.

How incredibly wrong she'd been.

"So, about that yarn," Lucas said.

"Um, right." Cora cleared her throat. "What type of yarn were you looking for."

"I'm not sure. I brought the lovely Addison along to help me since she's an expert like yourself," Lucas said.

Cora smiled at Addison. "She's probably even more of an expert than me. Addison knows her stuff when it comes to yarn."

"Then I guess I have the two best ladies in Harmony Falls to help me with my gift." Lucas's flirty grin brought a flush of colour to Cora's cheeks.

"What type of stuff does your mom usually knit?" Addison said.

"She used to do a lot of baby clothes and smaller stuff, but now she does mostly blankets for a few of the churches in town who hand them out to people in need in the community." Lucas's cheerful face darkened a smidge. "Mom's got arthritis in her hands. It's harder for her to knit now. She used to do intricate looking things, but now she can only do the easy stuff. It's gentler on her hands."

"Okay," Cora said. "Well, if that's the case, she probably uses bigger needles and a bulkier yarn. Blankets knit up faster with the bigger needles and bulkier yarn. It's over here."

Addison trailed after Cora and Lucas to the back of the store to the bulky yarn section. She stopped a few feet away, her fingers trailing lightly over a basket full of angora yarn and watched as Cora and Lucas perused the yarn wall.

"What's her favourite colour?" Cora asked. She stood a little closer than necessary to Lucas, and Addison hid her grin when Cora let her hand rest on Lucas's arm and thrust her small chest out just the tiniest bit. She was working the flirting hard, and Addison secretly cheered her on. Cora was a lovely woman, and her fun and flirty nature would perfectly fit Lucas's personality.

"Hey, Addison."

Addison smiled at Emma when she joined her. Emma wore a pair of dark green capris and a t-shirt with an image of two large balls of yarn and the phrase, 'I like big balls' across her ample chest.

"How are you, Emma?"

"Good, thanks." Emma eyed Lucas's ass before lowering her voice. "Who's that tall drink of water?"

"Lucas Wright. He just moved here from New Cassel, but he's originally from Willington. He works for that wealthy video game guy. I can't remember his name. The one who's opening up a company here in the Falls."

Emma's eyes widened. "Isaac Stark? He works for Isaac Stark of Stark Entertainment?"

"Yes. Why do you look like that?" Addison said.

Emma's eyes were wide, and a flush of excitement had darkened the birthmark on her face. "I am seriously addicted to his Shadow Series games. They're freaking amazing."

"You play video games?" Addison said.

"I do. I've loved them since I was a kid," Emma said. Her fingers traced the birthmark on her neck. "I knew Stark was starting an offshoot of his company here but didn't realize it was so soon."

"Well, technically, it doesn't start until September first, I think," Addison said. "Lucas moved here early because he has a month's worth of holidays to take."

Emma was staring at Lucas's ass again, and Addison nudged her. "He's single."

"Good for him." Emma's fingers moved from her neck to wander over the birthmark on her face. "From the looks of it, if Cora has her way, he won't be single for long."

"Not if you get in there and impress him with your yarn knowledge. He's looking for a gift for his mom," Addison said.

Emma rolled her eyes. "Girl, I saw his face when you guys came into the store. A man as pretty as he is would never be interested in someone who looks like me."

Before Addison could argue, Lucas and Cora turned around. Lucas smiled at Emma. "Hi there."

"Lucas, this is Emma Richardson. She owns Twisted Stitches. Emma, this is Lucas Wright. He just moved here from New Cassel," Addison said.

"Nice to meet you," Lucas said. His gaze fell to Emma's chest before he glanced at her face again.

Addison realized she desperately wanted Lucas to flirt with Emma like he flirted with every other woman he met. She didn't know Emma all that well, but she knew life wasn't easy for her.

Please, Lucas. Please flirt with her.

He didn't disappoint.

With the same flirty smile he'd given Cora, Lucas said, "I like your shirt, Emma."

"Thanks," Emma said.

He held up the two large balls of yarn he was holding. "I happen to have a couple of huge balls myself."

"Lucky you," Emma said in a brisk and almost cold tone that immediately deflated Addison's hopes that she and Lucas might hit it off.

"Emma?" A silver-haired woman wearing a caftan dress and fanning herself with a pattern book walked out of an aisle. "Do you still have time to look at that pattern I brought?"

"Sure," Emma said. "Nice to meet you, Lucas. Bye, Addison."

"Bye, Emma."

"She seems nice," Lucas said after Emma had walked away.

Cora was frowning slightly. "She's not usually like that. She must be having a bad day. Sorry, Lucas."

"Nothing to apologize for," Lucas said. "Addison, what do you think of this yarn?"

"It's beautiful," she said.

"I think Cora's helped me pick out the perfect yarn." Lucas winked at Cora, who blushed and handed him another four balls of yarn before grabbing four more.

"This should be enough to do a nice big blanket," she said. "Come to the front, and I'll ring you through."

Addison waited patiently as Lucas paid for his yarn. As they left the store, she said, "Did I see Cora writing her number on the back of your receipt?"

"Maybe," Lucas said with a lazy smile.

Addison laughed. "Cora's a lovely woman."

"She does seem sweet," Lucas said. "So, what are your plans for the rest of the afternoon?"

"Not much. I thought about going for a hike at the Falls, but it's way too frickin' hot," Addison said. "I'll probably just go home and knit and watch some Netflix."

She smiled up at him as they walked down the street. "Being the only schoolteacher in your group of friends means you spend a lot of time alone during the summer."

"I bet," Lucas said. "What grade do you teach again?"

"First grade," she said. "I love it. It's such a great age for kids, you know?"

"I haven't been around kids that much, to be honest," Lucas said. "Thanks again for going to the yarn shop with me, Addison. I appreciate it."

"Any time," she said. "I'll use any excuse to go to the yarn shop."

He laughed, and she smiled up at him again. "You know what? I have some cute wrapping paper at home with yarn and knitting needles printed on it. You should wrap your mom's gift in it. She'd love it."

"Hey, if you don't mind sharing, I'd love to snag some from you," Lucas said. "Mom's birthday isn't for another week and a half, but I'll pop by your place some time next week or so if that's okay?"

"Of course," Addison said. "Just text me when a day works for you."

They were approaching Preacher's tattoo shop, and she decided to casually glance in the window this time. If Preacher were near the window and happened to notice her, she would casually wave at him before casually walking on.

It would be all very... casual.

"Oh, hey," Lucas said. "Let's go into the Crimson Door for a minute."

"What?' She gave him a startled look and slowed to a stop. "You want to go into Preacher's shop?"

"You don't?" he said.

"Oh, um, well..."

"C'mon," he coaxed. "Just for a few minutes. I've been thinking about getting another tattoo."

"Sure, okay," she said. The butterflies bouncing around in panicked circles in her stomach, Addison followed Lucas into the shop.

She glanced at the three tattoo stations. Nolan was setting up some equipment at one, and Nix was tattooing a nervous looking man at the second one. The third one was empty. She glanced at the piercing room. The door was open, and unless

Preacher was hiding behind the door, he wasn't in that room either.

Disappointment rolled through her, but she masked it with a bright smile when Lucas glanced at her. "What kind of tattoo are you thinking of getting?" she said.

Nolan ambled over, glancing at her. "Hey, Addison, right?"

"Yes," she said. "Hi again."

"Hey. How's the tattoo?"

"It's good."

"You have a tattoo?" Lucas was obviously surprised.

"Yes. I just got it last week," Addie said as the bell on the door jingled behind them.

"Cool. Can I see it?" Lucas said.

"No."

The butterflies went on a real bender when they heard Preacher's deep voice behind them. She turned, trying to ignore the way her pussy went damp when she saw him. He held a bag from Nan's in one hand, and he looked a little tired and a lot pissed off. "Her ink is in a spot you don't get to fucking see."

WALKING INTO HIS SHOP TO SEE ADDISON STANDING THERE made the tension in his neck and shoulders dissipate almost instantly. Hearing Lucas ask to see her tattoo brought it back in full force.

He hadn't meant to say what he said, but even just the thought of Lucas seeing a glimpse of Addison's smooth back was driving him crazy. He'd never been the jealous type, and he had no goddamn idea how to process it. But from the look Addison gave him, his current method wasn't working.

"If I want to show Lucas my tattoo, I will," she said.

He brushed past them and set the bag from Nan's on the drawing table. He turned to see Lucas raising an eyebrow at Addie.

"Where exactly did you get inked, Addie?"

She rolled her eyes. "On my back. My upper back." She glanced at Preacher with a *you're being ridiculous* look that pissed him off even more.

"Can I help you with something?" Preacher said to Lucas.

"I was thinking about getting another tattoo. Since Addison and I were in the area, I thought I'd pop in and see some of your work," Lucas said. He glanced at Addison and then back to Preacher with an *I'm being your wingman* look that made Preacher grit his teeth.

"I'm fully booked until October," he said. "You should talk to Nix." He pointed at Nix, who was wiping down the tattoo he'd just finished.

Nix glanced up and nodded to Lucas. "Hey. Give me a few minutes, and we can chat."

"He can take a look at my ink," the dweeby tourist said. He was nearly vibrating with excitement. "Both of you can."

Before Nix could stop him, he'd jumped up and crossed the shop to Lucas and Addison. He stuck his arm out with a proud grin. "Bethany" was written across his forearm, and Lucas said, "That looks good."

"Thank you." The tourist turned to Addison. "It's my girl's name. I got it done as a surprise for her."

"I'm sure she'll love it," Addison said with a warm smile.

Great. Now Preacher was fucking jealous of a skinny little accountant.

"I hope so." He returned to Nix's station and sat down.

Nix pointed to some binders sitting on the edge of the

glass coffee table. "That's some of my art if you want to flip through it while I finish."

"Sure." Lucas grabbed a binder and started looking through it.

Preacher stood in front of Addie. "Hey."

"Hello."

She wasn't outright glaring at him, but the usual warmth in her eyes wasn't there, and it was fucking killing him. "You need me to look at your tattoo?"

"What? Uh, no, it's good," she said. "I'm only here because Lucas wanted to stop in."

"What about your piercing? Does it need to be looked at?" His gaze dropped to her perfect tits, a part of him soothed by the soft blush that immediately coloured her cheeks.

"No, it's fine."

"You sure about that?" He let his voice drop an octave. "Maybe I should have a quick look at it to check for infection."

She glanced around the shop before saying quietly, "You just saw it last night."

"I was distracted by your pretty pussy."

Her soft blush intensified, and she bit her bottom lip. "Don't be rude."

"I'm being honest, not rude," he said. "Besides, it's not my fault you have such a sweet tasting pussy."

"Behave," she said under her breath as Nix and the tourist walked to the counter.

"Thanks, man. I love it. I can't wait for my girl to see it." The tourist paid for his tattoo and left the shop, grinning from ear to ear.

Lucas joined them. "There goes a man who's getting lucky tonight."

Preacher snorted, and Lucas grinned at him. "What? Girls eat up that romantic stuff. Right, Addison?"

"It is kind of romantic," Addie said.

"No, it's stupid," Preacher said. "Nolan, what's the shop's number one tattoo cover-up request?"

Nolan looked up from his station. "Names. Fucking names. Unless it's your mama, never get a name tattooed on you. I don't care if you think you're gonna love that girl for fucking ever. Don't get her name tattooed on your body."

Preacher glanced at Lucas. "Only an idiot gets his woman's name tattooed on his body. It's not romantic. It's a mistake."

"Noted," Lucas said with another of his irritating grins. "Nix, you ready to talk?"

"Sure," Nix said.

"I'm going to go," Addison said.

"I can give you a ride home," Lucas said. "Connor mentioned you didn't have a car."

Before Preacher could spit out his immediate 'not a fucking chance', Addison said, "That's all right. I'll take the bus. The next one is in, like, two minutes."

"You sure?" Lucas said. "I can book an appointment to chat to Nix tomorrow." He glanced at Nix, who nodded.

"I'm sure," Addison said. "I'll talk to you later. Bye, everyone."

Without looking at Preacher, she walked out of the shop.

"Give me a few minutes to clean up my station, and then we'll chat," Nix said.

He walked away, and Lucas stared at Preacher. "Dude, I was trying to help you here. Gave you the opportunity to see her, and you act like you're going to rip everyone's head off, including hers. If you want a chance with her, you might want to act happy to see her, for God's sake."

"I don't need your fucking help with dating," Preacher said.

Lucas laughed and clapped him on the back. "Buddy, if this is you trying to make a good impression with the lady you like, then you do. You really do."

CHAPTER 19

"How long is your supper break?" Gideon slid into the booth at Nan's, adjusting his vest and turning down the radio on his belt.

"I'm done for the day," Preacher said.

"It's only five."

"My client was scheduled for four hours. Asshole tapped out after two," Preacher said.

"Hey, Sheriff." Georgia, a curvy redhead with a warm smile and a penchant for cursing that outmatched Preacher's, stopped at their booth. She wore a Nan's Diner t-shirt with a name tag just above her left breast and an apron around her waist, and she held a notepad in her left hand.

A slender blonde woman wearing an identical t-shirt and apron stood beside her, holding a tray with a beer. She set the beer in front of Preacher, who nodded in thanks.

"Hi, Georgia. Nice to see you," Gideon said.

"You too. This is Wren. She's the new server Nan hired."

Gideon shook Wren's hand. "Nice to meet you."

"You as well." Wren was soft-spoken and pretty, but Preacher barely gave her a second look. His obsession with

Addison meant that he compared every woman in Harmony Falls to her, and every single one failed to do a thing for him.

"Are you ready to order?" Georgia asked.

"Sure." Gideon placed his order, and Preacher ordered a steak sandwich and salad. He needed to eat something. After Addison left the shop, his appetite had disappeared, and he'd put the lunch he'd bought in the fridge. Despite not eating all day, he still wasn't hungry, but he'd choke down the food. The headache was lurking in the background, and not eating was a sure way to turn it into a goddamn migraine.

"You ever get tired of eating at Nan's?" Gideon said.

Wren was already returning with Gideon's iced tea, and she refilled Preacher's water glass before leaving.

"No," Preacher said. "The food's good here."

"The food is amazing," Gideon said. "But it's nice to have a home-cooked meal every once in a while."

"I go to your place when I want a home-cooked meal."

"A slab of meat thrown on the grill and some potato salad from the grocery store isn't exactly a home-cooked meal," Gideon said.

"Your cooking has improved since Grace moved in with you," Preacher said.

Gideon laughed. "It's all her. She's an amazing cook."

Preacher sipped his beer, waiting to see if his churning stomach would protest. It did, and with a grimace, he set the bottle down.

"What's going on with you?" Gideon said.

"I fucked up."

"How?"

"With Addison. I hurt her feelings."

Gideon waited patiently. There was no judgment on his face, and Preacher felt another rush of love and gratitude toward his best friend.

"We're still sleeping together," he said.

Surprise crossed Gideon's face. "Grace didn't mention it to me."

"She doesn't know. At least, I don't think she does. Addison said she wouldn't tell Grace or Kira."

"You're keeping it a secret," Gideon said.

"I didn't ask her to keep it a secret," Preacher said. "She wants it to be a secret."

Anger furrowed Gideon's forehead. "Why? If she's embarrassed to be seen with you, then she doesn't deserve to be with you, Preacher. Don't sell yourself short just because you think you don't deserve someone like Addison Moore. She's not better than you no matter what you fucking think and -"

"Christ, calm down," Preacher said. "It has nothing to do with that." His tone was exasperated, but fuck if he didn't appreciate how Gideon always had his back.

"Then why the secret?"

"Because it's just fucking. It doesn't mean anything."

"Still doesn't mean it has to be a secret. People have casual relationships all the time," Gideon said.

"Yeah, I know."

"What aren't you telling me?" Gideon leaned forward.

"Sometimes I hate that you're a fucking cop," Preacher said. "You can't leave shit alone."

"True," Gideon said with a grin. "So, you might as well tell me what I want to know."

Preacher glanced around the diner. It was crowded, and the hum of multiple conversations would mask their conversation if he kept his voice low. "She doesn't want people knowing because you know as well as I do that she's usually not the type of girl to have casual sex, and also because she asked me to give her lessons on fucking, and she's embarrassed about it."

"Oh." Gideon took a sip of iced tea, his features carefully schooled. "Okay."

"That prick of an ex-fiancé has her convinced that she sucks in bed. He broke off the engagement because he said she was terrible in bed."

"You're kidding me?"

"I'm not. He was fucking gaslighting her. Used it as an excuse for why he cheated on her. She's not terrible in bed. A little unsure maybe and shy, but the way she responds when I…"

He sat back, clearing his throat. "The motherfucker never went down on her."

Preacher almost laughed at the look of astonishment on Gideon's face.

"Seriously?"

"Dead fucking serious," Preacher said. "The asshole was perfectly fine with letting her go down on him but never once returned the favour, and they were together for how fucking long?"

"Since they were teenagers," Gideon said. "Jesus, I always thought Harrison was a self-involved blowhard and that Addie could do better. This confirms that."

"Anyway, she asked me for lessons once a week for a month, and I said yes. Nothing serious. Just fucking. Only…"

"Only what?" Gideon said.

Wren and Georgia arrived with their food, and Preacher waited until they left before saying, "Only I'm fucking jealous."

Gideon grinned at him. "It doesn't sound like Harrison was doing it for Addie in the bedroom, so you probably don't have to be jealous of him, pookie. Unless you're not going down on her either?"

"Fuck off," Preacher said before shoving a piece of steak in his mouth. This was his favourite meal at Nan's, and while it looked and smelled as delicious as it always did, it tasted like sawdust in his mouth.

Gideon laughed. "What are you jealous about?"

"She was hanging out with that Lucas guy today, helping him pick out a gift for his mother at the yarn shop down the street. They came into the shop after, and I was jealous even though Lucas told me he wasn't interested in her. But I was an asshole to Addison anyway and hurt her feelings."

He waited for Gideon to tease him, and when he didn't say anything, Preacher looked up from his food. The humour in Gideon's face had disappeared, and he stared solemnly at him.

"What?" Preacher said.

"Has Addison indicated that she wants this to be more than just lessons?" Gideon said.

"Of course she fucking hasn't," Preacher said. "Why would she? A woman like her doesn't want a relationship with someone like me."

Gideon snorted angrily. "How many times do I have to tell you that you're -"

"Yeah, yeah," Preacher said. "I know. I'm a good guy. A good guy who went to prison for four years, a good guy who almost made the same mistake a few years later, a good guy who needed his best friend to co-sign a loan for him so he could get his own fucking shop. Look, I appreciate that you always have my back, man, you know I do, but blowing this bullshit up my ass about how I'm just as good as someone like Addison Moore isn't what I need to hear."

"Too fucking bad," Gideon said. "I'll keep saying it until you believe it."

"I just need some advice on how to chill the fuck out around her."

Gideon ate some pasta. "You seriously want me to tell you how to stop being jealous?"

"Yeah." Preacher pushed at the bread under his steak before stabbing some lettuce from his salad and shoving it into his mouth.

"Dude, I love you, but the amount of denial you're swimming in is neck fucking deep. You like Addison, and you want to be her man. The jealousy isn't going to stop."

"No, I fucking don't," Preacher said.

Gideon rolled his eyes. "You can act as stupid about this as you want, but you know as well as I do that it's why you're so jealous."

Gideon was right, but Preacher wasn't giving him the satisfaction of agreeing. He hadn't talked to Gideon about this because he wanted advice on not being jealous. He'd talked to him about it because the way Addison had looked at him this afternoon was eating him up inside. What if she was so pissed that she never wanted to fuck him again?"

The little bit of appetite he had left immediately departed to parts unknown, and he pushed away his steak and salad. "She's pissed at me because of how I acted this afternoon."

"What exactly did you do?"

"Lucas asked to see her tattoo, and I told him no."

Gideon winced. "Yeah, telling a woman what she can and can't do with her own body is not a great idea, buddy."

"I know," he said. "It just fucking shot out of my goddamn mouth before I could stop it. I lose my fucking mind when I'm around her now."

"I can tell you how to stop being jealous around her,"

Gideon said. "End this thing you have going on with her. Stop giving her lessons, stop being with her. I know you like her, but now's the time to end it. Because trust me, the longer this goes on, the harder it'll be when it's finished."

Preacher didn't reply, and Gideon leaned closer. "Addison is a sweet girl, and I've no doubt she doesn't mean to hurt you, but she's also not over Harrison yet. She can't be. You don't get over the person you loved for over a decade in just a few months. And you deserve better than being the rebound guy. Okay?"

"Yeah," Preacher said.

"You're not going to stop, are you?" Gideon said.

He shrugged. "I told her I'd give her lessons for a month. That isn't that long."

"Preacher -"

"Look, you're right. She isn't over her dick ex-fiancé, and when she is over him, I'm not the man she's going to be looking at. I just needed to hear someone else say it."

"That isn't what I said," Gideon said.

"But it's the truth," Preacher said. "I'll give her the month I promised, and that'll be it for us. And if she wants to start dating that fucking gamer dude or some other guy before the month is up, more power to her."

"So, your little jealousy problem is finished. Just like that, huh?" Gideon said.

"Just like that," Preacher said.

JUST LIKE THAT, HIS FUCKING ASS.

He walked toward Addison's building. His stomach was still churning, and the sip of beer, bite of steak, and mouthful of salad were all bobbing around in his stomach acid and having a grand fucking time doing it.

He stared at the panel above the door, at the neatly typed 'Moore, A' next to number 427.

Go home, Simon.

Yeah, he would. This was a mistake. Going home and getting some sleep before the niggling headache became a migraine was exactly what he needed to do.

He reached out and pushed Addison's apartment button. His hands were sweating, and he wiped them on his jeans. It was almost six and still hot and muggy as shit. More sweat beaded up on his temples when Addison's voice came out of the speaker.

"Hello?"

"Hey, it's me."

When she didn't reply, he said, "It's Preacher," and then winced at how fucking stupid he was.

"What do you want?" she said.

"Can I come up?"

The pause was excruciatingly long. He was just about to buzz her apartment door again when the front door buzzed. He yanked it open before she could change her mind and took the stairs to the fourth floor.

He knocked on her door, and she immediately opened it and glared at him. He took one look at her and forgot to goddamn breathe.

Fuck.

Double fuck.

She wore the same pajama bottoms from last night and a thin white tank top without – fuck, he was getting a semi– a bra. He stared at her perfect nipples pressed against the thin fabric and could see the outline of the barbell in the right one. She backed up, and he stepped into her apartment, closing the door behind him.

She crossed her arms over her tits, and he mourned the loss of those perfect nipples. "What do you want?"

He cleared his throat. "It, uh, smells good in here."

It did smell good. So good that he felt a thread of hunger for the first time all day.

"I'm cooking chili in the slow cooker. Is that why you're here? To tell me that my place smells good?"

"No," he said.

Her look was frosty enough to make him lose his semi. Before he could say anything, she said, "I'm mad at you."

"I know."

"You had no right to say what you did to Lucas. It's my body, and if I want to show him my damn tattoo, I will. You don't get a say in it, Preacher."

"You're right. I apologize."

"And if you think – wait, what?"

"I'm sorry," he said.

She blinked at him, her stiff body softening as she slumped against the wall. "Did you just say you were sorry?"

"Yes," he said. "I fucked up. It won't happen again."

He didn't understand why she looked so shocked at his apology until she said, "I'm not used to a guy apologizing. Harrison always got so pissy if I pointed out something he did that was wrong."

"I'm not him," he said.

"Trust me, I realize that," she said.

There were a few seconds of awkward silence, and then she said, "Thank you for apologizing. I accept."

He grinned at how formal and weird she was making it. "You sure this is enough? Maybe I need to do something else to make up for it."

She licked her lips, her gaze dropping to the front of his crotch. "Uh, what did you have in mind?"

He picked her up, loving the little squeak of surprise she made and the way her arms wrapped around his neck. "Pussy eating. That work for you, Miss Moore?"

"Yes, Mr. Preacher." Her prim little schoolteacher voice made him grin. "Pussy eating works very well for me."

CHAPTER 20

Addison decided if pussy eating was Preacher's way of apologizing, he could try to dictate who looked at her tattoo every damn day.

She moaned and clutched at his head, little shockwaves of pleasure radiating up and down her spine as he licked a slow path over her clit. He'd had his face between her legs for almost twenty minutes now, and she arched her hips up, trying to urge him to give her exactly what she wanted, what she needed.

"Simon, please," she moaned when he stopped licking her clit and kissed her inner thigh. "Please, I'm so close."

"I know, baby." He stared up at her. "You need to come, don't you?"

"Yes." She pulled his hair before trying to press his face back against her throbbing pussy. "I needed to come like five minutes ago."

He laughed, and she cried out when he licked her clit. Her stomach tightened, and she dug her feet into the bed, her hips rising and falling against the pressure of Preacher's mouth. She was so close, so very close to…

"No!" She pouted at him when he lifted his head again. "Simon, stop teasing!"

"I don't want you going out with another guy while I'm in your bed, Sunshine."

She tried to focus past the need. "What?"

He licked her clit slowly and deliberately. "As long as I'm giving you lessons on fucking, no other guy gets to see your tits, eat your sweet pussy, or fuck it."

"Please," she whined. "I need to come."

He teased her clit with the tip of his tongue for a few seconds before lifting his head. "Look at me, Sunshine."

She forced her eyelids up and stared at him, her hands moving restlessly through his dark hair. "Simon, please."

"Say it, Sunshine. I'm the only guy who fucks your pussy. Say it, and then I'll let you come."

Her pussy aching, she nodded. "Yeah, okay, sure."

He kissed the top of her pussy. "Say it, baby."

"You're the only guy who fucks my pussy," she said. "Just you. Okay?"

"That's my good girl," he said with a wicked little grin. "You ready to come on my face, baby?"

"I was ready five minutes ago!" She gave his hair a hard tug and glared at him as he laughed.

She forgot her anger with him when he wrapped his lips around her swollen clit and sucked hard. His thick finger pushed inside of her, and she immediately came against his mouth, her hips bucking and her pussy squeezing around his finger.

When she was a limp noodle against the bed, Preacher sat up and wiped his mouth off on the sheet before squeezing her thigh. "Turn over, Sunshine."

She rolled to her stomach, jerking when Preacher nipped at her ass cheek before cupping her hips. He pulled her onto her hands and knees, and she looked over her shoulder at him with sudden apprehension.

Embarrassed by the admission, she said, "I've never, um, had sex this way before. I mean, there was that night at the tattoo shop with you, but this isn't exactly the same position, right? Well, I guess it's close to the same position, so I shouldn't be nervous. You know what? I'm fine. It's good, go ahead and -"

"Shh, Sunshine." He nestled his big body between her legs, pushing on her thighs until she parted them. "I'll go slow."

She was tense. She didn't want to be, but she couldn't help it.

He must have sensed it because he smoothed his hand over her ass. "Relax, Sunshine. I won't hurt you."

"I know," she said.

He rubbed the head of his dick over her sensitive clit, and she gasped, her hands digging into the sheets. He squeezed her hip, and when he pressed the head of his dick against her opening, she automatically spread her legs farther apart.

"Good, baby," he said. "Fuck, you're so gorgeous like this. I love watching your tight pussy swallow my dick."

She moaned, more turned on by his words than she wanted to admit. As he slowly pushed into her, she pushed back eagerly, suddenly wanting all of him, *needing* all of him.

He rubbed her lower back, his other hand holding her hip and keeping her still. "Patience, Sunshine."

"It doesn't hurt," she said. "Move faster."

His low chuckle made her flush with pleasure. "My girl is greedy for my dick, isn't she?"

"Maybe," she said.

He laughed again and made one final push, his pelvis

resting against her ass, his cock seated completely inside of her. "Better?"

She moaned in reply. God, she would never get tired of how it felt to have Preacher inside her.

Her hair hung in her face, and she was weirdly grateful when Preacher gathered her hair in one big fist. He tugged, and she lifted her head, arching her back when he pressed down just above her ass. He fucked her slowly at first, with long deep strokes that made her entire body shiver with anticipation.

"Good, baby?" His voice was low and filled with desire. Her pussy squeezed around him in response, and he groaned, a thick guttural sound that skyrocketed her arousal.

"So good," she breathed. "I want…"

She trailed off, suddenly feeling shy and uncertain.

Preacher's hand tightened in her hair and he leaned over and kissed between her shoulder blades. "Tell me what you want."

"Harder," she said, her face going red. "I want it harder."

He tugged on her hair until her face pointed toward him. He kissed her hard on the mouth, their tongues tasting and teasing until she was gasping and grinding her ass against him. He released her mouth and licked her bottom lip. "Whatever you want, Sunshine."

Both hands cupped her hips, and she cried out when he fucked her with hard, rough strokes. She gripped the sheets, taking every inch of his cock, enjoying the way he pounded into her, loving the sound of his low moans and gasps as he found pleasure in her body. He shifted her slightly, and on the next stroke, the head of his dick brushed across her g-spot.

She froze, her back arched and her head thrown back. "Oh my God!"

He thrust again, his dick pressing against that beautiful,

wonderful, amazing spot, and she cried his name before rocking back to meet each of his strokes. Her nerve endings on fire, she buried her face into her pillow and screamed when she climaxed with a jolting, sizzling burst of pure pleasure. It seemed to go on forever, infusing every molecule of her body with molten hot bliss.

She heard Preacher's hoarse shout, took the force of his final thrust that nearly flattened her onto the bed, and felt the hot warmth flooding her pussy when he spilled his seed into her. Her legs too weak to hold her weight, she collapsed on her face. Preacher pulled out, and his heavy weight landed beside her on the bed. She could hear him panting harshly. It matched the frantic pace of her breathing.

She was lying too close to him and needed to give him his space. She wiggled away, and Preacher's arm clamped around her waist, pulling her back. He turned her onto her side and – holy crap – spooned her.

She had no idea why he was cuddling, but she would enjoy it while it lasted. She relaxed against him and caught her breath as he cupped her breast and rested his face in the crook of her neck.

Ten minutes later, she was feeling pleasantly sleepy when Preacher lifted his head. "You okay?"

"Hmm," she said. It was so nice to lie against Preacher's hard body, even if the room was starting to be a little stuffy. She wanted to turn the ceiling fan on, but that would mean getting up. She'd much rather be too warm snuggling with Preacher than move.

Preacher kissed the back of her neck and squeezed her breast before he ran his fingers up and down her arm. Her eyes drifted shut. When Preacher was finished with her, when he started to find her as boring as Harrison did in bed, this right here would be one of her favourite memories. Being cuddled by Preacher was almost as good as being fucked by Preacher.

Almost.

He kissed the back of her shoulder, just above her tattoo, and she sighed with contentment. She could stay like this forever. Forever and –

"Addison, don't fall asleep."

She jerked awake, the sweet little fantasy she had of waking up in Preacher's arms destroyed in a heartbeat. Feeling stupid, she pulled away from him and slid across the bed. She sat up and grabbed her robe, belting it securely around her waist.

"Sorry," she said. "I didn't mean to do that."

She stared at the wall as Preacher got out of bed. Forcing a smile on her face, she turned around. "That was fun. Thank you. Do you, um, want to get together on the weekend for another lesson?"

She was proud of herself for making the suggestion. It was a massive step for her.

"Yeah, sure." Preacher stood naked by the bed, looking every bit like the tattooed god he was. She wished he'd get dressed before she did something stupid like try to lure him back into her bed.

"Okay, well…"

God, why wasn't he getting dressed already?

"You mind if I have a quick shower?" he said.

"Oh, uh, no. Go right ahead. The bathroom is just down the hall. There are fresh towels in the linen closet next to the bathroom."

"Great. Thanks." He walked out of her bedroom, still naked as a damn jaybird.

She stared at his clothes piled on the floor before studying her reflection in the mirror on the far wall. "Okay, this is kind of weird, right?"

Her reflection nodded, and, not entirely sure what she was supposed to do now, Addison pulled on some leggings and a t-shirt and left the bedroom.

FIFTEEN MINUTES LATER, WHEN A FRESHLY SHOWERED AND dressed Preacher joined her in the living room, she was knitting on the couch. She was starving, but it seemed rude to start eating while Preacher was in the shower.

She smiled tentatively at him as she set her knitting on the couch and stood. "Thank you again for, um…"

"Eating your pussy?" He grinned at her, and she could feel the stupid blush rising in her cheeks.

"I was going to say for apologizing, but that part was nice too."

"Sunshine, if it was just nice, then maybe I should be trying a little harder."

Still blushing, she said, "It was amazing."

His gaze dropped to her abdomen when her stomach growled. She pressed her hands against her stomach. "I haven't eaten dinner yet."

"It smells really good," he said.

They stood in awkward silence, and he scratched at his chest before staring at her.

"Would you like to stay and eat?" she said. "There's plenty."

"Sure." He followed her into the narrow galley kitchen, leaning against the wall and watching as she grabbed two bowls from the cupboard. "Can I help?"

She shook her head. "It's ready to go. What would you like to drink? I have water, juice, and wine."

"Water is fine."

She poured them two glasses of water, acutely aware of Preacher's big body making her small kitchen feel even tinier.

"You've got a nice place," he said.

"Thanks. It's small, just a one bedroom and den, but I like it." She lifted the lid off the slow cooker and stirred the chili. "So, uh, this is a vegetarian chili."

"You a vegetarian?"

"No, but my mom and dad are vegan. I usually eat a meatless meal once or twice a week," she said.

She spooned some chili into the two bowls and grabbed napkins and cutlery. "I don't have a kitchen table, but we can sit on the couch, and I'll set up TV trays."

She used to have a kitchen table. A small but perfectly lovely one that she'd sold because she was marrying Harrison and moving in with him, and they didn't need two kitchen tables.

"I can just hold the bowl," he said.

He took his food, cutlery, and water glass and followed her to the living room. Feeling supremely awkward, Addison set her glass of water on the coffee table and sat cross-legged on the couch as Preacher sat beside her.

He ate a few bites of the chili. "Fuck, this is good."

She flushed with pleasure. "Thanks. It's my mom's recipe, but I tweaked it a bit."

They ate silently for a few moments, and she laughed when their stomachs growled in unison. "I guess we're both hungry."

"Starving," he said. "Didn't eat all day."

"Were you busy at the shop?"

He was already scraping the last of the chili from his bowl. "Not bad. My last client tapped out after only a few hours, so I finished early."

She glanced at the clock. It was almost seven-thirty. She knew the shop was open until seven, which was why she'd been so surprised when Preacher had shown up just before six.

"Do you mind if I get some more?"

"Help yourself."

He left and returned with another heaping bowl. He settled beside her on the couch, and they ate silently. When they finished, he took both their bowls to the kitchen. She could hear him rinsing them in the sink, and she smiled when he said, "Is the dishwasher clean or dirty?"

"Dirty," she said. Holy crap, domestic Preacher was adorable.

He returned to the living room, and she smiled at him. "Thank you."

"Thanks for the food. It was really good."

"You're welcome."

He glanced at the door as a familiar awkward silence descended. She thought about inviting him to watch TV with her before dismissing the idea immediately. Preacher had stayed because he was hungry, that's all. The way he kept glancing at the door made it more than obvious he was ready to leave.

So, why isn't he?

She wasn't sure. He'd been acting weird all night. First, the apology, then the oddness in the bedroom when he wouldn't let her come until she said she wouldn't date anyone else, the spooning after sex, sticking around to eat dinner with her, and now this awkward moment.

Maybe he thought it was rude to eat and leave. Trying to help him out, she said, "Well, thank you again for -"

"You heard about that new show on Netflix. The one with the detective?" Preacher said.

"Yes."

"It's supposed to be pretty good. You watch it yet?"

"No, not yet," she said. "I was going to start it tonight."

He stared at her, and she cleared her throat. "Would you like to watch a couple of episodes with me?"

He shrugged. "Sure."

He sat down beside her, and she turned on the television and used the remote to switch to Netflix. She was a little embarrassed by how much she enjoyed the feel of Preacher's hard thigh against her knee.

As she waited for Netflix to load, by habit, she picked up her knitting bag and pulled out the scarf she was working on. Preacher glanced at her, and she paused with her knitting needles in her hand.

"Um, do you mind if I knit while we watch the show?"

"Why would I?" he said.

"The needles make a clicking sound. Harrison said it was distracting when we watched TV."

He just shrugged. "I don't care. Do your little grandma knitting."

She poked him in the thigh. "Knitting is cool now."

"Is it, though?" he said.

"No," she said.

He laughed, and heat pooled in her belly. God, she loved Preacher's laugh.

"What are you making?" he said.

"A scarf for Kira for Christmas," she said. "I like giving my friends homemade gifts."

"You still making the bracelets?" His gaze dropped to the six colourful bracelets she had around her wrist.

"No, not really. That was kind of a phase I was going through," she said.

"Oh. I saw you give Lucas a couple," he said.

"I have a bunch left over." She reached into her knitting bag and pulled out the handful that were in the bottom of it. "I made a lot while I was stressing about wedding stuff. I have so many of them floating around now. I try to tie bracelets around friends' wrists when they're not looking."

He laughed again. "Yeah, I noticed that most of your friends have more than one."

She studied the single bracelet around his wrist. "Would you, um, like another one?"

"Doesn't matter. If you have extra you're trying to get rid of, yeah, sure, I'll wear another one."

She spread the bracelets out on her leg. "Pick whichever one you want."

He studied them before picking up a grey and green one and a black and white one. "Which one do you like better?"

"You can have both," she said.

She tied them around his wrist, just above the blue one. He picked up a third one. "You care if I take this one, too?"

"Go ahead." She knew the surprise was showing on her face. Preacher had picked out a pink one.

"Guys wear pink now, you know," he said with a cute little grin.

She laughed. "I know. I just didn't know *you* wore pink."

"All the time, Sunshine," he said. "I have a dozen pink shirts."

"Of course you do." She tied the bracelet around his wrist with the others. The pink one matched one of the bracelets around her wrist, giving her a stupid thrill.

This isn't middle school, Addie. Wearing a matching bracelet with Preacher doesn't make you boyfriend and girlfriend.

Oh my God, she acted like a twelve-year-old with her first crush. If Preacher knew what she was thinking, she'd be mortified.

"Thanks," Preacher said.

"You're welcome." She stuffed the rest of the bracelets back into her knitting bag, found the show and hit play before picking up her needles again. She didn't know why Preacher was hanging out with her, but she had to admit it was nice not to spend another evening alone.

CHAPTER 21

"Did you want to watch another episode?" Addison said.

Preacher glanced at the clock. It was almost ten, and while he wasn't the least bit tired, he couldn't sit next to Addison for another episode without doing something dumb like resting his hand on her leg or pulling her into his lap or maybe fucking her on the couch.

"It's getting late," he said.

"Right, of course," she said. "Sorry, I become a bit of a night owl during the summer, but I forget that other people have to get up for work."

He shrugged. "Shop doesn't open until eleven."

"Right," she repeated. She stuffed her knitting into the bag and turned off the TV. "Well, thanks for hanging out with me tonight. It was fun."

"Thanks for dinner," he said.

"You're welcome."

He stood and walked to the door. Addison trailed after him and smiled hesitantly. "Bye, Preacher."

"Bye, Addie."

He told himself to put his boots on and leave. He'd been here long enough, and as it was, spooning Addison after sex, eating dinner with her, sitting on the couch and watching television with her sent the wrong message.

So, why did you do it?

The hell of it was, he didn't know why. The second Addison had started to move away in the bed, he'd pulled her closer without even thinking about it.

You liked cuddling with her.

Yeah, he fucking did. She smelled so good, and her skin was silky soft. The way she relaxed into him like a contented kitten was intoxicating.

Only, he'd fucked it up. He hadn't meant for her to pull away when he told her not to fall asleep, but she'd taken it that way. He'd felt a little guilty about it.

Is that why you hung around? Why you asked to shower as an excuse to stay a little longer? Why you hinted that you wanted food?

He was hungry. The food smelled delicious, and a man had to eat, didn't he? It was to stave off the migraine.

Bullshit. The orgasm you had got rid of your headache.

Hell, yeah, it did. He wanted to grin, just remembering how fucking good it felt when Addie had come around his cock. God, her little pussy squeezed so tight when she came. It had immediately made him climax, too. He could spend the rest of his life with his dick buried in her pussy every goddamn night.

"Preacher?" Addie was staring up at him, no doubt wondering why he was standing by the door with a blissed-out dumb expression.

He studied her silky hair and the lovely colour of her eyes before his gaze dipped to her tits. She was braless under that t-shirt, and every time he'd glanced at her while they were watching TV, the hint of nipple he could see against the fabric drove him crazy. He'd had a semi the entire fucking time they watched the show.

He glanced at the clock again. Fuck it. It was getting late, but Addie had just said she was a night owl. He'd fuck her one more time before leaving.

He put his arm around her waist and pulled her against him before dipping his head and pressing a kiss against her mouth. She responded immediately, parting her lips so he could slide his tongue between them. Fuck, he loved how responsive she was to him.

He pulled back and smoothed her hair away from her face. "What do you think about one more lesson tonight, Sunshine?"

"Yes." Her eagerness and the look of hot desire on her face made his cock press painfully against his jeans. "If I get to choose the lesson."

"What did you have in mind?"

"I want to give you a blowjob." Her face flushed red.

"You sure you want to do that instead of another pussy eating?" He was goddamn obsessed with eating her pussy. It was like his own personal mission to make up for how long she'd gone without a tongue in that perfect pussy of hers.

"I want to learn how to be better at giving oral sex," she said. "If you're okay with me, um, doing that?"

"Sunshine, any time you want to put your mouth on my cock, I am perfectly good with it," he said.

She giggled nervously, and he took her hand and led her back to the bedroom. He pulled her t-shirt off and cupped her left breast before toying with her nipple. He kissed her again, teasing her lips with small nips and licks as she moaned and rocked her pelvis against him.

He slid his hand inside her leggings and palmed her

pussy, grinding the heel of his hand against her clit. She gasped into his mouth, her nails digging into his back and her nipples hard as pearls.

He was beyond tempted to pull on the barbell in her right, but it was too early to touch it, no matter how healed it looked.

Instead, he bent and sucked on her left nipple while he trailed light fingers over and around the curve of her right breast. He'd been so anxious to eat her pussy earlier that he hadn't given nearly enough attention to her tits. The way her nipple swelled in his mouth, the little breathless cries she made when he sucked hard, made his cock ache.

"Preacher, wait." She tugged at his hair, and he growled against her breast before squeezing her pussy.

He didn't want to wait. He wanted to eat her sweet pussy until she screamed his name. Hell, maybe he'd make her say again that he was the only one who got to fuck her pussy. He liked hearing her say it, liked knowing that it was him and only him who would be between those smooth thighs of hers.

Good job on the not being jealous thing, asshole. You think forcing her to say she won't fuck anyone else before you let her come makes you a good guy? Because it fucking doesn't. You proud of the way you manipulated her?

He shoved the voice away as Addison pushed on his chest. "Preacher, wait."

He straightened, one hand still cupping her pussy, the other reaching down to squeeze her ass.

"You said I could give you a blowjob, remember?"

"Let me eat your pussy first," he said.

She shook her head. "No, it seems selfish of me to keep letting you do that without reciprocating."

He almost laughed out loud. She'd spent ten years never

getting her pussy eaten, and she was worried about being selfish?

"I want to go down on you," he said.

"Well, I want to go down on you."

They stared at each other, and when her lips twitched and she started giggling, he laughed, too.

"Are we seriously arguing about who gets oral sex?" she said.

"Your fault," he said. "You've got the sweetest pussy I've ever tasted."

She blushed like he knew she would, and he eased one finger into her narrow opening. She moaned, her pussy clenching around him as she clutched at his arms. "Hey, no distracting me."

He kissed her lightly and gave her clit a rub with his thumb before pulling his hand out from her leggings. "All right, Sunshine. You can have what you want."

Her smug smile made him laugh again, and he held his arms up when she tugged on the bottom of his t-shirt. She stripped it off of him, and he sucked in his breath when she trailed her fingers across his chest and down his abdomen.

She leaned forward and pressed soft kisses on his chest as she slipped her arms around him and made tiny circles on his lower back with the tips of her fingers. He groaned and squeezed her ass again when she ran her thumb over one flat nipple.

"Does that feel good?" she said.

He nodded and watched as she explored his chest with her mouth and her tongue. When she licked a circle around his nipple and then sucked on it, it was like a line of hot need straight to his aching dick.

"Fuck, Sunshine!" He cupped her breast and pinched her nipple.

She moaned before reaching for the button on his jeans. He helped her unbutton them and pushed them and his underwear down his legs. "Take off your leggings."

She hesitated, and he raised an eyebrow as he kicked off his clothes. "Take them off."

"I don't want you to be distracted by," she waved her hand in front of her crotch, "this. I feel like if I take them off, I'll be on my back with your head between my legs before I even get a chance to, you know…"

"Suck my cock?" he said.

God, would he ever get tired of watching that soft blush rise from her chest to her face?

He tugged on the waistband of her leggings. "I want you naked while you're sucking my cock, Sunshine. I promise to keep my tongue away from your pussy."

She giggled. "Okay, good. Lie on the bed."

He laid on his back in the middle of the bed, watching as she gracefully slipped out of her leggings before kneeling between his legs. When she leaned over him, and her soft hair brushed against his chest, he groaned and threaded his fingers through it.

She smiled at him and started a soft and meandering path of kisses down his body. When her tongue traced his v-line, he muttered a harsh curse, his hips bucking upward and the tip of his aching cock leaving precum smeared across her flat abdomen.

She licked his v-line on the right side, making him shudder and moan and more precum spill from his dick. She moved down a bit, and they both gasped when his cock brushed across her breast.

Her tiny hands pressed on his thighs, and he spread his legs further apart, groaning when she licked a slow path along his inner thigh. Her hand curled around the base of his dick, and he thrust upward. She smiled and squeezed lightly. "Hold still, Simon."

"Your mouth, Sunshine. Now," he moaned.

"In a minute," she said.

He glared at her, and she jacked him off with long, slow strokes that made his body shudder. His cock was weeping copious amounts of precum now, and he hissed out a breath when she licked the head of his cock clean.

"Fuck," he groaned. "Fuck, do that again."

She licked him again, this time licking around the ridge and down the thick vein that ran along the underside of his cock. His balls tightened, and when she slid her warm wet mouth around the head of his cock, he moaned and thrust his hips upward again.

She pulled back, denying him the heady heat of her mouth. "Hold still."

"You hold still," he muttered and then huffed out another groan when she giggled and licked his dick like it was a fucking lollipop.

"I like the way you taste," she announced before going in for another torturous lick. "I didn't like the taste of Har…"

She cleared her throat. "You taste good."

"Great. That's fucking awesome, I'm thrilled," he groaned. "Can you stop talking and start sucking again?"

She giggled her soft and sweet giggle. "So bossy, Preacher."

"Sunshine, you are killing me over here."

"Well, we can't have that, can we?" She slid her mouth down over his cock before sucking hard.

"Fuck!" His hands threaded into her hair, and he held tight as he watched her mouth move up and down his dick. She stroked the base of him, sliding her mouth down until her lips met her fingers and his cock touched the back of her throat.

To his surprise, she didn't gag or pull back. She took a deep breath and sucked hard, hollowing her cheeks.

Motherfuck, he had died and gone to heaven. As she bobbed her head up and down his dick, taking him deeper with every stroke, she cupped his balls and gave them a light tug.

"Fuck!" His voice was a hoarse rasp, and his entire world had narrowed down to the feel of Addison's wet, hot mouth. He was going to come. He was going to come in her mouth, he couldn't goddamn help it.

He opened his mouth to warn her, but she was already releasing him with a wet and loud pop.

"Baby, no," he groaned. "I was so close."

She licked his dick again, and her finger pressed that smooth spot just behind his balls. He cried out, and more precum dripped out of his cock. Addison licked him clean again as he moaned and twitched.

"Sunshine, suck my dick," He tried to tug her mouth back down, but she resisted, pulling free of his grip.

"Look at me, Simon." Her voice was low and sexy, and holy fuck, had he ever wanted to come so much in his life?

"Baby, please." Begging for her mouth no longer seemed like such a bad thing.

"Look at me," she repeated.

He squinted at her. Her lips were red and swollen, and it was way too fucking easy to remember how they looked stretched around his dick.

"As long as you're giving me lessons on sex, no other woman gets to suck or fuck your dick." She stroked him with a rough grip before sucking on the head of his cock again and then releasing him agonizingly quickly. "Do you hear me, Simon?"

"Yeah," he moaned, his hands trying to move her mouth back to his cock again.

"Say it, Simon," she said. "No one else fucks or sucks your dick but me."

"Addie, baby, please. I need your mouth." Her warm breath washing over his cock would be the death of him.

"Say it," she said.

"No one else fucks or sucks my dick but you," he said.

"That's right," she said with a smug little grin.

He groaned, his reply lost when her mouth slid over his dick again. She sucked hard for a few seconds before releasing him again. "Do you want me to finish you with my mouth or my pussy?"

"Your pussy," he said without hesitating.

As good as Addison's mouth felt, he couldn't resist being in her pussy. Any time she offered it up to him, he was going to fucking well take it.

She straddled his hips, and he helped her line up his dick to her pussy. When she pushed down, he grabbed her hips and thrust upward, making her take all of his cock in one hard stroke.

She cried out, her nails digging into his abdomen. He stopped moving immediately.

"Baby, did I hurt you?"

"No," she moaned. "God, no. It feels so good, Simon. You're so big. So damn thick and…"

She moaned again before bracing one hand on his abdomen and rubbing at her clit with the other. She rode him hard, her head thrown back, her beautiful tits bouncing with every one of his thrusts, and her inhibition completely gone.

She'd never looked more fucking beautiful.

When her pussy tightened around him, and her slender body stiffened, he made two more hard thrusts. She cried out as she came, her pussy clamping around his dick while she rubbed her clit furiously and ground her pelvis against his.

He shouted her name and came just as hard as she did. He shuddered beneath her, pumping his hips over and over, giving her every last bit of his seed as she rode out her orgasm. When she collapsed against his chest, he put his arms around her and stroked her back, smoothing away the hair from her sweaty face and staring at the fluttering pulse at the base of her neck.

When her breathing slowed, and the trembling in her limbs quieted, she eased off of him. He pulled her close before she could roll away, trapping her against his body with one arm around her. She slung a smooth thigh over his and rested her head on his chest again.

"That was really good." Her voice was sleepy and sated and sexy as hell.

"Hmm." He needed to get up, needed to get dressed and go the fuck home. Instead, he tugged Addison even closer and closed his eyes.

She yawned again and then kissed his chest. "Are you staying the night?"

"Yeah. If it's okay with you?"

"Yes. Night, Simon."

"Night, Sunshine."

CHAPTER 22

"Wait… you talked dirty to Preacher? Like, honest to God, dirty words? Words like fuck and pussy and cock?" Harper said.

Addison rested her feet on the edge of the coffee table and propped her iPad on her knees. "Well, not those exact words, but yeah."

"Oh my God," Harper grinned at her, "I wish I were there to hug you, maybe take you out for celebratory drinks or something."

"It's not even noon," Addison said with a laugh.

"Good point. So, what exactly did you say to Preacher to get him all hot and bothered?"

"I can't tell you that!"

"You can. You're choosing not to," Harper said. "I'm your best friend. You have to tell me, pinky-pie."

"When he was going down on me earlier, he made me say that he was the only one I would, um, have oral and, uh, sex with. I just made him say it back to me when I was going down on him. And no, I'm not saying my exact words because my head will explode from embarrassment."

When Harper didn't reply, Addison tapped the screen. "Hey, you still there? Crap, it's frozen."

"It's not frozen," Harper said. "I'm just surprised and maybe a little worried."

"What? Why?"

Harper took a sip of coffee. "If this is only a casual thing, why are you making each other promise not to fuck other people?"

"I don't – I mean… Preacher was the one who made me say it first. I figured it was only fair that the same rules apply to him."

"Oh, I'm not disagreeing. They should apply to him, too. I just find it strange that Preacher is asking you not to bang other guys if it's only casual sex between you two. Francisco and I don't have that agreement."

"Maybe it's a little more than casual sex," Addison said. "We've had sex three days in a row now, and the agreement was supposed to be a lesson a week for a month. Maybe Preacher wants… more."

"Honey, Preacher's not the kind of guy who will settle down with a woman. You know that, right?" Harper said.

"I know, but he spent the night with me," Addison said. "He stayed the night, and this morning, we had sex again before he left. He made me come three times, Harper. When I got out of the shower, I thought he would be gone, but he wasn't. He went down on me again, and then we had sex, and then when we were cuddling, he touched me until I had a third one. I told him he didn't have to, that two was more than enough, but he said something about a hat trick. I don't even know what that means."

"It's a hockey thing," Harper said. "Honey, look, just because he spent the night doesn't mean he wants more than sex. It probably means he was tired or still horny, or your bed is more comfortable than his. There are plenty of reasons why a guy you're only casually porking spends the night, and it's not because he's falling in love with you."

Trying not to let Harper see how her words crushed her, Addison said, "No, I know. You're right. I'm just hopped up on coffee and great sex."

Harper stared solemnly at her. "It's easy to mistake what's happening with Preacher as more than what it is. For the first time in your life, you're having amazing sex and trust me – all those orgasms do weird fucking things to your brain. But you did just get out of a long-term relationship, and I'm not sure that you're completely over -"

"I am completely over Harrison," Addison said. "I don't love him, Harper. I don't even want to ever see him again."

"Okay, but still… trying to start another relationship immediately after having your heart broken isn't a great idea. You need to have a couple of rebound relationships first. Trust me on this. What's happening with Preacher is a fun distraction, but don't start thinking it's anything more. Just enjoy it for what it is, okay?"

"Okay," Addison said.

"I'm not trying to upset you, honey," Harper said.

"You're not. I appreciate the dose of reality," Addison said.

"All right. What are your plans for today?"

"Not a lot," Addison said. "A woman is coming by tonight to look at my wedding dress."

Harper paused with her coffee cup in front of her mouth. "How does that make you feel?"

Addison smiled a little. "You sound like my mom. I Face-timed with her and Dad yesterday morning, and she said the same thing."

"You love that dress," Harper said. "I know you do."

"I do," Addison said. "But with my car dying, I could use the extra money. I can't return it to the dress shop because the alterations were already made, so selling it is my only option. I hate taking the bus, and once school starts again, it'll be inconvenient not to have a car."

"So, get a loan to buy a car. You don't need to sell your wedding dress. You'll marry the perfect guy someday, and don't you want your perfect dress when that happens?"

"I can't afford a car loan and my student loans," Addison said. "Besides, as much as I love that dress, it was meant to be for my wedding to Harrison, and wouldn't it be weird to marry someone else while wearing it?"

"If you didn't need the money for a car, would you sell the dress?" Harper said.

Addison shrugged. "I don't know. It doesn't matter though. I'm just being sentimental over it, and that's stupid. I'm glad I'm not marrying Harrison, so I shouldn't care one way or another about the dress. Anyway, why aren't you at work? Did you switch shifts again?"

Harper sighed. "I got laid off."

"What?" Addison sat forward. "When?"

"Monday."

"Oh my God. Honey, I'm sorry. Why didn't you say anything?"

"Because you've got your own thing going on, and I didn't want to go on and on about my problems."

"Stop it. You know I'm here for you no matter what. Have you already started looking for something else?"

"I think I might come home."

Addison stared at her in astonishment. "Harper, this is your dream. Just because you lost your job doesn't mean you give up on your dream. You can find another job and keep trying for a gallery show."

"I'm not good enough for a gallery show." Harper held up her hand when Addison started to protest. "I'm not, Addie. Trust me. I've seen other people's work here, and I'll never get my own show. My mom was right – I don't have the talent."

"You do," Addison said. "Stop letting your mother get in your head. She was wrong."

Harper shrugged. "It's not just that. I'm worried about my dad, you know? And maybe losing my job is a sign that I need to come home and take care of him."

"Your dad wouldn't want you giving up on your dream for him," Addison said. "I love you, honey, and I'd be lying if I said there wasn't a part of me that wants you to come home, but not at the expense of giving up your dream. You need to keep trying."

"It's been over a year," Harper said. "How much more time am I going to waste? Being a starving artist isn't nearly as romantic as it sounds. If I come home, I can work at the clinic again and at least make some money. I was barely making ends meet before I lost my job."

"Oh, Harper," Addison said.

"It's no big deal, honey. I haven't decided for sure one way or the other anyway. Listen, I gotta go. I'm meeting Angie at the deli in ten minutes. Love you, Addie."

"Love you too, Harper."

YOU KEEP DOING THIS, AND YOU'LL NEED YOUR OWN DAMN parking spot at Addison's place.

Preacher ignored his inner voice as he walked toward Addison's apartment building, but the damn thing kept talking.

You can't keep showing up at her house every goddamn night. She'll get the wrong impression.

What? That I want to fuck her? This is what she's asking me for, remember?

You going to spend the night again like you did last night?

He grimaced. Spending the night with Addie was a mistake, but he wouldn't make it again. He'd been exhausted last night, and it was easier to stay in her bed. He wouldn't stay as late tonight and wouldn't be weird and eat dinner or watch TV with her. He would fuck her and leave.

A woman walked out of Addie's building and paused by the door. She held a large black garment bag and talked animatedly on her phone.

"Yeah, I bought it. It's beautiful and fits me perfectly. I got a great deal on it." The woman paid no attention to him as he walked toward her. "Yeah, it's the one from that dinky little tourist town. I hated driving this far, but it was worth it. What are the odds that I would find a dress that's what I'm looking for and fits me? What? No, it's never been worn. She said her wedding was cancelled. I don't know why. I'm not going to ask a stranger why she isn't getting married."

She walked past Preacher, barely giving him a second look. "Are you home? I might stop by and show it to you. I'll be a couple of hours before I get there, but…"

He didn't hear the rest as she walked down the sidewalk. He waited until she climbed into her car before buzzing Addie's door.

"Hello?"

"Hey, it's me," he said.

She buzzed him in without replying, and he headed toward the stairs. He supposed he should have texted her first to see if she wanted him to come by.

So, why didn't you?

Because maybe she wouldn't see his text, or maybe she would ignore it, or maybe she would tell him not to come over.

Just showing up unannounced is a dick move, buddy. She's too sweet not to let you in if you're on her goddamn doorstep and you're taking advantage of that.

He opened the door to her floor and headed toward her apartment. No, he wasn't. She could say no but didn't because she wanted him just as much as he wanted her. He thought back to this morning and the way she'd looked when they were finished fucking. He'd brought her to orgasm three times, and her soft and perfect body was sated and limp when he left her in bed and dragged his ass to work.

He didn't want to admit that he'd been tempted to cancel all his appointments and spend the entire day in her bed. He couldn't get enough of her, and already his cock was hardening at just the thought of being inside her again.

He raised his hand to knock, but the door opened. His semi disappeared immediately at the look on Addison's face. "What's wrong?"

Her face was blotchy, her nose was red, and her eyes were watery. He stepped inside and shut the door. "Are you crying?"

"No, no," she said. "I just, um…"

"Why are you crying?"

"I'm not." Her eyes watered even more, and she turned away. "It's been a bit of a bad day. I'm going to get a drink. Would you like something?"

She walked to the kitchen without waiting for a reply, leaving him standing by the front door. What the fuck was going on? Why was she crying? Had that prick of an ex-fiancé upset her?

How fucking stupid are you, buddy? You really can't figure it out?

How the hell was he supposed to know what was making her cry? He wasn't a goddamn mind ...

Shit. The woman out front with the wedding dress. It was Addison's wedding dress. She was upset because she sold her dress.

Yeah, because she still loves that asshole.

She didn't. She couldn't. Not after what he'd done to her.

Why is she crying over selling her wedding dress if she doesn't? If she hated him, wouldn't she be happy to get rid of her dress?

He reached for the door handle. Addison was upset, and she wouldn't be in the mood for sex. And he wasn't in the mood to stick around and let her cry on his shoulder about how much she missed that asshole Harrison.

Don't be such a dick. Are you really going to walk out when she's upset and needs someone to talk to? She's a sweet girl and deserves better than that. Hell, she deserves better than you.

That was for fucking sure. Still, the thought of leaving while Addie sat in her apartment alone and cried made him feel pretty fucking awful. He realized that he wanted to make her feel better. That knowing she was upset was upsetting *him*. If making her feel better meant listening to her sob about how much she still loved that undeserving prick instead of having sex with her, he would do it. It wouldn't fucking kill him.

He took his boots off and walked into the kitchen. Addison was standing at the counter and pouring a glass of wine. "Would you like a glass?"

"No, thanks."

He watched as she took two healthy swallows of the wine.

She still had her back turned to him, and he said, "You okay?"

"Yes." She drank the rest of the wine and turned to face him. "Ready?"

He stared at her. "For what?"

She smiled, but it looked forced and unnatural. "Another lesson."

"You're obviously upset."

"I'll get over it. Let's have sex."

"Do you want to talk about why you're upset?" he said.

To his immense surprise, she shook her head. "No, I'm good."

She tried to slip by him, and he took her arm, tugging her to a stop. "Addie, you're not good."

"I am," she insisted. "Please, I don't want to talk. You're here for sex, right? So, let's have sex."

He pulled her into his arms. She was stiff and left her arms at her sides as he rubbed her back. He didn't say anything, and after only a minute or two, she relented and softened against him, burying her face in his neck. He waited for the tears to fall, but his little Sunshine surprised him again.

There were no tears. Instead, she let him hug her for a few minutes before trying to step away. He refused to let her go, and she patted his back. "I'm good now."

"Tell me why you're upset."

"I'd rather not," she said.

"Why?"

"Because I'm not going to bore you with my life."

"Maybe I want to be bored by you," he said.

She laughed, but there was a soft note of sadness to it that made his chest ache. "I know what you want from me. Come on, let's go to the bedroom."

"I'm hungry."

She leaned back and stared up at him. "What?"

"I didn't have a chance to eat supper. Do you have any leftover veggie chili?"

"Yes."

"Do you mind if I grab some?"

She hesitated and then shook her head. "No, but then we're having sex, right?"

"Yeah," he said. "Did you eat already?"

"I did."

He pushed her gently in the direction of the living room. "Go and knit or something. I'll grab my food and join you."

Confusion on her face, she left the kitchen. He grabbed a bowl from the cupboard and the leftover food from the fridge. He was hungry but mostly asked to eat to distract Addie.

He'd been prepared to listen to Addison cry and moan about selling her wedding dress, but now that she was refusing to tell him anything, he was oddly upset by it. He didn't like the idea of her using sex with him as a distraction from her life.

You want it to mean something more?

No, of course not. But as hard as he tried to deny it, she was already becoming more to him than just a warm place to put his dick. Right or wrong, he wanted to be more to her, too.

"How was your day?" Preacher said.

Addison stared blankly at him. He ate a spoonful of chili and said, "What did you do today?"

"Not much," she said. "Talked to Harper, cleaned the apartment."

Don't forget selling your wedding dress for a measly six hundred bucks. Oh, hey, you know you'll be alone forever, right? Even if you learn how to be better at sex, you'll never find someone. You'll die old and alone, surrounded by yarn and seventy-two cats.

"You sure you don't want to talk about what's upsetting you?" Preacher said.

She would die before she let Preacher hear how pathetic she was. Hell, she'd been tempted not to let him into her apartment because of how blotchy her face was, but sex would be a great distraction from her self-pity.

If she could get Preacher into the freaking bedroom.

"I'm sure." She glanced at his bowl. "Are you finished?"

"Almost."

She looked at the clock, trying to hide her sigh of impatience.

"My day was fine," Preacher said.

"That's good." Maybe he'd get the hint if she took off her bra and waved it at him.

"The new guy, Nix, seems to be working out okay. But he's from New Cassel, so we'll see if he can stick it out. It can be hard going from a city to a small town."

"Do you ever wish you still lived there?" Despite how much she just wanted to bang Preacher and forget about her pathetic life, her curiosity about Preacher's life was kicking in. She knew nothing about him other than he was originally from New Cassel. She would be an idiot not to take advantage of his weirdly chatty mood.

"Nah. I like small-town life. Once Gideon moved back here, he encouraged me to move here too. I was trying to open a shop in New Cassel, but it," he paused for a beat, "wasn't working out. Gideon convinced me to open a shop here instead."

"It seems to have worked out well for you," she said.

"I do okay."

She laughed. "You do better than okay, and you know it."

He grinned at her. "Hell, yeah, I do."

"How did you and Gideon meet?"

"He came into the shop I was working at, and I did his tattoo."

"So, just completely random," she said.

He nodded, and she smiled a little. "It's weird for me to hear about meeting your best friend in some random way. I've been friends with Harper since we were kids."

"You live your whole life in Harmony Falls?" Preacher ate the last bite of chili before setting the empty bowl on the coffee table and picking up his glass of water.

"I have. Pretty boring, I know, but both my parents grew up in Harmony Falls and never wanted to leave. They wanted Daniel and me to have the same childhood they had. And honestly, I have no real urge to leave either. I love it here and always have. Harper has an adventurous spirit, but I'm a homebody. Plus, I'm pretty close to my mom, and the thought of living more than half an hour from her makes me sad."

"What about your old man? You like him?" Preacher said.

"I do. He's an engineer, and he's travelled a lot for the last ten years or so for work, but he's a good dad, and I love him. What about you? Are you close to your parents?"

"No."

He didn't say anything else, and while she wasn't surprised, she wished he would give her something more.

As if he'd read her mind, he said, "My old man was in and out of prison a lot when I was a kid, and my mom was too busy shooting heroin to care much about what I was doing."

"I'm sorry," she said. "That must have been very upsetting and difficult."

He shrugged. "I had an aunt who looked out for me."

"Does she still live in New Cassel?"

"She died when I was seventeen," he said. "Drunk driver hit her car."

A flicker of pain flashed in his eyes, and without thinking about it, she scooted across the couch until she pressed against him. She took his hand, squeezing it gently. "I'm so sorry."

He studied their clasped hands. "It was a long time ago."

She didn't reply, and he rubbed his thumb absently against the palm of her hand. "After my aunt died, my mom started using every day. My aunt used to keep her somewhat in line, but with her gone... my dad was doing a stint in prison, and Mom was prostituting herself out to buy drugs. There was a lineup of strange men in and out of our fucking apartment every goddamn night."

She pressed even closer and rested her free hand on his arm, rubbing lightly as he stared at their clasped hands. "She was using all the money she got to buy more drugs, and eventually, we were evicted from our apartment. She went to live with some guy she knew."

"Where did you go?" she said.

"I was a couple of months from graduating high school, and a friend let me crash at his place until we graduated. But then his folks wanted me out, so I lived on the street for a while."

"You were homeless?"

"Yeah, for about six months. I was good at art, and I'd go to one of the dog parks and sketch people's dogs in exchange for cash. One day, this big dude covered head to toe in tattoos is at the park, and he's got this ridiculous tiny dog. It was one of those miniature poodle crosses, some yappy little shit, and he's fucking babying this thing. You know? Like, the dog's got on a damn leather jacket, and the collar around its neck probably cost more than any of my clothes ever did."

She smiled at him. "People love their pets."

"I sketched out his dog and then showed it to him, did my usual song and dance, and the guy looked at my drawing and then looked at me, and said, 'Son, you got some fucking talent, don't you?'"

He traced more patterns on her palm with his thumb. "He asked if I ever drew anything other than dogs. I said yeah and showed him a few of my other sketches. He gave me a business card for his shop. Told me to come by the next day, and we'd talk about a job opportunity."

"He was a tattoo artist?" Addison said.

Preacher nodded. "One of the best in the city, although I didn't know that at the time. I showed up at the shop the next morning, and he offered me the chance to apprentice."

"That's what Nolan does at your shop, right?" she said.

"Right. An apprentice cleans the shop, books appointments, and takes out the trash. Basically, you do all the grunt work in the shop in exchange for being taught how to tattoo. Jorge even let me sleep on a cot in the back of the shop."

"That was nice of him," she said.

"Yeah." A smile crossed his face. "Until his wife, Maria, found out. He caught so much hell from her. I was eighteen by then, but she said a tattoo shop was no place for a kid to be sleeping."

"Where did you stay once Maria kicked you out of the shop?"

His slight smile became a full-grown grin. "Maria and Jorge's house."

She laughed and squeezed his hand. "Seriously?"

"Maria gave Jorge shit for not bringing me back to their place where I would have a proper bed and food to eat. I lived with them until I finished apprenticing a few years later and got my tattooing licence."

"They sound like good people."

"They are. Better than I deserved."

She frowned at him. "Don't say that."

He just shrugged. "Anyway, then I met Gideon, and we became friends. He moved back here to take care of Kira, and about a year later, I moved here and opened up the Crimson Door."

She knew that Preacher was around Gideon's age, which meant he had skipped over a significant chunk of time between becoming a tattoo artist and moving to Harmony Falls. She was intensely curious about what had happened in those years but wouldn't push him for details. It was a miracle he'd even told her this much. Besides Gideon, she didn't think anyone in Harmony Falls knew anything about Preacher's life.

"What about your parents?" she said.

"My mother died when I was twenty, and I don't have a clue where my father is," Preacher said. "I saw him at the funeral and gave him my cell number. He said he'd call, but he never did."

Another flash of pain, and she pressed a kiss against the bulge of his upper arm. "I'm sorry. Your dad is stupid."

"He was a drunk. He's probably dead from fucking liver disease by now. It's why I don't drink much."

"That's understandable," she said. "I know it might be hard to believe because of the way I sucked back that glass of wine tonight, but I don't generally drink that much either. I hate going to the bars – always have. They're too loud and too crowded, and men and women are only looking for one thing. I can't even remember the last time I went to a bar."

He squeezed her hand. "You wanna talk about what's upsetting you now?"

While she liked that Preacher had opened up to her, telling him her problems would bore him to death and he might leave. She didn't want to sit here alone, feeling sorry for herself. She wanted to be in bed with Preacher and forget how pathetic her life was for a little while.

Yeah, because it's not at all pathetic asking Preacher to teach you how to bang.

"Addison?" Preacher said.

She let go of his hand and pressed her palm against his crotch, rubbing gently and smiling when she felt him harden. "What I want is to go into my bedroom and practice my blowjob skills again."

The look on his face suggested that he might argue with her. She gave him a light squeeze and leaned forward to lick a slow path up his thick neck to his ear. She sucked on his earlobe, her hand still circling over his dick. "Don't you want my mouth again, Simon?"

He groaned, and she squeaked in surprise when he stood abruptly and pulled her to her feet. "I think it's my turn to eat your pussy. You got a problem with that, Miss Moore?"

She grinned and followed him eagerly toward the bedroom. "No problem at all, Mr. Preacher."

CHAPTER 23

Preacher climbed off his bike and slipped off his helmet. He ran a hand through his hair, groaning inwardly when Gideon's SUV pulled into an empty spot in the street in front of his bike. He glanced at Addison's apartment building before walking to the driver's side of Gideon's vehicle.

Gideon was wearing his sheriff's vest, and as Wanda's voice crackled over the radio, he turned it down. "Hey, buddy."

"Hey," Preacher said. "What are you doing here?"

"Just doing my rounds through town," he said. "The better question is – what are you doing here?"

"You know what I'm doing here," Preacher said.

"Yeah, the same thing you were doing here last night and the night before," Gideon said.

Preacher brushed imaginary dirt off the front of his leather vest. "When did you start being such a creeper?"

Gideon grinned. "I was just doing my job until I saw your bike here Tuesday night. That got me curious, so I drove by last night during my shift. I thought it was a once a week thing with you two."

"You done telling me where I was last night?"

"I'm working the night shift this week," Gideon said.

"I know."

"I drove by here at four this morning, and your bike was still parked on the street. You spent the night with Addie."

"Nice work, detective. You've cracked the case."

"God, you're a fucking ass when you want to be," Gideon said. "Since when did you spend the night at a woman's house, Preacher?"

Since he couldn't get enough of Addison or her soft sweetness. He *could* have left last night. It was only ten when he was finished making her come on his mouth and his cock. But Addison's bed was comfortable, and she had already fallen asleep against him, and it was just fucking easier to stay the night.

You also wanted to give her the chance to tell you what was wrong this morning. Admit it.

No, he didn't. If Addison didn't want to confide in him, so what? It wasn't that kind of relationship, and he should be fucking happy she wasn't sharing every goddamn detail of her life with him.

It didn't matter anyway. Addison was quieter than usual this morning, but she still hadn't told him about selling her wedding dress. Honestly, she'd looked a little on the tired side, and she'd had a rasp in her throat.

She looked exhausted. Probably because you woke her up at three and then at five for sex again. Jesus Christ, it's a wonder she can even fucking walk.

Guilt trickled through him. Addison did seem sore this morning. He'd seen her rubbing her thighs after her shower, and she'd winced when she sat down on the bed. He'd immediately nixed his plan to fuck her again before he had to leave for work.

"I stayed the night because I was tired," Preacher said. "Stop reading into shit that isn't there. And stop stalking me like a fucking weirdo."

"Never," Gideon said. "I gotta make sure my pookie-bear is safe."

"Jesus, I fucking hate you today," Preacher said.

Gideon laughed before sobering. "Be careful, Simon. You have a good life here, and I don't want it destroyed because Addison Moore breaks your heart."

A bus pulled up at the bus stop across the street, the sound of its engine and brakes giving Preacher a reason not to answer Gideon. The bus pulled away, and Addison, looking even worse than this morning, trudged across the street. She twitched in surprise when she saw Preacher and Gideon and stopped in the middle of the street before joining them.

"Hi," she said. Her voice was hoarse, and her eyes were rimmed in red.

"Hello, Addison," Gideon said. "How are you?"

"Good," she said.

"Still no car, huh?" Gideon said.

Her smile was strained. "No, not yet. Hi, Preacher."

"Hey," he said.

She didn't look good. She looked fucking terrible. Before Preacher could ask what was wrong, she gave them an awkward wave. "Nice to see you both. If you'll excuse me, I'm pretty tired."

She coughed into her hand before walking down the sidewalk toward her apartment building. Preacher heard her sneeze as Gideon started up the SUV. "See you later, pookie-bear."

Preacher gave him the bird, and Gideon laughed and drove away. Preacher waited for a beat and then walked after Addison. He caught up to her at her building door.

"Addison, wait," he said.

She turned to face him. Her eyes were watery, and he knew damn well she'd been crying again.

"Tell me what's wrong," he said.

She shook her head and fumbled in her purse for her keys. "It's been a shitty evening, and I'm tired and don't feel like talking about it."

"Sunshine, please tell me why you're upset."

She blinked rapidly before coughing into her hand. "I – it's nothing important."

"I want to know."

She pulled a tissue out of her purse and dabbed at her eyes. "Daniel was supposed to go car shopping with me tonight. I sold my – some stuff yesterday and thought I might have enough money now to purchase a secondhand one. But he blew me off to drink with that idiot Brad and the other firefighters."

She swallowed, wincing a little before clearing her throat again. "He's drinking too much. I don't know what to do about it. I tried to talk to him tonight about how much he's been drinking, and he got pissed at me and stopped answering any of my calls or my texts. I'm worried about him, but I don't want to tell Mom and Dad because they won't be home for a while yet, and I don't want them worrying about him if I'm overreacting like Daniel said I am."

She rubbed at her forehead, her eyes watering again. "Anyway, I should have asked Grace or Kira to go with me instead, but I... I need to get used to doing stuff on my own now, right? So, I decided to go alone, and it was awful. The sales guy was a total jerk and acted like I was an idiot, and all of the cars on the lot were completely out of my price range. So, then he was pressuring me to apply for a loan through them, but I can't afford a car loan and my student loans, you know?"

He nodded, and she leaned against the door to her building, looking defeated. "My choices are to buy some awful beater car that will probably break down on me in the first month or take the bus to work for the next year while I try to save more money for a car. Taking the bus is a huge pain in the butt because the schedule is stupid, and I -"

She stopped and rubbed away the tear that was sliding down her cheek. "Anyway, it's been a terrible day."

"Did you eat dinner yet?" he said.

"No, I'm not very hungry. Would you be upset if I begged off on our lesson tonight?"

"No," he said. "I can order us something to eat, and we can watch some TV."

"It's probably better if you don't come in," she said. "I'm getting a cold, and I'd feel terrible if I gave it to you."

He tried to ignore the immediate hurt that washed over him. "Yeah, okay."

She fished her keys out of her purse before sneezing into the crook of her arm. "Bye, Preacher. I'll text you when I'm feeling better."

She stepped into her building, waving again before heading toward the elevator. Disgruntled and worried about Addison, Preacher walked away.

"HOLD THE FUCK STILL," PREACHER SAID.

Brad glanced at him. "Sorry."

He shifted in the tattoo chair, and Preacher glared at him.

"You keep squirming, and your tattoo will be fucked up."

"Right." The firefighter gave him a shit-eating grin, and

Preacher was tempted to stop tattooing and tell the idiot to get the fuck out of his shop. Instead, gritting his teeth, he went back to tattooing Brad's arm, concentrating on the shading as Brad watched Nix clean his station.

"Where's the guy with the green hair?" Brad said.

"Off today," Preacher said. If Brad didn't stop being so fucking chatty, he really would tell him to get the fuck out.

"Shop's busy today," Brad said. "Is that why you hired the new guy?"

"You want a fucking tattoo, or you want a goddamn cup of tea and a chat?" Preacher said.

"Sorry, man," Brad said sheepishly.

Preacher started up the gun again. He wasn't being an asshole to Brad because he'd been sitting at the table that night with Addison at the Thirsty Beaver and let her go outside without any fucking thought to her safety. He was being an asshole because Brad was a jacked-up dickhead without a single fucking coherent thought in his head.

The bell over the shop door chimed, and Preacher looked up when Brad said, "About fucking time you got here. Where the hell you been?"

Daniel, his blond hair too long and his usual clean-shaven jaw covered with two days of stubble, grabbed a stool near the drawing station and brought it over. He sat down next to Brad. "Sorry, my car is still at the Beaver, so I took an Uber over here."

"Jesus, you fucking reek. You still hung over from last night?" Brad said.

The scent of stale beer clung to Daniel like a musty overcoat.

"Nah, I'm good," Daniel said.

Preacher glanced at Addison's brother. He didn't think he imagined the beer smell intensified when Daniel talked or that he'd staggered a little when he walked. He glanced at the clock on the wall. It was just after eleven on a Friday morning, and the guy was already fucking drunk.

"Christ, my thighs still hurt from ball Wednesday night," Brad said. "Swear to fucking God, I was doing all the work. I don't even know why we put Martin in center field. Fucker can't catch or run worth shit."

Daniel shrugged as a few tourists entered the shop and studied the artwork on the walls. Nix joined them, their conversation drowned out by the sound of Preacher's tattoo gun. "Martin was just having an off night."

"Every fucking night is an off night for him," Brad said. "Jesse ask if you could take his shifts tomorrow and Sunday?"

"Yeah. I said I would."

"Sucker," Brad said. "Hey, can I borrow your phone for a minute? Forgot to fucking charge mine."

Daniel handed Brad his phone, and Preacher grunted in annoyance when Brad shifted in the chair again.

"I gotta look up when that -" Daniel's phone chimed, and Brad squinted at the screen. "Gross, your sister's asking you to get tampons for her."

Brad moved his arm again, and Preacher stifled his urge to slap the idiot across the head.

"Hold still," he growled.

"Right, sorry," Brad said.

Daniel took his phone back and texted rapidly. "She's been a real pain in my ass lately."

"Send her my way, I'll be a real pain in *her* ass," Brad said with a laugh.

"Talk about my sister like that again, and I'll shove my foot up *your* ass," Daniel said.

"Whatever, man. Your sister's got that hot good girl thing

going on. Swear to God, ever since her loser fiancé dumped her, half the guys in town have been dying to get between her -"

Brad bellowed a curse and glared at Preacher. "Fuck, that hurt! Are you tattooing to the goddamn bone?"

Preacher stared at him until Brad dropped his gaze. Daniel scowled at his friend. "Keep your mouth shut about Addie, or I'll kick your fucking head in. I mean it."

"Yeah, yeah. You're the one who was complaining about her."

"I can complain about her. She's my sister."

"Why's she texting you for this shit, anyway?" Brad said.

"Because my parents are gone, and her friends are working, and as you keep pointing the fuck out, she's not with Harrison anymore."

"Jesus," Brad snorted. "That lawyer was pussy-whipped if your sister got him to pick up that type of shit for her. If I had a girlfriend who even texted the fucking word tampon to me, I'd kick her out the door. Keep your goddamn monthly blood bath problems to yourself, you know?"

Preacher stopped tattooing and wiped the smears of ink away before placing plastic wrap over Brad's arm and taping it into place. If he had to hear Addison's name come out of this shit stain's mouth one more time, he'd stab the tattoo gun into his own goddamn eye.

"What are you doing?" Brad said

"Lunch break," Preacher said. "Come back in an hour."

"Are you fucking kidding me?" Brad glared at him as Daniel's cell dinged again.

"No, I'm fucking not," Preacher said. "You got a problem with that?"

Brad cleared his throat. "Nah, man, that's fine."

"Good. Get out."

Brad slid off the tattoo bed and turned to Daniel. "Let's head over to Nan's and get a bite. Unless you need me to drive you to your car so you can do a fucking tampon run for your sister?"

Daniel shook his head. "She's doing it herself. Let's go. See you in an hour, Preacher."

Preacher just nodded. The two men left the shop, and Preacher joined Nix, who was still with the tourists. Nix glanced at him. "Hey, what's up?"

"You okay for a while on your own?" Preacher said.

"Not a problem," Nix said.

"Just text me if it gets busier," Preacher said. Leaving Nix to deal with the tourists, he went upstairs to his apartment. He was feeling anxious and unsettled, and he studied the leftover pizza in his fridge before closing the door and moving to the window.

He stared at the people scurrying down the sidewalk. He wasn't worried about Addison, he told himself grimly. He didn't fucking care if she was sick. He didn't miss her either. Besides, he didn't want to be around her if she was sick.

Still, the fact that she was reduced to asking her brother to bring her tampons had to mean she was really sick, right? Not that the useless twit could help her. He supposed he should have been relieved that Daniel had enough common sense not to drive when he was drunk, but Preacher was mostly just pissed that he was leaving Addison to fend for herself.

He sat down on the couch and scrolled through Facebook for twenty minutes. He needed to eat, but he had no appetite. He stood and paced his small apartment for another few minutes before returning to the window.

He stared blankly across the street. An older woman sat on the bus stop bench outside of Walgreens. She climbed painfully to her feet and adjusted her hat as the bus pulled up and blocked her from his view. After a moment, the bus drove away, and he studied the woman who had stepped off the bus and stood next to the bench. She wore a baggy sweatshirt, yoga pants, and flip-flops, and her hair was in a messy ponytail on top of her head.

Her ass reminded him of Addison's ass, he thought before snorting. Addison wouldn't be caught dead outside of the house in a sweatshirt and yoga pants. His little Sunshine liked to wear -

His eyes widened as the woman turned to grab the back of the bench, and he saw her face. She coughed harshly, her body bending with the force of it. Even from his apartment, he could see the flush of fever in her cheeks. She straightened and walked slowly into the Walgreens.

He paced back and forth in front of the window with his hands clenched into fists. After a few minutes, he cursed and stomped down the stairs, striding across the shop and stepping out into the hot sunshine.

ADDIE SNEEZED AND THEN GROANED IN PAIN. SHE DIDN'T know whether to grab her stomach or her head. She settled for rubbing her forehead with one hand and pressing on her abdomen with the other.

She was completely stuffed up, she had the mother of all sinus headaches, and her throat felt like razor blades lined it. As if the world's worst summer cold wasn't bad enough, her period had started this morning, and she was cramping like a bitch.

She picked up a basket, staggered down the aisle, and grabbed a box of tampons. She tossed it in the basket before wobbling toward the cold medicine aisle. She squinted at the cold medicine boxes, trying to think past the agony of her headache as she sneezed again. She winced and wiped her dripping nose with a tissue before squinting at the boxes again.

Her head hurt so bad. It was hard to think. She wanted to cry, and she cursed her stupid brother in her head. He wasn't working today but still refused to bring her some tampons and cold medicine. She hated to ask him, but with her parents out of town and Grace and Kira at work, she had no one else. The thought of dragging her ass out of bed had made her cringe. She shouldn't have even bothered asking him, though. She loved Daniel, but sometimes he was a selfish ass. Asking him for help was a stupid idea.

She sneezed again and clutched at her head, moaning quietly as it sent a wave of throbbing pain through her sinuses. God, her head hurt. Her throat hurt, her stomach hurt – hell, every part of her body hurt. She blinked back the hot tears of self-pity. She didn't even have a boyfriend anymore to take care of her.

She thought she would burst into tears right in the middle of Walgreens for one black moment. The idea of picking out meds, walking to the counter, paying the cashier, and then waiting in the hot sun for the bus was horribly overwhelming. She leaned forward and rested her burning forehead against the cool cement pillar beside the cold medicine shelf.

Stop feeling sorry for yourself. So you don't have a boyfriend to care for you when you're sick. Boo fucking hoo. Take care of yourself, and don't be such a baby about it. Plenty of women don't have –

"Addison?"

Shit. Please, let it be someone else who sounds exactly like Preacher.

She lifted her head from the pillar and stared at the man beside her.

The gods of luck were actively working against her today.

"Hi, Preacher. How are you?"

He touched her forehead. "Jesus, you're burning up."

She jerked back from his touch and stumbled away a couple of steps. "It's only a cold, but I think I'm pretty contagious, so don't get too close."

He ignored her and took her arm, drawing her up next to him. "You should be in bed and resting."

She blinked owlishly at him as she tried to think past the pain pulsing in her head. "Yeah, I was. I needed some cold medicine and some other, uh… stuff."

He stared at the basket with the box of tampons lying in the bottom of it. Embarrassment flooded through her, and she jerked the basket behind her body. It smashed into the shelf beside her, and the tampon box flew out of the basket and landed at Preacher's feet.

"Oh gosh," she said. "Oh gosh, I'm so sorry."

He bent and picked up the box, tossing it back into the basket and taking it from her before she could move away.

"Thank you." She stared at the floor. "Um, I should go now. Bye, Preacher."

He refused to let go of her arm when she tugged. He scanned the cold medicine boxes before picking up one box and reading the back. "Relieves congestion, sinus headache, sore throat, fever and coughing. Any of those apply to you?"

"Yeah, all of them."

His look was surprisingly sympathetic. "Come on, Sunshine."

Keeping a firm hold on her arm, he headed toward the front of the store. He picked up two bottles of orange juice and then stopped to pick out a heating pad.

"Oh, I have a heating pad at home," she said. Her voice was nasally and hoarse, and she winced when she caught sight of her reflection in the milk cooler. She hadn't showered this morning, her hair was a rat's nest on her head, and her nose was bright red and swollen. She was bloated looking with dark circles under her eyes.

God, why did she have to run into Preacher today? What exactly had she done to have karma bite her so cruelly in the ass?

Still holding her arm, he led her to the tills.

"Hello, Miss Addison." Shelly was standing at the till, and Addie groaned inwardly. The chunky woman had worked at the Walgreens for years. She was sweet enough but also shockingly dumb, and it took her forever to ring through even the simplest of transactions.

Shelly turned her gaze to Preacher. Addie watched in numb disbelief as she giggled and reached across to squeeze Preacher's arm.

"Hi there, Preacher. I ain't seen you in a while."

Preacher piled the items from the basket onto the belt. "Hello, Ms. Dicks."

"Oh, call me Shelly, hon," she cooed.

Her head pounding, Addison stared at the cashier. The woman was in her mid-fifties, but apparently, she had a thing for younger men.

"I've been thinking about getting a tattoo," Shelly said as she slowly scanned the items and stuffed them into a plastic bag. "I was thinking I might get one right here."

She pulled the neckline of her shirt down, and Addison blinked at the neon orange bra that encased the cashier's oversized breasts. Shelly caressed the top of her right boob. "Thought I might get me a little heart right here. What do you think, Preacher? Would you tattoo a heart on me?"

"Sure," Preacher said. "Call the shop, and Nolan will book you in. We're booking for three months from now."

"I was thinking," Shelly leaned forward until her breasts were nearly falling out of her shirt, "that maybe you could squeeze me in sometime this weekend. To say thank you, you could drop by my place later for a piece of my famous meatloaf."

Addison would have giggled if her head hadn't hurt so much. She watched silently as Preacher said, "Sorry, Ms. Dicks, I can't do that. It's not fair to the other customers. But you call Nolan and book an appointment, and I'll be happy to tattoo you then."

Disappointment flickered across Shelly's face, and she straightened before giving him a strained smile. "I'll do that, hon."

She glanced at Addison. "You look real bad, hon. You got that cold that's been going around? Your face is some red, and your nose is so swollen. Tricia Rathen came in this morning with the same thing. She didn't look near as bad as you look, though."

"Thanks." Addison rummaged in her purse, cursing under her breath when she couldn't find her wallet. She reached past the wad of tissue she had stuffed in before she left her apartment and shoved her bus pass into one of the side pockets. Her phone was lying on the bottom. Where was her damn wallet?

"What are you looking for?" Preacher said.

Her eyes watering with unshed tears, she said, "I can't find my wallet."

"I'm paying for it anyway." Preacher pulled his wallet from his pocket and handed Shelly some cash.

"Aren't you just the sweetest," Shelly said. She gave him his change – she had to count it out three times before she got it right – and smiled again at Preacher. "You got a big heart under that tough guy exterior, doncha, hon?"

Preacher took the plastic bag. "Have a good day."

"You too, hon. You too."

He started toward the door, and Shelly glanced at his ass before smiling at Addie. "See you later, hon. And don't you worry about what folks are saying about Harrison dumping you. You'll find yourself a new man soon."

Addison couldn't even manage a polite smile. She followed Preacher out the door of the Walgreens. The hot sun brought a wave of nausea to her stomach, and she grimaced and raised her hand to shade her eyes.

She reached for the bag that Preacher still held. He didn't let it go, and she smiled tentatively. "Thank you for buying the stuff. I'll drop by the shop when I feel better and pay you back."

He just grunted, and she tried to take the bag again. "Um, the bus will be here soon so…"

"Let's go," he said. Ignoring the tourists swarming around them, he took her arm and marched her across the street to his shop. He opened the door, and she could have wept with relief at the air conditioning when he ushered her inside.

The shop was blessedly empty of customers. She didn't need everyone in the damn town seeing what a gross snotty mess she was. Nix sat at the drawing table sketching onto a tablet and glanced up when they walked in.

"Hey," he said. "Addison, right?"

She tried to smile. "Yes. Hello again."

"Give me five minutes, and then you can take your lunch break," Preacher told Nix.

"Take your time," Nix said.

He returned to his sketch as Preacher led her down the hallway to the stairs.

"Preacher, what -"

She shook free of Preacher's grip and bent over as a coughing fit racked her body. Groaning, trying not to cry, she covered her mouth with one hand and held her aching head with the other as she coughed wretchedly.

A warm hand rubbed her back, and as she straightened and wiped her mouth with the back of her hand, Preacher said, "You okay?"

"Yeah," she said. "I'm -"

She sneezed three times in rapid succession. This time, she grabbed her cramping stomach and tried not to moan too loudly before fishing a tissue out of her purse and wiping her nose.

"Listen, I'd better go," she wheezed. "I need to lie down, and I'll make you sick if I stay here much longer. Thank you again for – oh my goodness!"

Preacher had scooped her up, and she stared wide-eyed at him as he carried her up the narrow staircase to his apartment.

"What are you doing?" she said.

He carried her to his bed and set her down next to it. He pulled her sweatshirt over her head. She was wearing a stained t-shirt under it, but before she could be embarrassed, he had pulled it over her head, too.

Suddenly too damn tired to protest, she let him take off her bra, her flip-flops, and her yoga pants. He pulled the covers back and made her climb into bed. She rubbed at her forehead and kept her eyes closed as he rifled through the Walgreens bag.

"Sunshine, do you need these right now?"

She cracked open an eye. Preacher held the tampon box, and she wanted to pull the covers over her head with embarrassment. "Uh, no, I'm okay for now."

"I'll put them in the bathroom for you," he said.

She squeezed her eyes shut as he turned and carried them into the bathroom before returning. She heard him moving around in the kitchen, and after a few minutes, he said, "Sit up."

"I'm tired," she said. "My head hurts so bad, Preacher."

"I know, baby." The bed dipped as he sat beside her and slid a hand under her neck. "Sit up for me, just for a minute."

He tugged lightly until she sat up. Despite how hot she felt, she was shivering, and he gently squeezed her neck. "Open your eyes."

She blinked at him as he pushed the glass of orange juice into her hand. "Drink."

She drank some juice. It was cold and painful on her sore throat, but she took the pills Preacher gave her without protest. She washed them down with more juice, and he smoothed back the strands of hair that had fallen out of her ponytail and were plastered across her sweaty cheeks.

"Hot," she said.

"You have a fever," he said. "The medicine will help you feel better. Okay?"

"Okay," she mumbled.

"I have to go back to work," he said. "I'll put your phone on the nightstand. Just text me if you need anything, and I'll come upstairs."

Tears slid down her cheeks, and he wiped them away. "Don't cry, baby."

"Why are you being so nice to me?" she whispered.

He rubbed her cheekbone with his thumb before pressing a kiss against her forehead. "Get some rest. I'll check on you in a bit."

She curled up on her side, and he tucked the covers around her, closed the blinds on the window so the apartment was shrouded in comforting darkness, and left.

CHAPTER 24

W hen she woke, he was sitting beside her on the bed, scrolling through his phone. She sat up and scrubbed at her face.

"What time is it?" Her voice sounded like a shovel scraped over gravel, and she swallowed gingerly. She didn't object when he pressed his hand against her forehead.

"Just after seven," he said. "Do you feel better?"

"A little, I think. My head doesn't hurt as bad."

"Good. Your fever is gone."

She rubbed again at her forehead. "Are you finished work?"

"Yeah."

"Oh," she said.

There was a moment of awkward silence, and then she threw the covers back. "Okay, well, thank you for your help."

He frowned when she climbed out of bed and grabbed her yoga pants and sweatshirt from the floor. He stood and moved around the bed to stand in front of her. She covered her breasts with the sweatshirt. "I just need to use the bathroom quickly, and then I'll get out of here."

"You're staying the night," he said.

"I appreciate your help," she said, "but do you think I could give you a rain check for the thank you sex? I feel better than I did, but I'm still pretty stuffed up and achy, and I would feel bad if I gave you my cold. Plus, as I'm sure you've figured out, I have my period. I prefer not to have sex during my period."

"You think I want you to stay for sex?" he said.

"Uh, maybe?"

He scowled at her. "I'm not going to make you have sex with me. You need someone to look after you, and your fucking brother is useless."

She cocked her head at him. "How do you know that?"

"Never mind. You're spending the night, Addison. No arguing."

She opened her mouth to argue and barely had time to cover her mouth before sneezing.

He leaned down and picked up an overnight bag tucked at the end of the bed. She gave it a look of confusion. "That – is that my bag from my bedroom closet?"

He nodded. "During my supper break, I went to your apartment and grabbed some of your stuff for you."

Her mouth dropped open, and he stared at her in irritation. "What?"

"You went to my apartment? How did you get in?"

"Your keys were in your purse." He set the duffel bag on the bed. "I'll run a bath for you and then get us something to eat."

ADDISON WIPED HER DRIPPING NOSE BEFORE STARING INTO the overnight bag on the bed. The bag had most of her toiletries from her bathroom – it looked like Preacher had just grabbed everything on the shelves. She picked up a narrow tube and studied it before giggling despite her aching belly. Did Preacher think she might want to do a relaxing mud mask tonight? She tossed it back into the bag and reached for a pair of panties.

"How many pairs of panties does he think I need for one night?"

Preacher had stuffed a week's worth of underwear into the bag. All of them were her plain, practical cotton ones, and while she was grateful for that, she was also surprised. Her lacy, silk panties were in the same drawer, and she would have bet a thousand bucks that Preacher would have picked those out. Guys liked sexy underwear on a woman, and he didn't strike her as the type of guy who would think about the fact that she was on her period and might want more practical underwear.

Yeah, but you didn't think he would be the type of guy to pay for your tampons, run you a bath, and look after you when you were sick, either.

She sneezed and wiped her nose again. Her inner voice made a good point. She had no idea what Preacher was thinking but felt so horrible that she didn't want to think much about it. It was just nice to have someone take care of her.

Of course, she had told Preacher she didn't want a boyfriend, and she didn't need him to do any of this stuff. As much as she enjoyed being cared for, she needed to leave when he returned. If she gave him her cold, he'd be pissed and would probably never have sex with her again.

Seriously? Is sex with Preacher the only thing you can think about?

It wasn't the only thing, but hell, for the first time in her life, she was genuinely enjoying sex. The things Preacher did and said to her made her so hot, was it any wonder she had a difficult time thinking about anything else?

Too bad he doesn't feel the same way. You're not making a very good impression, Addie.

No, she supposed she wasn't. But that's why she was sleeping with him – to get better at sex. He seemed to enjoy the blowjob, but he hadn't asked her to go down on him again since. Before giving him the next one, she would ask him for clear instructions on what he liked and didn't like. She'd be better at it once she knew exactly what he wanted.

While she was at it, she needed to ask him for more instructions regarding sex. All the lessons so far were him teasing her and making her come so hard she nearly blacked out. While she supposed that was good for teaching her to be more responsive, it didn't help her with being sexier or making sure the guy was having a good time. Hell, half the time, she didn't even notice when Preacher came. She was too busy being off in la-la land from the mind-blowing orgasms he gave her. She wondered bleakly if he would even put up with her dismal skills in the bedroom for the entire month before he simply lost interest.

Does it matter? You can find another guy and get more lessons if you don't learn enough from Preacher.

The thought of sleeping with someone else made her already-aching stomach roll with nausea. She shoved the idea of sleeping with someone else - of *Preacher* sleeping with someone else – out of her head. She rubbed her stomach and then wiped her nose for a third time. The hot bath had cleared her sinuses somewhat, but she could feel the headache lurking behind her eyes. As soon as the cold meds wore off, she'd be right back to feeling like death.

She searched through the bag even though she could see

everything in it. Oddly enough, Preacher hadn't brought her any clothes, just underwear.

She hesitated and then opened the second drawer of Preacher's dresser. His t-shirts were folded in neat layers in the drawer, and she picked one from the top. It was dark blue with a Crimson Door Tattoo logo on the chest.

She dropped her towel and slipped into her panties before pulling his shirt over her head. It was much too big, but she liked wearing his shirt. Liked it a little too much, she supposed. She briefly considered putting her other clothes back on, cringed at the thought of wearing the dirty pants and t-shirt, and instead grabbed her comb from the bag. She combed her wet hair, gently pulling out the snarls and then braided it.

God, she felt so much better after her bath. She grabbed some orange juice from the fridge and took a swig as the apartment door opened and Preacher entered.

"Hi," she said.

"Hey." He placed the bag on the counter. "How do you feel?"

"Better," she said. "The bath really helped. I'll head home after dinner. The cold meds and the -"

She clapped her hand over her mouth before erupting into a coughing fit that bent her over with the force of it. She coughed and coughed, trying to catch her breath as Preacher pressed his hand on her upper back.

He rubbed slowly as her coughing fit eased, then pushed the juice bottle into her hand. "Drink."

She drank a few swallows, the acidic juice burning her throat. "Better, thanks."

He nodded and headed to the bathroom. Her eyes widened. She had left a bunch of her toiletries in the bathroom right next to his, like she had moved in, for God's sake. He would be pissed. She set the juice down and hurried forward, squeezing past him just as he got to the bathroom.

"I'm so sorry," she said as she scooped up her toiletries. He frowned as she snatched her shampoo, conditioner, and body wash from the tub's edge, juggling her toothbrush, toothpaste, and antiperspirant in one hand.

"Sorry," she repeated as she hurried out of the bathroom. The box of tampons was still in his bathroom, but she would need them again before she left. Hopefully, he wouldn't be too bothered by the box sitting on the sink.

He watched silently as she dumped her toiletries into the bag. "Thank you again for picking those up for me. It was nice to have a bath."

He just nodded and disappeared into the bathroom. She wandered over to the window and peeked through the blinds, people watching until Preacher returned. He opened the bag and pulled out a few containers. "Go sit on the couch."

She sat on the couch as he brought the food over and set it on the coffee table in front of them.

"Here." He handed her one container.

She took the lid off and smiled a little. It was chicken noodle soup. "You brought me soup."

"You're sick," he said. "It's from Nan's."

"Thank you." She spooned a few mouthfuls into her mouth. She was so stuffed up that she couldn't taste a thing, but she ate the entire container of soup as he ate a steak sandwich and salad.

"You want some of mine?" he asked when she was finished.

"No, I'm full. It was good."

"You're so stuffed up you probably can't taste anything." He studied her face, and hating that he saw her looking so awful, she looked down and picked away some non-existent lint from the front of his shirt.

"I borrowed one of your shirts. I hope that's okay."

"It's fine." He gave no explanation for why he hadn't brought her any clothes but underwear.

He handed her a bottle of water. "You should drink some water. You're dehydrated."

"Thanks."

She drank half the bottle of water before setting it on the coffee table. Her stomach was cramping from her period, and she was shivering from a combination of cold and exhaustion. She closed her eyes and rubbed her forehead as Preacher finished his meal. Her headache had returned, just as she had predicted. She didn't look up when Preacher stood from the couch. He returned a few minutes later.

"Take these."

He was holding some cold medicine, and she shook her head. "I'd better not. They make me sleepy, and I don't want to pass out on the bus. I'll take some as soon as I get home."

She tried to smile at him, but it died on her lips when he glared at her. "I told you – you're staying here tonight."

"Preacher -"

"Take the pills, Addison," he said.

She washed down the pills with a swallow of water. Part of her wanted to be thrilled at the idea that Preacher cared enough about her to watch over her while she was sick, but she couldn't seem to accept it. He had to have another motive, but her head was aching too badly for her to figure out what it was.

He'd disappeared again, and she curled into a small ball and pressed her hands against her aching abdomen. She would sleep on the couch, at least. It wasn't as comfortable as Preacher's bed, but the cold meds would knock her out. She could hear Preacher rustling behind her, but she was suddenly so damn tired. She yawned and shivered wildly, curled into a tighter ball before falling asleep.

———————

SHE WOKE UP A COUPLE OF HOURS LATER. SHE HAD A blanket on top of her, a crick in her neck, and her bladder was screaming at her. She sat up and stared at Preacher in the soft glow of the TV. He was sitting at the other end of the loveseat, his head tipped back and his body relaxed. He was snoring softly. The alarm clock by his bed said it was almost midnight. She coughed quietly and grabbed her toothbrush and toothpaste from the overnight bag before entering the bathroom. When she was finished, she washed her hands and brushed her teeth. She studied her reflection in the mirror before making a low "ugh". Her face was still bloated, her nose still swollen and red, and her eyes were rimmed with red. God, she looked like a nightmare.

She sneezed and blew her nose before washing her hands again and leaving the bathroom. The TV was off, and the apartment was pitch black. She could just make out the large shape of Preacher's body stretched out in the bed. Holding her hands out in front of her and hoping she didn't trip, she shuffled toward the couch.

The light on the bedstand clicked on, and Preacher sat up. "What are you doing?"

"Going back to the couch," she said. "I'm sorry. I didn't mean to wake you."

He got out of bed, and she said, "Do you have an extra pillow I could borrow?"

He sighed in annoyance and took her arm. "Get in the bed, Addison."

"I can take the couch," she said as he tugged her toward his bed. "I don't mind at all."

"My bed, now," he said.

She climbed into his bed without further argument as he shut the light off. Her stomach was cramping, and his bed was much more comfortable than the loveseat. She curled on her side on the edge of the bed and pressed her hand against her stomach as another cramp went through it.

She made a startled "eep" when Preacher pulled her into the center of the bed and up against him. His large body was deliciously warm against her back and ass.

"Move your hand," he said.

She moved her hand away from her stomach, and he reached over her and pressed the heating pad against her belly. He must have plugged it in when she got up from the couch because it was already warm. He held it there with one big hand as he rested his head on the pillow behind hers.

"Thank you," she whispered. She felt a little weepy at how nice he was to her but held back the tears grimly. Crying would stuff her up even more.

"Go to sleep," he said.

"Okay," she said. "Good night, Preacher."

"Night, Sunshine."

"Pinky-pie, you're not looking so hot."

Addison laughed and tried a different angle with her phone. "Better?"

"Nope. You sound terrible, too," Harper said.

"Remind me again why I answered your video call?"

"Because you love me and because when you didn't

answer three of my texts in a row, I threatened to text Gideon and have him do a wellness check on you?"

"I've been passed out on cold medicine for the past two days," Addison said.

"My poor girl. Summer colds are the worst," Harper said.

"They really are. But as awful as I look, I'm feeling better today," Addison said. "My sinus headache is gone, and I'm not sneezing every thirty seconds."

"Where are you?" Harper said.

"What do you mean?"

"I mean, where are you?"

"I'm in bed."

"I can see you're in bed," Harper said. "But it ain't your bed. So, whose bed is it?"

"Why do you think it's not my bed?" Addison hedged.

"Addison Mabel Moore, I know what the wall behind your bed looks like." Harper squinted into the camera. "I also know your quilt is a blue checkered pattern, not a plain gray. So, answer the question you're so blatantly avoiding."

"Fine," Addison said. "I'm at Preacher's apartment above the shop."

Harper's mouth dropped open. "The fuck you are."

"It's not a big deal," she said.

"Show me his apartment," Harper said.

"What? Why?"

"Just do it."

Addison flipped the camera around and did a slow scan of the apartment before reversing the camera to face her. "There, satisfied?"

"It's a small place," Harper said. "I like the shag carpet and the avocado fridge… very seventies retro."

"It's a studio apartment," Addie said. "He doesn't even have a stove or a microwave."

"Okay, I have some questions. First – where is Preacher?"

"Downstairs in the shop," she said.

"On a Sunday? I thought his shop was closed on Sunday and Monday."

"It is. He uses the washer and dryer in the shop to do his laundry. And he said he had a sketch he wanted to work on."

"Okay. Second – why are you at Preacher's place?"

"On Friday, I took the bus to Walgreens to pick up some cold meds and tampons, and Preacher was in the store. I had a bad fever and was feeling awful, and he…"

"He what?"

"He brought me back to his apartment. He said I needed someone to look after me while I was sick. I thought he just wanted sex again, so I tried to leave Friday night after I'd slept in his bed for the day. I have my period, and between that and this stupid cold, I am so not into trying to be sexy, you know? But he said he didn't want sex."

"So, you've been staying with Preacher while you're sick and have your period in his tiny little apartment since Friday?"

"Yes."

"In his tiny apartment with only one bathroom where he might hear or smell you doing certain unsexy things in said bathroom?" Harper said.

"It's not that big of a deal."

"Okay, so your body has definitely been invaded by an alien who is now controlling your every move. Addie, if you can hear me, hang tight. I'll be there in seventeen hours with a team of scientists to save your life."

"You're being weird, Harper," Addison said.

"Pinky-pie, you refused to poop if Harrison was within a two-mile radius of you the first five years you dated him. Now, you're practically living with Preacher in his apartment that's even smaller than this crack hole I'm living in, and you're pooping all willy-nilly like it ain't no thing. Don't act like I'm being the crazy one."

"There's a fan in the bathroom," Addison said.

Harper laughed until tears ran down her cheeks, and she had to hold onto her stomach with one hand. "Oh my God, Addie, I love you so much."

"Have you found another job yet?" Addie said.

"No, but stop changing the subject. Are you and Preacher dating?"

"Of course not," she said. "Why would you think that?"

"You're pooping in -"

"Oh my God, enough with the pooping," Addison said. "We're not dating. He's just being nice. Preacher has a sweet side to him, okay?"

"Okay, but Addie, just remember that -"

She could hear Preacher's footsteps on the stairs and said, "Harper, I have to go. Preacher's on his way up. I love you."

"Love you too. Text me later."

She ended the call and smiled at Preacher when he walked in with a clothes basket. "Hi. That didn't take long."

He set the basket of clean clothes on the bed. "How are you feeling?"

"Better," she said.

"Good. You ready?" He glanced at the watch on his wrist.

"Ready for what?" she said.

"To go home."

Dismay mixed with a healthy dose of embarrassment made her face red. "Right, of course. Yes, I'm good."

She slid out of his bed and grabbed her clothes sitting on top of the basket. "Thank you for washing my clothes."

"No problem." He had grabbed his phone and was scrolling through it.

She hurried into the bathroom and quickly got dressed. Her stomach was churning, and she couldn't believe how stupid she was being. She should be grateful that Preacher let her stay this long, not be upset and close to tears that he was kicking her out. He had done more than enough for her over the last two days, and she would plaster a smile on her face and make sure he knew how grateful she was for his help.

Blowing him would be a nice thank you gesture.

She gathered up her toiletries. Yeah, it would be, but even though she was feeling better, she still had her period, and she wasn't up for sex tonight anyway. Hopefully, she'd be over her cold by the weekend and invite him over to say thanks.

If he's still interested in giving you lessons. Maybe this is it for you. Did you think of that? He said you would want more, and he was right. He's come to his senses and is ending it before you start believing you guys are a couple or something.

Being upset that he was ending it was probably a good indication that it was time to finish it. This thing between them always had an expiry date. That expiration date had been moved up, and Addie had no one to blame but herself. She should have gone home Friday night instead of staying with him all weekend.

She took a deep breath and arranged her face into a semblance of a smile. She joined Preacher by the bed and dumped her toiletries into her bag. She stuffed the shirt she'd been wearing into the bag as well. "I'll wash this and return it to you."

"Sure." He had a scuffed and worn leather newsletter bag crossed over his chest, and he tugged absently on the long strap.

Her face flushed as she put on her flip-flops. She had no

intention of returning it to him unless he specifically asked for it. She wanted something to remind her of him.

Jesus, you'll see him at the barbeques and ball games, you idiot. Stop being so dramatic.

Her stomach clenched tight. She *would* see him, and how awful was that going to be? Worse, how would it feel when she saw him with another woman?

She wanted to barf. She wanted to cry. She wanted to do something extremely dumb, like ask Preacher if he wanted to try dating.

Instead, she took another deep breath, slung her bag over her shoulder, and grabbed her purse. "Okay, well, thank you again, Preacher. I appreciate all of your help. I'll pop by later this week when I'm feeling better and pay you for the stuff from Walgreens."

He frowned at her. "Why are you acting like you're taking the bus home, Addison?"

"Well, I know you're busy and..."

"You're not taking the bus home," he said in the now familiar *stop arguing with me* tone. He took her bag and put it over his shoulder. "Let's go."

CHAPTER 25

"Thank you for carrying my bag in," Addison said.

"You're welcome. Be right back." Preacher dropped Addison's bag in her bedroom. When he returned, Addison stood by the door and looked weirdly upset.

"What's wrong?" he said.

"Nothing. Um, so thank you again. I appreciate you helping me this weekend and letting me invade your space."

"No problem," he said.

"Okay, well, bye then."

"You want me to leave?" he said.

Shit. He sounded like an idiot. He'd brought Addison back to her place because his apartment was a shithole compared to hers, and he figured she'd prefer to be in her own bed. But he assumed he'd stay with her. He would have kept her at his place if he'd thought she'd asked him to leave.

Oh my God. You know how pathetic you sound right now, right? She doesn't want you to stay. Go home before you make an even bigger fool of yourself.

"See you around," he said. He sounded sulky and like the

world's biggest fucking baby, and he winced inwardly before pushing past Addison.

"Preacher, wait!" Addison's soft hand grabbed his arm. "I don't want you to leave."

He turned to face her, wondering if his relief was plastered all over his face. "No?"

"No," she said. "I thought – I mean, when you said it was time for me to go home, I thought that you didn't want to be around me anymore. Which, I understand because if I were you, I wouldn't want to get sick with this cold either, and with my period, I can't, um, *do* anything for you."

"I brought you home because I figured you would want your own bed, and your own stuff, and maybe some food that wasn't takeout. You know, like vegetables and fruit."

She started to giggle, which almost immediately became a coughing fit, but to his relief, it wasn't that deep booming rasp of a cough, even from two days ago.

He rubbed her back until she stopped coughing and said, "Get into bed. I'll make you tea for your throat."

"Thank you." She disappeared into the bedroom, and he made her some tea before taking off his boots and joining her. She was sitting up in the bed, already knitting, and she took the cup of tea from him with a small smile.

"Thank you. It smells good."

He sat on the bed beside her, propping a pillow behind his back before opening his bag. He pushed past the extra pair of underwear and the antiperspirant he'd shoved into the bag and grabbed his tablet and stylus.

What? No toothbrush?

He didn't need a toothbrush. The first time he'd stayed overnight, Addison gave him a new toothbrush she had in the medicine cabinet. It was still sitting in the holder next to hers in the bathroom.

Just moving right in, aren't you? Making yourself completely at home. You going to ask her to clear a space in her closet for your fucking clothes?

He turned on his tablet. Addison's knitting needles clicking, the warmth of her small body next to his in the bed, hell, even the occasional sniff she made, were stupidly comforting.

"What are you working on?" Addison said.

He showed her his sketch. It was a bear's skull surrounded by colourful flowers. A flush of pride went through him when Addison said, "Wow. That's amazing. You're such an incredible artist. You and Harper would have a lot to chat about when it comes to art."

"Thanks," he said.

For a while, the only sound in the room was the clicking of Addison's knitting needles. He made a few adjustments to his sketch before googling some images of flowers. As he studied them, he rested one hand on Addison's thigh. Her apartment was a bit warm even with the air conditioning, and she had changed from her yoga pants into cotton shorts before climbing into bed. He couldn't resist touching the smooth softness of her skin.

When his phone dinged, he dug it out of his pocket and checked his messages before texting back. Addison didn't ask, but he said, "It's Gideon."

"Is he asking you about the barbeque at Kira's tonight? Grace texted earlier to see if I was feeling better and if I needed a ride."

"You probably shouldn't go," he said. "You're still sick."

He supposed she was probably well enough to go for a little while, but he selfishly wanted to keep her to himself for a while longer. If they went to the barbeque, he wouldn't be able to touch her whenever he wanted.

"I know. I told her I was skipping out on this one."

Addison gave him a quick sideways glance. "What time are you headed over there?"

"I'm not," he said. "I told Gideon I couldn't make it."

"You shouldn't miss out on the barbeque because of me," she said. "I'm better now and -"

"You shouldn't be alone," he said. "You still have coughing fits that almost make you pass out."

"Does that mean you're spending the night?" she said with another sideways glance.

"Probably a good idea," he said. "Just to be on the safe side. If you're good with it?"

"Yes," she said. "I, um, I'd prefer that. You know, to be on the safe side."

He grinned at her and rested his hand on her thigh again, gently squeezing it. After a few minutes, she picked up her knitting, and the soft clicking sound started.

As he scanned the internet for flower images, Preacher tried to identify the weird feeling inside him. After a moment, it dawned on him.

Holy fuck. He was happy.

———

"You're right. This wrapping paper is adorable, and my mom will love it."

Addison laughed. "I know when you're mocking me, Lucas."

He grinned at her. "I'm not mocking you. She really will love it. Thanks for letting me have some of it."

"No problem," she said.

He glanced around her living room. "Your place is nice. You like the neighbourhood?"

"I do," she said. "It's mostly rentals in this area, but it's quiet and not too far from downtown."

"Some of the guys transferring from the New Cassel office to the one here are looking for places to rent. I'll mention this neighbourhood," Lucas said. "According to Kira, my neighbourhood is a hot spot and hard to get into. Which makes it even more impressive that she found me something."

"I was texting with Kira today, and she said she had an appointment this afternoon with your boss to look at a few houses."

Lucas nodded. "Yeah, Stark's in town this week. Construction on the office building is almost complete, so he's doing a final check. He mentioned he was looking at houses today when I had coffee with him this morning."

He glanced at his watch. "Anyway, I should get going. It's almost seven-thirty, and I said I'd meet Connor for a drink at the Thirsty Otter."

She laughed. "It's the Thirsty Beaver."

"I know," he said with a grin. "Do you mind if I use your washroom before I go?"

"Not at all," she said. "Second door on the left."

He headed down the hallway as there was a light knock on the door. She checked the peephole, and happiness flooded through her. Preacher was standing in the hallway. He had stayed with her Sunday night and all of Monday and spent last night with her, too. But when he'd left this morning to go to work, he hadn't said if he would come by tonight or not.

Honestly, she'd assumed he wouldn't. They'd spent the last two days holed up in her apartment doing nothing but napping and binge-watching television shows on Netflix. He hadn't once asked her for sex.

On Monday afternoon, feeling more like herself for the first time since Thursday, she tried to give him a blowjob. At the beginning of her relationship with Harrison, before he decided she was boring in bed, he'd often try to convince her to have sex during her period. He became pouty and dismissive when she refused. She'd learned quickly that giving him a blowjob was the only way to bring him out of his bad mood with her.

To her surprise, Preacher refused to let her go down on him. Confused and slightly upset by his refusal, she'd pushed past her embarrassment and asked him why. His explanation that he wasn't into it if she didn't get anything in return was still a concept she was trying to grasp fully.

She opened the door. "Hi. Snuck past the security in the lobby again, huh?"

He grinned at her. "Your neighbours think nothing of holding the door for a tattooed biker. You busy?"

"No, come in." She shut the door behind him. "Did you eat dinner?"

"Nah, worked through it."

"I made chicken stir-fry for dinner, and there are leftovers. Do you want some?"

"Sure." He followed her into the kitchen, leaning against the counter as she pulled the stir-fry out of the fridge. "How was your day?"

"Good. I stayed home and gave myself one more day of rest, but I think tomorrow I might venture into the real world and have lunch with Kira and Grace. Kira said she'd swing by and pick me up, and we'd have lunch close to the dental clinic. Kira's got a showing right after lunch, so she can't drive me home, but there's a bus stop outside of Grace's clinic."

She popped the leftovers into the microwave. "Do you want water or juice?"

"Water is -"

"Addison? Thanks again for – oh, hey, **Preacher**." Lucas returned to the narrow kitchen.

Preacher's face paled and then turned red. "What the fuck are you doing here?"

"Preacher," Addison said, "stop it."

"What the fuck is he doing in your apartment, Addison?" Preacher said. Without waiting for her reply, he turned to Lucas. "Get the fuck out of here, asshole."

"Stop it!" Addison glared at him. "You're being rude."

"I don't fucking care. I don't want him here with you alone," Preacher said.

Pissed at his behaviour, she stared pointedly at him. "It's not your decision to make."

"Like hell it isn't," he said.

"Like hell it is," she said.

"I'm gonna go." Lucas grabbed the wrapping paper from the counter, and Addison followed him toward the door, shaking off Preacher's hand when he touched her arm.

"Lucas, I'm so sorry."

"Don't worry about it," he said.

"You don't have to leave."

He laughed and glanced at Preacher, standing at the edge of the kitchen with his arms folded across his chest. "That's nice of you to say, but I'm pretty fond of my head being exactly where it is, and if I stay any longer, your boyfriend is gonna shove it right up my own ass."

"I'm not her boyfriend," Preacher snarled.

A healthy dose of hurt mixed in with the anger. She shoved it ruthlessly aside. Two days of Preacher being nice to her didn't make him her boyfriend.

Lucas opened the door. "See you later, Addie."

"Bye, Lucas."

The minute the door shut, she turned and glared at Preacher. "Are you freaking kidding me?"

"What?"

"You can't just dictate who comes to my place, Simon."

"I don't want you alone with him. I don't fucking trust him."

"Lucas is a nice guy, and even if you *were* my boyfriend, you still wouldn't get to tell me who I can and cannot be friends with."

"I'm not your boyfriend."

"I *know*," she said. "You're making that clear. It's just sex between us, I get it."

"Why the fuck was Lucas here anyway? The lessons I'm giving you on fucking not enough? You gotta bring in a pinch hitter?"

"You asshole," she said. "I told you I wouldn't have sex with anyone else while we were… were together. Stop being such a dick."

"This is who I am, sweetheart. You don't like it, that's not my problem."

"This isn't who you are," she said. "It's who you pretend to be because God forbid anyone should see the real Simon."

"You know what?" He pushed away from the counter. "I don't need this fucking bullshit. I'm done giving you sex lessons."

"Fine by me," she said.

He stomped past her, jerked open the door and slammed it shut behind him.

She cursed in frustration before stalking back to the kitchen. The microwave beeped, and she yanked the stir fry out and set it on the counter. She stared blankly at it before bursting into tears.

"You okay? You don't look so hot."

Preacher glanced up from his tablet. The shimmering lights hovering at the edge of his vision brought on a dull sense of panic. "I'm fine."

"You sure?" Nix leaned against the table. "Seriously, man, you look sick."

He gave up trying to work and shut off his tablet. He had maybe thirty minutes before the pain started. Another wave of panic washed over him, and the shimmery light of the aura flashed briefly. "I'm getting a migraine."

"Shit." Nolan had joined them. "I'll cancel your appointment for this afternoon. You want me to cancel tomorrow's appointments, too?"

"Yeah." It was going to be a bad one, he could tell. He had no one to blame but himself. He'd barely slept since storming out of Addison's house three days ago, and lack of sleep was his biggest trigger. He pulled out his phone and quickly texted Gideon, squinting at the screen.

"He get migraines a lot?" Nix said to Nolan.

Nolan nodded. "Yeah. Fucking lays him flat on his back. You going to go to the sheriff's?"

Preacher nodded before squinting at his screen again. He needed to call an Uber. The pain was starting, and he wouldn't make it to Gideon's if he drove himself.

"Fuck," he muttered as the throbbing in his head increased.

"Give me your phone. I'll call you an Uber." Nolan took his phone. "What's the sheriff's address again?"

Preacher mumbled out the address as the door swung open, and a man wearing a cowboy hat and boots walked in.

"That's my two-thirty appointment," Nix said. "Feel

better, man." He clapped Preacher lightly on the back before walking over and greeting the client.

Nolan handed him his phone. "Uber's on the way. I'll close up the shop tonight and open tomorrow."

"Thanks, Nolan." He felt a wave of gratitude for his apprentice. The guy might never shut the fuck up, but more than once, he'd taken care of the shop when Preacher was suffering from a migraine.

"It's no problem. Your Uber will be here in two minutes. Text me if you need anything." Nolan squeezed his shoulder and left.

His phone dinged. The aura was so strong now that he could barely read Gideon's reply text. His head throbbing and sick to his stomach, he considered going to his apartment and riding out the migraine alone rather than brave the drive to Gideon's house, but ultimately headed outside.

He hated being alone when he had a migraine. He needed Gideon there, needed him checking on him every few hours, bringing him water and ice packs, and making sure he wasn't fucking dead from a goddamn aneurism or something. His not quite articulated fear that the migraine would never end, that he would spend the rest of his life in agony, was dimmed somewhat when he wasn't alone.

The Uber was waiting for him, and he staggered forward and climbed into the back seat, trying to keep the sudden nausea at bay.

"Hello," the driver said.

He mumbled out a hello and closed his eyes. He'd be okay. He just needed to get to Gideon's, and then he'd be okay.

PREACHER SQUINTED OUT THE WINDOW AT THE BUILDING THEY were parked in front of.

"What the fuck?" he muttered. "Why are we here?"

"This is the address you gave me." The Uber driver twisted in his seat to stare at him.

"What?" Preacher tried to think past the throbbing pain in his head. "No, I didn't."

"Yeah, you did," the guy said. His cell phone rang loud and shrill, and Preacher could barely stop from grabbing it and throwing it out the window. The driver stared at his phone as it rang but didn't answer it.

"For fuck's sake," Preacher growled. "Answer the goddamn thing."

The driver stared cautiously at him. "What's your problem, man? You're sweaty, and you look fucked up. You on drugs or something?"

"No," Preacher gritted out.

The phone rang repeatedly, and with a small groan of pain, Preacher opened the car door. "Thanks."

"Sure, yeah," the driver said.

He nearly fell out of the car in his haste to get out. He shut the door and braced his hands on his knees as the car pulled away. The exhaust made his gorge rise, and he fought bitterly against vomiting. After a few seconds, he won, and he straightened and staggered down the sidewalk to the building.

He should call Gideon and ask him to come pick him up, but the thought of trying to use his cell phone, of sitting outside with the hot sun beating down on his aching, pounding head, made him want to cry like a fucking baby.

He couldn't do it. He needed a soft bed and darkness before his fucking head exploded. He had given Nolan the wrong address to type in by accident, and now he just had to hope she was home and would let him inside.

He buzzed her apartment number. The sound made new pain burst through his head, and he lowered it and clung grimly to the wall as he waited.

"Hello?"

"It's me," he gritted out. "Can I come in?"

There was silence, and he was getting ready to beg when the door buzzed open. He yanked on the door handle and staggered into the blessed coolness of the lobby. In too much pain to climb the stairs, he took the elevator. He rubbed the back of his neck as the fire in his brain burned bright. He lurched out of the elevator and down the hallway to her apartment. Before he could knock, the door opened, and he squinted at her as he swayed back and forth.

"Preacher? What's wrong?" Even Addison's soft voice seemed too loud.

He grimaced and gripped the doorframe for support. "Migraine," he managed to spit out.

"Come in."

Thank Christ, she didn't ask more questions or say anything else.

He stumbled into her small apartment and leaned against the wall. He needed to remove his boots, but his stomach was churning, and his head was on fire. If he leaned down, he would either pass out or throw up.

He realized that Addison had crouched and was unlacing his boots. She tugged them off his feet before taking his hand. "Come lie down, Preacher."

Squinting, trying not to vomit all over the back of her head, he stumbled down the hallway to her bedroom. Sunlight streamed through the window, and he groaned and shielded his eyes.

Addison quickly pulled the blinds, plunging the room into darkness. He breathed a sigh of relief as she led him to the bed. Remaining silent, she helped him strip off his clothes. When he was naked, she urged him into her bed. She pulled the covers to his waist and left the room.

He kept his eyes closed as his head pulsed and throbbed. It would only worsen, and he wondered if he should ask Addison to take him to the hospital. He didn't want to go. He knew from experience that it would be too loud and too bright, and the pain meds they gave would maybe dull the pain if he were lucky. He didn't need that. He just needed dark and quiet. His head felt like it would explode, but it would get better. It always did...eventually.

Sex will help.

Yeah, it would. For some migraine sufferers, orgasms helped to ease the pain. Sometimes, it even made the pain disappear completely. That didn't usually happen to him, but an orgasm did provide enough relief that he might avoid going to the hospital. He wondered if Addison would freak out if he masturbated in her bed. He pictured the look of horror on her sweet face when she returned to find him yanking one out and would have laughed if he didn't believe it would make his head detonate like a bomb. Even thinking about moving his goddamn arm back and forth made him queasy.

Ask Addison to do it. You don't have to move – she'll do all the work.

Jesus, he wished his inner voice would just shut the fuck up. He could only imagine what Addison would say if he asked her for a hand job. At best, she'd think he was a fucking idiot. At worst, she'd think he was faking the migraine just to get laid.

She was back. He could smell her sweet scent in the room, and he tried not to wince when she sat on the bed, and it jostled his aching head. A cold cloth was placed on his forehead, and he groaned at the pressure but didn't move it. Sometimes, cold helped.

"Do you have medication?" she said.

"Doesn't work," he grunted out before clenching his hands into fists. Fuck, he was going to vomit. He struggled to sit up as the cloth fell to his lap with a wet plop. She pressed her hand against his chest.

"What's wrong?"

"Gonna barf." He was about three seconds from throwing up all over Addison and her bed. He'd never make it to the bathroom in time.

A bucket was pushed into his hands, and he immediately vomited into it. He threw up again and again until his stomach was empty, and he felt shaky and weak. He dry-heaved a few times as she rubbed the back of his neck with her cool hand. When he was done, she helped him ease back onto the bed. The bucket was pulled from his hands, and a cool cloth wiped his mouth.

"Okay?" Her tiny hands stroked his chest.

"Yeah," he grunted. It was a lie. While his stomach was no longer churning, the vomiting had made his head hurt even more, and the pain was fucking blinding him. "Sorry."

"It's fine," she said. "I'll be right back."

She disappeared, and the foul smell of his vomit vanished with her. Faintly, he heard the sound of a toilet flushing and a few minutes later, Addison was back.

"Sorry," he rasped again.

"It's okay." Her cool hand rested on his forehead. "What about the hospital? I can call Gideon and ask him to give us a ride to the hospital. They can give you stronger pain meds and maybe some oxygen."

"Not going to the hospital," he said waspishly. "Just need to be left alone."

"Do orgasms help?"

He opened his eyes. She stared at him with no embarrassment, and he closed his eyes again. "Yeah."

"Okay." Her soft little hand slipped under the covers and wrapped around his dick, and he groped blindly for it.

"No."

"Why not?" she said.

"I can't do anything for you," he said.

"You don't have to."

"Not fair," he muttered.

Jesus Christ, you idiot! Shut the fuck up!

"I want to do this," she said before pulling her hand free of his. "Let me help you, Simon."

He relented when she said his name, letting his hands fall to his sides as she pulled the covers down to his knees.

"If you need me to stop, just say so." Her warm breath washed over his cock, and despite the dragon spewing fire in his brain, his cock twitched. Christ, was she going to blow him? At this point, he would be happy with a hand job. Giving him a damn blowjob was going above and beyond the

—

Her warm mouth slid over his cock, and he groaned. His hips arched automatically, and he made another low groan of pain as the movement sent bolts of agony through his head. She stopped immediately and massaged his thick thighs.

"Simon, can you do this?"

"Yes," he whispered without opening his eyes. "Please try. It'll help if I come."

She took his cock into her mouth again, sucking him firmly until he was hard and throbbing despite the agony in his brain. She didn't waste time teasing or tormenting. She set a firm and steady pace of sucking, her hand squeezing and stroking the base. He gave in to the sensation completely. He wanted to come – fuck, he needed to come – and he wasn't even embarrassed when his body shuddered, and he climaxed after only a few minutes. She swallowed his seed and licked him clean before sitting up on the side of the bed.

"Turn over," she said.

He turned onto his stomach. His head was still pounding, but the rush of endorphins from his orgasm had helped to dull it to a more manageable pain. He groaned when her soft but surprisingly strong hands kneaded his tense upper back muscles and shoulders.

"Any better?"

"A little," he groaned.

"Good. Try to relax, Simon."

He would never relax. The orgasm had helped. He no longer felt like his head was going to simply shatter apart at the slightest touch, but it still hurt like motherfucking hell. Still, her rubbing and massaging were helping. It was impossible to stay tense with her hands rubbing out every knot in his shoulders and neck.

"Feels good, Sunshine," he mumbled.

"I'm glad. Go to sleep, honey."

"Yeah, sleep." He made a soft snorting sound and drifted.

CHAPTER 26

Addison studied Preacher in the dim light. His face was pale and sweaty, and even in sleep, the pain was still etched into it. She used the cool cloth to wipe his upper back and neck before pulling the sheets up to his waist.

His clothes were lying on the floor, and she picked them up and carried them to the dresser. She was about to drape them over the dresser when his jeans vibrated. She fished in his pocket and pulled out his cell phone. The screen was lit up with two missed calls from Gideon and a flurry of texts.

Where are you?

Call me, for God's sake.

If you stayed at home, then call me and let me know.

She nearly dropped his phone when it vibrated in her hand. Gideon was calling again, and she hurried out of the bedroom before answering it.

"Hi Gideon, it's Addie."

"Addie? Where's Preacher?" Gideon asked.

"He's here at my place. He has a migraine."

"I know," Gideon said. "He usually comes to my place

when he has one. He texted me and said he was on his way over."

"He showed up at my place about half an hour ago," Addie said.

"Why? I didn't think it was serious between you two. Preacher told me it was just fuc -"

He stopped abruptly, and Addison felt a moment of shame. She swallowed it down and said, "We are just, um, screwing. He probably came here because the pain got too bad, and my place is closer. It's a bad one – he can barely walk, and he's throwing up."

"Well, I can come get him if you want," Gideon said. "I've been through this with him more times than I can count, and he can be a real asshole when he's got a migraine. Not that I blame him."

"It's fine," Addison said. "He's sleeping right now, and I don't want to wake him up. If he wants to go to your place later, can I call you to pick him up? I still don't have a car."

"Yes," Gideon said. "If you need anything, just call me. Okay?"

"I will. Thanks, Gideon."

She hit the end button and went back into the bedroom. She returned Preacher's phone to his pocket and turned on the ceiling fan. It was starting to get stuffy in the bedroom, but she didn't want to open the window. The noise from the street might wake him. She stood by the side of the bed and studied Preacher. Why was he here? In the last three days, he hadn't tried to contact her.

A small part of her – okay, a very large part - had hoped he would show up at her place on Wednesday night with another apology. Even Thursday night, she was still holding out hope. He liked having sex with her. Maybe that would be enough to get him to admit he'd been acting stupid about Lucas.

But by this morning, she'd had to admit the truth to herself. Preacher was finished giving her lessons. The sex was over between them.

Oh yeah? He showed up at your apartment, didn't he? You just gave him a goddamn blow job.

Preacher had shown up at her place instead of Gideon's because he was one of those migraine sufferers who could find some relief from the pain with an orgasm. He knew she would give him one, so he came to her place.

You sure about that? He never mentioned an orgasm. You brought it up. Remember?

She ignored her inner voice and brushed her lips across his cheek. He didn't move, and she crept out of the bedroom and into the kitchen to finish making dinner.

SHE PROBABLY SHOULDN'T SLEEP IN THE BED NEXT TO HIM, but it was almost midnight, and she was tired. Preacher had been sleeping for hours and would probably sleep through the night. She could have taken the couch, but it was uncomfortable, and there was enough room next to him in the bed. Besides, she reasoned as she undressed to a nightshirt and her panties, she should be close by in case he needed the bucket to vomit again or wanted to go to the hospital.

Or in case he needs another blow job.

She flushed as she slipped carefully into the bed next to him. Yeah, that, too. What kind of person did it make her to hope that Preacher would need another orgasm? She'd watched her mother suffer for years with migraines, and she knew how horrible they were. She shouldn't be wishing something like that on him just because it gave her a thrill to make him climax.

She eased up the covers, trying not to jostle him as she lay on her side and stared at the wall. She shouldn't be so happy that Preacher came to her when he was sick. It didn't mean anything. Maybe he thought she owed him because he cared for her when she was sick. Yes, that was probably it. Which was fair enough. He had taken very good –

She jerked when Preacher shifted closer until his body was pressed against hers. He put his arm around her waist, and she didn't object when his big hand cupped her breast and kneaded it lightly. It didn't take long before his erection was pushing against her ass. He was lying very still behind her. Only his hand moved as he squeezed and caressed her breast, and she touched his forearm.

"Do you still have a migraine?" she whispered.

"Yeah."

"I'm sorry. I hoped an orgasm would help."

"It did," he said in a low voice.

He didn't say anything else, and after a moment, she said, "Do you want another one?"

More silence, and then, sounding unsure and nothing like the usual brash Preacher, he said, "Yeah. If you don't mind?"

"I don't," she said immediately. Before she could twist around, his hand was sliding under the waistband of her panties and cupping her pussy. His rough fingers rubbed at her clit, and she moaned before grabbing his wrist. "Hey, this is about you, remember?"

"I want to fuck you this time," he muttered.

His words sent pleasure spiraling through her belly. "Okay," she said, "but I can touch myself until I'm wet enough to take you."

"No," he said. His head didn't move at all from the pillow. "Let me make you come, Sunshine."

She gave in and shoved her panties down her legs and off her feet. She spread her thighs to give him better access. His fingers rubbed and stroked and pulled on her clit as she clutched at his wrist.

"Oh gosh," she whispered, "oh gosh, it feels so good."

She bit at her bottom lip. His head was pounding, and he didn't need to hear her talking. She concentrated on keeping quiet, but as she grew closer and closer, low moans and whimpers spilled from her lips.

"That's right," Preacher said in a low voice. His hips were rocking ever so slightly, pushing his cock up and down the crack of her ass. "I fucking love it when you come on my fingers, on my cock, on my face. Did you know that, baby?"

She moaned again, and her hips arched as his words pushed her over the edge. She tried not to shake the bed too much as she came and kept her mouth closed against the loud moans that wanted to escape.

When she could think straight again, she sat up. "Your turn. Lie on your back, and I'll ride you."

He shifted onto his back and worry trickled through her when he made a groan of pain. "Keep your eyes closed," she said. "I'm turning on the bedside lamp."

She turned it on and studied his face. His tanned skin was pale, and pain was etched into every line of his face. She cursed under her breath. She shouldn't have let him give her an orgasm.

"Oh, honey," she said as she stroked his broad chest, "how bad is it?"

"Not as bad as before," he said. "But still pretty fucking bad."

"You shouldn't have given me an orgasm."

"I wanted to," he said.

She carefully straddled him. His hands cupped her thighs as she pressed his cock against her entrance. "Are you sure you want this and not a blowjob?"

"Yes," he said. "Please, Sunshine."

She pushed firmly. Her wet pussy slid down his cock, and he groaned, his hands digging into her thighs.

"I think you'll have to do all the work," he muttered.

"I know," she said. "Don't move, honey."

She rode him slowly, trying not to jiggle the bed too much. He groaned, his hands kneading at her thighs but the rest of his body remaining still as she rocked up and down. She braced her hands on his chest and rode him a little harder, watching his face carefully. The pain was easing from it, and his breathing was becoming laboured.

"Okay?" she said.

"Fuck, yeah," he whispered. "Your little pussy feels so good, Sunshine. Can you go harder?"

She did what he asked, squeezing her inner muscles with every downward stroke. He groaned. "Fuck, you keep doing that, and I'm gonna come."

"Don't hold back, honey." She moved faster. The motion of the bed didn't seem to bother him, and she squeezed and released him as his hips arched beneath her. Like before, he didn't last long, and she ground her pelvis against him when he came with a hoarse moan. His entire body tensed, and he moaned again before collapsing on the bed.

She climbed off of him and slid off the bed. He was lying motionless on the bed, and she patted his thigh. "I'll be right back."

She used the bathroom quickly and then went to the kitchen. She returned with a glass of water and rubbed

Preacher's leg. "Can you sit up for a minute and drink some water? I think you're dehydrated."

He sat up slowly, and she rubbed the back of his neck as he drank the water. He kept his eyes closed, and she rubbed his neck again. "Is it better?"

"Yes," he said. Addison could hear the relief in his voice, and she pressed a quick kiss against his cheek.

"Good. Drink more water, and then you can sleep, okay?"

He drank the rest of the water, and she set the glass on the nightstand before pulling the covers up.

"Are you getting into bed?" he said.

"I can sleep on the couch if you prefer."

"No," he said. "Get in the bed."

She shut off the light and climbed into the bed next to him. He grunted with annoyance when he felt the soft material of her nightshirt.

"Lose this," he said.

He was starting to sound like Preacher again, and that made her so happy that she stripped off the nightshirt without protesting. She normally didn't sleep naked, but it was hard to resist Preacher, even when he didn't feel well.

She curled on her side again, and he molded his body to hers. He cupped her breast and kissed the back of her neck. "Thank you, Sunshine."

"You're welcome, Simon."

WHEN SHE WOKE, IT WAS JUST AFTER NINE, AND PREACHER'S side of the bed was empty. She swallowed her disappointment and slid out of bed, yanking her nightshirt over her head before starting toward the door. She had to pee like crazy, and she needed a coffee. She would get her caffeine hit, then have a long hot shower to wash away Preacher's scent. If she didn't, she'd be distracted all day.

Her eyes widened when Preacher stepped into the room. He was naked except for a towel tucked around his hips. His dark hair was wet, and he smelled like her body wash.

"Um, hi," she said.

"Hey. I used your shower."

"That's fine," she said. "Your toothbrush is still in the bathroom."

"I used it," he said.

"Do you feel better?"

He nodded. "Yeah. The migraine is gone."

"Good, that's really good," she said. "Um, excuse me, I'm just going to use the bathroom."

She hurried past him, tamping down her urge to trail her fingers along all that gorgeous tattooed skin, and nearly ran to the bathroom. She used the toilet and then brushed her teeth. She thought about having a quick shower but decided to wait. Preacher might get impatient and leave while she was showering, and as pathetic as this made her, she was hoping to convince him to stay a little longer by offering to make him breakfast.

She left the washroom and headed back into the bedroom. She expected Preacher to be dressed, but he stood beside the bed with his back to her as he studied the rumpled sheets. He was still wearing just the towel, and she looked at the big muscles in his broad back, beyond tempted to sneak up behind him and lick each of his tattoos.

Addison, enough! You got sex from him last night when you didn't think you'd ever get to fuck him again. Be happy with that.

Yes, she needed to accept that her lessons with Preacher were over. Sex with him last night was just a nice bonus.

Maybe if she were lucky, he'd come to her whenever he had a migraine, and she could bang him. It wasn't much, but it was better than nothing, right?

Nice, Addison. Could you be more pathetic?

She joined him by the bed. "Preacher? Are you hungry? I can make you some breakfast."

He turned to face her, and she couldn't help but lick her lips as she stared at his broad chest. God, he had an amazing body. He dropped the towel, and she stared at his cock. It was half-hard, and she didn't protest when he curved his arm around her waist and pulled her closer. She rubbed her abdomen against his cock, and he groaned and squeezed her ass through her nightshirt. He bent his head and nipped at her throat as his big hand curled in her hair and pulled her head back.

"Are you hungry?" she said.

"Yes," he muttered before sucking on her earlobe.

She gasped and rose on her tiptoes, arching her body into him as he squeezed her ass again. "I – I'll make you breakfast."

He stripped off her nightshirt and dropped it next to the towel. "That's not what I'm hungry for, Sunshine."

He teased her nipple with his thumb before kissing her hard on the mouth. She returned his kiss eagerly, sucking at his tongue when he pushed it between her lips. He kissed her until she was breathless and trembling before turning her around. He cupped both her breasts and pressed kisses against her upper back before trailing his fingers down her belly. He traced a circle around her belly button before touching the small patch of hair at the apex of her thighs.

"Open," he said into her ear.

She spread her legs immediately, and he rewarded her by cupping her pussy and rubbing at her clit with his thumb.

"Oh my gosh! That feels so good, Simon. You're like a rock star at touching me and -"

She shut her mouth with a snap as Preacher made a low chuckle in her ear.

"I'm sorry," she said as her face flamed with embarrassment. Fuck, what was it about Preacher that made her babble like an insane woman whenever he touched her?

"Don't be," he said before kissing her neck. He rubbed her clit again, and she arched against his fingers. One thick finger pushed into her, and he made a low sound of approval.

"So wet for me, baby."

"Oh please," she moaned as she rocked her pelvis against his hand.

"My little Sunshine needs to come, doesn't she?"

She nodded, and he rubbed her clit again as he nibbled at her ear. "First, you're going to come on my hand, and then you're going to come on my cock."

"Yes," she said eagerly. "Yes, please."

He laughed and licked her neck before cupping her breast with his other hand. She moaned again, and he tweaked her nipple as he rubbed firmly at her clit. Shamefully, the pleasure was already building in her belly, and she arched into him, flinging her hand over her mouth to muffle her scream of pleasure as she climaxed. Her body shook against his, and he held her up when her knees gave out, and she sagged against him.

"Oh, oh God, oh God," she muttered as he slid his finger in and out of her clenching pussy.

"Ready for my cock, baby?"

"Yes, please," she said.

He laughed again before turning her and pushing her gently onto the bed. She relaxed on the bed, and he kneeled between her thighs. He rubbed her soft skin as he stared at her pussy.

"Simon, please," she said as she reached for him.

He propped himself up above her on one hand before reaching between them and guiding his dick to her pussy. He entered her with one firm push, and she squeezed her legs against his hips as her inner walls stretched around him. God, she had missed this.

PREACHER COULD HARDLY STOP HIS LOUD MOAN WHEN HE pushed into Addison's tight pussy. She squeezed her legs against his hips, and he stared worriedly at her. "Did I hurt you?"

She wrapped her small hands around his forearms. "No. Fuck me."

She blushed immediately, but his hips jerked, and a low moan escaped his throat. "Christ, hearing you ask to be fucked is way hotter than it should be."

She smiled up at him and traced the tattoos on his arms. "I like it when you fuck me, Simon."

He made two helpless thrusts, his breath hissing out between his teeth before he leaned down and nipped at her jaw. "Do you know what you do to me, Sunshine?"

She moaned when he slid in and out of her with slow, deep strokes. "So good," she gasped out.

He bent his head and pulled on her nipple with his teeth. She cried out, bucking her hips against him as he licked her nipple and then sucked on it.

He groaned and lifted his head. "Your little pussy squeezes my dick so hard when I do that."

"Feels good," she panted as he fucked her with slow, deep thrusts.

He rested on his forearms above her, pressing his chest against hers as he nuzzled her ear. She wrapped her legs around his waist and met each of his slow thrusts as she put her arms around his shoulders and clung to him.

"Have you missed my cock, baby?" he said into her ear.

"Yes," she moaned.

"Say it."

"I've missed your cock," she said.

"Good."

"Have you missed my – my pussy?"

"Fuck, yes," he said. "You're all I've thought about, Sunshine."

She squeezed her inner muscles around him. He groaned and bit her throat before lifting his head and staring at her.

"Have you let anyone else fuck you?"

"No."

"Good," he muttered before kissing her.

When he released her mouth, she said, "Have you fucked anyone else?"

"No."

Before she could say anything else, he propped himself on his hands above her again and fucked her hard and rough. She met each of his thrusts with reckless abandonment. When she slid her hand between them and rubbed at her clit, he made a growl of approval.

"Good girl. Touch yourself while I fuck you."

She stroked her clit as her hips rose to meet him. Her soft cries of pleasure mixed with his louder groans, and a smile crossed his face when she began to babble at him.

"Oh God, Simon, so big. So thick. Oh God, I've missed your cock. Please fuck me harder. Please, Simon!"

He moved faster, driving into her with hard strokes that rocked her small body into the bed. She tossed her head back and forth, her fingers pulling at her clit until her babbling ceased, and her body stiffened under him. She climaxed with a loud cry as she squeezed compulsively around his dick.

He shouted with pleasure and threw his head back, the cords standing out in his neck as his climax rushed over him. He thrust deep, pinning her to the bed as his large body shook. Panting, he pulled out of her and collapsed on the bed next to her. He pulled her into his embrace. She rested her head on his chest and traced the tiger tattoo on his ribs as he rubbed her back. She jerked when the door buzzed. She half-sat up and stared at him.

"You expecting someone, Sunshine?" he said.

She shook her head, and he pulled her back into his arms as the door buzzed again. "Then ignore it."

He rubbed her lower back again as she studied the skull tattoo inside his right forearm. She'd never really commented on his tattoos, but she seemed fascinated by them this morning.

She touched the skull tattoo, and he turned his arm so she could see all of it. She traced her fingers over it before touching the snake tattooed on the inside of his bicep.

"That must have hurt," she said as the door buzzed for a third time.

He shrugged and ran his fingers over her flower tattoo. "The ones on my ribs hurt worse."

"Is it the most painful spot?"

"Skull is probably more painful," he said, "but the ribs are pretty bad. You thinking of getting more ink?"

"I don't know," she said. "I'm not sure what to get, and I have to have it somewhere hidden from my students. Maybe I could get a favourite quote or something on my upper thigh?"

His hand squeezed her ass. "I could create a script for you."

"Really? It would be cool to have an original script. Now I need to figure out what quote I'll use."

He stroked her satin skin above the small patch of her pubic hair.

"You could put something right here," he said. "I've got the perfect quote."

"Oh yeah?" Her voice was a bit breathless. "What would it say?"

He stroked her skin again. "Preacher's pussy."

She gaped at him before bursting into giggles. "That is so cheesy."

He laughed, and she sat up and leaned over him. He rubbed her silky hair between his fingers as she arched her eyebrows at him. "Do you try to brand every woman you have sex with, Mr. Preacher?"

His gaze dropped to the barbell in her right nipple, and she followed his gaze. "What?"

"Nothing," he said. If Addison knew what the SW engraved in the barbell meant, she'd freak out. Still, it wouldn't stop him from doing the same thing when he pierced her other nipple.

She touched his forehead. "How often do you get migraines?"

He shrugged. "Once a month, sometimes more."

"I'm sorry."

"I'm sorry I showed up on your doorstep like that," he said. "Thanks for not telling me to fuck off and die like I deserved."

She stroked his forehead again. "I wouldn't have done that. Migraines are horrible, and I'm glad I could help you."

"Do you get migraines? Is that why you knew what to do?" he said.

"No, my mom suffers from them. I've done a lot of research on migraines."

He studied her for a few seconds before saying, "I'm sorry about Tuesday, I shouldn't have -"

"Addison? You home, babe?"

She froze in the bed as Harrison's voice echoed down the hallway. Anger shot through him. "What the fuck is that prick doing here?"

"I don't know," she said.

"How the hell did he even get in here?"

"I forgot to get his keys back from him," she said as she threw back the covers. "Stay here. I'll get rid of him."

"Don't let him touch you."

"What?"

He sat up and put his arm around her waist, pulling her closer until their faces were only inches apart. "Don't let him touch you, Addison."

"I won't," she said.

"Good." He kissed her hard before letting her go and relaxing on the bed. She touched her mouth as Harrison's voice drifted down the hallway.

"Babe? Are you up?"

CHAPTER 27

Addison snatched her robe from the closet and belted it securely before opening the door. Harrison was almost to her bedroom, and she slipped into the hallway and shut the door.

"Hey," Harrison said. "You're here. Are you still sleeping? You never sleep in."

"What are you doing here?" she said.

"I came to talk."

"And you just let yourself in?" She glanced at the bedroom before pushing past Harrison toward the kitchen. Thankfully, he followed her, and she glared at him as she grabbed a pod of coffee and stuck it into the machine.

"It's almost ten. Why are you still in bed?" Harrison said. "And what's going on with your hair?"

"I just woke up," she said as the smell of coffee filled the kitchen. "Why are you here?"

"I told you – I wanted to talk."

"You can't just come into my apartment, Harrison." She grabbed the milk from the fridge and added some to her coffee.

"Babe, we've been together since high school. You don't care if I let myself into your apartment."

"Actually, I do," she said. "We're not together anymore, remember?"

"That's what I'm here to talk about," he said as he reached for the coffee. "Thanks, babe."

"This isn't for you." She backed away. "Jesus, Harrison."

He stared at her in surprise as she sipped at the coffee. "Addie? You're acting differently."

"What do you want?"

"I miss you, babe. I'm ready to end this break we're on."

Her mouth dropped open, and she stared silently at him.

He cleared his throat. "I told you I needed time to get some stuff out of my system. It's out now, and I'm ready to be with you again."

"Are you fucking kidding me?"

His eyes widened. "Since when do you talk like a trucker?"

"I don't know. Since I walked in on my fiancé wearing a dog collar and being spanked by his damn legal assistant?"

Harrison's face turned bright red. "You don't have to be crude."

"You cheated on me!" She slammed her coffee cup in the sink so hard that coffee splattered across her arm and the counter. "Multiple times! You think I'm just going to forgive and forget that?"

"I cheated because you weren't willing to give me what I needed in bed," Harrison said. "I only slept with Crystal because she wasn't weirded out by – "

"Weirded out? How could I be weirded out by your kinks in bed when I didn't even know about them?" Addison said.

"I couldn't tell you about them," Harrison said. "You're

too strait-laced, and you're not that adventurous in bed. You know you're not."

"If I suck so much in bed, why do you want to get back together with me?"

"I can show you some things," he said delicately. "I realize now that having you in my life is worth the sex problems. You can speak to a therapist about your intimacy issues, and we'll get through this together, babe."

"My intimacy issues," she said.

He sighed. "Babe, stop focusing on the negative, okay? I love you, and I want to be with you. I don't care if you're not good in bed. Do you understand? Sex isn't everything and -"

There was a knock on the front door of her apartment before it opened, and Grace said, "Addie? You home? Sorry to show up unannounced, but for once, both Kira and I have a Saturday off. We're headed to the farmer's market, and you're coming. No arguments or... oh, hell no." Grace glared at Harrison. "Why is this asshole here?"

Before Addie could reply, Grace cocked her head. "Why do you have 'just been fucked' hair, Addie?"

"This isn't a good time," Addison said. "Can I text you later and -"

"Nope." Gracie glared at Harrison again. "What the hell are you doing here?"

"Addison and I are back together," Harrison said.

"What?" Kira and Grace shouted in unison.

"You're back together with Harrison?" Kira said.

"No!" Addison said.

Grace scowled at her. "But you're sleeping with him? Addie, honey, I don't know what this mouthbreather said to convince you to sleep with him again, but it's a mistake. You don't need him in your life."

"I'm not sleeping with Harrison," Addison said.

Grace studied her hair. "Your hair would suggest otherwise."

"Gracie, I'm not."

When both Kira and Grace continued to stare at her skeptically, she glared at Harrison. "Harrison, tell them we're not having sex!"

He grinned at her and leaned against the counter. "Babe, it's nothing to be ashamed of."

"You asshole," she said. "Tell the truth."

He grinned again, and she wanted to punch him in his smug face. What she'd ever seen him in, she'd never know.

"Babe," he said placatingly, "you might as well just tell them that we're – what the hell?"

Harrison stared at Preacher, who was standing behind Kira and Grace. "What are you doing here?"

Grace and Kira turned. Addison didn't know whether to laugh or cry when Preacher grinned cockily at them. "Ladies."

"Hi, Preacher," Kira said hesitantly as he slipped past them and grabbed an apple from the fruit bowl on the counter. He tossed it into the air and caught it as he stared at Harrison. Harrison stepped back, and Preacher grinned at him before turning to Addison.

She made a weird squeaking sound when his arm snaked around her waist, and he pulled her into his embrace. His hand cupped her ass and squeezed as he dropped his mouth onto hers. He kissed her deeply, pushing his tongue past her lips to stroke the inside of her mouth. Despite their audience, Addison could barely stop from moaning when she felt his cock harden against her.

He released her and stepped back. He adjusted the obvious bulge in his jeans before winking at her. "Thanks for last night, Sunshine."

"I... you're welcome," she said.

He bit into his apple and chewed noisily before nodding to Grace and Kira. "Bye, ladies."

"Bye, Preacher," Kira said as, with a final hard look at Harrison, Preacher left the kitchen. The front door shut, and Addison sagged against the counter as Harrison, Grace, and Kira stared at her.

Harrison finally broke the silence. "What was Preacher doing here?"

Grace laughed, the look of delight on her face nearly lighting up the kitchen. "Are you blind or just stupid? I think what he was doing was obvious, Harrison. Or should I say, who?"

"No," Harrison said in a low voice. "Addison, no. You-you wouldn't sleep with someone like him."

"What's that supposed to mean?" Addison said.

"He – he's below us," Harrison said. "He's a tattoo artist, and he...look at him!"

"Oh, I think she's been looking at him a lot," Grace said.

Kira laughed, and Harrison's face turned red. "Look, I know I gave you permission to sleep with another guy, but Preacher? Did you go crazy because we're on a break, Addison? Is that it?"

Now, it was Addison's turn to laugh. "Are you serious? Get out of here, Harrison. Leave your keys and go."

"Addison -"

"Get out!" she shouted.

He flinched and started for the doorway.

"Your keys," Addison said.

He pulled them out of his pocket and dropped them on the counter. "We're not done with this conversation, Addison."

"Whatever," she said.

"Bye, Felicia," Grace said.

Harrison's upper lip curled, and he glared at Grace as she waved her hand at him. He stomped toward the front door, slamming it shut behind him. Addison moved to the living room, Kira and Grace trailing after her, and sat on the couch.

"Holy shit!" Grace crowed. "Did you see the look on Harrison's face when Preacher came strolling into the kitchen?"

"Forget Harrison," Kira said as she sat beside Addison. "Did you see my face? Addison, you're sleeping with Preacher again?"

"Based on the size of her sex hair, they're boinking like crazed bunnies," Grace said with a laugh. "Why didn't you tell us you were still banging Preacher?"

"Because it doesn't mean anything, and we agreed to keep it a secret," Addison said.

"A secret?" Grace said. "Then why did he just do a "this is my woman, stay away from her" grab and kiss in the kitchen?"

"I… I don't know what that was about."

"I thought it was just a one-time rebound thing," Kira said. "When did you start up with him again?"

Grace sat down beside Kira as Addison cleared her throat. "A couple of days after we had sex the first time."

Kira's eyes widened. "Holy shit." She stared at Grace. "Why do you not look that surprised?"

Grace shrugged. "Preacher was at our place one Saturday, and he freaked out when he heard us talking about Addison getting pierced in Willington. It seemed like an overreaction for a guy who barely knew her. He made me tell him where she was getting pierced, then he left and never came back. I'm pretty sure he went after Addie. Did he?"

Addison nodded as Kira's mouth dropped open. "You got a piercing?"

"No, not that day," Addison said. "Preacher wouldn't let the other guy pierce me."

"Oh," Kira said. "Wait – what do you mean not that day? Did you get a piercing?"

"Yes, Preacher pierced me."

"Holy shit," Kira repeated. "Did you get your belly button pierced?"

"Um…"

"Let me see it," Kira said. "I've been thinking about piercing mine."

"It's not my belly button," Addison said. "Preacher pierced my nipple."

The look on Kira's face was priceless. "Your *nipple*?"

"Yes. I booked an appointment with Preacher a few days after I got my tattoo. After he pierced my nipple, we, uh, had sex in his shop again. A couple of days later, I asked him if he would give me some lessons on sex, but he refused because he said I would want more from him than just sex."

"So, why are the two of you still having sex?" Kira said.

"After he turned me down, I went to the shop in Willington to get my other nipple pierced. I like the way it looks and figured why not, you know? But Preacher showed up, literally threw me over his shoulder like a caveman, and carried me out of there before I could. He said I wasn't allowed to let anyone pierce my body but him."

"Oh, he likes to pierce you, all right," Grace said.

"Gracie, behave," Addison said.

"That still doesn't explain why you're sleeping with him now. You got a tattoo, your nipples pierced, and you're sleeping with my brother's best friend – the town's," Kira made air quotes with her fingers, "'bad boy'. Who are you, and what have you done with Addison?"

"Not nipples. *Nipple*," Addison said. "I only have one pierced."

"But you're gonna get Preacher to pierce your other one?" Kira said.

"Yeah, probably."

Kira turned to Grace. "This is an *Invasion of the Body Snatchers* situation, right?"

Grace studied Addison. "Tell us everything, honey. Start from the beginning."

"OKAY, SO IF YOU GOT INTO A FIGHT ON TUESDAY AND agreed to end the lessons," Grace said half an hour later, "why was he in your bed last night?"

Addison sipped at her second cup of coffee. "He had a migraine. He showed up at my door yesterday afternoon."

"He knew you had experience with migraines because of your mom?" Kira said.

"He didn't know about my mom," Addison said. "He texted Gideon and said he was on his way – I guess he usually stays with Gideon when he has a migraine – but he ended up at my house."

"That's kind of sweet. He wanted to be with you when he wasn't feeling well," Kira said.

Addison shook her head. "No, he wanted sex."

Kira stared at her. "When he had a migraine?"

"Yeah. Sometimes a migraine can be stopped, or the pain is eased a little, with an orgasm."

"You're kidding me."

"I'm not," Addison said. "It's the rush of endorphins."

"So, you fucked his migraine away?" Kira said with a

grin. "I wish I could have been there for the conversation when Preacher came in."

She puffed out her chest and mimicked Preacher's deep voice. "Hey, Sunshine. I got me a big bad migraine, so why don't you ride my dick and make it all better."

"It wasn't like that. When Preacher first arrived, he was in a lot of pain and could hardly walk. I barely got him into bed before he was vomiting."

"Poor Preacher," Kira said.

"And he didn't ask me for sex," Addison said. "I was the one who asked him if an orgasm would help – it doesn't work for everyone. He said yes, but I knew he was in too much pain to have sex, so I, uh, gave him a blowjob."

"Aren't you a sweetheart," Kira said.

"Wait – so he didn't ask you to make him come?" Grace said.

"No."

"So, he showed up at your place instead of Gideon's so that you could give him sex and make his migraine go away, but then he didn't tell you that sex would help him. Is that what you're saying?"

"Well, I…" Addison studied her coffee cup. "Maybe he just came to my place because it's closer. Anyway, the orgasm helped enough for him to sleep. Around midnight, he woke up and still had a migraine. It wasn't as bad, so this time we had sex."

"So, he still had a migraine this morning?" Grace asked. "Because he looked pretty chipper when he walked into the kitchen, grabbed your ass, and stuck his tongue down your throat in front of your ex-fiancé."

"Grace!" Addison said as her cheeks flamed hotter.

"Well, did he?"

"No, he was feeling better this morning."

"But you still had sex," Grace said.

"Maybe?" Addison said.

Kira laughed, and Grace grinned at her. "They had sex."

"Fine! We had sex this morning, too, but he initiated it," Addison said. "He, um, he has a large sex drive, I think."

"Does that bother you?" Grace asked.

"God, no, I like it." Addie paused. "Does that make me a slut?"

Gracie laughed. "Oh, honey, no. You are not a slut. Spill it, Addie. I know you're dying to give us details."

"You can't say anything to anyone."

"We won't," Kira said. "Tell us, Addie."

"Sex with Preacher is amazing," Addison said. "He has a really large, uh, penis, but he always makes sure I'm ready first, and it never hurts to have sex. I didn't think that was possible, you know? I have an orgasm every time we have sex. Usually, I have two. One time, I had three!"

Grace grinned and said, "Atta boy, Preacher."

"I'd never had oral sex before and -"

"Wait, what?" Grace stared at her. "Harrison never went down on you? Is that what you just said?"

"He said proper women didn't want that sort of thing," Addison said.

"Jesus Christ," Grace said. "That guy is such a fuckhead."

"Preacher, um, goes down on me all the time. Like almost every time we have sex," Addison said, "and you would not believe the different sex positions he knows. Harrison would only do two – missionary and me on top."

"Boring," Grace said.

"So, are your sex lessons with Preacher back on?" Kira said.

"I... well, I don't think so," Addison said. "He didn't

bring up the topic of more lessons, and he doesn't want a relationship with me, so…"

"Do you want a relationship with him?" Grace said.

"No, of course not," Addison said.

"You sure?"

"Positive," Addison said. "Preacher and I don't have anything in common other than sex, and he's been very clear all along that he doesn't want to be my boyfriend."

"From what you told us, the way he acted when he realized Lucas was at your place was boyfriend-like," Kira said.

Addison shook her head. "No, he just doesn't like Lucas. It had nothing to do with me."

She chewed on her bottom lip as Kira and Grace glanced at each other. She hadn't told them about Preacher demanding she not sleep with anyone else. What was the point? It didn't mean he wanted to be exclusive. They weren't using condoms… of course, neither of them wanted the other to sleep with someone else. That was a quick way to an STI.

"Okay, since your lessons with Preacher are over, who will you wow with your new skills?" Kira said.

Addison held onto her smile with grim determination. "Oh, uh, I don't know. I hadn't thought about it."

"You should," Kira said. "Why don't we have a ladies' night out tonight?"

Addie's stomach dropped, but if she and Preacher were finished, and she was pretty sure they were, sitting around feeling sorry for herself wasn't the way to go.

He might want to have sex again if he gets another migraine.

Yeah, maybe, but how pathetic did it make her not to sleep with anyone else while she waited to see if Preacher might come to her for sex when he had a migraine.

"Addie? Do you want to? You don't have to," Kira said.

"Yeah, let's," Addie said. "It'll be good for me to, uh, experiment sexually."

"We should go to The Hitching Post," Kira said. "We can find a sexy cowboy for Addie to ride."

"Okay," Addison said.

"Honey," Grace said, "are you sure that's what you want?"

Addison stared into her coffee. "Yeah."

"Really?"

"Yes," Addie said. "It's over with Preacher now, so why shouldn't I have some fun with someone else? I've spent the last decade having boring sex with Harrison – don't I deserve to have fun?"

"Yes," Grace said. "If that's what you want. Are you certain it's over with Preacher?"

"Of course I am."

"I only ask because he showed up at your apartment yesterday, and you had sex twice."

"Because he had a migraine. We wouldn't have had sex if he didn't have a migraine, okay? I won't sit around and wait for Preacher to have a migraine, hoping I might get laid. I'm young, and I'm single and I... I want to have meaningless sex with a damn cowboy who I'll never see again." Her voice was too loud.

"All right," Grace said.

"Good. I'll shower quickly, and then we'll go to the farmer's market."

She gulped down the rest of her coffee and escaped to the bathroom. She turned on the shower and stared at herself in the mirror. Her cheeks were red, and she felt sick to her stomach. What was she doing? She didn't want to have sex with anyone but Preacher.

If you keep thinking that way, you'll die a spinster.

Preacher doesn't want you for anything more than sex, and even that is done. It was only because of his migraine that he —

I know! Shut up! she snarled at her inner voice.

She rubbed at her suddenly aching forehead. She didn't want to date Preacher. Well, maybe she did, but that was just stupid. Even if he were interested in something more than sex, things would never work out between them. She was too much of a goody-two-shoes for him, and sooner or later, he would get bored. It was best to stop now before she got attached to him.

Attached? That's a funny word for love, Addison.

She froze before taking a deep breath. God, she didn't love Preacher. She was just being... stupid.

She took off her robe and stepped into the shower. She was young and single, and her nights of mind-blowing sex with Preacher were over. She had just broken off a ten-year relationship, and jumping right into another wasn't smart. She would do what young, single women did and find a few different guys to bang. She had the skills now, thanks to Preacher. She didn't have to worry that they would find her boring.

Do you, though? Are you any better in bed? What kind of lessons did he give you besides making you come repeatedly?

She was better. She knew she was. She could make Preacher come, and he was the hottest guy she knew. She just had to act with other men like she did with Preacher in bed.

What if they can't make you come the way he does?

She swallowed hard. They would. Probably. Preacher couldn't be the only guy who made her come. He just couldn't be. The gods wouldn't be that cruel, would they?

What do you think Preacher will do when he finds out you

went to a bar to pick up a guy? He told you that you weren't allowed to sleep with anyone else, remember?

She ducked her head under the hot spray and ignored the butterflies fluttering in her stomach. She and Preacher were finished. She wasn't doing anything wrong by going to the bar tonight.

CHAPTER 28

"Hey," Gideon said when Preacher strolled into his backyard. Preacher grabbed a beer from the cooler and opened it as Gideon flipped the steaks on the barbeque. "You look pretty good for a guy who had a migraine yesterday. I was surprised when you agreed to come over. Normally, you sleep most of the day after a migraine."

Preacher shrugged. "I called Mark in so I could work on his sleeve. He was supposed to come in yesterday afternoon, and I felt bad about cancelling."

"You did a tattoo today?" Gideon paused with a foil-wrapped potato in each hand.

"Yeah, it's why I'm a little late. I just finished up the appointment."

"You tattooed?" Gideon repeated.

"Yes. What's the big deal?"

"When I talked to Addison yesterday, she said your migraine was bad. Said you were throwing up and could barely walk."

"I feel fine now," Preacher said. "Addison helped me."

"Oh yeah?" Gideon raised his eyebrow at him. "What did she do for you that I don't?"

An image of Addison riding him flickered through his head. He cleared his throat as Gideon laughed.

"Jesus, you're blushing, Preacher. What did she do to you?"

"Fuck off, Gideon."

"Why did you go to Addison's place anyway? You told me Wednesday that it was over with her."

"Her place was closer," Preacher said.

"Not that much closer."

"Close enough."

"Or maybe you went over there because you're falling in love with her," Gideon said.

"Have you lost your fucking mind? It was just a fling, okay? She wanted to try fucking a guy who wasn't a goddamn pussy like her ex-fiancé. I agreed. Now it's over."

"Then why did you go to her place when you had a migraine?"

"Did you miss the part where I told you to fuck off, Gideon?" Preacher said.

"Answer the question, Preacher."

"Don't pull that cop shit on me," Preacher said. "It was just sex, and now it's over. I only went there last night because her place was closer, and I didn't feel like barfing in the goddamn car."

"Right," Gideon said as he flipped the steaks again.

Preacher scowled at his back before taking a drink of beer. "Where's your woman tonight?"

"Grace went out with Kira and Addison for a ladies' night."

Preacher stiffened. "What do you mean a ladies' night?"

"You know what a ladies' night is," Gideon said.

Preacher relaxed in his chair, petting Tank's side when the big dog wandered over and leaned against him. Addison hated going to the bar, and she didn't drink much. Neither did Grace or Kira. They were probably knitting and watching those ridiculous chick flicks at Addison's place. He took another drink of beer and smiled inwardly. Maybe when Grace got back, he'd head over to Addison's. Remind her how to have fun that didn't involve yarn. He would eat her sweet pussy to say thank you for helping him with his migraine.

"What time do you expect Grace home?" he said.

"We're supposed to hike at the Falls early tomorrow morning to beat the heat, so she said she'd be home by eleven. Of course, The Hitching Post is ten miles outside of town, and she never factors in driving time, so it'll probably be closer to eleven thirty or midnight."

"They're at The Hitching Post?" Preacher said.

"Yeah."

"Why?"

"What?"

"Why are they at the goddamn Hitching Post?" Preacher snapped.

"Ladies night, remember?" Gideon said with a shrewd look at him. "I believe they're looking for a cowboy for Addison to take home and... ride."

Preacher stood up so quickly he knocked his chair over, and Tank made a startled 'woof'. "Like fucking hell, she is."

He was so pissed he was pretty sure he might start foaming at the mouth.

"What do you care?" Gideon said. "You and Addison were just fucking, remember?"

"She is not going anywhere near a fucking cowboy." Preacher set his beer down. "I gotta go."

"What are you doing, Simon?" Gideon said. "You and Addison won't work."

"I have to go," Preacher repeated.

He knew what Gideon said was true, but he didn't care. The thought that some fucking cowboy had his hands all over Addison was filling him with pure rage. He stalked out of the yard, climbed onto his bike, and roared down the road in a cloud of exhaust fumes and dust.

"ADDISON?"

Addison looked up from her glass of wine and smiled at the man beside her. "Sorry. What did you say?"

"I asked if you wanted another glass of wine."

"Oh no, thank you. I'm good with this one."

"Okay." The man gave her a generous smile, and she studied his tanned face and white teeth. He was handsome enough – okay, fine, he was downright sexy, and his tall, lean body was the stuff that sex dreams were made of – but she felt nothing for him.

She looked around discreetly for Grace and Kira. They had gone to the ladies' room half an hour ago and hadn't returned. They'd only been here for a few hours, but she was ready to go home. This was a mistake. She couldn't think of anything but Preacher, and it wasn't fair to the handsome and very nice cowboy sitting next to her.

"Your friends are on the other side of the bar, studiously pretending to ignore us," the cowboy said with another smile. "Go on and join them. I won't be insulted. Disappointed but not insulted."

"I'm sorry, uh…"

Shit! What was his name?

"Nathan," the cowboy said.

"I'm sorry, Nathan," Addison said. "It's not you, it's me."

He made a face before laughing, and she blushed.

"Oh God, I'm such an idiot. Listen, you're good looking and nice, but… this isn't right for me."

"What isn't right for you?" Nathan said.

"Finding some random cowboy, taking him home, and riding him," she blurted out before giving him a horrified look. "Oh God, tell me I didn't just say that out loud."

Nathan grinned again at her. "You did."

She took a big swallow of wine before closing her eyes and breathing deeply. "My dirtbag fiancé cheated on me. My friends convinced me that what I needed was to have sex with a random guy. I thought they were right, but I can't do it. Not with you."

"Ouch," Nathan said.

"No!" Addison squeezed his forearm. "No, not because there's something wrong with you. There isn't. You're funny, smart, handsome, and wow, do you smell good, but there's this guy and…"

"Still got a thing for your dirtbag fiancé, huh?"

"No. There's another guy. He's a tattoo artist, and I feel like I'm cheating on him just talking with you."

"So, you're dating someone else?" Nathan's confusion was written all over his face.

"No. We were having casual sex, and he was giving me some sex pointers because my fiancé said I sucked in bed. Oh shit! Forget I said that last part."

Nathan laughed, and she blushed furiously. "You're easy to talk to, and I don't drink very often, so two glasses of wine are making me say things I shouldn't."

"Let's get this straight. You're having casual sex with a tattoo artist, but now you're here trying to have casual sex with me? Which makes you feel like you're cheating on the tattoo artist?"

"Yes. Which is stupid because Preacher is finished with me," Addison said. "I asked him for some lessons, and he gave them to me, and then he – we – ended it."

"Ah." Nathan leaned back in his chair. "Well, if you think you haven't had enough lessons, I'm happy to help."

Oh God, her face was going to burst into flames.

"Oh, and casual sex is just fine with me. I'm not looking for anything permanent either," Nathan said.

"I'm sorry," Addison said. "I can't."

"Right – you're smitten with the tattoo artist."

"Smitten?" She laughed. "I'm not trying to be rude, but how old are you? You don't look like you're from the fifties."

He grinned and squeezed her hand playfully. "I'm probably an old man compared to you."

"How old?" she said.

"Thirty-five."

She shrugged. "That's not old. I'm twenty-five."

He winced and let go of her hand. "And now I feel like a dirty old man."

"Ten years is not that big of a deal."

"Doesn't matter anyway," he said. "Unless you've changed your mind about taking me home and riding me? Which I am agreeable to, by the way. Even with the age difference."

She sighed. "Honestly, Nathan? I wish I were attracted to you."

"Sorry, Addison."

"Yeah, me too."

She glanced across the bar. She saw Grace and Kira sitting at a small table on the other side of the bar and smiled when they gave her matching grins.

"My friends will think I'm an idiot," she said.

Nathan stood up and held out his hand as the music turned soft and slow. "C'mon, Addison."

"Where?"

"Dance with me."

"Just a dance?" she said.

"Just a dance."

She took his hand and let him lead her to the dance floor. He put his arm around her waist and held her close but not so close that she was uncomfortable. She stared at him as he steered her around the dance floor.

"You're a good dancer."

"Thanks," he said. "Took some lessons in my youth. My dad told me the ladies loved a man who could dance."

"They do," she said.

"My old man always gave good advice," Nathan said.

"Do you live in Harmony Falls?" she said.

"I do. I just moved here about six months ago," he said.

"Do you like our town?"

"Yes," he said. "I was living in the city for quite a few years, but I grew up in a small town very much like this one, and it feels a little bit like coming home."

"What do you do for a living?" They'd sat and talked for nearly an hour, but Nathan mostly asked about her life.

"I'm a vet. I work over at… well, this must be your tattoo artist."

"What?" Addison said.

Nathan stared over her head, and she craned her neck to see Preacher standing behind her.

"Preacher? What are you doing here?"

Preacher stared at Nathan and said, "Can I cut in?"

His tone was low and perfectly polite, but Addison was pretty certain there was murder in his eyes.

Nathan gave Preacher an easy grin. "Sure, if the lady is agreeable to it. Addison?"

Preacher made a low growl of anger when Nathan said her name. He held out his hand. "Take my hand, Sunshine."

She automatically reached for his hand, smiling apologetically at Nathan. "I'm sorry, Nathan."

Nathan nodded to her as he released her and stepped back. Preacher pulled her into his arms, pressing every inch of her body against his before splaying his hand across her lower back in a possessive grip.

Nathan walked away, and Preacher glared at her. "What are you doing here?"

She returned his scowl. "What are *you* doing here?"

"I asked you first."

She rolled her eyes and then winced when Preacher stepped on her foot. He cursed and muttered an apology before resuming his awkward swaying.

"You don't even like country music," she said.

"You don't know that."

She just stared at him, and he said, "Why are you at this bar?"

"It's ladies' night, okay? Which you've ruined by showing up here."

She supposed that statement would have stung him a little more if she hadn't sounded so pathetically excited about him showing up.

"You don't go to bars," he said. "You should be home knitting or some stupid shit like that."

"One – you're not the boss of me, and two – knitting is not stupid." She winced again when he stepped on her foot for a second time.

He cursed and lifted her until her feet were dangling.

"What are you doing? Put me down – this isn't dancing."

"I can't fucking dance," he said.

"Then why did you cut in? Nathan was a perfectly good dancer."

"Because I know exactly what you were planning to do with that prick, and it is not fucking happening," he snarled. "Do I make myself clear, Sunshine? If you let him anywhere near your pussy, I'll break both his arms."

She stared silently at him. He had given up on moving and stood on the dance floor, holding her tightly as the other couples moved around them. His face was red, and the usual calm and collected Preacher had disappeared. He acted like a jealous lover, and a tingle of excitement went through her. Maybe Preacher wasn't done with her after all. She bit back a smile as a truly wicked idea flashed in her head.

No, Addie! No, that is a very, very bad idea. Maybe he still wants you, but there's no point in continuing to sleep with him. Tell him he has no say over who you can sleep with, then go and find that nice cowboy and take him home. You'll forget all about Preacher when Nathan's in your bed.

She almost laughed out loud. She'd never been a good liar – not even to herself.

"Did you hear me, Addison?" Preacher said.

"I heard you," she said sweetly. "But I'm still not feeling confident about my bedroom abilities, and since my lessons are over with you, I'm looking for a new teacher."

Preacher's arm tightened around her until she gasped and smacked his back. "Can't breathe!"

When he loosened his grip, she said, "I've already talked to Nathan about my problem, and he's more than happy to continue my lessons. So, if you don't mind…"

She stared pointedly at him. His face was a mask of fury, and his eyes glittered angrily.

Shit. Maybe she had pushed him too far.

He pressed his mouth to her ear and said in a dangerously calm voice, "You want another lesson, Sunshine? Fine. I'll give you another lesson tonight. But I'm going to fuck you until your voice is hoarse from screaming my name, until you're begging me to stop because you can't take one more orgasm. I'll fuck you until your thighs are so sore you can't fucking walk tomorrow. When I'm finished with you, your tight little pussy will know who it belongs to. I promise."

He dropped her to her feet and took her hand. "Let's go."

"Preacher," she whispered. Her limbs were trembling, her pussy was throbbing, and Preacher's damn speech had made her so hot she couldn't think straight.

"Let's go, Sunshine."

CHAPTER 29

"**P**reacher, are -"
"Bedroom, Addie."

She shivered, her stomach clenching with pleasure as Preacher closed her apartment door. He took his boots off, and she slipped out of her heels.

"Do you want something to drink?"

"Bedroom," he said.

Another shiver, another stomach-clenching burst of pleasure. Without another word, she walked to her bedroom, awareness tingling through every nerve ending.

She was barely in the room before Preacher unzipped her dress. She turned around when he stepped away, giving him a questioning look. He smiled lazily at her. "Strip, Addie."

Her nerves singing an award-worthy opera, she shimmied out of her dress, letting it fall to the floor. Thanks to her nipple piercing, she wore a cotton bra, but she'd put on one of her silk thongs.

Her excitement that Preacher would see her in sexy panties for once dimmed when he said, "Lose the bra and panties."

She ran her hand over the scrap of silk material. "You seriously aren't going to comment on the fact that I'm wearing sexy underwear for you for the first time?"

"You didn't wear them for me," he said, "you wore them for that dickhead at the bar."

She wanted to argue, but he made a valid point.

To her utter shock, he said, "I like your cotton ones better. They're soft and sweet and perfect, like you."

Something in her chest tightened, and she swallowed hard. "That's the nicest thing anyone's ever said to me, Simon."

He smiled at her. "I meant every word. Now, get naked."

She giggled and took off her bra and underwear. Preacher stripped off his clothes, and her mouth watered when she saw his cock. It was already shiny with precum, and she wanted to drop to her knees and take him into her mouth.

She reached for the clasp on the pearls around her throat, faltering to a stop when Preacher shook his head. "Leave them."

She let her hands drop to her sides, her body vibrating, and her nipples already peaked and waiting for Preacher's mouth. He stepped toward her, hooking one finger around the string of pearls and tugging her closer until his cock brushed against her abdomen.

He threaded his other hand in her hair and pulled her head back before pressing his mouth against hers. She parted her lips immediately, sliding her arms around his waist and pressing up against him as she sucked on his tongue.

He groaned into her mouth, his hips thrusting against her, rubbing his cock across her stomach. She reached between them, but before she could curl her fingers around his shaft, he pushed away from her.

"Hands and knees on the bed," he rasped.

She complied quickly, her heart beating out a quick rhythm that made her feel a little lightheaded. Preacher trailed his fingers down the back of her thighs, and she spread them immediately. She reached between her legs to rub her clit. She was wet but not quite wet enough to take him in this position.

Preacher knocked her hand away, making a low growl that sent fresh heat zinging through her lower body. "Don't touch your pussy, Addison. It's my pussy, remember? Only I get to touch it."

He stroked her inner thighs, her ass, the back of her calves. She squirmed on the bed, her need for him a raging, out-of-control flame. She suddenly didn't care if she was wet enough or not. If she didn't get his dick inside of her in the next few minutes, she'd lose her damn mind.

"Simon, please."

"Please, what?" Those rough fingers made slow torturous strokes in the crease between her thigh and her pussy.

"Please fuck me."

She smiled to herself. Cursing, asking to be fucked, still felt a little embarrassing, but she knew it would be the way to get what she wanted.

"You're not wet enough to be fucked."

"I am." She wasn't completely lying. If he kept touching her inner thighs the way he was, she'd be wet enough in approximately thirty seconds.

"You're not," he said.

She cried out, her body arching and her hands digging into the sheets when she felt his wet tongue glide across her slit.

"Simon!" Her voice was strangled, surprised, stunned.

His hands pushed on her thighs, spreading them wider and opening her up to him. She ground against his mouth, babbling incoherent words of need as he licked and sucked and nipped. He tongued her opening, making her gasp and moan and plead. He nipped at her inner thigh and then sucked hard on her clit.

She moaned his name, her body already beginning its climb to the peak she was straining for. Before she could get there, he lifted his head, his hands sliding around her hips and squeezing.

"Simon, I'm so close!" She reached between her legs, cursing at him when he grabbed her wrist and pulled her hand away.

"Look at me, Addison."

"I need to come," she whined. "Simon, I can't wait."

"Look at me," he said.

"Fuck," she snapped.

He laughed, and she whipped her head around to glare at him. "You're the worst."

"Whose pussy is this?" He rubbed her clit with his free hand, and she pushed back against his rough fingers, grinding against him without any shame.

He immediately stopped touching her and gave her ass a light slap. "Answer the question, Sunshine."

"Yours," she said. "It's yours."

"That's right," he said.

She waited breathlessly for his mouth on her clit again, whining in disappointment when he knelt on the bed behind her and pushed on her lower back. "Simon, I want your mouth."

"I know you do, but only good girls get their pussy eaten until they come," he said.

"I'm a good girl," she said.

"You weren't being my good girl tonight," he said.

She cried out when he pushed the head of his cock into

her pussy and then made another slow thrust. Her inner walls stretched around his thickness, and she gripped the sheets, her back arching as he sheathed himself completely.

"Fuck," she moaned. "You're so thick."

He made a few long, slow pumps in and out of her. She was more than wet enough for him now, and she met each of his strokes with eager enthusiasm. She tried to shift a little, tried to make the blunt head of his cock brush against her g-spot.

He made a low chuckle and slapped her butt again. "Not yet, Sunshine. Bad girls like you don't get to come until I say you do."

"I only went to the bar to have a couple of drinks with my friends," she panted.

He leaned over her and slipped his fingers around the string of pearls. When he tugged, she straightened to her knees, moaning in need when he splayed one hand across her abdomen and tangled her pearls around his fingers until they pressed against her throat.

He made a few deep thrusts, his warm breath stirring her hair, his hard chest and abdomen pressed flat against her back. He lowered his mouth to her ear and nipped at her earlobe as he cupped her left breast and toyed with her nipple. "If you keep lying to me, Sunshine, I won't let you come."

"Simon," she gasped, "I need to come."

"I know you do," he said. He pinched her nipple before his hand moved to the curls between her thighs and tugged lightly. "You told me you wouldn't fuck another guy. Remember?"

"I thought you were done with me," she moaned. "You said the lessons were over."

He rubbed her clit with the ball of his thumb as he tugged

on the pearls around her neck. "So, you immediately tried to find another guy to fuck."

"I wouldn't have fucked him," she said. "I swear. I thought that's what I wanted, but I couldn't."

"Why?" He rubbed her clit again.

"Because I…"

"Say it, Sunshine. Say it or I won't let you come."

She moaned her displeasure when he stopped rubbing her clit, her nails digging into his forearm. "Simon, please touch me."

"Why couldn't you fuck him?" He tugged on her curls teasingly, his fingers grazing her wet pussy lips but not going where she needed them.

Her clit aching, her entire body on fire with need, she said, "Because he wasn't you. I don't want to fuck anyone but you, Simon."

"That's my good girl." The smug satisfaction in his voice was drowned out by her scream of pleasure when he rubbed her clit, and she climaxed hard against his fingers. Her body shook, and she grasped at Preacher's arm like a woman drowning as pleasure drenched her body.

His fingers tightened around the pearls, and he clamped his other arm around her waist as he fucked her with hard, deep thrusts that sent fresh new flutters of pleasure shuddering down her body.

She cried out when the head of his cock pressed against her g-spot and tried to squirm away from the intense pleasure. It was too much, too soon, after her orgasm.

Preacher growled and pulled on the pearls until her head was forced back. His free hand held her hip in a tight grip, and he fucked her with rough and almost punishing strokes. The pleasure built inside of her again, and she squirmed and writhed in his tight grip, unable to get away, the pressure against her throat and hip a sensual turn on she never thought possible.

He drove deep, and she screamed his name like a prayer, her entire body tensing as her second orgasm roared through her. She shook and quivered against him as the pleasure went on and on. When it finally dimmed, she sagged forward like a boneless kitten. Preacher slid his arm around her waist and kissed the middle of her back before lowering her to the bed. She collapsed on her side, breathing harshly as her legs twitched and jerked.

Preacher rubbed her hip and thigh, pressing kisses against her upper shoulders and the nape of her neck. He nuzzled the pearls around her neck before kissing her throat. "You okay?"

"Oh my God," she moaned. "I've never come that hard in my life."

He kissed her throat again before spooning her. "Good."

She relaxed against him, closing her eyes and letting him soothe her trembling body with long, gentle strokes of his hand. "I feel so good. Thank you, Simon."

"You're welcome, baby."

After a few minutes, she became aware of two things... Simon's fingers tugging on her nipple and the hard length of his cock between her ass cheeks. She opened her eyes and craned her head to stare at him. "Simon, you didn't..."

"Not yet." He pressed a kiss against her mouth.

"Why not? I came twice. It's your turn to come."

His grin turned wicked. "You're going to come again for me."

"I don't think I can come again," she said. "Those last two were... intense."

He flipped her onto her back and kissed the tip of her nipple. "Trust me, Sunshine. Before this night ends, you'll lose track of how many times you come."

"SIT UP, SUNSHINE."

"No."

Preacher laughed. She groaned when he opened the blinds, and bright sunlight speared into the room.

Preacher set a cup of tea on the nightstand beside her before sliding into his side of the bed, tucking a pillow behind his back, and leaning against the wall. Grumbling, she sat up and then winced and grabbed at her thighs.

"It took me ten minutes to walk to the bathroom earlier," she said. "My thighs hurt so freaking bad."

Her voice was raspy, and Preacher grinned at her. "Drink some tea. It'll help your throat."

She tucked the sheet and quilt around her naked body before sipping at the tea. She rubbed at her thighs through the quilt. "What time is it?"

"Almost eleven." He pushed some pillows behind her, and she leaned back, smiling a little when Preacher rested his hand on her thigh while he scrolled through Facebook on his phone.

She was tired, God, was she tired, and her throat was sore, and her thighs hurt and...

Your pussy hurts.

Not exactly hurt... more like ached.

Because Preacher did what he said he would do. Didn't he? He fucked you until you screamed yourself hoarse, made you come over and over until you begged him to stop, and ruined you for any other dick but his for the rest of your damn life.

That thought should have scared her. So why wasn't it?

She took another sip of tea before studying Preacher. He glanced over at her. "You hungry?"

"Getting there," she said.

"We have an errand to run, but we can grab lunch at Nan's first."

"We have an errand?" she said.

He nodded, and she grinned at him. "Are you going to tell me what this errand is?"

"No."

She laughed. "So secretive this morning, Simon."

She studied the tattoos across his upper chest. "Are you ever going to ask me how I know your real name?"

"Figured Gideon told Grace or Kira, and they told you," he said.

"Grace told me. She only told me because after we kissed that first time, I was kind of freaking out about kissing a guy whose actual name I didn't know. Otherwise, she wouldn't have told me," Addie said.

"It's fine," he said. "It's not that big of a deal."

"How many people in Harmony Falls know your real name?" Addison said.

"You and Gideon and Grace. Probably Kira if Gideon told her."

"He hasn't. I asked her once if she knew your real name, and she didn't. She said Gideon wouldn't tell her. Why do you go by Preacher?"

She could almost feel his discomfort. He looked away from her. "It's just a nickname."

He wasn't telling her the entire truth, but she let it go. "What's your last name?"

"Wells."

"Simon Wells," she said. "I like it. It has a good…"

"What?" he said when she trailed off.

"Your initials are SW," she said.

He didn't reply, and she tugged the sheet down to stare at the barbell in her nipple. "SW is engraved in the barbell."

She glanced at him. "You had your initials engraved in the barbell before you put it in my nipple."

His cheeks turned red, and he cleared his throat before pushing back the covers. "I'm gonna have a quick shower."

He pressed a kiss against her mouth and left the bedroom. She stared at the SW on either end of the barbell before leaning against her pillow and staring at the ceiling. Preacher had his initials engraved in her body jewelry. He got pissy and jealous as hell if he even thought another guy was interested in her. He went to the bar last night to stop her when he thought she might sleep with another man and then made her come so many times she forgot her own damn name.

A slow smile crossed her lips. Preacher could deny it all he wanted, but he was into her. Hell, he might even be developing some feelings for her.

Maybe. But don't confuse that with love.

She wouldn't. But if Preacher wanted to date her, she was all for it. Why shouldn't they date?

Because you're completely different? Because he'll eventually get bored with you? Because you're already in love with him, and it'll break your heart when he ends it?

She pushed those thoughts away immediately. She wouldn't dwell on negative crap like that. It was like she told her students… positive thinking leads to a positive life.

Maybe she and Preacher were complete opposites to other people, but she'd seen glimpses of the real Preacher. She'd seen *Simon*, the sweet and kind guy who brought her tea in bed and looked after her when she was sick. The man who made her laugh, made her come, made her feel alive for the first time in her life.

Who cared what other people thought anyway? Let them

gossip. Spending time with Preacher – that's what mattered.

"WHY ARE WE AT A STORAGE PLACE?" ADDIE SAID AS Preacher punched in the code, and the gate swung open.

She followed him inside, and they walked toward his storage unit in the hot sunshine. She was walking slowly, and he grinned at her. "Hurry up, slowpoke."

"My thighs hurt," she reminded him. "And it's all your fault."

"Technically, it's your fault for thinking you could fuck someone other than me. If you'd been my good girl, you wouldn't have been fucked last night until your thighs hurt."

She stuck her delectable tongue out at him. "Be nice, Preacher."

"I am being nice. I got us an Uber instead of making you ride the bike to Nan's or here, didn't I?"

She shuddered and reached down to rub at one thigh. "Oh my God, I would have died."

He glanced around. The storage place was empty, with not even an employee lurking in the lot. He took her hand, linking their fingers together as they walked. He didn't want to admit how fucking nice it'd been to have lunch at Nan's with her. Sitting in a booth, eating lunch and chatting about the tattoos he would be doing this week and how Addison was looking forward to returning to work on Tuesday and wishing she had a few more days of holidays.

She'd done most of the talking, but he preferred that. Hell, he'd enjoyed the cute stories she was telling about the kids she taught and when, at one point, she'd apologized for her boring stories, he'd been quick to tell her they weren't boring. They should have been boring – he liked kids and wanted a couple of his own, but stories about other people's kids weren't his usual thing.

But it didn't seem to matter what Addison said or talked about. She could read the fucking dictionary to him, and he'd be mesmerized by her.

That's what love does to a person.

He squeezed Addie's hand so hard she made a soft squeak of pain.

"Sorry," he said.

"That's okay." She smiled at him, and he studied how the sunlight turned her auburn hair a muted red.

"Your hair looks pretty," he said a bit gruffly.

"Thank you." Her smile widened, and he couldn't resist leaning down and pressing a kiss against her perfect mouth.

She returned his kiss, even parting her mouth when he licked her bottom lip. He loved how responsive she was to him, even when it was obvious that she was tired and sore. He pulled back and kissed her forehead. "Sorry your legs hurt, Sunshine."

"It's fine," she said. "It was worth it."

She followed him a few more feet to his storage unit. He unlocked the padlock and slipped the lock into his pocket before lifting the heavy garage door. She watched as he pulled the slip cover off the SUV.

"You have a car?" she said.

"Yeah. Use it in the winter."

"Oh, right. That makes sense," she said. "You can't ride the bike in the winter."

He folded the slipcover as she walked around the SUV. "It's nice. Not what I expected you would drive."

"What did you think I would drive?" he said.

She shrugged. "A muscle car like a Dodge Charger, maybe? Definitely not a Toyota RAV. It's very… practical."

He laughed and tossed her the keys. She caught them neatly, and he winked at her. "Let's go, Sunshine."

"Go where?" she said.

"Back to your place. I just took it for a drive a week or so ago, so it'll start fine, but you'll have to move the seat forward. My legs are a fuck of a lot longer than yours."

"Why am I driving?"

"Might as well get used to it," he said.

She stared at him. "What am I missing?"

He pulled her into his arms and kissed her forehead. "You can use the car until we find you a new one."

Her eyes widened. "Simon, I can't... I mean..."

"What?" he said.

"I can't just use your car. What if you need it?"

"I have the bike," he said.

She chewed at her bottom lip. "This is too generous of a gift, Simon. I can buy a secondhand car and -"

"I'm not letting you drive some piece of shit car that could break down and leave you stranded in the middle of nowhere again," he said. "We'll go car shopping this weekend and see if we can find something reliable and in your price range. I know a guy who might have something."

She stared at the SUV again before hugging him hard and kissing him. "Thank you, Simon. This is amazing, and I so appreciate it."

"You're welcome, Sunshine." He kissed her again before squeezing her ass. "C'mon, let's get out of here. It's too fucking hot to stand outside."

She laughed and pinched his cheek. "If you're a very good boy, I might just stop at the Dairy Queen on the way home and get us ice cream cones."

"Sunshine," he squeezed her firm ass again, "I'm always a very good boy."

CHAPTER 30

"Man, if it gets any busier in here, we'll need to hire a receptionist. I can't keep up with the calls and the walk-ins," Nolan said.

"Might be an idea." Preacher pulled his phone out of his pocket, smiling when he saw the message from Addie. She returned to work today but texted him during lunch to say hi and ask if he was coming by tonight.

Before he could text back, Nolan nudged Nix and said, "See, I told you."

"You told him what?" Preacher looked up from his phone.

"That you must be getting laid on the regular. You've never been this cheerful the entire fucking time I've known you."

"Fuck off, Nolan," Preacher said.

Nolan laughed. "Even your 'fuck off's' are cute right now."

Preacher rolled his eyes as Nolan said, "Just the fact that you're agreeing to a receptionist is a goddamn miracle."

"I said it might be an idea. I didn't say I agreed to it,"

Preacher said. "Keep running your mouth, and I'll put you on reception duties full fucking time."

"He doesn't mean it," Nolan said to Nix. "Look at that sparkle in his eye. He's like a kid in a fucking candy store, am I right?"

Nix didn't reply, and Nolan grinned at Preacher. "C'mon, dude, who are you playing hide the salami with? Anyone I know?"

Preacher glanced at Nix. The tattoo artist had been in the shop the day he'd brought Addison to his apartment when she was sick. He was the only one in town besides Gideon, Grace, and Kira who knew he and Addison were together. He hadn't said anything to Nolan, and as far as Preacher was concerned, that upped Nix's cool factor.

Yeah, yeah, Nix is a good guy. Let's get back to that you and Addison being together bullshit. You're not dating, asshole, and don't start thinking you are. This isn't going to work out between the two of you. Besides, do you think she's over her ex yet? He still had a fucking key to her place.

"You seriously not gonna tell me?" Nolan said.

Preacher just shrugged. "I'm not with anyone, and even if I were, it wouldn't be any of your fucking business. Don't you have some floors to mop?"

Nolan laughed. "There's the asshole Preacher I know and love. I'll mop the floors after lunch. Nix, you want to run to Nan's and grab a bite to eat?"

"Sure," Nix said. "You locking up the shop and coming with, Preacher?"

Preacher shook his head. Addison had sent him home with leftovers from the dinner she had made them the previous night. "Nah, I'm good. I got some food upstairs."

"See you in an hour," Nolan said.

He and Nix left the shop. Preacher checked Facebook

before typing in Addison's name. He had less than thirty friends on Facebook. Hell, he only had an account because he'd needed one to attach the Crimson Door business page to, and he rarely posted anything other than tattoos he'd done.

He hovered over the add friend request button, staring at the cute picture of Addison with Grace, Harper, and Kira that she had as her profile picture. After a few seconds, he snorted and closed the app. Jesus, he was acting like an idiot.

The bell over the door jingled, and without looking up, he said, "Shop is closed for lunch but will open at one-thirty."

"This won't take long."

He glanced up, anger and irritation flooding through him when he saw that prick Harrison standing in his shop. "What the fuck do you want?"

"Is that any way to treat a potential client?" Harrison said.

"Fuck off. I'm not tattooing you," Preacher said.

He stood and felt a twinge of satisfaction when Harrison stepped back. "No need to be rude. I'm only here to have a quick chat."

"I've got nothing to say to you," Preacher said.

"I bet you thought I didn't notice how you looked at her at the barbeques," Harrison said. "I bet you think I'm too stupid to know when some asshole is after my girl."

Heat prickled along the back of Preacher's neck. "She's not your girl anymore."

"I saw how you looked at her, but I found it amusing. As if a man like you would ever have a chance with a woman like Addison."

"Guess it must have fucking stung when you realized you were wrong," Preacher said.

Harrison laughed. "You mean the other morning? Just because you slept with Addison doesn't mean she loves you.

She still loves me. We've been together since she was fifteen years old. We were meant to be together."

"If you believe that, then you shouldn't have fucking cheated on her," Preacher said.

"I'll admit it was a mistake, but it's over now. I'm ready to be with Addison for the rest of my life, and she's ready to be with me."

"Oh yeah? Then what's she doing with me?"

Harrison leaned against the door. His once perfect nose was slightly crooked now. The smug look on Harrison's face made Preacher want to slam his fist into that nose and finish the job of ruining it.

"She's with you because I gave her permission."

"What the fuck are you talking about?" Preacher said. Christ, could the little asshole see how badly he'd just rattled him?

"When Addie and I decided to take a break, I told her to find a random guy and fuck him. A freebie, if you will, before she settles down and marries me. She'd only been with me, and I thought it was fair that she had a," Harrison paused, "new experience. Especially since she was willing to over-look what happened with me and Crystal. Addison agreed."

He looked Preacher up and down. "I'll admit that I'm surprised she chose you to be her free pass, but maybe she knew you wanted her, and she felt sorry for you?"

He studied Preacher's face. "You okay, Preacher? You look nauseous. I imagine it's a bit of a shock to know that I was aware Addison would sleep with someone else and that she had my permission."

His head spinning, Preacher tried to school his features. The little fuckwit had told Addie to sleep with someone else, and she had. She'd slept with him. Was everything she'd told him a lie?

"Look, maybe you thought this could be something more. Addison's a sweet girl, and she wouldn't want to hurt your feelings, but she's not in this for the long run with you. I guarantee she'll be back with me before the month ends. You need to walk away, Preacher."

"Thanks for the fucking suggestion, but I'll talk to Addison about what she wants," Preacher said. "Now get the fuck out of my shop."

Harrison's look of pity shredded his already frayed nerves. "You think what she wants is an ex-convict?"

All of the air sucked out of Preacher's lungs, and the shop suddenly seemed too small and too hot.

"I know you went to prison, *Simon*," Harrison said. "Simon Wells, a proud inmate of the New Cassel Correctional Center for four years."

He wanted to tell Harrison to get out of his shop. He wanted to punch his fucking face in, but his legs were wobbly, and there was still no goddamn air in his lungs.

"You're probably wondering how I found out, right? Trust me, it wasn't that difficult. I'm a lawyer. We deal with the scum of the earth like you all the fucking time. One phone call to a private detective and a shockingly cheap amount of money, and I know everything there is to know about you, Preacher. What do you think Addison will say when she finds out you're a convict?"

Preacher's fucking stomach was somewhere near his feet, and he couldn't get the image of Addison's sweet face out of his head. Of the look of horror and disgust that would cover it when she discovered his past.

"Even if Addison were willing to overlook your criminal past," the fucking dipshit wouldn't stop his yapping, "her parents never would. She's close to her mom and dad, and if she chooses you over me, they'll cut her out of their life.

They're important to her, maybe almost as important as I am to her, and do you want to be the guy who destroys her relationship with them? They love me, Simon. Do you know why? Because I'm a good guy."

"Get out of my shop." Preacher's heart was thudding, and the adrenaline rush made him feel sick. His ears were starting to ring, and he could barely hear Harrison, but the fucker still wouldn't shut up.

"You don't have a future with her, and you know it. Do the right thing and walk away," Harrison said. "Don't destroy her life just because you think you deserve someone like Addison. You don't. You never will."

Preacher's hands clenched into fists. He stared Harrison in the eye, and Harrison's face paled. He groped for the door handle as Preacher said, "Get the fuck out of my shop and don't come back. I won't tell you again."

Harrison's groping, trembling hand finally found the handle. He yanked open the door, and when it was obvious that he was going to say something else, Preacher said, "Say one more word, and I will rip your fucking tongue out of your mouth."

Harrison's mouth shut with a snap, and he quickly left the shop, letting the door slam shut behind him. Preacher locked the door and staggered the few steps to his tattoo station. He sank onto the stool, the adrenaline fading and his heartbeat slowing. He stared at his trembling hands as his stomach churned before reaching for his phone. He sent a quick text to Addie and then turned off his phone.

ADDISON, DON'T DO THIS. HE DOESN'T WANT TO SEE YOU.

She ignored her inner voice as she slipped her shoes on.

Okay, so Preacher had been avoiding her since the weird text she got from him last night. So, yeah, maybe driving over to his tattoo shop was a mistake, but what else was she supposed to do?

She opened her messages and stared at the text from Preacher.

Something's come up. I can't make it tonight.

She hadn't heard from him since. She'd only managed a few hours last night before she'd texted him. Just a casual, *hey, no problem, hope your day was okay*, message that she obsessed over for half an hour before sending.

When she still hadn't heard from him this morning, she'd texted him again, another brilliant and casually worded, *good morning, hope your night went okay, are you free for dinner*, message that he'd seen but not answered.

Girl, he's ghosting you. Are you going to be that pathetic and go to his shop when it's obvious he's over you?

She hesitated with her purse in her hand. Maybe she shouldn't go. It was barely twenty-four hours since he texted her. Maybe he'd just had a bad day. Maybe he just needed some alone time. Being the clingy, needy girlfriend would not be a good look. Preacher would be annoyed as hell by that.

Girlfriend?

She blew her breath out in a frustrated rush. Okay, maybe not girlfriend, but they had to be something more than just fuck buddies, right? He spent his time off with her, stayed overnight in her bed, and they'd eaten out together where anyone in the town could see them. Hell, he was letting her borrow his car. That was more than just a casual thing. It had to be.

Besides, this didn't feel like a ghosting thing. Something was wrong. Something had upset Preacher, and asking him if he was okay wasn't being clingy or needy. It was thoughtful and kind.

She opened the door, letting out a soft shriek when she saw Harrison standing in the doorway with his hand raised to knock. She staggered back, glaring at him when he stepped into her apartment.

"What are you doing here, Harrison?"

"I came to talk," he said.

"I'm on my way out," she said. "And I have nothing left to say to you."

"Are you going to see Preacher?"

"That's none of your business," she said.

"You need to get over this Preacher thing," he said. "Look, I made a mistake, all right? I know I did. I should never have been involved with Crystal, but it's over now, and I know that it's you I want. So, let's get married, babe. Let's start our lives together."

"Are you seriously that arrogant?" she said. "We're finished, Harrison. I want nothing to do with you. You're a horrible person. You're selfish and cruel, and the way you treat other people who you think are below you is awful. I'm glad we're not together anymore. I hated that I ever put up with your behaviour."

His laugh was bitter and angry. "Is that why you fucked Preacher, Addison? Because you knew it would piss me off?"

"It's none of your business why I slept with him, and Preacher is a way better man than you'll ever be."

"I told Preacher you only slept with him because I said to sleep with a random guy. He knows you only did it to get back at me."

"You asshole." She wanted to shove him in the chest and stuck her hands behind her back instead. "What is wrong with you?"

"What? Does the truth hurt? Admit it, **Addie**. You only slept with him because you knew he wanted you, and you thought it would be the perfect way to get back at me. Sleeping with someone like him, lowering yourself like that, you knew I'd hate it. You're right, you know. I do hate it. I hate that you let any part of that loser touch you. But you know what? I'm willing to forgive you because that's how much I love you."

The laughter came spilling out of her, loud and harsh and unstoppable. "Are you fucking kidding me? Preacher is twice the man you are. He's kind and sweet and generous and everything you're not. I have sex with him because he is amazing in bed, and he can make me come. Every single time, Harrison. I finally know what good sex is because of him."

His face turned bright red, and a vein popped out at his temple. "You stupid little bitch. You're the fucking cold fish, but you're going to blame me for our sex problems?"

Feeling both exhilarated and sick, she said, "I'm not bad or cold in bed. The problem was never me. I just needed a man who knew what he was doing. A man like Preacher."

"Are you in love with him?" The shock in Harrison's voice made her urge to punch him even stronger.

"Get out of my apartment," she said.

"He's a convict, Addison."

Shock infused her system, making her spine rigid and her legs quiver. But beneath the initial surprise, she wasn't really surprised at all, was she?

You're not that shocked because deep down, you knew. Didn't you, Addie? The years he skipped over, the way he avoided certain topics or questions. A man like Preacher, a man who grew up the way he did, would have a past, and that past wouldn't be all sunshine and roses.

"How do you know that?" she said.

"Does it matter? It's true. His real name is Simon Wells, and he was a prisoner at New Cassel Correctional Center for armed robbery. He's a felon and a dangerous one. Is that the guy you want to be with?"

"Get out," she said. "Leave, Harrison."

"Your parents are back tomorrow, aren't they?" Harrison said. "What do you think they'll say when they find out their precious baby girl has been sleeping with a convicted criminal? Do you think they'll be proud of you? Do you think they'll welcome him into the family with open arms? Think, Addison! This little crush you have on him will destroy your life. Do the right thing and marry me. I love you and -"

"I don't love you," she said. "I don't love you, and I never will again. Leave right now, or I swear to God, I'll call the cops."

"Addison -"

"Leave! Right now!" she shrieked.

He winced and backed out of her apartment. "We'll talk later when you're not so upset."

"No, we won't," she said. "I hate you. If you come near me again, if you ever speak to me again, I'll tell everyone in this fucking town about how you let Crystal leash you like a dog and spank you. Do you hear me? Do you think you'll still make partner at the firm when everyone in town knows all the dirty details of your sex life?"

"You wouldn't," he breathed.

"Yes, I fucking would," she said. "You don't want to fuck with me, Harrison. I will destroy you and your career."

She slammed the door in his face, leaning against the cool wood and trying not to cry as she listened to Harrison's footsteps fade down the hallway.

She needed to talk to Preacher.

"Yo, Nix has left, and I'm leaving too. You good to lock up?" Nolan said.

Preacher nodded and sprayed his tattoo chair with disinfectant for the second time. It didn't need it, but the ritual of disinfecting and cleaning was soothing to him.

It also meant giving him a little more time before he walked upstairs to his empty apartment. He cursed under his breath as he wiped the seat of the chair. He used to love his fucking crappy little apartment, just like he loved the fucking food at Nan's. Now, both of them held zero appeal to him.

He wanted to be at Addison's apartment, to sit on her couch next to her while they ate dinner and talked about their day. He wanted to binge watch stupid TV shows with her and then crawl into her bed and fall asleep with every part of him touching every part of her.

He sprayed the seat again, wiping it with hard and savage strokes as the bell jingled over the door, signaling Nolan's exit. It hadn't even been forty-eight hours since he'd seen her last, and he already felt like he was going crazy. She'd only texted him twice before giving up, and despite knowing that it was for the best, a part of him was hurt she hadn't tried harder. Hurt that she hadn't –

"Preacher?"

The disinfectant bottle slipped from his suddenly nerveless fingers. He left it on the floor as he stood and turned. Addison stood just a few feet away, looking nervous and uncertain. He had to fight against his immediate urge to scoop her up and carry her upstairs. He wanted nothing more than to strip her naked and bury himself in her soft body, to forget that they could never be together again.

"What are you doing here?" he said.

"I was worried about you."

"I'm fine."

"You don't look fine."

"Well, I am." His stomach churning, he said, "I'm done giving you lessons."

She didn't look surprised. Instead, she said, "Harrison was wrong about why I slept with you. When I confronted him about cheating on me with Crystal, he said he wanted a break to experiment with other women who could give him what he needed in bed. He said I was free to sleep with another man, even though he knew I was satisfied with him."

She made a bitter little laugh that hurt his heart. "I gave him back his engagement ring and told him goodbye. I thought he understood we were through, but obviously, he didn't. I don't love him, Preacher. I stopped loving him the moment I found out he was cheating on me. I'm not inter-ested in having a relationship with him again. Anyway, I didn't sleep with you because Harrison gave me permission. I had no intention of doing anything he told me to do ever again."

"So, why did you sleep with me?" he said.

"Because I'd been attracted to you for a long time. Even when I was with Harrison. It made me feel bad and like I was cheating on him, but I couldn't help it. I wanted you, Simon. When we kissed that night outside the bar, it was... well, incredible. I'd never felt so alive, and I know that sounds stupid and like a cliché, but it's true."

She took a few steps toward him. "When I had the chance to sleep with you, I took it because I wanted you. No other reason. And it's good between us, isn't it?"

He looked away. "Yeah."

"It's not just the sex either. We're good together. I have more fun with and enjoy spending time with you than anyone else. And that includes Harper. Don't ever tell her I said that, though."

Her smile faltered when he didn't return it. "I think there could be something more between us than just sex. Don't you?"

He wanted to say yes. More than anything in his life, he wanted to say yes. Instead, he shook his head and said, "No."

Hurt flickered across her face before she straightened her shoulders and stared directly at him. He had to hand it to his little Sunshine. When she wanted something, she went after it.

"Is it because of your past? Because I don't care about what happened or... or where you've been."

He'd expected this. Had been expecting it since the minute Harrison told him he knew he was an ex-convict. There was no way the prick wouldn't tell Addison. Still, his heart dropped into his stomach, and his mouth went dry, and his stomach clenched like he was anticipating a punch to the gut.

"You know I was in prison," he said.

"Yes."

"Then you know why we can't be together."

"Your past doesn't define you, Simon. Just like my past doesn't define me. Do you think I'm proud that I was in love with someone like Harrison? That I looked past his bigotry, and his cruelty, and his arrogance? That I convinced myself he was the person I deserved? I'm not proud of that or the way I justified his actions. But it's my past, and I can only move forward and try to be better. The way you have."

"It's not the same thing," he said. "I have a criminal record, Addison. Everything in my life will be a little harder because of that. Traveling, working, everything. You don't want to be dragged into that with me. I'm not a better man now than I was then. Don't start thinking I am."

"You are," she insisted. "You've learned from your mistakes, and you're a good person. You were a good person before, too. You just made some mistakes. But look at you now. You have your own business, and you -"

"I have my own business because of my best friend. Not because of anything I did. You know why I moved here, Addison? Because it was the only way to get my shop. There wasn't a single fucking bank in all of New Cassel that would give an ex-convict a loan, not even if Gideon co-signed with me. The only reason I have my shop is because Gideon co-signed the loan that the Harmony Falls bank manager would only give me because he owed Gideon a goddamn favour."

"What does that matter?" Addison said. "I can't even afford a crappy secondhand car. Do you think I'm less because of that?"

"It isn't the same!" he shouted. "You will never understand why, and I'm glad you won't. You shouldn't live your life with someone like me. I'm no fucking good, Addison."

"You are," she said. "You're the best man I know, Simon Wells, and I think I'm in love with you."

He froze, his lungs seizing and his brain going blank. After a few minutes, Addison said, "Say something, Simon. Please."

"You're not in love with me."

"I am," she said. Her voice was full of certainty, of utter surety and belief.

"Your family will hate me," he said. "This isn't some goddamn Hallmark movie, remember? What do you think your folks will say when you tell them you're in love with an ex-convict?"

"Well, maybe that won't be the first thing I tell them

about you, but my parents are good people and won't judge you for your past."

"They will," he said. "You're their baby girl, and being with someone like me will destroy your relationship with them."

"You haven't even met them." There was the slightest tinge of anger in her voice. "Don't judge them the way you think they'll judge you when you haven't met them yet. Give them a chance, okay? Give us a chance. Please. I know you feel something for me more than just lust. Don't be afraid, okay? Be with me."

He wanted to agree with her. He wanted to fall to his knees and tell her he loved her and fucking beg her never to leave him. But what good would that do? Over time, when the relationship with her parents was fractured, when that prick Harrison spread his past to the rest of the town, and he and Addison were the fucking town gossip for the next decade, her love for him would dim. She'd find someone worthy of her, and Preacher would be left with only her memory.

He took a deep breath. "It won't work, Sunshine. You and me? We're finished. Do me a favour and lose my number."

Her bottom lip trembled, and he could see the shine of tears in her eyes. She swallowed hard and walked toward the door. She paused in the doorway and looked back at him, searing him with her gaze. "I never took you for a coward, Simon."

The door shut behind her and he watched the only woman he'd ever love walk out of his life forever.

CHAPTER 31

"What are you doing here?" Gideon pulled up short in the doorway of the kitchen.

"Gideon," Grace said, "don't."

"It's fine," Addison said. She knew that Gideon would be angry with her. He was Preacher's best friend, and she'd be disappointed with him if he wasn't kind of an asshole to her.

"I came by to talk and ask you for a favour," Addison said.

"I'm not asking Preacher to forgive you," Gideon said. "Not when you fucked him over the way you did."

"Gideon!" Grace's look was half-exasperation and half-love. "I know Preacher is your best friend, but don't be a dick, okay?"

"It's fine," Addison repeated. "Grace, honey, can you give me and Gideon a minute?"

Grace nodded and stood up before calling for Tank, sitting in Addie's lap. "I'll be in the living room if you need me."

The big dog lumbered out of the kitchen, but Grace paused in the doorway next to Gideon. She cupped his jaw and tugged his head down before pressing a kiss against his mouth and whispering into his ear.

He nodded, and while Addison couldn't hear what Grace had said to him, the look of anger on Gideon's face dimmed a little. He even sat beside her at the table as Grace left the kitchen.

"How is he?" Addison said.

"Since you broke his goddam heart a week ago? Not so fucking hot, to tell you the truth," Gideon said. "Tell me something, Addie, did you give him any chance to explain his past, or did you immediately tell him the two of you were finished as soon as your prick of a fiancé told you and the rest of the goddamn town he was an ex-convict?"

"Ex-fiancé," she said. "How do you know he told other people in town?"

"Oh, I don't know, maybe the dozens of phone calls from people asking me if what Harrison said is true and if they needed to be worried about a man like Preacher in their town."

She rubbed at her forehead. "Has it affected his business?"

Gideon laughed bitterly. "No. If anything, it's fucking increased business. I guess for some folks, the idea of being tattooed by an ex-convict gives them a fucking thrill."

She could see his anger seeping back into him, and he tapped his fingers on the table with a hard *rat-tat-tat*. "I knew it was a bad idea for the two of you to get together. I knew you'd break his heart, but I thought it was because you weren't over Harrison. I never imagined it would be because you judged him for his past."

"What exactly did he tell you?" she said.

"He won't tell me shit," Gideon said. "He's barely fucking talking at all. He just said that you found out he was an ex-convict and that it was over between the two of you. Did you even give him a chance to explain or -"

"Gideon, he broke up with me," she said. "I told him I didn't care about his past, and I loved him. He said it wouldn't work and that it was over."

The hard rhythm of his fingers slowed on the table. "I – what?"

"Simon ended it with me," she said.

He scrubbed his hand through his hair. "Fuck! Jesus Christ, I'm sorry, Addie. I shouldn't have assumed like that, but I..."

"You see your best friend hurting," she said, "and you want to protect him."

She squeezed Gideon's forearm. "You're a good friend, Gideon."

He shook his head. "Not that good of a friend. I told him repeatedly not to get involved with you."

That stung, but she knew why he'd done it, and she tried not to take it personally. "You were just trying to protect him."

"I was, but it was still a shit thing to do. I could see how much he liked you," Gideon said. "Did he tell you anything about his past?"

"No," she said. "Harrison said he went to prison for armed robbery, but that's all I know."

"He was the driver," Gideon said. "He never went into the bank, and he never had a weapon on him. He fell in with the wrong people, who convinced him to do the job with them. They were arrested a few days later. Preacher was given ten years but released after four for good behaviour. He kept his nose clean, and he finished his parole. He's a good man who made a mistake, Addie."

"I know," she said. "Kira told me once that Preacher said you saved his life. Will you tell me how?"

He hesitated, a look of discomfort crossing his face. "Did Simon ever tell you why he's called Preacher?"

"I asked him, but he avoided the question."

"He got the nickname in prison. His cellmate was an old man who went by Preacher. He used to be a pastor back in the day, I guess. He got into drugs, did some robberies to pay for the drugs, and in one of the robberies, a man was killed. By the time Simon met him, he'd been clean for years and ran the prison church group, which is how he got the nickname Preacher."

Gideon leaned back in his chair. "One of the other prisoners started after the pastor. No particular reason why. Just decided he could make his life miserable, so he did. Eventually, it turned to physical violence. He went after the old man, and Preacher stopped him. Beat the shit out of the guy and threatened to kill him if he ever tried to hurt the pastor again."

"Simon didn't get in trouble with the guards?" Addison said.

"None of the other prisoners ratted Simon out. This guy was a real shit, and Preacher said he'd had the beating coming to him for a while. Anyway, they started calling Simon the preacher's son because of the way he looked out for the old man."

"What happened to the pastor when Simon got out of prison?" Addison said.

"He'd died two years before, colon cancer. After he died, Simon went from the preacher's son to just Preacher. One of his fellow inmates got out on parole around the same time as Simon. They actually worked at the same tattoo place together until the guy went back to prison for drug trafficking. But he called Simon by his nickname at the shop, and it stuck. He's been Preacher ever since."

"How did you save his life?" She knew Gideon wanted to avoid the question, but she needed to know.

"He's a good man, Addie. He just made a bad decision, okay?" Gideon said.

"I know. Tell me the story," she said.

"He wanted his own shop and couldn't get a business loan because of his criminal record. He," Gideon hesitated, "took a job again. As the driver."

"What happened?" Addie whispered.

"I stumbled onto him by stupid luck while patrolling and talked him out of it. Told him to drive away, and he did. I arrested the other guys. They tried to say Preacher was there, too, but there was no proof. It was their word against Preacher's. I said I never saw Preacher at the scene, and my partner, Martin, backed me up."

"Why?" Addie said.

"Because I asked him to back me up," Gideon said. "Martin knew Preacher was a good man who made a mistake."

He glanced at her. "That's all it was, Addie. A stupid mistake born out of desperation."

"I know. Do you know about Jorge and Maria?" Addison said.

"Yeah. Preacher doesn't talk much to them anymore. I thought it was because they rejected him, but I met them once, and Maria said Preacher stopped talking to them. They took him in and gave him a career he loved, and he believes he disappointed them by going to prison. Maria said they tried to tell him it didn't matter, that they loved him and were still proud of him, but…"

"But he wouldn't listen," Addie said. "At least we know it's a pattern with him."

Gideon sighed. "I tell him every fucking day that he deserves to be happy, that he's not below me or anyone else in this town, but it's like talking to a brick wall."

"He is pretty stubborn," Addie said. While she was glad that she had talked to Gideon and had gotten even a small piece of Preacher's history, she was feeling depressed and sick to her stomach. If Preacher had abandoned Jorge and Maria, two people he loved and admired, what chance did she have? None. He had never said he loved her.

"You okay?" Gideon said.

"No. I miss him, and I'm worried about him. He's all alone in that tiny apartment and…"

Her eyes watered, and she cleared her throat before dabbing at her eyes with a tissue. "Anyway, I was wondering if you could do me a favour and return his car to him? He gave it to me to use because I didn't have a car, but it's just been sitting in my parking spot. It doesn't feel right to use it. I'd return it to him, but he's made it clear he doesn't want to see me again."

"Yeah, I can return it to him," Gideon said. "I'm sorry, Addison. Sorry for being a dick, sorry it didn't work out."

"Thanks, Gideon." She squeezed his arm again. "Can you make sure he knows I won't be going to Kira and Connor's barbeques? He won't go if he thinks I'm there, and he needs our friends, you know?"

"You need them, too," Gideon said.

"It's okay," she said. "It's more important for him to have the support right now. I have my family, he only has us… I mean, you guys."

She set the keys to Preacher's car on the table before standing and kissing Gideon's cheek. "His car is parked outside on the street. Thanks, Gideon. Take care of him for me, okay? Make sure he doesn't spend all his time alone, all right?"

"I will. Bye, Addie."

"Bye, Gideon."

PREACHER SWALLOWED THE LAST OF HIS BEER AS THE tourists sitting across from him made a loud and raucous cheer. It was Friday night, which meant the Thirsty Beaver was busy as fucking hell with tourists and locals. It was noisy, crowded, and hot, and coming here was a huge mistake.

But sitting in his apartment alone wasn't exactly a fucking walk in the park either. He'd thought being at the Beaver, where it would be crowded and loud and drowning out the sound of his inner thoughts, would be a relief.

It wasn't. He could sit in the middle of a fucking tornado, and his inner voice would still be talking about Addison Moore and just how badly Preacher had fucked up.

He pushed back his chair with a loud grunt and stood. He needed to get out of here. If he had to listen to the assholes at the table across from him talk about baseball for one more minute, he'd lose his fucking mind.

He strode across the pub, people automatically stepping out of his way. The *don't fuck with me* look on his face worked great as a people deterrent. Just before he reached the door, his steps slowed. The jostling and shouting to his left drew his attention.

He watched the two men shout and shove at each other before walking toward them with a harsh sigh. The idiot was going to get himself fucking killed, or at the very least have his ass handed to him on a fucking tray.

Just as he reached them, the bigger man cocked his hand back to throw a punch. Preacher caught him by the wrist, grinning at the man when he whipped around and glared at him. "What the fuck do you…"

The man trailed off. He was big, at least 6'3", but whether it was the grin on Preacher's face or the *don't fuck with me* vibe, he didn't try to do something extraordinarily stupid like punch Preacher.

"There a problem here?" Preacher said.

"This asshole insulted me and my friend," the man said.

"The fuck I did," the smaller man said. "It's not my fault you stink like beef and cheese, and your friend looks like Captain Kangaroo on a bender."

"Shut up, Daniel," Preacher said without looking at Addison's brother. He squeezed the bigger man's wrist before dropping it. "The idiot's drunk. Walk away, brother."

"He needs to be taught a lesson," the man said. "His fucking mouth is gonna get him in some real trouble someday."

"You think you're the one to teach it to me, you smelly little leprechaun?" Daniel taunted. "I'll kick your ass so hard you'll be tasting my fucking boot in your throat."

The man surged forward. Preacher shoved his way between them, pushing the man back. "Get the fuck outta here."

"What are you, his fucking boyfriend?" the man spat.

"I said leave. Now," Preacher said. He grabbed Daniel's arm, squeezing it hard when he tried to move past Preacher. "Keep your fucking mouth shut, Daniel."

When the man continued to stand there, his chest puffed out like an angry raccoon and his nostrils flaring, Preacher said, "Walk away, asshole. Last chance."

"You're lucky your boyfriend showed up, you fucking dickhead," the man said to Daniel.

Daniel flipped him the bird and laughed, swaying on his feet as the man and his friends walked away. "Nice, Preacher. Pound it, baby."

He held his fist out to Preacher. Preacher ignored it and, still holding Daniel by the arm, started toward the door. "Let's go."

"I'm not done my fucking beer," Daniel slurred. "Preacher, lemme go."

"Move," Preacher said. He half dragged, half-carried Daniel out into the warm night air.

Daniel slung his arm around Preacher's shoulders and grinned up at him. "Hey, who's the firefighter here? I should be carrying you."

Preacher rolled his eyes as Daniel said, "Can you give me a ride home, man? I've had a bit too much to drink and shouldn't drive."

"Like you could even stay on my fucking bike," Preacher said. "Give me your keys."

Daniel handed him his keys. "It's the red truck over there."

Sighing, Preacher headed toward the truck, dragging Daniel with him.

CHAPTER 32

"Where the fuck is your house key?" Preacher said. He had leaned Daniel against the house, and he prodded him in the chest. "Daniel, wake up."

Daniel cracked open one eye. "Wha? Whassup?"

"Where's your house key? None of these keys are working."

Daniel squinted at the house. "Wha' the fuck? This ain't my house, man."

"Are you fucking kidding me? This is the address you gave me," Preacher said.

"Nah, couldn't be. This isn't my house, this is my -"

The porch light turned on, nearly blinding Preacher, and Daniel lifted his hand to block the light. "Jesus, turn down the sun, would ya?"

The front door opened, and Preacher stared at the auburn-haired woman standing in the doorway in a silk robe. "Oh, Daniel," she said.

"Hey, Ma." Daniel waved at her. "What's happening? You got any toast? I'm hungry."

She sighed and stepped back. "Can you bring him inside?"

Preacher hesitated before helping Daniel into the house. He leaned Daniel against the wall as a man came down the stairs, belting a robe around his waist. "Belinda, who is… Daniel, is that you, son?"

"Hey, Dad!" Daniel stumbled forward, laughing when his Dad caught him around the waist. "You wanna make me some toast?"

His dad brushed the hair out of Daniel's eyes. "Son, you're drunk."

"Nah, just a little tipsy."

His father slid his arm around his waist. "C'mon, kid, let's get you into the bed in the spare room."

"Yeah, sure, okay. Hey, thanks for the ride home, Preacher." Daniel waved at him. "You're all right, man."

As Addison's father helped Daniel up the stairs, her mother smiled at Preacher. "So, you're our Addie's Preacher. I'm so happy to meet you. I know it's late, but will you come into the kitchen and have some tea?"

He stared blankly at her. Addie's Preacher? What the hell was happening?

He had no idea, but having tea with Addison's mother was number one on the list of very bad ideas. "Oh, uh… I should probably get going."

"Just one cup," she said. She walked down the hallway and disappeared into the kitchen. After a moment, feeling like a large sandbag had been dropped onto his head, Preacher followed her.

She turned on the electric kettle and put tea bags into three mugs. "I guess I should ask if you like tea," she said.

"I do."

"Good," she said. "Sit down, Preacher."

He sat, or rather his knees unhinged, and he mostly fell into the chair. He watched in stunned disbelief as Addison's mother set out a delicate porcelain cream and sugar set and a plate of ginger cookies before pouring hot water into the mug and handing it to him.

She smiled when she caught him staring at the cream and sugar set. "Isn't it divine? I bought it at a flea market in this little town in England. Clark and I went to Europe for our fifteenth anniversary. Have you ever been to Europe?"

"No," he said.

"Have a cookie," she said, pushing the plate toward him.

"Mrs. Moore, I appreciate the cookies, but -"

"Call me Belinda," she said. "Thank you so much for giving Daniel a ride home. Clark and I do appreciate you looking out for our boy."

"It was no problem." He shifted in his chair. "He, uh, he gave me this address by mistake."

"I'm not surprised," she said. "He seems to have had a terrible lot to drink."

She sipped at her tea. "So, it is lovely to meet you. Addison has told us so much about you."

"She has?"

"Yes. She hasn't stopped talking about you since we got home. It's a shame that it didn't work out between you. It's clear that Addison is very taken with you. Why, she wasn't this upset when she found out that dirty dink Harrison cheated on her."

"I... she... what?" he said.

Addison's father walked into the kitchen. Preacher stood and shook his hand when he held it out to him. "Clark Moore."

"Simon Wells," Preacher said.

"Good to meet you," Clark said. "Are you a friend of Daniel's?"

"Honey, Simon is Addie's Preacher."

"Oh, right, of course!" Clark pumped his hand a couple more times. "Real nice to meet you then. Addie hasn't stopped talking about you since we got home. Have a seat. Did you try some of Belinda's ginger cookies? They're delicious."

Preacher sat down again as Clark sat next to Belinda. She pushed the cookies closer to Preacher. "Try one, Preacher."

He took a cookie and bit into it. "Thank you."

"You're welcome." She smiled at her husband. "Did you get Daniel settled?"

"Yes. He's in bed and on his side with a bucket beside the bed. I'll check on him again in a few minutes. Thanks for bringing him home, Preacher."

"You're welcome," Preacher said.

"Do you prefer to be called Simon or Preacher?" Belinda said.

"Either is fine," Preacher said.

"So, we were just talking about Addie and how upset she was that she and Preacher weren't seeing each other anymore," Belinda said to Clark.

"She is pretty upset," Clark said. "She didn't cry that much when she told us that dirty dink Harrison had cheated on her."

"She showed us the tattoo you did for her," Belinda said. "It's so pretty. I might book an appointment with you to get a tattoo. Maybe a heart with mine and Clark's initials inside of it."

"Uh, sure, call the shop, and we'll book you in," Preacher said.

"I'll do that," Belinda said before squeezing Clark's hand.

"How's that cookie?"

"It's delicious," Preacher said.

"Addison is an amazing baker and cook, just like her mother," Clark said. "A man never goes hungry when they're around. Isn't that right, honey?

"Yes," Belinda said. "She's a fantastic cook. Much better than me." She hesitated before smiling at Preacher. "I realize this isn't our business, but would you consider giving her another chance?"

Preacher choked on his bite of cookie. Belinda stood and pounded him on the back as Clark poured a glass of water and handed it to him. He coughed and coughed some more before drinking some of the water.

"Are you all right, dear?" Belinda said.

"Yes," he croaked out.

She and Clark sat down again and stared at him expectantly. "Well, what do you think? Would you consider giving our Addie another chance? She really is the most marvelous girl," Belinda said.

"She obviously didn't tell you I'm an ex-convict," he said and then winced. Fuck, he sounded like an asshole, but it was better her parents knew the truth now.

"She did," Clark said.

There was a moment of silence before Belinda said, "Addie has many wonderful qualities, Preacher. She's the sweetest and kindest girl you'll ever meet. She's also creative, sensitive, and amazing with children. Kids love her. She's ridiculously good at her job, you know."

"She is," Clark said. "She's a fantastic teacher. You really should consider rethinking your decision not to date her."

"You want a man like me with your daughter?" Preacher said.

He was in the Twilight Zone. He had to be. There was no

other explanation for it.

"We want a man who's loyal and good to her. You looked after her when she was sick, you gave her your car to use, you just gave her brother a ride home when he was too drunk to drive," Clark said.

"I'm not a good guy," Preacher said.

"Nonsense," Belinda said. "Addison adores you and has nothing but good things to say about you. That dirty dink Harrison aside, our girl has very good instincts about people, and we trust her. She says you're a good man, that you take care of her, and that she loves you. That's all we want for our girl. Someone to be good to her and treat her how she deserves."

He swallowed hard. "I screwed up with her. She won't want to be with me now."

"It isn't too late," Belinda said. "You can fix this. One of Addie's most admirable qualities is her forgiving nature. Isn't it, honey?"

"Yes," Clark said. "Our girl is very forgiving."

Preacher stared at Addison's parents. The weight on his chest that appeared when Addison walked out of his life lifted the tiniest bit. "You sure you want me in your daughter's life?"

"Positive," Belinda said. "Now, have another cookie, dear. There's plenty."

"OH, HARPER," ADDIE SAID. "I'M SO SORRY."

Harper shrugged before tossing another shirt into the suit-case. She adjusted her phone screen so it was pointed more toward her face. "It's no big deal. Moving to New York and making it as an artist was a long shot, right?"

"Are you sure you want to come home, though? I mean, it's only been a year."

"I'm sure," Harper said. "It isn't just being a failure, you know? I'm really worried about Dad. He told me on Thursday that he's selling the clinic to this Dr. Henshaw. They're having the paperwork drawn up. I couldn't talk him out of it, pinky pie. The most I could get him to agree to was to wait until I got home so I could look over the paperwork."

"Shit. I'm so sorry."

"Yeah, me too. If this asshole Dr. Henshaw thinks he can just take the clinic from my dad, he's in for a big fucking surprise. I'm not letting some hotshot city vet destroy my dad's life."

"Honey, I get wanting to be there for your dad and protecting him, but you need to live your dream, too. Leaving New York, not pursuing your art is -"

"The right thing to do," Harper said. "Trust me, Addison, I can't cut it here. My work is terrible compared to the others. I was stupid to think I was good enough."

"Don't say that," Addison said.

"It's true. Listen, I'll be there next weekend, and we can discuss in great detail why my dream failed, okay? Now, how are you doing? Have you talked to Preacher at all?"

"No, I told you he wants nothing to do with me."

"The barbeque is gonna be real awkward tomorrow."

"I'm not going," Addison said.

Harper frowned at her. "So, Preacher just automatically wins our friends? That's not fair. You've been friends with them your whole life. Preacher has only lived here for a few years. You win the friend war, Addison. Let Preacher find new friends."

She shook her head. "He needs them, Harper. I'm worried about him. He's alone and doesn't even have a stove in his apartment. He eats out all the time, and he works too many hours. What will he do the next time he gets a migraine?"

"Honey, I love how compassionate you are, but the asshole broke up with you. Let him worry about his own life."

"We were never actually dating, so technically, he didn't break up with me," Addison said.

There was a knock on her door, and Harper frowned at her through the screen. "Jesus, I swear you have the worst security in your apartment building. What's the use of a locked lobby if anyone can stroll in? Are you expecting someone?"

Addison picked up her phone and walked toward the door. "You've been living in New York for too long, Harper. I ordered a pizza because I'm too depressed to cook."

She opened the door with her free hand. "Thank you so…"

"Addison? What's wrong?" Harper peered at her through her phone screen. "Why are you so pale? Who's at the door? What's going on?"

Addison turned the phone until it was pointed at the door.

"Oh look, it's the asshole," Harper said. "What the fuck do you want, Preacher?"

"Harper, stop." Addison turned the phone back to face her. "I have to go. I'll talk to you later."

"Make him beg for forgiveness!" Harper hollered before Addison could hit the end button.

She shoved her phone into her pocket as Preacher stepped into her apartment. There was a bandage on his right forearm, and she said, "What happened to your arm?"

"New tattoo," he said. "Nix did it for me tonight after the shop closed."

"Oh."

There was an awkward silence, and she said, "My mom called this morning. She told me you helped Daniel last night. Thank you."

"Your parents are nice," he said.

"They're amazing. Are you here to tell me how nice my parents are?"

"No," he said. "I screwed up, and I'm sorry. I love you, Addison."

She blinked at him before pulling at the friendship bracelets around her wrist. "I – what did you just say?"

"I love you. I feel like I'm a good man when I'm with you. You help me to be a good man. I know I'm not perfect, but being with you makes me think maybe I'm not such a fuck up, after all." He peeled back the bandage covering his arm, and she stared at the ink, fresh new shock pouring through her.

"Is that... oh my God, did you..." She stared at her name written in a script font on Preacher's forearm. "Preacher... what did you do?"

"I got your name tattooed on my arm because even if you don't want to be with me anymore, I'll never stop wanting you. I'll never stop loving you. You'll always be mine, Sunshine, and I want everyone in this fucking town to know it. I love you."

She stared at her name on his arm before lifting her gaze to him. The warmth and the love in his dark eyes made tears slide down her cheeks. "I love you too, Simon."

She could see the relief sliding over his body, feel it in the way he crushed her to him when she threw her arms around him. He kissed her face and mouth repeatedly before resting his forehead against hers. "I love you, Sunshine. I won't ever let you go again."

EPILOGUE

"Sunshine, I'm home."

"In the kitchen," she called. Would she ever get tired of hearing Preacher say he was home? She suspected not. Sure, he'd only moved in two weeks ago, but holy crap, it'd been the best two weeks of her life.

"How was your day?" Preacher slid his arms around her and nuzzled her throat above the pearls.

"Good. Busy. The kids were super hyper today. How was your day?" She traced her name on his forearm.

"Not bad. Finished up Rick's tattoo. It looks good."

"I bet it looks amazing." She stirred the sauce in the pot.

"That smells really good," he said.

"Thanks. It should be ready in about ten minutes. Guess what?" She turned in his arms and kissed his broad chest.

"What's that?"

"You and I are no longer the gossip of the town."

"You're kidding me," Preacher said. "It's only been a couple of weeks. I figured they'd talk about us for six months."

"Something juicier has pushed us right off the gossip map," Addison said.

"Oh yeah? You going to tell me what it is or keep looking like the cat who swallowed the canary?"

She giggled. "I'll tell you, but you can't judge me for how mean I'm being about this or how happy it makes me."

"Sunshine, this is a judgment-free zone, you know that."

"You know how Harrison told me he and Crystal weren't together anymore?"

"Yup."

"Well, that was a lie. He was still banging her. But not just her. He's been having sex with some other woman from Willington, and Crystal found out he was cheating on her too because…" she paused for dramatic effect, wiggling her eyebrows at Preacher.

He squeezed her ass. "Don't leave me twisting in the wind here."

"Harrison gave her herpes. He caught it from this other woman apparently and gave it to Crystal. Crystal told everyone. His entire firm knows, and I guess the partners had a long talk with Harrison about proper behaviour with his legal assistants, and they pushed his promotion to partner to the back burner."

Preacher laughed. "Couldn't have happened to a nicer fucking guy."

"He definitely deserves to have herpes and have his career screwed over," Addison said. "But don't tell anyone I said that because I have my sweet reputation to protect."

"Your secret is safe with me, Sunshine. Now," he reached over and shut off the burner, "what do you say we let this sauce sit for a bit, and I'll take you to the bedroom and eat your sweet pussy for you."

"Why, Mr. Preacher," she said, "what kind of girl do you think I am?"

"I know exactly what kind of girl you are, Miss Moore, and I love every sweet, dirty part of you."

She giggled and put her arms around him when he picked her up. "I love you too, Simon."

Keep reading for an excerpt from Redeeming Harmony, Book Four in the Harmony Falls Series.

REDEEMING HARMONY EXCERPT

BOOK FOUR, HARMONY FALLS SERIES

Harper cursed and wiped the condensation off the windshield. The weather was getting worse, with the rain bouncing off the windshield until, even with the wipers on full blast, she could barely see more than a few feet in front of her. She slowed to a crawl and squinted through the glass. Her hands clenched around the steering wheel, and the beginnings of a tension headache lurked behind her forehead.

Sheets of water poured from the angry, dark sky. It was almost eleven, and Harper cursed again, wishing she had stopped at the motel a few hours back. Anxious to see her dad and just wanting to be home, she'd decided to push forward… a decision she was regretting.

She was barely doing twenty miles an hour and considered pulling over and waiting for the rain to abate when bright headlights shone behind her. The driver honked two long, loud blasts, but Harper ignored him until the car pulled around and flew past her with a screech of tires and the gunning of his engine. She caught a quick glimpse of his angry, red face before he sped past and dipped back into her lane, narrowly missing her front bumper.

"You smelly taint crotch hound!" Harper shouted as his taillights disappeared into the stormy darkness. A few minutes later, she breathed a sigh of relief. The rain was letting up a little, and she could see the dark, winding road in front of her. After another twenty minutes or so, she would be at her dad's place. Hell, she could almost taste the strong, dark coffee he made.

She breasted a small hill and slammed on the brakes. The brakes, way past their prime, squealed in protest but did their job. She stopped inches from the back bumper of the dark car that had sped around her earlier. It was stopped in the middle of the road, its engine idling roughly.

"What the hell?" She threw the car into park and picked up her phone, ready to dial 9-1-1 if the asshole even took one step out of his car. With a squeal of tires and a belch of dirty smoke from the tailpipe, the vehicle took off down the road. Harper shook her head and shifted back into drive. She had just stepped on the gas when her headlights caught the reflection of eyes in the ditch beside the road.

"Shit."

She parked her car well onto the side of the road before grabbing the silk scarf she'd been wearing earlier off the passenger seat. She stepped out into the pouring rain, not bothering to grab her jacket from the back seat. She was soaked to the skin instantly by the pelting rain. Goosebumps screamed to life all over her body, and her blonde hair was plastered to her skull within seconds. She slipped and slid into the ditch, wincing as the ankle-deep water soaked her tennis shoes.

The dog lying in the ditch whimpered pitifully as she approached it.

"Easy, boy," she said. Holding the scarf in one hand, she approached the whining dog.

It tried to get to its feet, and Harper winced when it fell back on its side with a bone-jarring thud. She crouched beside its prone body and rested a hand on its thin side, squinting as she waited for her eyes to adjust to the darkness. The dog returned her stare, its body trembling under her palm. When it made no attempt to move, she cautiously moved her hand to scratch behind its ears.

He lay passively, and she scratched his cheek and under his chin. "Steady, boy."

Moving slowly, she twirled the scarf into a rope and then eased it around his muzzle, wrapping it several times before tying it in a knot. It didn't matter how friendly the dog was, an injury could make even the sweetest dog bite. Muzzling an injured dog to minimize the risk was one of the first lessons her father had taught her.

"Steady, boy," she repeated before running her hands over its thin sides. The dog whimpered again but didn't try to get up. Water had soaked into his thick fur, and his body was shivering as wildly as hers. She moved her hands down to his back leg, and he made a sharp yelp of pain that pierced her heart. He tried to lurch to his feet before sinking into the rain and mud-soaked ditch.

"It's okay, big guy. It's okay." Keeping one hand on the mutt's flank, she sat back on her heels and tried to decide what to do. It was impossible to confirm what type of dog it was in the darkness and pouring rain, but she suspected it was a shepherd or at least a shepherd cross. She could feel every rib with chilling clarity. He was obviously a stray, but even in his emancipated state, he was still much too big for her to carry to her car. She was small but strong and knew how to handle animals, thanks to working at her father's vet clinic for years. However, even she could recognize the impossibility of the task in front of her.

"Hold on, buddy. I'm going to get my phone and call Dad," she said to the dog.

She stood, pausing when headlights splashed across the road behind her. She squinted at the truck as it stopped behind her car, and the driver climbed out. He jogged over to her, and she stood protectively in front of the dog.

"I just want to help," he said.

Harper stared up at him in the pouring rain. Even cold and worried about the injured dog, she couldn't help but notice his body's lean, hard length or the – sweet baby Jeebus – sexiest lips she'd ever seen. There was no way this guy was from Harmony Falls. She wouldn't ever forget a mouth like that.

Harper! Now is not the time.

She stepped aside, crouching next to the stranger when he kneeled beside the dog and ran his hand over its flank. He made his own murmured reassurances to the dog before running his hand over his hind leg. The dog whined, lifting its head to give them a weary, accusing look of pain before dropping it with a squishy thud against the wet ground.

"Did you muzzle the dog?"

Harper nodded. "Yeah. I didn't want him biting me."

"Smart. Is it your dog?"

"No. There was an asshole driving like a moron in front of me. I think it hit the dog and then took off. He looks like a stray to me."

The stranger nodded as his large hands moved quickly over the rest of the dog's body, searching for obvious injuries.

The rain had slowed to a drizzle, and Harper jumped when there was a big boom of thunder, and the rain became a torrential downpour again. Shivering, water dripping from her nose and chin, she leaned forward and spoke directly into his ear so he would hear her over the rain.

"I need you to help me carry him to my car. There's a vet about ten minutes from here."

He turned his head, and Harper blinked at the closeness of his face to hers. She caught a glimpse of his dark eyes and tanned face before he tilted his head and spoke into her ear. "We'll take my truck. There's more room."

His biceps bulging against his t-shirt, he carefully picked up the stray, cradling it against his chest as he headed toward his truck. She splashed ahead of him and opened the passenger door. The truck was high, and she felt like a little kid, stepping onto the running board and using the handles to help herself climb in before scooting over to the middle. The man eased the shivering, whimpering dog into the truck until his head rested on Harper's lap.

The dog cried out again when the man shifted his back leg into a more secure position before closing the door. He slid behind the wheel and slammed the door shut. Now that she was sitting beside him, she was acutely aware of how big Mr. Sexy Lips was.

He was lean but well over six feet, and the hands gripping the steering wheel were twice the size of hers. She could feel every brush of his thigh against hers as he started the truck and drove down the road, peering through the windshield.

Both of them were shivering, and he turned the heat to high. She enjoyed the warm air blasting against her body for a few seconds before reaching across and angling the vent to blow directly onto the trembling dog draped in her lap.

"Steady, boy. Steady." She rubbed the thick, wet fur of his forehead and neck when he shifted and yelped.

"I'm Nathan."

"Harper." She peered out the windshield into the darkness. "You're going to take your next right in about five minutes. It's a long, winding driveway. Try to go slow. There are lots of potholes."

She glanced up at Nathan. "Can I use your cell phone? I left mine in my car."

He pointed to the phone mounted on the dashboard, and she grabbed it.

"Code is 175636," Nathan said.

She punched it in and then dialed the number from memory, smiling a little as she held the phone to her ear. Her dad and Addie's numbers were the only ones she knew.

Her father's voice on the phone chased away some of the chill she felt. "Hey, it's me. I'm about three minutes away, and I have a dog just hit by a car. Maybe a broken hind leg or some internal injuries. Can you meet me at the clinic?"

"Yes. See you soon, sweetheart."

Her dad ended the call without asking other questions, and her smile grew. God, she loved him.

She stuck the phone back in its holder on the dashboard. "Once you reach the top of the driveway, take a left. You'll see a brick building you can park in front of."

He nodded but didn't say anything. She petted the injured dog, her teeth clacking together and her body quaking from the cold. She was tempted to lean into Nathan to try to leech some of his body heat, but he was just as wet as she was and wouldn't provide much warmth.

He turned right and drove slowly down the bumpy gravel driveway. Harper held the injured dog and tried to minimize his movements, breathing a sigh of relief when they parked in front of the clinic. It was already lit with light, and a sense of being home covered Harper like a warm blanket, chasing away some of the chill she felt.

Nathan jumped out and hurried around to the other side of

the truck, opening the door and easing the dog out, doing his best not to bump the injured leg as he shifted him in his arms. Harper slid across the seat towards the door and jumped the considerable distance to the ground. She slammed the door shut as the door to the clinic opened.

Leaving Nathan and the injured dog behind, she hugged her father, burying her face in his shoulder. He smelled the same, a combination of antiseptic and coffee, and her throat started to burn as she blinked back tears. God, she'd missed him. She hadn't been home in the last year, and he'd only visited her once in the year she'd been gone.

"Hi, sweetheart."

"Hi, Dad." She kissed his cheek and scooted past him into the clinic, her sneakers making rubber squeaks on the tile floor with every step.

Harper crossed the foyer to the swinging door that separated the waiting area and exam rooms from the clinic's treatment area. She held the door open as Nathan and her father walked through. A green blanket covered one of the steel examination tables, and Nathan eased the dog onto it as her father brought over a muzzle.

He untied Harper's scarf, setting it on the long counter that held the lab equipment, before petting the old dog's cheek and chin. He slipped the muzzle on and secured it, then examined the dog's eyes and ears.

"Pupils look normal. Harper, step around here and hold his head while I examine him, please."

How many times had she done this before? Too many to count. It might have been over a year since she'd last helped her father in the clinic, but she fell into the familiar routine without missing a step. She buried her fingers in the shaggy fur of the dog's throat and scratched gently.

She was right. The dog was a shepherd cross. He was

horribly thin. His hip bones and ribs stuck out, and he had lost large clumps of fur across his body. She wondered idly when he had eaten last as he made a low sigh and closed his eyes.

She watched her father's hands, crisscrossed with large blue veins, ease their way down the dog's body. He prodded the dog's stomach, and when the dog whined, he said, "Steady, boy. Steady."

She rubbed the dog's head again, picking out small burrs and twigs from his fur, murmuring soft assurances to the frightened animal. The initial warmth of the clinic had faded, and she clenched her jaw to keep her teeth from chattering as water dripped from her hair down the back of her neck.

Nathan stood slightly behind her, and she was more aware of his body than she should have been. Man, how tall was the guy anyway?

Her father hummed softly to himself, muttering small, unintelligible words to the dog as he pressed around the dog's back hips.

The dog whimpered and tried to sit up. Harper pressed against his head and shoulders, but the dog was starting to slip free despite how emancipated and weak he was. Before she could shout a warning to her father, she felt the hard, warm bulk of Nathan press up against her. His big hand pushed against the dog's shoulders next to hers, his other hand bracing the dog's head against the table.

The dog struggled for a few seconds longer before giving up the fight. With Nathan holding him down, Harper could pet and scratch the dog's neck.

"Good boy. That's a good boy," she said when he whimpered again.

The dog settled, and she was suddenly much too aware of Nathan's body against hers, of his warm breath on the side of her neck. His chest brushed lightly against her back, but he kept his lower body away from hers. She should have been pleased that he wasn't using her need for his assistance as an excuse to be a total perv. Instead, she wished his crotch was pressed up against her ass, wished that grinding up against a complete stranger in front of her father was a perfectly a-okay move to make.

Who's the perv now?

She was. With a capital P. Still, his politeness wouldn't stop her from asking out Mr. Tall, Dark, and Sexy Lips the minute she had a chance. He would be a nice distraction from her life's current mess.

"Okay. You can ease up now," her father said.

Nathan stepped away, and she mourned the loss of his warmth. She cautiously stepped back from the dog, waiting to see if he would try to get up. He didn't move, keeping his head on the blanket and his eyes closed.

"No break in the leg, but that hip's dislocated," her father said. "We'll sedate him, do some x-rays and then pop the hip back in. Nathan, can you stay and help?"

"Wait, what?" Harper stared at her father. "You know this guy?"

Her father nodded as Nathan stuck his hand out. "Hi, Harper. I'm Nathan Henshaw. I work with your dad. I've heard a lot about you."

Harper stared mutely at him.

Mr. Tall, Dark, and Sexy Lips was Dr. Henshaw.

The asshole veterinarian who was trying to steal her father's practice and send him into early retirement.

The man she'd never met but already hated.

Well, shit.

ABOUT THE AUTHOR

Elizabeth Kelly was born and raised in Ontario, Canada. She moved west as a teenager and now lives in Alberta with her husband and a menagerie of pets. She firmly believes that a person can survive solely on sushi and coffee, and only her husband's mad cooking skills prevents her from proving that theory.

For more information about Elizabeth, check out her website at

www.elizabethkelly.ca

facebook.com/EKellyBooks

twitter.com/ElizabethKBooks

instagram.com/elizabethkelly_author

amazon.com/Elizabeth-Kelly/e/B00EOHZ0MS

bookbub.com/authors/elizabeth-kelly

ALSO BY ELIZABETH KELLY

Tempted Series

Tempted

Twice Tempted

Forever Tempted

Breathless

Tempted Trilogy (Books 1-3)

Red Moon Series

Red Moon

Red Moon Rising

Dark Moon

Alpha Moon

Pale Moon

The Recruit Series

The Recruit (Book One)

The Recruit (Book Two)

The Recruit (Book Three)

The Recruit (Book Four)

The Recruit (Book Five)

The Recruit (Book Six)

The Shifters Series

Willow and the Wolf (Book One)

Ava and the Bear (Book Two)

Katarina and the Bird (Book Three)

Porter's Mate (Book Four)

Bria and the Tiger (Book Five)

Rosalie Undone (Book Six)

The Dragon's Mate (Book Seven)

Rise of the Jaguar (Book Eight)

The Assassin and the Bear (Book Nine)

The Draax Series

Reign (Book One)

Rule (Book Two)

Rebel (Book Three)

Surrender (Book Four)

Survive (Book Five)

Salvation (Book Six)

Harmony Falls Series

Sweet Harmony (Book One)

Perfect Harmony (Book Two)

Forbidden Harmony (Book Three)

Redeeming Harmony (Book Four)

Absolute Harmony (Novella)

Beautiful Harmony (Book Five)

Seasoned Romance Series

Bet Your Heart on Me (Book One)

Take a Chance on Me (Book Two)

Place Your Trust in Me (Book Three)

Individual Books

The Necessary Engagement

Amelia's Touch

The Rancher's Daughter

Healing Gabriel

The Contract

A Home for Lily

Saving Charlotte

Shameless

The Fairy Tales Collection

Broken

An Unlikely Seduction

Holiday Romance

The Christmas Wife

The Christmas Rescue

The Christmas Nanny

The Christmas Boss

Sordid Games

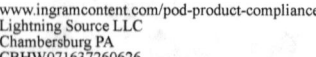